The Chariot Stone

Pamela Lamb

Agneau Press
2011

First published August 2011 by
Agneau Press, Qld. Australia
Email: agneaupress@optusnet.com.au

ISBN 978 0 9580489 9 6

Cover illustration: Wall painting from Boscoreale, 2nd century
BC, held in Metropolitan Museum of Art, New York
Cover design by Chris Platt

This book tells the story of a woman living in the years following the collapse of the Mycenean and Minoan civilisations around 1,300 BC. These years are known today as the Greek Dark Ages but I don't suppose the people alive at the time had any idea they were living in a dark age of civilisation. Like the rest of us, they were just getting on with life as best they could.

There was one strange thing that happened during the writing of this book. In my imagination Lily's farm lay in the shadow of the ruined palace of Mycenae. In 2006 I went to Greece with my mother and, of course, we visited Mycenae. To walk under the Lion Gate was the fulfillment of a lifelong dream. When we climbed up into the palace I pointed out to Mum where Lily's farm would have been. It was exactly as I had imagined it!

On that trip we also visited the island of Santorina, or ancient Thera, where there had been a volcanic eruption at the time the palace cultures died - some say it was the cause of their collapse. Santorina was not a bit as I had imagined, in fact it is like nowhere else on earth. So I was able to come home and rewrite that bit.

The Chariot Stone was a heap of fun to write. I hope you enjoy reading it.

Pamela Lamb
August 2011

Part One

Achaea

1

At first she was reluctant to take off her night shift. The thin linen garment still held the warmth of the bed she had just left. But the dawn light was growing stronger beyond the window and, if he was coming today, it would be soon. Yesterday's clothes pulled on quickly over bare skin. Fingers tugged impatiently through the tangle of her hair. The stone floor of the kitchen was cold against her bare feet.

Time to blow life into the fire and swing the blackened pot over the new flames. Then out into the garden, startling a pair of doves into clattering flight onto the low roof. She stood on the wet grass and shivered, tucking her hands under opposite arms. She could smell the sea in the air, hear the calls of gulls and men. The gate opened. Her heart turned over in her chest.

He was a tall, powerful man. Dark hair cut short. Blue eyes set in a sailor's face. She saw his hand flinch towards the dagger in his belt as she catapulted herself towards him. Her hands went around his waist, under his cloak where the warmth was. She had grown but he was still taller.

'Lilleth?' He pushed her away, then tugged gently at her hair until he could see her face. 'What are you doing out here in your bare feet?'

His eyes told her what she wanted to know. Not little Lilleth. Not this time.

He put his arm around her shoulders and pulled her to him. Began walking towards the kitchen door. 'How did you know I'd come today?'

Lilleth shook her head. 'I didn't know. I counted the days since the last time you were here until I could count no more. Then yesterday Sylos said some ships had come in so I thought the way might be clear. He said one had a mast down. Is it yours? Has there been fighting? There's water ...'

She was breathless. Held so close, she could feel the hard leather vest he wore next to his skin.

'Hot?' He was laughing at her.

She nodded. 'You can use my room, if you like. It's warmer in there.'

She sat on her bed and drew her knees up under her chin. Watched him strip down to the leather vest which he unbuckled and dropped on the floor. It had left red weals where the leather had rubbed. His body was white next to the skin of his arms and neck. The water steamed into the cold air. When he had finished washing he pulled on his shirt, leaving the leather vest on the floor. Came across to the bed. Bent and kissed her on the mouth. Paused, then kissed her again.

'Now I must find your mistress.'

'She's not up yet.'

'Not up, eh? I've been sailing through the night looking forward to a welcome from this house and nobody is up?'

'I welcomed you, Lord Xander.'

'Yes, and it was a good greeting, little one. But now I need a bed to sleep in and a good dinner when I wake.' Xander strode towards the kitchen door and the three shallow stone steps that led up into the bright garden. 'I suppose I can find a room for myself. I've been here often enough to know the way.' He turned on the top step and ducked his head to see into the gloomy kitchen. 'There are rooms free?'

Lilleth nodded. These days there were always rooms free. 'You'll come and see me before you leave?'

'If you're awake.'

'I will be.'

Xander went out, whistling through his teeth.

Sylos came into the kitchen with a basket of wood. Crouched by the fire, feeding the flames. His bony knees stuck out from under the too-short embroidered shift he had acquired when its owner had no further use for it, or for anything else in this world. He stood up and peered into the black pot.

'You'd better put some more water in this or you'll burn the bottom out of it.'

Lilleth cut the end off the loaf on the table and gnawed at the stale bread. 'I'll do it in a minute.'

Sylos straightened up. 'She'll be wanting hot water herself in a minute. Who's going to tell her there isn't any?'

'There will be by the time she wakes up. Lazy sow.'

'And that sailor you're so keen on will want his dinner, even if he is the only guest in the house.'

Lilleth stared at Sylos through the tangle of her hair, chewing her bread. 'He's beautiful, isn't he?'

Sylos flicked her a look. 'Forget it, sweetheart. He's not interested in kitchen sluts like you.'

'He might be.'

Lilleth was still warmed by the look Xander had given her in the garden.

'And you'd do it for nothing, too, wouldn't you? For love?' Sylos crossed the kitchen, took two pottery beakers from a shelf and filled them with watered wine from a pitcher standing in a basin of water. 'You can't live on love, sweetheart. Not in this world.' He pushed one beaker across the table to Lilleth and drank from the other, perched on the corner of the table like a grubby stork. 'If you get the chance, ask him for something. A silver piece.'

'What would I want with a silver piece?'

He grinned. 'Buy yourself a comb to drag through that hair of yours. Do yourself a favour. That's all I'm saying. Because nobody else will.'

That afternoon Lilleth was sitting in the big pomegranate tree at the bottom of the garden. Its branches overhung the pig pen but Lilleth didn't mind. She liked the smell of pigs. It reminded her of home. From where she sat she could see over the high wall of the garden, over the huddled mossy roofs of the town and down into the harbour where the afternoon sun struck sparks from rolling blue water that rocked the ships at anchor and made the little boats toss up and down like beetles in bath water. The sun was hot on the back of her neck and the insects hummed and stung. She'd picked a pomegranate, warm from the sun, and her small teeth were busy stripping the sweet, pink flesh from the yellow rind.

'Lilleth!'

She looked down through the crowded leaves and saw Xander standing at the foot of the tree.

'Come down!'

He reached up and grabbed one foot and she allowed herself to slip from the branch and descend swiftly, catching the skin of arms and legs on sharp twigs as she went, until she arrived in his arms. She wrapped her arms around his neck before he had a chance to drop her on the ground. It was he who pulled her dress down over her thighs but not before he had seen what she wanted him to see. She laughed, suddenly a woman, and kissed him.

He loved her hard as she knew he would with the dappled sunlight lying like drops of gold on the ground and the pigs grunting sleepily from the other side of the wall. He was not her first. A kitchen slut in a harbour inn had little chance to grow up gracefully and she had done it sometimes with the upstairs customers who had gold in their pockets and the will to spend it and sometimes with Sylos just for the warmth of another body close to hers. But she felt this man invade her soul where no one had ever been before and she cried out with something that was both exhilaration and melancholy, and the knowledge that nothing would ever be the same again.

'Ah, Lilleth, what did you make me do that for?' Xander rolled onto one elbow so that he could stare down into her face.

'Not Lilleth. I am Lily now.'

'So you are. A beautiful lily.' His fingers traced a line from her throat down between her breasts until she shivered. 'White and slender. But strong. Be strong, my Lily. Bad times are coming.'

He lifted his head and stared up at the sky, now shot through with the rose and gold of evening, and she could see where the life leaped in his throat. And then, 'I don't have anything to give you.'

She shook her head. 'I don't want anything.' She was his slave in any case, didn't he know that? Then, remembering Sylos, 'Bring me a comb. Next time you come.'

He laughed. 'For this hair of yours?' He grabbed a handful. 'Don't comb it, Lily. I don't care for fine ladies with jewelled nets in their hair. Wild girls at the bottom of the garden are more my taste. Anyway there might not be a next time. You wait here and I'll never come. Or else I'll come and you won't be here.'

'Yes, I will.'

He shook his head. 'Not this time, sweetling.'

'But you've always come back!'

'It's not me coming back that's the problem. It's what I'll find when I get here.'

'What will you find?' And, when he didn't answer, 'There have always been pirates, Lord Xander, ever since the bull ships left the sea. And that was in my great-grandfather's day. If they come here, we'll chase them away. Or welcome them!' She grinned, showing her small white teeth.

'Let's hope that's all you have to worry about.' Xander stood up and pulled the girl to her feet. 'Hold out your hand!'

He reached into the soft leather purse hanging from his belt and pulled out a dull yellow stone the size of a walnut which he dropped into Lily's open palm.

'What is it?' It felt warm and smooth.

'It's amber. Hold it up to the light.'

Lily did so and saw the sunlight strike golden sparks through the strange rock.

'See? It's the colour of your hair.' Xander's face was close to hers. 'Keep it for me, Lily. One day I'll come back and claim it.'

Lily got her piece of silver. It had been her choice not to take the herbal draft that brought on the bleeding when it was late and, when she became too sick to do her chores, the mistress of the house who was also her aunt, gave her the silver and sent her home. She found a ride on a wagon going north with an old man who said she reminded him of his daughter and treated her kindly, stopping the cart when she needed to be sick and standing as patiently as his oxen while she crouched miserably in the roadside dust.

They were two days plodding along lonely roads and three nights sleeping under the wagon with a bright fire burning to keep the wolves away and a short bronze sword with the tip broken off lying by the old man's hand. Then, on the third morning, they went around a bend in the road and Lily saw the ruins of the old palace like broken teeth at the top of a rocky hill.

'There,' she said, pointing. 'I can walk from here.'

Carrying her bundle, Lily trudged through a thicket of trees and emerged to a view of a wide valley. On her right the hillside rose steeply to where the huge stones of the old palace lay tumbled among sapling trees and flowering weeds. The bleating of goats came down to her in the hot air.

Suddenly there was an explosion of movement. Out of the black shade of a thorn tree halfway up the slope a man came leaping and jumping, calling out in a strange, high voice. He slipped down the last of the hill, his feet skidding on the rough ground, and arrived panting almost on top of the girl.

He was a broad, muscular young man who would have been handsome if it had not been for the vacant look in his eyes and the string of spittle hanging from his grinning, gap-toothed mouth. One arm hung useless by his side, the hand shrunk and clawed. He grabbed hold of Lily and stuck his face into hers. Gabbling excitedly and drooling spittle onto his stained tunic, he reached out a grubby hand and touched her face, her hair and then her breasts.

'Don't, Quin.' Lily grabbed his hand. She reached out and took him in her arms and felt him lean heavily against her. The sour smell of him made her stomach heave and turn. The goats arrived, skipping nimbly down the slope and milling around on the dusty track.

'Go on, go back up the hill.' Lily pointed. 'Go on, Quin. You don't want a beating, do you?'

Quin rolled his eyes in his head and mumbled through untidy teeth. He grabbed a thin branch from a dusty bush growing by the track and waved it in the direction of the goats. Taking the hint, the animals trooped unhurriedly back up the slope.

The smells greeted her first - pigs and cooking - then the dog, squirming her pleasure as she came up and sniffed Lily's dusty toes. She dumped her cloth-wrapped bundle at the doorway and went inside, eyes squinting in the gloom. The fire was burnt down to a red glimmer. On the table a pot of cooked beans, congealing. Chickens on the dirt floor, pecking scraps. Lily's mother, Cleia, was sitting by the fire, her hands buried in the pile of white fleece on her lap. She was asleep, her chin sunk onto her chest, her mouth slightly open. Her breath was raspy in her chest.

Lily crossed the room and shook her mother by the shoulder. The older woman raised her head. Saw Lily. Saw what there was to see about her although Lily had no idea how - the baby lay invisible, the only sign a slight roundness in her breasts. But, then, Quin had known, too.

'So you're home then.' A brisk nod of the head. 'Did you bring me anything?'

The bundle revealed a small round cheese with a hard yellow rind and a flask of oil. Cleia pulled out the stopper. 'Yech! It's perfumed. What use is that to me?' She rummaged through Lily's clothes. 'So you've been pleasing yourself instead of your mistress? Still I'm not sorry to see you home. I could do with another pair of hands.' She reached for a wooden bowl and ladled some of the half-cold bean mess out of the pot. 'You're hungry, I suppose?'

Just at that moment Lily was, and she ate quickly, shovelling the beans down with a hunk of bread.

'Where's my father?'

'You might well ask where your father is. I ask myself the same question every day.' Cleia dumped a beaker of watered wine next to her daughter's plate. 'Gone off soldiering. Him and all the men from hereabouts.'

'*Soldiering*? Where?'

A gesture with her thumb. 'Up yonder. He's been gone since the new moon was out and that was many a day ago.'

'And the boys?'

'Aye, them too.'

'But not Quin. I saw him.'

The woman's face softened. 'No, not Quin. And I'm glad of him, too, let me tell you. He's good company at night when the wolves are howling.'

'So who's working the land?'

'Me. Eumeus. Until he decides to run away like the rest of them.'

'The slaves? They've run away? How did that happen?'

Cleia slumped on a stool and rested her elbows on the table. She ran one hand through thin, greying hair.

'They just up and left. Not a thought to us that's fed and housed them all these years. And don't say why didn't you lock 'em up because I did, ever since your father left. But they made such a racket at night, thumping and banging and singing those songs that sound like nightmares in your head.'

She shuddered. 'And they died, too, some of 'em. Just died in the night as if they couldn't stand the thought of being alive any more. In the end I let 'em go.'

Lily stood up and reached under the table for the scrap bucket. 'I'll go and feed the pigs.'

2

Lily crouched down and ran her finger around the familiar patterns carved on the stones that made up the pig pen's walls. This one was her favourite. A man in a chariot - she know it was a chariot because her father told her. Two horses prancing. A long hunting spear. Her father said the stones were grave markers. He and Lily's brothers had brought them down from the old palace on the hill, the only stones they could manage to manoeuvre down the slope, and the carvings had been part of Lily's world ever since she was a little girl.

She remembered nothing of the palace as it had been before the burning. Had never seen the fine gentlemen in their carved chariots, prancing down the hill from the palace gates. Or the priestesses, gold jingling on their white tunics, driving the goats down to their sanctuary hidden on the far side of the hill. Always down the hill, Lily's father said. That was the way of the high and mighty. It was ordinary folk who took things up the hill - oil and grain and the thin local wine - for the clerks to tally on their clay tablets.

She didn't remember the burning either. On the night it happened she had been just a small scrap of a baby lying in her cradle by the fire. But she had heard the stories from her father Haro. How the palace people had sent their clerks to knock on the doors of everyone in the valley and take away every scrap of metal they could find, even the carved bronze cup which had been part of her mother's dowry. She had kept it, polished and gleaming, on the shelf above the fire place all her married life and never used it. After it was gone, she said she wished she had let it get dirty and then perhaps they wouldn't have known what it was because who would expect a poor woman like her to own something so fine?

And then the smithy in the village ringing all day to the

sound of pounding hammers as spear-tips and arrow heads were forged from poor folks' treasures. And for what? Men marched away. The chariots came and went, always in a hurry. There was smoke on the horizon, the smudge of flame at night, far away. Tales came of crops burnt, stock driven off, women raped.

It was a poor harvest that year but still the palace demanded its share of the crop. Haro had joined the crowd of men queuing at the store rooms inside the palace gates waiting to hand over their precious oil to the clerks who stared down their noses as if a pig was loose. It was the last time he would do so. A few nights later when the harvest moon was full and yellow in the star-filled sky, the raiders attacked the palace.

Haro had woken to the sound of voices in the still night and the pounding of feet on the paved road that led up the hill to the palace gate. He had stumbled to the doorway of the house, grabbing the only weapon he had - the long-handled hoe he used for weeding. There were about twenty of them. Big men, wild men, long hair streaming like the smoke from their torches. And, above, the hasty blare of trumpets as the palace woke to the attack.

'The palace folk didn't have much idea how to defend the place. They'd never had to do it before.' Lily's father used to say, telling the story as they sat half-way up the slope and watched the cloud shadows swoop across the valley, or crouched over the fire on cold winter nights. 'They thought their strength, their power was protection enough. They never imagined an attack at their very gate.'

There was a brief struggle at the gate. The thrum of arrows in the dark. Then a roar of triumph going up and up into the night sky and the sudden bloom of yellow fire. The oil store by the gate was the first to go, exploding with a whoosh of flame which spread like a red flood to engulf the other buildings. It must have been then that Quin went out, slipping by his father as he stood in the doorway watching the flames licking the sky.

They found him the next day sprawled in the gateway, his head a red mess of blood and bone and his arm almost hacked through above the elbow. At first they thought he was dead. Haro carried him down the hill and laid him on the bed by the fire and Cleia piled the blankets on him, topped by the old wolf skin with the bare patches on it. His eyes flickered once when she was washing the blood from his head but he made no other movement.

And Haro sat by the fire and stared at the thing he had picked up from the ground next to Quin's body. A small knife with a carved bone handle and a narrow blade made from some grey metal that he had never seen before. He ran his thumb along the blade then reached forward and knocked the knife against the hearth, watching it strike sparks from the stone.

'What is it?' Cleia turned from the bed.

Haro handed the knife to his wife. 'I don't know what it is. See where I hit it against the hearth? You'd knock the edge off a bronze knife, doing that. But this one isn't even marked.'

Cleia handed it back. 'It's an ugly thing.'

'Ugly maybe. But I'll tell you one thing. Whoever comes against us with weapons like this will be our masters.' Haro nodded his head in the direction of the smouldering palace on the hill. 'Last night was the proof of that.'

The following day, when the fire on the hill had died down, Haro and his two remaining sons went up to the palace to see what they could find. The fire had been thorough and there was little left of the vast palace. Haro and the boys scrambled over piles of tumbled masonry until they stood in the great hall where the king and his household had feasted and entertained their guests. Most of the great wooden columns had burnt through and collapsed, pulling the walls down with them. One column, half burnt, lay at an angle across the room. It had dragged down the roof beams and tiles which lay scattered across the tiled floor. The mellow light of early morning shone down on bodies burnt so badly that it was impossible to tell whether they had been nobles, or slaves, or the hated clerks from the store.

Haro led his sons back to the store room at the front of the palace. Here the exploding heat from the great storage jars had destroyed both roof and walls. Nothing remained but scattered shards of pottery, baked black by the heat. Haro bent down and picked up a small square of clay. On it were lines of markings in neat rows from top to bottom. He showed it to the boys.

'This is what the clerks used when I brought up the oil. They marked who I was and how much I'd paid. They were always busy scratching away. You never saw their eyes.'

The boys crowded round. 'I can't see,' said the younger boy.

But Haro grasped the tablet firmly and snapped it in half. He threw the pieces onto the floor. 'There's nothing to see.' He put his arm across his sons' shoulders. 'Come on, lads. Let's go home for our dinner. There's nothing up here for the likes of us.'

In the afternoon Haro and his oldest son went back up to the palace. They dragged all the bodies they could find into the great hall and laid them out on the bright red and black tiles. Then they went down to the sanctuary on the other side of the hill to look for the priestess. She wasn't hard to find. She lay in the doorway of her small stone temple with her throat slashed and her white linen dress hitched up to her waist. Haro bent down and, with the small grey-bladed knife, cut off all the little gold discs that hung from her dress, dropping them one by one into his son's cupped hands. Then he picked up the body, slung it over his shoulder and carried it up the hill to join the rest.

They piled stones and timber on top of the bodies to keep away the wolves and kites, then walked back down the hill with the skin between their shoulder blades prickling at the thought of the dead ones' souls unreleased by a priestess' words. In the night the wind blew up, setting alight the smouldering timbers, and by morning, the bodies were no more than grey ash feathering across the brightly coloured floor of the king's hall.

It was almost spring before Quin stirred from his sleep. All winter his mother fed him grain porridge and bean mess, and poured goat's milk spoon by spoon down his throat. She sat next to him crooning lullabies while Lily learned to crawl on the dirt floor and played with a litter of puppies in a basket on the hearth. And finally, with the sunshine falling through the open doorway and lying across his bed in a solid block of warmth, Quin opened his eyes.

But it was not the old Quin who came back to them slowly as the sun strengthened in the sky and the heat lay on the land. His speech was a high-pitched mutter that only his mother could understand. His damaged arm hung broken and withered by his side and his good hand was slow and clumsy, and Lily learned to feed her brother almost before she could feed herself. When he was back on his feet, Quin was sent up the hillside to mind the goats, usually the job of the youngest son, and made no complaint when his younger brothers teased him and ordered him around.

He grew into a big man, a great, gentle giant of a man with a slow smile and faded blue eyes behind which things came and went that nobody could grasp, least of all himself. His mother loved him fiercely and his father found her love harder to bear than the boy himself.

'Here you are then.'

The voice, gently spoken, roused Lily from her half slumber by the pig pen. She opened her eyes and squinted up at the man who stood in front of her. He was of middle years, tall and slender, dressed in an old brown tunic tied around the waist with a rope belt. His face was smooth and unlined, burned dark by the sun, his long elegant hands hardened by work. His straight, dark hair, streaked with grey, was hacked off below his ears. This was Eumeus, their slave.

He squatted down in front of Lily and nodded towards the carvings on the pig pen wall. 'Been visited old friends?'

Lily smiled. 'How's it going, Eumeus?'

The slave shook his head. 'Not good. Your father's been gone too long. Your mother will be pleased to have another pair of hands.'

'I'm pregnant.'

The slave's expression didn't alter. 'We'll manage.'

He stood up and held out his hand. Lily grabbed it and he pulled her to her feet.

'Now come and eat.' His long, serious face lit into a smile. 'Your mother wanted to kill a kid. Quin's been trying to stop her.'

Lily returned the smile. 'It's good to be home.'

3

If Lily thought it was hard work being a kitchen slut in her aunt's inn, she soon changed her mind. At least she'd had hot water to wash in and good food to eat. Kid meat seethed with vegetables, fresh bread, eggs and cheese. Grapes and pomegranates from the garden. Turkish delight, pink and sweet, that she sometimes bought from the market stalls set up along the harbour wall.

Once her sickness was gone, Lily was ravenously hungry. But there was little food to be had. Dried beans boiled up with whatever herbs her mother could find along the dry stream bed. The tough, stringy flesh of an old hen, gone off the lay. Curdy goats cheese, strained through a cloth and eaten with the flat grey bread her mother baked on the hot stone hearth. And the work was unremitting.

The small farm had been run quite comfortably by Lily's father and brothers, helped by their handful of slaves. It had left Cleia with leisure for spinning and weaving, and for the fancy embroidery she could exchange at the market for the occasional luxury when the trading caravans passed through. But now, as summer turned to autumn, there was only Lily and Cleia to help Eumeus cut and stook the wheat, harvest the olives and crush them into oil and pick the small sweet grapes ready for making into wine.

Wine crushing was a festive occasion for the whole village, even in those hard times. It was Lily's first visit to the village since her return home and she found it a strange, melancholy experience. The pressing tub had been dragged out into the square, the tables set up under the trees and laid with bread and cheese, and jars of well-watered wine, just as usual. But there were no men left any more to do the crushing. Only the old, recruited from their sunny benches to lend a hand, and young boys doing the hard work in the tub which had always been the privilege of older brothers.

Young women watched the little lads' scrawny legs crushing the grapes and sighed for other years when the young men, sweaty and wine-scented, would take them by the hand and whirl them in dance around the square and then push them into dark corners where the real business of the day was done. But there would be no new life created at this wine-crushing. In fact there was no new life at all. Staring round at the other girls, Lily realised that she was the only one who was expecting a child and she plucked nervously at her thin tunic to hide the rounding of her belly.

All the talk was of invasion. Somebody's son who had come home to nurse a broken wrist said there was trouble at the northern edge of the old kingdom where a narrow strait of water divided the king's land from that which, so far as anybody knew, belonged to nobody. There were people on the far shore building wooden ships as fast as they were able and, every time one was finished, it was laden with folk and set afloat.

'What's the point of that?' Lily asked. 'There's nothing left for them to take.'

'They're not after palace treasure,' said the lad. 'Not these people. It's land they want.'

'They should stay where they are then,' said Lily, suppressing the urge to break wind, 'there's plenty of land up there that nobody wants.'

But the story made her nervous as the days shortened and the cold wind blew down from the hills. Huddled under the blankets with her mother while the baby skipped and turned inside her, she listened to the howl of the wind and remembered Xander's face that day in the orchard. 'There's trouble coming,' he had said and, although he hadn't told her what form the trouble would take, she was sure that boatloads of barbarians coming into an unprotected land would bring trouble indeed.

'They should come home,' she said to her mother one night when the baby's kicking had woken them both. 'My father and brothers. We need them here.'

But Cleia, who had reached the time in her life when she preferred her daughter's company in bed to that of her husband, turned over and took Lily awkwardly in her arms.

'We'll just have to manage the best we can.'

It was Quin who saw them first. He came down the hill at a run, scattering the hens scratching by the doorway and arrived in the house, panting and running with sweat.

'Fire! Men!'

He grabbed Lily painfully by the arm and dragged her outside. Cleia followed, wiping her hands on the front of her tunic. From the middle of the valley, where the village lay, thick grey smoke billowed into the hot afternoon sky. Eumeus hurried up from the bean field, wiping his forehead with the back of his hand.

'You'd better go inside,' he said to Lily and Cleia.

'What's going on, Eumeus?' asked Lily.

'Trouble,' he said briefly, nodding towards the thin ribbon of road that ran along the floor of the valley. There were people on it. Men, moving swiftly. Lily could hear the sound of their shouting, thin and far away.

Eumeus bundled the two women into the house and shut them in. The door was seldom shut, summer or winter, and it took the combined efforts of both Eumeus and Quin to drag the heavy timber door scraping and shuddering across the dirt floor. In the sudden darkness Lily reached for her mother and the two women huddled together, eyes straining towards the cracks of light around the edge of the doorway.

Several hours later, with the hearth fire burned down to a sullen red glow, Lily heard heavy footsteps outside the door, followed by the exchange of voices, back and forth. That of strangers, talking in a language she couldn't understand. The high pitched mumble of Quin, cut short. Then Eumeus' voice, calm and serious as it always was, replying in the strange language. There was a swift exchange, followed by laughter from the strangers. Lily felt her heart pounding slowly in her chest and the sudden nervous skip of the child under her ribs. The door shuddered open, letting in the glory of a golden sunset.

'They want wine, mistress.'

Cleia put her hand against her chest. 'Then give it to them. Watered, mind. We don't want any trouble.

Eumeus inclined his head. 'I think you'd better come outside.'

He herded the two women out of the house, much as he had herded them in several hours previously. Sprawled on the bench beside the door were two young men. It almost made Lily laugh to see them because they were not much older than she was. They were handsome enough in their own way, dark-skinned with long, shaggy hair framing their beardless faces. They were dressed in dusty sheepskin tunics and thick leggings tied up with strips of leather. Propped up against the bench were two swords with heavy blades made of the same grey metal as the knife Lily's father had found after the palace burning.

The men turned their faces away from the setting sun and stared at the women. There was some more of the rapid speech and then one of them leapt up from the bench and bounded towards Lily. Fearfully she took a step backwards and suddenly Quin was there, pushing his way between Lily and the man. The man was no taller than Lily, and slightly made. He stared up at the red-faced giant and spoke angrily. Lily saw the swift movement of the man's hand towards his belt.

'No, Quin. It's all right.' She put her arm around him and pushed him to one side. Stepped forward and faced the man. He spoke. Smiled, showing white teeth against his dark skin. Reached forward and touched the round globe of her belly.

Lily turned her head. 'What is he saying, Eumeus?'

'That you are very beautiful and he will care for you and the child you carry.'

'*Care* for me? What are you talking about?'

'Mistress, this farm is theirs now.' He waved his hand in the direction of the darkening valley where the smoke lay along the ground, amethyst in the light from the dying sun. 'All the valley belongs to their chief. We should think ourselves lucky they are letting us stay.'

'So what does that make me? His *slave*?'

'On the contrary, mistress. You are his wife.'

If Lily imagined the arrival of the barbarian brothers would make life easier for the rest of them, she was sadly mistaken.

They were, after all, conquerors and although a poor farm on the slopes of an anonymous valley might not have been what they had been hoping for, they were determined to enjoy the spoils of their victory. The fact that it had been against a slave, a fool and two women did nothing to change their attitude. It became clear early on that Lily's so-called husband Fen and his brother Ger knew nothing about farming and had no intention of learning. The two men took a liking to the bench where Lily had first seen them, stretching out their long legs and passing the wine jug between them, while they admired the play of sun and shadow in the valley below and waited for the next meal to arrive.

Come spring, Lily took over Quin's duty with the goats so that he could help Cleia and Eumeus plough the small, stony fields and plant the summer crop. It became Fen's fancy to climb the hill to where Lily sat uncomfortably in the shade of a thorn tree. He would lie beside her with his hands behind his head, staring up at the sky. To Lily, watching her mother bent double in the fields below, Fen's behaviour was intensely irritating but she had her child to think of and she never forgot that Fen had the power to decide its fate. When they understood a little of each other's language, Fen asked Lily about the old palace. He said that they had heard about the palaces and the rich lands they ruled, had grown up on the stories of them told around the fire on winter's nights. It's what had decided them to come south, to seek their fortunes in softer lands.

'You're too late,' said Lily. 'The raiders took everything the night the palace burned.'

'But what about the gold? The stories said there was gold buried in the hills. D'you mean to say you've never looked for it?'

Lily shuddered. 'I wouldn't go up there, not if the whole hill was made of gold.'

'But why?'

'Because the place is full of ghosts, that's why. After the fire there was nobody to help the dead into the next life and they are up there still.'

Fen grinned, showing white teeth. 'I don't know what you're frightened of. We like the souls of our ancestors around us.' He turned on his elbow to face Lily. 'Wouldn't you like gold around your neck, Lily? In your ears?' He reached out his hand. 'I'd like to put it there.'

Lily shrugged, thinking about Xander's piece of amber, hidden under a loose stone in the hearth. 'It wouldn't stop my stomach growling.'

After that Fen used to go up to the ruined palace from time to time, poking around among the fallen walls and the dusty, crumbling timber, grown over with weeds. One time he found a necklace set with turquoise but it wasn't gold. He sat on the bench with the wine jug beside him and polished the dull metal links with a bit of cloth, as if it was the most important job he could find to do, while Eumeus and Cleia struggled to keep the new crop alive, carrying jars of water from the small, green pool under the shadow of the hill which was all that remained of the winter rains.

Lily's labour was short and painful, the child a sturdy boy. It amazed Lily, when Cleia put him in her arms, that such long, rounded limbs, such dark, knowing eyes, could have been contained within her body all that time. The two women had been alone in the house during the luminous spring night, the men who crowded their lives having taken themselves off to sleep elsewhere.

In the morning, as custom demanded, Cleia took the child and showed him to Fen who was sprawled impatiently on the bench outside the door. Fen reached over and unwrapped the child, making him whimper as the cold air touched his skin. The whimper turned to a wail which brought Quin stumbling from the shed, followed closely by Eumeus. Quin wanted to hold the child, his big hand reaching forward eagerly, but memories of spilled drinks and broken pots caused Cleia to push his hand away.

'Later, Quin. Now I'll get your breakfast.'

Lily was awake when Cleia took the child back inside.

'What did he say?'

Cleia shrugged. 'Not much. He said he and Ger were going down to the village later to celebrate.' She snorted. 'As if he doesn't celebrate every day of his life right here at home.'

4

Lily called her son Lex, after his father. Once she had recovered from his birth she thought it prudent to give Fen a child of his own. But she found it difficult to conceive again and Lex was two years old when the new baby was born. The baby suffered from the twin disadvantages of being a girl and sickly, exhausting her mother night after night which pleased Fen not at all who wanted to use Lily for his own purposes. Lily sometimes wondered if she had wasted her time having Roza, or if Fen even remembered that Lex was not his son. He treated both children the same way he treated all the other members of the little household over which he ruled with a lazy indifference.

By then, Fen's brother Ger had married a girl from one of the neighbouring farms, a handsome, dark-haired wench who turned shrew the minute the wedding feast was eaten. Forced to make himself useful and keen to stay out of her way, Ger took to hunting in the forest beyond the valley and often Fen went with him. Hunted out in the palace's heyday, the forest was now well stocked with wild pig and deer, providing excellent hunting for the two young men and the added bonus of praise from their women folk when they returned home with meat for the pot. Lily found life a lot easier to bear when Fen was not around and the meat helped her recover from her long and painful labour and kept her milk in while she struggled to keep her tiny daughter alive.

The winter after Roza's birth was bitterly cold and Cleia developed a dry rattling cough which not even the warm days of spring could dispel. Cold winter turned to hot summer and there was no rain. By midsummer Cleia had taken to her bed, so ill and weak she hardly had the strength to lift her head to sup at the thin barley broth that Lily kept warm on the hearth. She needed someone to nurse her, someone to sit her up and hold her when she had a coughing fit, someone to wipe her face and bathe her body when the night sweats hit her. But there was nobody to do it. It was all Lily could do to work in the fields, care for her children and give Fen what satisfaction she could spare before sleep possessed her.

With that strange intuition small children often possess, Lex took to spending part of each day sitting on the floor in his grandmother's line of sight playing with his collection of pebbles, his latest obsession, and babbling cheerfully to himself, neither wanting nor expecting any reply from the old lady in the bed. But he ran outside when she started to cough, frightened by the noise, and left her to get on with it as best she could.

It was on the day the well ran dry that Lily realised the extent of her misery. The well drew its water from an underground stream and Lily knew with a sinking heart that the lack of anything but a brown trickle was not because the stream had failed but because the well was choked with leaves and debris. It had always been the job of the slaves to clean out the well and it had not been done since they took themselves off more than three years ago. Lily knew there was only one person who could go down and clean it out now. Quin was too big. Lex was too small. Cleia, who would have done anything to ease the burden on her daughter, was far too sick even to be told.

Early the following morning, with Eumeus on the end of the rope, Lily climbed down into the narrow, stinking shaft, banging her knuckles on the slimy stone walls until her feet connected with a narrow ledge near the level of the water. She looked up and saw Eumeus' anxious face filling up the small bright circle at the top of the shaft. Below her feet was the stench of drowned leaves and the dark, secret smell of water. Eumeus had rigged up a square of heavy cloth, tied at the corners, to hold the leaves and Lily had to load it several times before the well was clear.

Each time the slave heaved the heavy, dripping cloth to the surface, Lily crouched in the darkness at the bottom of the well while the black, stinking water fell onto her head and showers of dead leaves covered her head and shoulders. Then, when she felt that she could endure no more, the rope came snaking down out of the bright circle of the sky and Eumeus, as exhausted as she was, dragged her out.

He laughed when he saw her. She cried. He made her sit in the shade and brought her a fresh-cooked barley cake dribbled with honey. He made her feel like a child again and, looking up at him, Lily realised that the old slave was one of the very few sure things that she had in her life. It made her smile to realise how much she had come to depend on him, this strange, quiet man who worked her fields and slept in the shed where the farm tools were kept.

On a still morning in late summer Cleia died peacefully in her sleep, leaving behind a body that was little more than bones held together with fine, white skin. She had been a beautiful woman once and, with the weariness gone from her face, she was suddenly beautiful again. Cleia's funeral, held on a day of fierce heat, was the first Lily had attended since the coming of Fen's people to the valley. It was a day of strange contrasts. The almost overwhelming feeling of despair at the loss of her mother was tempered by the pleasure she found in the company of several of her neighbours, including Ger and his wife and a gaggle of small children whose presence at the farm seemed to echo the occasions which had marked her own childhood.

Several small boys teamed up with Lex to chase the hens into cackling displeasure on the branches of the nearest tree, leaving behind one small, white egg over which the boys fought fiercely. Roza, now nine months old and beginning to thrive, was admired by the woman causing Fen to pick her up and toss her about energetically in a sudden excess of fatherly zeal.

With the backing of the other men of his tribe, Fen had insisted that Cleia be cremated. Despite local custom, the idea of burying a body in the ground was completely abhorrent to Fen's people who had been wandering herdsmen before they invaded the land of the old king. For once, Lily was fervently grateful for her status as a woman because cremations were men's business in Fen's tribe and she could stay with the woman and children some distance from the carefully built fire which was going to consume her mother's body. However it was not as dreadful as Lily imagined. The fire caught and burned quickly and she found herself being congratulated by her neighbours when the thin column of smoke rose straight up into the hot afternoon sky, a sign that her mother's soul had been accepted by whatever gods lived there.

Afterwards there was food to eat and gossip to share. Lily found herself talking to Jen who had been a child in the village when Lily left to work for her aunt but who was now heavy with a child of her own. Sitting in the thin shade of a tree and mopping her brow, Jen was staring across the valley to where white clouds were gathering on the horizon.

'D'you think it's going to rain?' asked Lily, handing her a beaker of watered wine.

Jen shrugged. 'It never rains. Or, if it does, it never stops. It's a stinking place, this.' She turned to face Lily. 'You got away, didn't you? Why did you come back? I wouldn't.'

Lily opened the front of her shift to let Roza suckle. 'I had nowhere else to go.'

'What was it like? Where you went?'

'I don't know how to describe it.'

How could you describe the sea to someone who had never seen it? Lily remembered her first glimpse of it, vast and shiny like the sky had fallen onto the land. Even at night it looked like the sky was upside down, crossed by the golden path of the moon. Lily gave up the attempt.

'My aunt's house was very big. I worked in the kitchen. It had a stone floor.'

Jen's eyes were like pebbles in her face. 'A stone *floor*? My man Ryn had never lived in a house before he came here. He says they used to live in shelters made with willow withies and the hides of animals.' She wrinkled her nose. 'Imagine that!'

'They were travellers, that's what Fen says. That's why they burn people instead of burying them. Because they didn't have any land of their own to put them in.'

'They're still travellers,' said Jen. 'Ryn wants to move on. He says there are places across the sea. Rich places. Better than here.' She turned to face Lily. 'Would you go over the sea? On a ship?'

'Yes. Why not?' Lily felt her heart skip in her chest. The baby woke suddenly and started to cry.

'Why don't you ask Fen? He might want to go.'

But the thought of Fen stirring himself sufficiently to move his family even as far as the coast was so improbable that Lily laughed.

'That'll be the day.'

Gradually people drifted home until finally it was just Fen and his brother sitting on the bench, drinking away the last of the day. Lily, going into the house to settle an exhausted Lex, realised for the first time that her mother had gone for ever and it was up to her now to do for her own children what Cleia had always done for her. It was a desolate thought. That afternoon the idea of leaving, of going somewhere - anywhere - had awoken in her chest a slow-beating excitement. Now, standing wearily in the dark house listening to the slow murmur of Fen's voice beyond the door and the quiet whimper of the sleeping baby, she felt her excitement die like yesterday's ashes as she realised that escape was as impossible for her as it was for Eumeus, her slave. She stared down at her son who, suddenly sleepy, was blinking at her from the bed. She bent her head and kissed his warm cheek.

'Sweet dreams, darling.'

'What are you doing out here?'

Crouched by the pig pen wall, Lily hadn't heard Eumeus' approach until he loomed over her, black against the luminous sky. The clouds were higher now, great pale shapes heaped in the sky, and full of lightning.

Eumeus crouched next to her. 'You should be in bed. Not out here in the dark.'

She turned her face towards his. 'In bed asleep so I can get up in the morning and work again?'

'You need your sleep. The baby ...'

But Lily wasn't listening. 'You know something, Eumeus? We're two of a kind, you and me. We're both working for someone else. Is this what it's been like for you all these years? I don't know why you didn't run away. Or ... or end it all. That's what I feel like doing.'

Eumeus reached out and touched her arm. 'It's only because of your mother you feel this way.'

Lily ignored his words. 'Do you know what I own, Eumeus?

In the whole world? A turquoise necklace. A lump of amber ...' Lily opened her hand and showed him the stone, black and anonymous in the darkness. '... and *you.*' She shook her head. 'It's ridiculous, don't you think? A slave owning a slave? Because that's what I am. I didn't choose to live this way. Or *him* for a husband.' She gestured with her head towards the house.

'Can I see it? The amber.' Eumeus held out his hand and Lily dropped the stone into his open palm. He held it up to the luminous sky. 'You know where amber comes from, don't you, Lily?' Eumeus' voice was gentle in the darkness. 'If you follow the sun towards the west you come to a people who know nothing of farming or towns. Who only hunt and follow the herds ...'

'Like Fen. That's what his people used to do.'

'Ah, yes, but these people are different. They draw pictures on the walls of caves. Fantastic pictures. Yet they know nothing of metal or pottery. They find this precious stuff - this amber - in the ground and sell it to the traders in exchange for the things we have and think nothing of.' Eumeus put the amber back into Lily's outstretched hand. 'It's the colour of the setting sun, you see, because that's where it comes from.'

'Someone once said it was the colour of my hair.'

'And he was quite right. Exactly the colour of your hair. I presume it was a man who said that?'

Lily nodded. 'It was Lex's father.'

'Who was he, Lily?'

She shrugged. 'A sailor. An adventurer. I think he was probably a pirate, too, when it suited him. He used to come to my aunt's house when his ship was in port.'

'But I thought ... I didn't think ...'

Lily laughed softly. 'No, no, I wasn't one of my aunt's girls. I was working in the kitchen, that's all. But I loved him, see? He was so ... so beautiful. And the last time ...'

'He loved you.'

'Yes, he loved me. And when I knew I was carrying his child, I didn't stop it. I could have. The girls would have told me what to do. But I didn't want to lose the child, too.' Suddenly Lily couldn't stop talking. 'He told me ... Xander told me that there was going to be trouble. That we might never see each other again. He gave me the amber to keep for him. I think it was his way of saying that one day we'd be together again.'

'Well, he was right about the trouble.'

Lily bent forward and scratched a hole in the damp ground. She pushed the piece of amber into the hole as far as it would go and covered it with earth, forcing it down with the heel of her hand. Lightening as bright as day lit up the sky. Pushing a strand of hair from her face, she looked up at Eumeus' puzzled expression.

'If I leave it here it means I'll come back one day to find it.'

'Are you thinking of going somewhere?'

'I might be.' She reached out and grabbed the slave's arm. 'Eumeus, they were talking today. Some of them from the village. They're going away. Across the sea. I want to go, too.'

'You'll never persuade that husband of yours to shift himself further than the bean field.'

'I'm going, Eumeus. I've made up my mind.' Lily pushed back her hair with the heel of her hand. 'There's something I have to do first. I was going to wait until morning but I can do it now.' She reached out her hand and touched Eumeus on the shoulder. 'I free you, Eumeus.'

Eumeus turned and looked at his shoulder where the girl's hand lay. 'What did you do that for?'

'I told you. Because it's madness for a slave to own a slave. Anyway I need your help. As a friend.'

'What do you want me to do?' Eumeus' voice was cautious.

'Go, if you want to, of *course*. There's nothing to hold you any more.'

'And you want me to go? Is that the idea?'

Lily shook her head. 'No, of course I don't want you to go. Why on earth would I want you to do that?'

'So why did you say it?'

'Look, Eumeus, you're free.' Lily took her hand from Eumeus' shoulder and dragged it through her hair. 'You can choose to go or stay. That's all I'm saying. What *I* want doesn't count. Not any more.'

Eumeus was silent for a long moment. Thunder growled, far away. Several large drops of rain fell onto the ground.

'I was born a slave,' Eumeus said quietly. 'I don't think I'd know what to do with freedom. It's frightening more than anything.'

A sudden spurt of laughter. 'Well, I can't make you a slave again. I couldn't afford you, for a start. I just gave away most of what I own. And buried the rest.'

'So what happens now?'

'I'm going up the hill to dig up the gold. That's what I want you to help me with.'

'What gold? I didn't think there was anything left.'

'Not in the palace, Eumeus. In the graves. I remember my father telling me how the palace folk used to bury their dead with all the things they'd need to be comfortable in the life to come. It's what we do, too. My mother's spindle went with her into the fire today. It was all I could spare. If I'd put in her cooking pot too, there'd be nothing for me to boil the porridge in tomorrow. But rich folk could put everything in - cups and bowls and weapons. Oil and wine. All the fine things they wore everyday.'

'So why haven't you dug it up before? If you knew it was there?'

'Because I was too scared. Scared of what would happen if I started digging up people's graves. But now ... now I'm more scared of staying here and fading into dust, like my mother did.'

'When are you going?'

'Now. Tonight.'

'And you want me to come with you?'

'*Yes*. Will you?'

Eumeus stood up and wiped his hand carefully on the back of his tunic. Reached down to help Lily to her feet.

'Come on, then. Before it starts to rain.'

5

At the top of the hill Lily stepped through the ruined gateway and stood in the paved courtyard where her father used to wait to pay his tribute to the king's clerks.

Eumeus came up behind her. 'This way.'

But Lily knew where the graves were. Away from the palace buildings but enclosed within the encircling walls, they straggled down the hill, buried in long grass. It was where she and her brothers had played while her father and Quin manhandled the carved grave markers they had used to build the pig pen walls. The remaining stones lay flat on the ground or leaned at a drunken angle, marking the graves of kings and nobles long since gone and forgotten.

Somewhere behind the clouds the moon was shining, casting a grey luminescence over the desolate scene. The light from Eumeus' clay lamp was like a golden teardrop in his hand. He put it onto the nearest grave stone.

'Newest first, I think. They'll be shallower and easier to dig.'

Lily shivered.

'Are you cold, mistress?'

She shook her head.

'No. Not cold. And don't call me 'mistress', Eumeus. It'd better be Lily from now on.'

'I'll dig.' Eumeus thrust his spade into the ground. 'You sit over there and hold the lamp. I'll let you know when I want it.'

Lily squatted on the grave stone and held the small clay lamp cupped in her hands. She watched Eumeus digging in the ground.

'Eumeus ...'

'What?' A grunt.

'If you have been a slave all your life how did you end up being *our* slave?'

Yesterday it would have been impossible to ask. Tonight it was different. But Lily was still not sure if Eumeus would reply.

He straightened up and wiped his forehead with the back of his hand. 'It's a long story, Lily.'

'Where did you come from? You can tell me that at least. Is it from the setting sun? Where the amber comes from?'

Eumeus laughed and shook his head. He bent to the digging again. 'Far from it. I was born in the east. In a great city a long way from the sea.'

'So how did you know about the amber?'

'If you are so rich that you have everything you want of the things that are around you, then you start wanting things that come from far away. That's what it was like in that city. Traders went to the setting sun. To the south where the hot lands are and the people are the colour of the earth. To kill the great, grey beasts and steal their teeth.'

'Their *teeth*?'

'One long tooth, either side. The length of a man standing. *Damn*. Bring the lamp, Lily.'

The golden gleam of the lamp showed a broken pottery vessel with something dark and damp seeping out.

'Oil. Hang on, there's something else.' Eumeus bent down.

'What is it?'

'Bone.' Eumeus sent the object spinning away into the darkness. 'I knew things were getting bad even before the palace burnt down. I didn't think they had got this bad.'

'What d'you mean?'

'There's nothing here. No gold, at any rate.' He grinned, showing his teeth. 'Not even a spindle We'd better try the ones down the hill. Bring the lamp.'

The oldest graves were huddled in the shadow of the great wall. Here the ground was hard and littered with great slabs of stone. In some places sapling trees had taken root, their strange, black moon-shadows motionless on the ground. Eumeus grabbed the nearest tree and began shaking it backwards and forwards. He put his foot on its thin trunk and pushed hard. There was a cracking sound and the tree slumped over. Eumeus grunted.

'Come on, girl. Lend me a hand.'

Lily grabbed a handful of leaves from the tree's crown

and pulled hard. The leaves came away in her hand and she staggered backwards, almost falling.

'No, not there. Round here. With me.'

Lily ran around to where Eumeus was pushing on the tree. She placed her hands below his and tensed her arms.

'Ready? *Now!*'

For a while the tree resisted. Lily could feel the heat from Eumeus' body, smell his sweat, hear his breath whistling in and out. She felt a sudden weariness and the sting of milk in her breasts. Then, with one final push, the tree laid itself out on the ground like its own shadow, revealing a tangle of roots and the rich smell of disturbed earth.

Lily sank to the ground and sat with her head between her arms, struggling to regain her breath. Finally she spoke. 'Eumeus, why did we knock that tree down?'

'In this country trees grow where the soil is deepest. I thought you would have known that.'

'And the soil is deepest where the graves are?'

'That's what I'm hoping. Plus, the tree's done our digging for us. Now, where's the lamp?'

After a search, Lily found the lamp tangled among the branches of the tree. The light had gone out.

'We won't be able to see anything.'

Eumeus climbed into the dark hole underneath the tree's roots. 'We can see enough to tell the difference between bone and gold, which is all that matters.' He lifted his head. 'We'd better hurry. That storm's not far away.'

Bent double, Eumeus dug into the soft dirt. Kneeling by the hole, Lily scooped up the damp earth in armfuls and dumped it on the grass. A warm damp wind swept over the hill, cooling the sweat on the back of her neck. With it came the sound of distant thunder and the sweet smell of rain.

'There!' Eumeus was down on his hands and knees scrabbling in the soil, his breath coming in whistles and grunts.

'What is it?' Lily crouched on the edge of the hole, leaning forward as far as she dared.

'Something. I saw it just then. Hang on ...' Eumeus straightened up and put something into Lily's hand.

It was a goblet. Through the dirt Lily could see the pale gleam of metal.

'What is it?'

Eumeus laughed. 'What do you think it is? A cup.'

'To drink from?' Even in her aunt's house there had only been pottery beakers. Painted, some of them, with fantastic designs of plants or sea creatures. But pottery nevertheless.

'Of course to drink from,' said Eumeus. 'What do you think it's for? To look at?'

'That's what I'd do with it. Like my mother's bronze pot that the soldiers took.' Lily rubbed the goblet on the sleeve of her gown and held it up to the sky, twisting it this way and that to catch the strange half-light of the storm. 'Is it gold?'

'Aye, it's gold sure enough.' Eumeus was back on his knees, scrabbling in the dirt. 'Put it down, Lily. There's plenty more where that came from.'

For a while there was no sound but the grumble of the thunder, suddenly close at hand. Lightening ripped the sky above their heads, lighting up the scene like day. Then the rain came, freezing rain like cold pebbles on Lily's skin. Instantly she was soaked through, her hair plastered to her head, the dirt on her hands running like rivulets down her arms.

Eumeus knelt in the hole, half-sheltered by the roots of the tree. His hand reached up again. Another goblet, the rain revealing the sunset gleam of ancient gold. Then more. Plates and bowls. Neck rings and arm rings, laden with gems. A round shield, embossed with loops and swirls like the patterns on the pig-pen walls.

Suddenly Lily thought about the time she had been down the well and the water and muck had soaked her and made Eumeus laugh.

'Remember when I was down the well?'

She was heaping the stuff, streaming with mud and rain, onto the shield where it lay in a slippery, gleaming pile.

Eumeus grunted. 'It's a bit different tonight.'

'Perhaps I'll laugh at you this time.'

'Will you give me a honey cake if I do?' And then, suddenly, 'Oh, Lily, *Lily!*'

Lily looked up, suddenly afraid. Eumeus stood in the dark, wet hole. His head was up, rain pouring down the familiar planes of his face. He lifted up his arms to the storm. For a moment Lily thought he was crying. But it was laughter. Standing chest-deep in an ancient grave, the freed man laughed, shaking his fists at the sky where some say the gods dwelt.

'Here, give me a hand.' Eumeus was himself again. He held his hand up to Lily and she pulled him from the hole. The rain was easing now, dripping heavily from the trees and Lily could hear the hush of the small stream at the bottom of the hill.

'We'd better go home.' She bent to shovel the jewellery into a loop of her skirt 'Can you manage the rest?' She turned to see Eumeus carrying the piled shield. 'What are we going to do with it?'

'Put it somewhere it won't be seen. Now, come on. You must be frozen.'

They climbed over a gap in the wall and took the short way down the hill, slipping and sliding through the wet grass until they arrived, soaked and exhausted, behind the goat shed at the back of the farm. Lily was shivering with cold and she could feel the milk heavy in her breasts.

'I hope Roza's still asleep.'

'If she was awake, that man of yours would be out here looking for you. There's not much he can do for her.'

'If she was awake, he'd let her cry. He's done it often enough.'

'Go on, then. You'd better get yourself inside.' He indicated Lily's sodden, dripping skirt. 'Dump that lot on the ground. I'll see to it.'

'Where are you going to put it?'

'Over the pig pen wall for now, and hope the pigs don't take it into their heads to eat it before morning.'

'Would pigs eat gold?'

'Pigs will eat anything, in my experience. Now, goodnight.'

The baby was asleep, her small face pink and peaceful in the dim glow from the banked fire. Lily kicked off her clothes and sat on the stool by the hearth while she wrung the rain from her hair. Then she climbed into bed, dragged the covers over herself and lay shivering. Her husband turned and murmured in his sleep.

'Lily? Where have you been? You're freezing.'

'Out in the storm. Listen to the rain! There's water in the stream.'

'What did you want to do a thing like that for? You'll catch your death of cold.' Fen reached out and gathered Lily in his arms, tucking her damp head under his chin and wrapping his warm legs around her cold ones.

'Better?'

It was the only kind thing Fen had ever done in all their time together and, coming as it did on top of the excitement of the night, Lily felt the tears thick in her throat. But she was too tired to cry, however much she felt like doing it, and it was too near morning to delay sleep any longer. Already the sky beyond the doorway was washed with grey. She pushed her face into the soft hollow of Fen's neck and, with the delicious warmth creeping up from her feet, closed her eyes and fell instantly asleep.

6

The hardest part about packing up was selling Quin's goats.
The most surprising was how much they were worth. Lily had
long known that Quin liked to breed his animals for the pretty
colours he could get but that his goats were bigger and gave
more milk she found out only when she and Eumeus drove
the herd down into the village on market day, leaving Quin
behind to mope on the hillside. In the end she allowed Quin to
keep several of his favourites to form the basis of a new herd
in whatever land they came to. With the palace gold hidden
in crates of garden tools, dropped into the bottom of oil jars
and sewn into the hems of blankets and shawls there was no
need for them to travel with the gaggle of animals that was
to accompany their neighbours, and it would have been much
easier not to, but Quin's look of despair was more than Lily
could bear.

Still they travelled light compared with the families that
straggled up the road from the village on the appointed
morning. Fen, following Lily up the hill with Lex on his
shoulders, greeted his brother loudly and the two men walked
together in the middle of the untidy procession made by the
half dozen migrating families. They made no attempt to help
their wives who struggled to keep their little parties together
in between refastening bundles that had come undone and
stopping by the wayside to attend to small children's urgent
needs.

Encouraged by their women, the two men had come to view
the approaching migration with approval. Fen had taken it
upon himself to visit the village most days in the weeks leading
up to their departure to attend to the heavy matter of planning
while Lily and Eumeus gathered in the harvest, helped by Lex
whose sturdy little legs ran up and down the fields throughout

those endless late summer days, his small face alight with joy from the few gruff words of praise he received from the old slave.

The day of the wine pressing was one of mingled celebration and sadness as families prepared to be parted. But there was food and wine, and dancing to the music of the small wooden flutes which the newcomers had brought into the valley. Sitting in the shade with Roza sprawled asleep on her lap Lily watched the old people holding and kissing their precious grandchildren, soon to be lost to them forever, and wondered if they remembered that the fathers of those same children had come into the valley as conquerors only five years previously. Or if they ever thought about the other men who had gone off to fight and never returned.

What with goats wandering off in search of greener pickings and children growing tired and wanting to be carried, it took them a full five days to make the journey to the coast and it was late in the afternoon when they came to the top of the hill and looked down on the little harbour town where Lily's aunt kept her house.

Most of the valley people had never seen the sea and their eyes were drawn to the sight of the shining water but Lily, who had seen it all before, said to Eumeus, 'There's something wrong.'

Eumeus shaded his eyes with his hand. 'No ships in the harbour.'

'Yes, that. But look, Eumeus. The town's been burnt. And not long ago.'

Squinting in the sea-glitter, Eumeus followed Lily's pointing finger and saw the huddle of houses around the harbour, all roofless with blackened beams and collapsed tiles.

'Where's your aunt's house?'

'Halfway up the hill. You can't see it from here.' She turned her head. 'Eumeus, it's what Xander said was going to happen. Lex's father. Who do you think it was?'

'Pirates. Invaders. Who knows?'

'What are we going to do?'

'Not go into the town. At least not now. Let's get a fire going. We'll sleep up here tonight.'

Quin ambled up with a small, grubby child astride his shoulders. 'Water,' he said, nodding his head in the direction of the glittering sea.

'Never mind about that now, Quin,' said Lily. 'Put that child down and find some wood for a fire. It'll be cold soon.'

In the morning the scene at the bottom of the hill had changed. A ship had arrived in the night and was tied up at the end of the harbour wall. Fen, Ger and the other men decided to go down and find out what was going on.

While they were away, Lily and Eumeus went in search of Lily's aunt's house. It took a while for Lily to get her bearings in the deserted streets but finally she found the long high wall and, halfway along, the gate that led into the garden. The gate was open.

Inside, the garden was as she remembered it. Doves making love on the low roof. The pomegranate tree hung with orange globes. The grass a little long and starred with flowers. But the kitchen door hung on its hinges showing an interior black with fire. As they approached, the stench of death came to them and made Lily retch. It was Sylos, grown to a man, but Sylos nevertheless, dressed in one of his ridiculous embroidered tunics and lying on his back just inside the doorway, legs asprawl, with a great, black wound in his chest, crawling with flies.

Eumeus bent over the body. 'Was he a friend of yours?'

Lily nodded. She remembered Sylos' scrawny body next to hers in the narrow bed, and the swift, sweaty coupling that passed for love. Remembered how he used to share the things he stole, crouched by the windy fire on cold nights with all the knobs of his backbone sticking out underneath his clothes.

'How long has he been dead?'

'Three or four days by the look of him.' Eumeus looked up. 'Do you want to look any further?'

Lily shook her head. 'What do you suppose happened to the girls?'

Eumeus shrugged. 'Plying their trade for different masters.'

Lily shivered. 'If I'd still been here, it would have been me.'

'If we'd arrived three days earlier, it would have been all of us.'

She giggled suddenly. 'I don't suppose Fen and his brother thought about it in all that planning they did. Us getting killed before we even went anywhere.'

'No, probably not.' Eumeus allowed himself a small smile.

Outside the gate Lily paused with her hands on the latch.

'What's wrong?'

'Nothing. It's just ...'

'Just what?'

She turned her head. 'It's just that Xander won't know where to find me now. I thought ...'

'Thought what? Come on, Lily! You don't still expect him to come back, do you?' Eumeus put his hands on her shoulders and turned her gently to face him. 'Look at me, Lily. Look at me! The world's gone mad, don't you see? It's not a safe place any more. Not for any of us. Think of yourself, that's what you need to do. Forget about the things that will never happen.'

A gulp. 'That's what Sylos told me to do.' She nodded her head. 'Him, in there.' She pushed the back of her hand across her eyes. 'I suppose you're right. It's no good crying over what you can't have.' She pulled the gate shut behind her. 'Let's go and see what the men have found out about that ship. They should be back by now.'

Half way up the hill Lily paused for breath. She turned round and gazed out at the glittering sea.

'Are you glad we're going, Eumeus? You'll be nearer your own home, won't you? You said you came from the east. Where the sun rises.'

Eumeus squatted on his haunches and hung his arms over his legs.

'The farm was my home. And now ... wherever you are.'

'But, *why*?'

Eumeus smiled his slow serious smile. 'Because I was happy there, that's why. The last few years I've been happier than I've ever been in my life.'

'Since my father left?'

'Well, yes, I suppose so.'

'He used to beat you. I know that.'

Eumeus shrugged. 'I never minded being beaten. Sometimes it was all there was to show I was still alive.'

'What, then?'

He turned and stared at her. Didn't speak for a long moment. Then, 'It's just that I felt needed. Wanted. Like I was part of a ...'

'A family?'

'Yes. A family.'

'But you must have your own family, surely? Wouldn't you like to see them again?'

Eumeus shook his head. 'Impossible.'

'Because they're slaves?'

'No, because I'm one.' He bent his head forward and pushed his hair away from one ear. 'See?'

It was a raised mark, a strange pink scar in a shape that Lily didn't understand. She reached out her finger and touched it gently.

'What is it?'

'A slave mark. Put on me by my master.'

'But you're free now.'

He shook the hair back into place. 'With that mark on my body I'll never be truly free. Anyway I doubt if there's anyone left to remember me now. I haven't seen my mother since I was eight.' He indicated with his hand. 'This high.' He stood up. 'Now, come on, or they'll be looking for us.'

'Tell me about it, Eumeus.'

An early memory. A dark night, the hiss of sleet against wooden shutters. Curled up in a warm bed against his mother's perfumed flank. He must have been very young. When they were two years old, the children were taken from their mothers and put into a big nursery. That was where the other memory came from. Sunlight falling through the fretwork frame of a big arched window, making strange shadows on a cool tiled floor. A necklace of blue painted beads. A hand reaching down to yank him up by one arm. The beads breaking, bouncing over the floor. His own yell, echoing in the big room. One hard slap, enough to shut him up. Old enough to have learned that lesson, then.

'When we reached our eighth birthday, we were taken from the nursery and allocated our roles in the palace. The great thing was to be picked as a *castrato*, a eunuch, you know what that is, I suppose? It was the softest life of all and some of the *castrati* became very powerful, in their own way. Of course, what happened to them didn't stop them enjoying the pleasures of the flesh and they had their pick of the women, no questions asked. But you had to be a special sort of boy to be chosen as a eunuch. And they didn't choose me.'

Eumeus turned his head

'I had something they didn't like, a spark of independence, defiance, call it what you will. They tried to breed it out of us, like Quin and his goats. Breed us to be dull and obedient, interested only in the room they put us in and the task they wanted us to perform. But it didn't always work out that way.'

'So what happened to you?'

Eumeus shrugged. 'I suppose they thought that, if I had my eyes on the far horizon I might as well lift them higher, so they set me to study astronomy. I enjoyed the work and learned quickly. The old men were pleased with me, I remember that. And it's a funny thing but that teaching turned out to be the most precious thing they could have given me, the one thing that has brought me comfort in the life I have lead since I left the palace.'

'They let you leave?'

'I didn't choose to go, Lily. It was them that got rid of me. Looking back, I don't think things were going well for them just then. They gained their wealth from trade, you see, and trade has been difficult since the bull-ships left the seas.. Although it would have been hard to notice the hardship in a place like that. Except for the new pleasure-garden put off for another year and a few palace-born slaves standing in the market place with all the rest.'

'You must have been scared.' Lily thought of the slave market in the next village where her father went to buy field workers.

Eumeus shook his head. 'No, I wasn't scared, although I probably should have been. I was fourteen years old, well-educated, with hands like a baby. The thought of manual labour never crossed my mind. I didn't even know such a thing existed. How was I supposed to know about farms and mines and rowers' benches? I'd hardly ever been outside the palace. But it didn't take me long to find out, nor to discover that a nice, clean boy like me was worth a lot less than the rough crew standing with me who knew the meaning of a day's work.'

'Where did you go?'

'Many places. And everywhere I went the stars came with me. You see what I mean about them being a comfort? After a while it didn't really matter where I slept whether it was curled up on a bit of old sacking in the corner of a field, or in a leaky barn with a hundred other men, or laid out on the rowing benches in the middle of the ocean - and I've done that a few times, too, let me tell you, with the boat wallowing under sail and us too exhausted to care about pirates, or reefs, or even whether we woke up in the morning - because the stars were always there and always mine. The first thing I did when I arrived on your father's farm was knock a hole in the shed roof so I could see the stars from my bed. I had to fight a couple of the other men before I could do it but I was a good fighter by then and I wasn't scared of being hurt.'

Lily took a couple of swift steps to catch him up and laid her hand on his arm.

'I'm sorry.'

'What for?'

'For sleeping in a leaky shed and working the fields when you could have been ... '

'Could have been what, Lily?'

'Well, it doesn't seem right. A man like you. You should have been up at the palace with the tally clerks.'

A great bellow of laughter.

'What's so funny?'

'The palace. I was just thinking about the palace. You know, the first time I saw it, I thought it belonged to your father. I remember thinking, that's not half bad. Better than a lot of places I've been. And then we turned off from the road and I saw your house. It looked like somewhere you'd keep the pigs. But I thought, well, at least it'll be dry.' Another guffaw. 'And then I found out that was my master's house. Can you imagine? And I was in the shed with six other men.' He shook his head. 'That was before you were born. Quin was around the place though. He used to run in and out of the shed and gabble away in all the languages he heard us speaking. He could speak them well enough to make himself understood and, of course, he understood every word we said. Bright as a pebble he was. I've always thought it was a pity what happened to him the night the palace burned. Although I've never been convinced he's as daft as he looks.'

'Poor Quin.'

'Yes, poor Quin. Poor Lily. Poor Eumeus.' He grinned suddenly. 'Let's see what gold will do to make things better.'

7

The town was not as deserted as it first appeared. Cooking smells and the flap of washing greeted Lily and Eumeus as they descended the hill with the rest of the travellers. In a small, sunny plaza next to the harbour a market was in progress. Fruit and vegetables, still on the cart that had brought them from the farm, fresh fish laid out in rows and a tangle of squid and octopus drowning in their own ink, chickens with their necks rung, hung up by their feet. Tall jars of wine stood in the shelter of a hastily erected sail, serving women busy among the crowded benches of men. Not surprisingly, Fen and Ger were in the thick of it. From the middle of the crowded tent, Fen raised his arm and beckoned to Lily and, when there was no response, stood up and threaded his way unsteadily between the tables.

'It'll take us,' he said. 'The ship. We leave tomorrow.'

'Where are we going?'

Fen waved his arm at the glittering sea. 'To the other side.' He frowned. 'Isn't that where we want to go?' He shrugged his shoulders when he got no response and went back to his drinking.

Eumeus had turned away while Fen talked to his wife. Even though he was a free man now and Lily's partner in this enterprise, Eumeus was not about to display his independence to the man who still thought himself his master. Lily found him standing by a market stall close to the harbour wall. He was turning something over in his hands. He looked up briefly when Lily came up to him and then returned to his study of the small object held in the palm of his hand. The stall was covered with a grubby linen cloth and was set out with an array of rings, pins and brooches made of gold or crystal. Some were carved intricately, others decorated with vivid enamelling. They were all breathtakingly beautiful, like nothing Lily had ever seen in her life before.

She reached out her hand and was aware of a sudden movement behind the stall. There was a man sitting on an upturned barrel, gnawing on a piece of cooked meat. He was powerfully built, black-haired, deeply sunburned, his face crossed with old scars. Not the sort of man Lily would expect to be the guardian of such treasures. She pulled her hand back but, at a nod from Eumeus, the man approached, wiping grease from his face with the back of his hand.

Lily picked up a small, flat stone. It was a cool, translucent white, showing the colour of the sea when she lifted it from the linen cloth. The design, cunningly executed to fit the circular shape, was of a large bull, head erect, horns curving around the rim of the stone. The man held out his hand, then moved the stone close to his face to squint at the design. He returned the stone to Lily's hand.

'My lady has good taste. A fine example of the craft.'

'Where did it come from?'

An eye-brow lifted. 'From the palace itself, of course.'

'The palace?' Lily was puzzled.

'He's talking about the bull palace, Lily.' Eumeus moved closer to the girl's side.

'The bull palace?' Lily stared up at the stall holder. 'You've been there?'

The man inclined his head. 'I was there two, three days ago. Called in here for supplies and to off load some of these little trinkets. Seems I am too late. The luxury trade has fallen off since the last time I was here.'

Lily stared down the little object, now warm from her flesh, and tried to remember what she knew about the bull palace. Her father had told her the tales: how the palace had existed on its green jewel of an island for as many years as there were stars in the sky and how it had been destroyed by an earthquake in the time of her great grandfather.

The people who lived there had been more like gods than humans. Small, dark and exquisitely beautiful. Able to command the seas in their small, swift ships. So powerful that the people in the area they controlled forgot about war and prospered under their benign rule. However, they exacted a payment for the prosperity they bestowed, or so the story went. A payment of pretty girls and boys for their bull dancing and the raw materials - gold, jasper, agate and green porphyry - for their art.

Lily knew they decorated everything with designs of incredible artistry, adorned their bodies with fine cloth and rich jewellery, lived in a palace so vast that it took a lifetime to learn how to cross from one side to the other. And that they worshipped the bull - a powerful creature with a black hide and golden horns who was both god and king. She was not sure she believed any of it.

She stared up into the man's pale blue eyes. 'What's it like?'

He shrugged. This was hard work, he thought, for the sale of something so small. Still, he'd get a good price for it. It was a fine piece, one of his best, and the old man obviously knew quality when he saw it. The girl, too, was beautiful and no doubt earned his generosity.

'Vast,' he said. 'Ruined. Deserted.'

'Doesn't anyone live there?'

He shuddered. 'Only ghosts.'

'Is there nobody left at all?'

'My lady, the people who inhabited the palace are gone. Dead, or sailed away. Some say they went towards the setting sun to found a new city. Some say they went south to live in the court of the Nile king. Those that are left on the island are the ancient ones who came from the womb of the earth. They served the palace folk for as long as the palace stood on the hill. Now they have nobody to serve but still they farm the fields, setting aside the tribute of oil and grain to stand by the road and go rotten in the sun.' The man stared down at Lily's startled face. 'They can afford it, lady. The land is rich. And they are too stupid to realise they don't have to do it any more.' He turned around and spat into the harbour waters. 'They are like dogs without a master. You can kill them for sport, if you care to, and they will stand there and let you do it.'

'And ... these things?'

'They pick them up when they find them. Plough them out of the fields. Give them to you, if you ask for them. They are happy to do it, grateful even that they have a chance to serve. I'll tell you, it's not a place to visit often. It makes your skin crawl. And then when you get back to your ship it's loaded with jars of grain and wine. Chuck them overboard as soon as you're at sea. Not just because they're a hundred years old but would you touch it?'

Lily dropped the stone back onto the table. 'I don't think I want it now.'

Eumeus picked it up and enclosed it in her hand. He was enjoying himself. Just to hold these beautiful things in his hand. To be allowed to touch them, encouraged to touch them. He had seen the look in the other man's eyes and knew what he thought about his relationship with Lily, and even that was a pleasure. Slave or no slave, in his secret heart Eumeus belonged to Lily and the acknowledgement of a connection between them was sweet, even though the man had assumed a physical dimension to their relationship which Eumeus shrunk from imagining.

But the purchase had another purpose apart from the pleasure of buying Lily a gift. He wanted information. He reached into the small leather pouch hanging from his belt and extracted a handful of gold links broken from one of the ancient necklaces he and Lily had stolen from the dead. Dropped them one by one into the stall holder's hand until he saw a flicker in the other man's eyes that showed he had paid enough. Added two more.

'We're looking for a ship.'

The man shook his head. 'I don't take passengers.'

'So that's not yours?' Eumeus nodded towards the small wooden vessel tied up at the end of the harbour wall.

The man turned his head and spat into the water behind him. 'I could smell the stench of pirates two stades out. I'm not that stupid.'

'Not a person to trust your life to, then? The boat's owner?'

'He's sound enough. Give him enough gold and he'll take you anywhere you want to go. It's not him I'd worry about.'

'What, then?'

'That lot. Men, women, children. *Goats*.' The man rolled his eyes skywards. 'He'll have his work cut out if he has to outrun another ship.'

'There are only four of us. Two children.'

'Goats?'

47

'No goats.'

He could deal with Quin later.

'And where d'you want to go?'

'Across the sea. They say there's good land along the coast and none to claim it.'

The man shrugged. 'The Lydians face towards the rising sun. They don't see what lies at their back. You can pay?'

'As you see.'

'Tomorrow morning.' The man's thumb stabbed north. 'There's a small bay on the other side of the headland. High tide's just after sunrise.' He held out his hand. 'The name's Ugar.'

The two men shook hands. 'See you in the morning, then.' Eumeus dropped his hand onto Lily's shoulder. 'We'd better go and tell the others.'

More than half full of cheap wine, Fen's only reaction to the news that he was to travel separately from the rest of the group was to offer his brother impossible odds that he would get there first. Neither of them had much idea where 'there' was except that it was other than here and therefore worth the journey. Five years in one place had sparked the travel lust even in these most indolent of men.

Quin was another matter.

'The ship's too small to take them,' explained Eumeus. 'Turn them loose and we'll send for them later.'

Quin's bottom lip drooped dangerously. 'We can go on the bigger ship.'

Lily leaned forward and placed her hand on her brother's knee. 'The bigger ship's full, Quin. There's no room for us.'

Sleepy and smelling of wood-smoke, Lex blundered into the small, earnest gathering looking for his uncle Quin. He climbed onto Quin's lap. Turned and patted the big man's face with one small, brown hand. He had a smear of dirt on his face, Lily noticed, and his hair was matted and unkempt. Suddenly she was tired of living on the road. She knew the feeling of home-hunger, having felt it in the long-ago days when she worked in her aunt's house. Now she just longed to be clean.

'Stay here, then, Quin. I don't care what you do.'

Lex turned around at his mother's voice. That sharp tone was something he thought she kept exclusively for him. But Quin, who knew his sister's moods quite as well as his young nephew, picked up the little lad and tucked him under one arm.

'Bed time now, Lexy-boy,' he mumbled. 'Big day tomorrow.'

In the pearl grey light of dawn the small party made its way down the steep slope to the small bay where Ugar's ship lay at anchor. It was a pretty vessel, clean and neatly painted with a strong enigmatic eye picked out on the bow that served as both good luck and a warning. As they watched, there was movement in the waist of the vessel and the sides bristled suddenly with oars.

Eumeus shifted his bundle to the other hand. Gold might be useful but it was heavy stuff to lug around. 'We'd better get a move on.'

A grin showing broken teeth was all the greeting Ugar gave them. He stowed people and gear aboard with equal efficiency then sent a small, wild-eyed boy over the side to pull the anchor from the sand. The ship lifted in the water, floating high like a sea bird. An order was given. Oars dug in. The sun lifted over the horizon, pouring liquid gold onto the sea. Within minutes the bay had been left behind and the vessel was hit by the strong, sea-smelling breeze of the open water. On the high stern, the steersman heaved on the big wooden rudder. Up went the sail, flapping vigorously. The oars were shipped, dripping green sea water. The wind filled the sail and sent the ship skipping over the choppy water.

Lily glanced down at her son. His eyes, reflecting the intense light of that brilliant early morning, were turned up to the top of the mast. She reached down, grabbed the hem of her gown and scrubbed his grubby face.

Part Two

Thera

8

The island humped out of the sea like a raw red rock. As the boat came closer, huge naked cliffs reared against the sky. Fist-sized pumice stones bobbed in the sluggish water and tapped against the wooden hull like ghostly fingers. The smell of sulphur hung in the cool morning air.

Lily emerged from the canvas shelter where her family slept. She stared around in astonishment.

'What is this place?' she asked Ugar.

'Thera,' he answered shortly.

'We're not going to land here, are we?'

Ugar flicked her a glance then returned his gaze to the sea. 'We are.'

'But how?'

'You'll see.' Ugar turned on his heels and walked away, his bare feet slapping on the warm wooden boards of the deck.

Lily remained where she was and stared in astonishment at the raw cliffs that were towering closer and closer to the small boat. Now she could see they were made of layer upon layer of tiny stones that flowed in places like red rivers and stained the sea a dull brown. Not a thing grew. Not a thing moved, except for a pair of eagles gliding on the warm updrafts at the top of the cliff.

Behind her Ugar shouted a command. At a touch from the helmsman the boat came about and wallowed, sails flapping. It seemed to Lily as if the boat was going to sail straight into the cliffs themselves but then she could see that they were rounding a steep headland and in front of them lay a huge natural harbour. The great bare cliffs grew from the sea in a vast circle, broken only in the place where the boat now sailed, making slow headway as the headland blocked the wind from the sea. Eumeus came out from the shelter and stood next to Lily at the rails.

'It's amazing, isn't it?'

Lily turned her head. 'You've been here before?'

'Once or twice.'

'What happened, Eumeus?'

'It's a volcano. Was a volcano,' he amended. 'It blew its top in the time of the bull ships. The harbour – where we're sailing now – is all that's left of the top of the mountain. They say it was blown into the sky in pieces so small they coloured the sunsets for years afterwards.'

Lily nodded. 'I remember my father telling me about it. It happened when my great grandfather was a young man. A great wave came from the sea and flooded the valley. Everything was washed away. And then the red sunsets every night. My great grandfather thought the world was coming to an end, but it didn't. What happened was the salt water got into the soil and spoiled the crops.'

'The world ended for these people,' said Eumeus. 'They say it was a great city, second only to the bull palace for the richness of its art. The houses were all destroyed. Some were washed away in the flood that followed the explosion or were buried under the thick blanket of ash that fell from the sky. The rest tumbled into the crater and disappeared under the sea.' Eumeus stared down into the green depths. 'They say there's a whole city down there with gold and treasure beyond imagining.' He touched Lily's arm and pointed. 'Look, we're getting closer.'

The boat was under oar now, heading across the choppy water towards the shore. Lily could see wooden wharfs built out from a place where the cliffs were less steep. Fat trading vessels and sleek war ships were tied up against them. Other boats rocked at anchor with small rowing boats busy between them and the shore. As they came closer, she could see white-washed houses dug into the cliffs and the zig-zag of a donkey track leading upwards. Shading her eyes, she followed the track to the top where the cliff was pockmarked with doors and windows, like swallows' nests in a muddy bank. Between the houses were flashes of colour from poppy and heliotrope giving the impression at last that there was some life in this desolate place.

Ugar had taken the helm now and was occupied with bringing his boat into a vacant berth at the end of one of the long, overcrowded jetties, not an easy task as he had to manoeuvre his vessel among the small skiffs and rowing boats that crowded the harbour. He was cursing under his breath, a steady stream of invective that included the old man who had chartered his vessel and forced him to put in to this place laden with children and household goods. Thank the gods he'd refused to take the goats, he thought, or he'd be a laughing stock in the harbour-side taverns that night.

With a bit of luck he'd be able to get rid of them now. Thera was the crossroads of the Aegean and it would be easy enough for them to find another ship that would take them to the eastern shore. For himself, he was going back to cargo and he wasn't fussy what he carried. Pumice for preference. It was nice and light, and it didn't require him to make polite conversation.

It was not that his passengers had been any trouble, quite the reverse. They had made no objection to the quality of the food, had slept on deck under the sail he had rigged for their shelter, had kept out of the way of the crew, as he had requested. They had marvelled at the daily sight of dolphins cruising the bow waves, pointed out the small rocky islands that humped up from the horizon and were left behind, watched the sea birds diving into the sea after scraps. But, still, it had been unsettling to have passengers on board.

The man, Fen, when he was not nose-down in a beaker of wine, stood hour upon hour in the stern of the boat, staring back the way they'd come. Ugar explained that the bigger boat carrying his brother would hug the coastline and take several more days to do the journey but this information did not deter Fen from his pastime. Doing nothing was obviously an art Fen had perfected with much practice and, eventually, Ugar left him to it.

The older man, Eumeus, whom Ugar had mistaken for Lily's lover, had revealed himself unexpectedly as an ex-galley slave. He squatted patiently in the shade of the sail and showed the small boy how to tie elaborate knots or stood on the deck, feet balanced against the swell, while he answered the child's endless questions.

The giant simpleton sat in the middle of the ship, as far away from the edge as he could get, watching the sky and rocking himself to and fro. The bright-faced youngster, when he was not being amused by Eumeus, ran about the ship, always contriving to occupy the one piece of deck that Ugar wished to stand on.

It was the girl that bothered him most. She was very young, slender, and fair skinned with that mass of red-gold hair that untangled itself from every knot she tied it in and flew about her head like fantastic snakes. The dark haired infant she had with her was sickly, unsettled by the movement of the ship and wailed often, causing the young girl to bare one perfect, pink-tipped breast and offer it suck. How was a man supposed to run a ship with that sort of thing going on? The eyes of the galley slaves were all a-swivel and a-slant and the creamy wake behind the boat was like a donkey's hind leg. Not the way he liked it. Not the way he liked it at all.

While Eumeus and Lily, with an excited Lex in tow, explored the jumble of harbour side shops, Fen was coming to a decision. He'd eaten a plate of fried squid washed down with a krater of wine and enjoyed the company of the sailors with whom he'd spend the afternoon under the shade of a tattered sail. The sail was set up over the entrance to a small, dark room dug into the pumice and Fen liked the cool, damp smell of the hillside mingled with the aroma of frying fish and the tangy harbour reek brought to his nostrils by a lively sea breeze. When he got back to the boat he announced that he didn't want to go any further. He was going to wait on Thera until his brother arrived. Suppressing a grin of triumph, Ugar negotiated a generous payment from Eumeus for their passage so far. Then the family's bundles and jars with their hidden cargo of gold and precious stones were unloaded from the ship and stacked carelessly on the dock.

By then it was late afternoon and the sun was sinking behind the stark black cliffs on the far side of the harbour. They found an inn several streets back from the wharves where the stench from the door didn't knock them off their feet and the straw mattresses seemed relatively vermin free. From the arched window of their room they had a view over the drowned caldera to where the last of the light was turning the rim of the cliffs into pure gold. Leaning her elbows on the rough stone sill, Lily felt suddenly happy, a feeling that persisted through

Fen's wine-fuddled coupling and several trips from her bed during the night to comfort an unsettled Lex.

They waited a week and the other ship did not come in. The morning after their arrival Eumeus had taken a donkey up the steep zig-zag path to the top of the cliff. Here he found the dome-roofed houses of the rich merchants and ship owners dug into the pumice with their backs to the cliff and their windows open to the view of sea and sky. There were temples here, too, to all the gods of the sea, and shops filled with jewellery and perfume and fine cloth. Eumeus secured rooms for the family in a boarding house at the edge of the town where donkeys grazed in a steep field and the sun gleamed from the beaten gold of a temple roof further down the cliff.

With nothing to do, Lily took to walking every morning along the edge of the cliffs until she reached a place where the pumice had slipped down the slope and she could go no further. One day she visited a beauty shop where a disdainful young woman attempted to manicure her broken fingernails and smooth sweet-smelling oil into her work-soiled skin. The young woman admired Lily's hair, gave her some cream to tame its unruliness and sold her a jewelled net, wildly expensive, into which it could be gathered neatly. It made her look older somehow, Lily thought, staring at her reflection in a polished silver mirror held up by a small slave.

At the end of the second week they had to accept that the second ship was lost or had simply gone somewhere else. Eumeus joined Lily on her walk along the cliff and they sat together on a smooth white boulder staring out at the sun-drenched sea. From where they sat, they could see along the curve of the cliff to another promontory on the other side of the town.

'There are two houses over there.' Eumeus shaded his eyes and pointed to the far hilltop. 'Side by side and both for sale. I had a look yesterday.'

Lily stared at him. 'What do we want with two houses?'

'I was thinking we might set up business here. We would need two houses for what I have in mind. One for us and one for the girls.'

'*Girls*? You mean a brothel?'

'I was thinking of something a little more … exclusive, Lily. Fine dining. Good wine. Beautiful girls. The sort of thing the right person would be prepared to pay a good price to enjoy.'

'The right person?'

Eumeus raised one eye-brow. 'I was thinking of invitation only.'

'Invitation only? To a *brothel*?'

'People always want what they think they cannot have. If a man sees his fellow enjoying something from which he is excluded, what will he do to gain admittance?'

'We'll have to make it something worth the craving.'

'It will be, Lily. Trust me.'

Lily's house was far too exclusive to be the talk of the town. What was noticed, however, was the small quiet man with the straight hair cropped below his ears who stalked the markets and emporia of Thera seeking the strange, the exotic, the wonderful. After a while Eumeus didn't have to leave home because the merchandise came to him, brought up the zig-zag path on the backs of sweating donkeys, or men. He was more circumspect in the choice of his girls. These he acquired by word of mouth, by recommendation, by his own eye for a beautiful face in the teeming harbour side alleys. Some were slaves, some freeborn, the daughters of houses overflowing with girls and no money for dowries who were only too happy to climb the hillside and leave their sisters behind to mourn their ill-luck.

His greatest find was a dark-skinned girl from south of the Nile kingdom just landed on the wharf and lying in her own stench from drinking foul water. Her owner knew well enough what she would be worth at the slave market the following week but doubted she would live long enough for him to make his profit. He accepted Eumeus' offer on condition he took her away immediately. She was indeed close to death, her eyes sunk and dull, her belly a pitiful hollow under her ribs. Eumeus handed her over to Quin who nursed her like one of his orphan kids, feeding her on thin barley gruel and wiping away what she could not keep down until finally she was strong enough to sit up and take the spoon from his big, gentle hand. She was not grateful, however. Having willed herself to die ever since the slavers took her from her village and having come so close to success, her life was not something she was grateful to have restored to her.

She was, however, extremely beautiful: her body lisson, her skin a rich glossy brown, her teeth pure white against lips like dark rose petals. Eumeus dressed her in fine pale silks and asked no more of her except that she should sit in the girls' salon after dinner. He had no intention of allowing her to take her own life after all the effort he'd put in to saving it and he knew well enough that she was capable of taking herself beyond his reach, if he tried to force her into something she didn't want to do. Knew also that she was the jewel of his collection, made more precious because she remained untouched.

Lily's house opened for business the following spring and was an instant success. Not for nothing had Eumeus been raised in the harem of a minor Babylonian princeling. Minor he may have been in the high society of that, the richest and most exalted of cities, but what was on offer to Lily's special guests was beyond anything ever seen on Thera. A man rich enough, or lucky enough to receive an invitation to the white house on the hill climbed off his donkey in a paved courtyard lit by scented torches flaring against the velvet blackness of the sky. Quin stood in front of a heavy, metal-studded door. Clean and well-groomed, the half-light disguising the somewhat daft expression in his eyes, he made a formidable sight. He wore a custom-made costume consisting of a short silk tunic, an enamelled breastplate and a leather kilt, edged with gold discs. Gold-plated greaves moulded his heavy calves. A short bronze sword in an embroidered sheath hung at his side. His helmet, crowned with a pure-white horsehair crest, was more often carried under one arm that worn on his head because he didn't like the way it squashed his ears but still it added to the somewhat theatrical effect although few people imagined that Quin was there just for show.

The evening began with dinner taken on a wide veranda roofed with a vine-covered trellis and with a view of the glittering harbour far below. Eumeus had imported a chef from the east, someone who was escaping from something, or someone, or why would he accept work in a place like Thera? He had a taste for very young slave boys which Eumeus supplied on request, never querying what happened to the one before. He behaved like a petty princeling, bemoaned every aspect of his job from the lack of fresh spices to the quality of the kitchen slaves and cooked like one of the immortals.

The amount of waste and extravagance behind the presentation of those perfect meals would have driven Lily frantic, had she known about it. The fact that they were fed to Lily's wealthy clients as part of the service was something else of which she was not aware but was nevertheless a clever ploy on Eumeus' part.

He knew how much rich men valued something that cost them nothing and he cared little whether they were parted from their gold sooner or later, it all arriving inevitably in the same purse. The meal was served by young boys, immaculately dressed and highly trained. Music played behind a fretted screen. There were no dancers, no jugglers, no pretty whores to sit half-clad at the end of the client's couch, nothing but anticipation of the moment when, with one appetite sated, Eumeus himself arrived silently to lead his guests to the satisfaction of the other.

The girls' salon was based on Eumeus' recollection of the harem where he had spent the first two years of his life. It took up the full width of the house farthest from the road and overlooked the steep cliff overgrown with stunted bushes and sweet-scented herbs. Eumeus had replaced the fretted window screens of his memory with bronze grills, cunningly wrought with patterns from the sea which reflected the designs set into the cool blue and white tiles on the floor. Despite the cliff, Eumeus felt it necessary to guard his investments carefully.

The room was furnished comfortably to give the impression of private living quarters and the girls were trained to set aside their weaving and embroidery when the men entered and to serve them with sugared almonds and Turkish delight from pretty dishes. All except Afrikka, Eumeus' dark-skinned treasure, who sat by the darkened window like a tethered bird.

Anyone who found himself an overnight guest at Lily's house was served a small, exquisite breakfast early the following morning by the same boys who had waited on table the night before. By then, the girls were nowhere to be seen. As Lily's satisfied customers said to each other in dining salons and drinking clubs throughout the island, it was all so damned civilised it was a pity they couldn't take their wives.

9

On a hot summer afternoon Lily sat in the window of her salon waiting for the cool breeze to blow in from the sea. She was dressed in a simple linen shift, her hair smoothed into a net at the back of her neck. Her soft, white hands lay idle in her lap. Her loom stood by her side holding a piece of fine wool work half finished. It was intended for Lex and she had been inserting a coloured meander pattern but had realised that she had made an error - glaring now she had noticed it - and she was ill inclined for the trouble of undoing it.

I could leave it, she thought with a sigh, and nobody would even notice. The only reason she did the work was because it was what women were supposed to do. And because it was better than doing nothing at all. Finer fabric than she could create was hers for the asking. Like the linen of the dress she was wearing. Eumeus had acquired it as a job lot dirt cheap from some merchant down on his luck who only wanted the price of his fare home.

At Lily's feet lay her daughter Roza, now four years old. She had been working on her own miniature loom but had fallen asleep with her head in the pile of soft white wool and her arm flung across a half-grown striped cat who didn't mind staying where she was for now but had one eye half open in case a better opportunity came along.

The breeze arrived and with it a subtle change in the light heralding the slow death of the day. Lily leaned forward and began to unpick her work. She was desperately lonely. Despite her wealth and her status as a married women, she was shunned by most of the women of the upper town because of the nature of her business and she kept herself aloof from the rest because their husbands were her clients and would not be pleased to discover her sitting in their wives' salons. It was a strange business, this male duplicity, Lily thought. That men could take such pride and pleasure in cheating with the finest whores in town and yet refuse to acknowledge to their wives something so universally known.

The women with whom Lily would have been most comfortable were those of the lower town: the young wives and daughters of the harbour side merchants and navy personnel. But these women were the kin of many of her working girls and could not accept her as a friend. So she sat in her high, white house teaching her small daughter useless housewifely skills and waiting for the afternoon sea breeze to cool her scented skin while the members of her family went about their daily business.

Eumeus and Quin were engrossed in the affairs of the house next door from which bursts of girlish laughter and the tinkle of music made Lily wish she had insisted on taking a more personal interest in her business. Lex, rising seven years old, spent most of his time running wild in the town. Eumeus insisted on spending an hour with him in the morning teaching him counting skills with the abacus he used for the household accounts but, as soon as the coloured beads finished clicking along the rods, the boy was gone. One of his favourite routes was out of his bedroom window onto the narrow stone wall that divided the kitchen yard from the street, down into the neighbour's tiny garden via the branches of an olive tree and thence along a steep goat track that ran down to the harbour through the rough grass and gnarled bushes of the cliff face. It was a dangerous path and one that turned into a torrent in wet weather but it had the advantage of keeping his whereabouts a secret from Uncle Quin and Eumeus.

His playmates were the brothers of Eumeus' girls and he was treated kindly by their families, fed on bread and honey, patched up when he fell and skinned his knees, and sent home before sun set. Many of these boys had older brother at sea and the dockside was their playground. Often when a ship came in he went on board with the other boys to help unload the cargo, be it fish or fine silks, and watch the men fix nets or rigging. He told the boys his own father was a sailor and was coming soon but he didn't really know if it were true. All he knew was that Fen was not his father, something which gave him quiet pleasure and another reason to pity his sister Roza.

Lex often saw his step-father in the taverns and harbour side bars. Fen took no interest in the affairs of his wife's ex-slave or her idiot brother, except that they allowed him to be as idle as he chose. The only thing that concerned him was the fate of his brother Ger. He alone remembered the ship that was lost and retained a fierce faith that one day he would find out what had happened to it. That searching for news of his brother could best be done in the drinking houses frequented by sailors was a happy coincidence, and a ready supply of small gold ensured that he was never short of drinking companions, a role for which he missed his brother most of all.

One night Fen did not come home for dinner. His absence was not noticed by Eumeus and Quin, who had a busy night ahead of them in the house next door. Lily was unconcerned and relished her sleep alone in the big bed. The following morning Eumeus went down to the harbour to select fresh fish, a task he refused to trust to anyone else, and was accosted by one of the harbour layabouts who pointed out Fen's body lying in a narrow alleyway with a knife buried in his back. The man was rewarded handsomely for his trouble and Eumeus hurried up the hill to tell Lily the news. And so Lily became a widow as suddenly and unexpectedly as she had become a wife.

On the occasional quiet night Eumeus would send Quin down to the docks to see if there were any new ships in port. Quin had an unerring eye for the gentleman who could appreciate, and afford, what Lily's house had to offer, even if he was straight off a ship and mired to the eyebrows. On this particular night it was no wonder that Lily's house had fewer clients than normal. The rain, blowing from the sea, had turned to sleet with the ending of the day and the town was huddled on its hillside in chill misery.

There was a new ship in the harbour all the same, a slim vessel painted black and almost invisible in the windy darkness. A man, stepping from deck to wharf, collided with Quin who was hurrying along the quayside with his face muffled in a thick cloak. The man was tall and powerfully built. His dark hair, cut short, was tipped white with salt. He stepped back and dipped his head to Quin. 'I apologise. Too keen on my supper to watch where I was going.'

For once Quin's discernment deserted him. This man was a gentleman sure enough. That he was possessed of sufficient funds to enjoy the delights of Lily's house was less apparent. But dinner was a-cooking and it would go to waste if there was nobody to eat it. The man accepted Quin's invitation gratefully and followed his broad back up the zig-zag path to the top of the hill.

With the house closed up against the rising gale, Eumeus served dinner in the hall where a brazier was burning. At the end of the meal the man, wishing to relieve himself and having no desire to brave the elements in order to do so, went in search of indoor facilities through the door he had seen Eumeus use. This door was the only link between the two houses, and was usually kept locked but it was opened during the dinner hour so that the family could be served with its meal.

What the man found on the other side of the door was a large, comfortable salon. Heavy shutters covered the windows where the wind whistled and probed for entry. There were patterned rugs on the tiled floor. A woman's loom and that of a child were set up in one corner. In the mellow lamplight he saw a woman seated alone before a large table. The remains of a meal lay in front of her. The woman was leaning back in her big, carved chair, her hands playing with the stem of a heavy wine glass. She was dressed in a white silk gown and her hair, which was an extraordinary colour somewhere between red and gold, was gathered in a jewelled net. She lifted her head and saw him standing in the doorway. The expression on her face went from bored enquiry to recognition to an incredible joy.

'Xander!' She was up and running across the room. Her arms slid around his waist and she laid her head on his chest. She looked up. 'Lord Xander, don't you recognise me?'

He held her away from him and peered down into her face. Suddenly she reached up and pulled the net from her hair. Shook it out so it fell around her face in wild disarray.

'Is that better? Last time we met you said you didn't care for fine ladies with jewelled nets in their hair.'

'Lily? Is it really you?' Xander wrapped his arms around Lily's body and plucked her from her feet. 'It is you! What are you doing here?'

It was at that moment that Eumeus hurried in, having found the connecting door open and his guest missing. He thought for a moment that Lily was being attacked by the huge, dark-haired sailor and moved forward, not quite sure what he was going to do to save her. But then he saw that she was laughing joyfully and the man was laughing too. The man put her carefully onto her feet and she caught his hand.

'Eumeus, this is Xander, can you believe it? He is Lex's father.'

Lex lifted the latch on his mother's bedroom door and tip-toed inside. The gale had blown itself out during the night and he could see sunshine in the gaps between the heavy wooden shutters that covered the window. He was wearing a soft linen nightshift, several sizes too small, revealing his small, pink penis and the round cheeks of his bottom. Every morning he came to Lily's room and climbed into her bed. Every morning he rubbed his body against the warm, scented flesh of her thigh while she struggled to free herself from sleep's grasp. It was his special time and one he guarded jealously from Roza who had their mother to herself during the daylight hours. He always made sure he closed the door to their room behind him and Roza was too small to reach the latch.

Despite the sunshine, the room was dark. His mother's big carved bed seemed like a huge monster crouched in the middle of the floor. He pattered barefoot across the cold tiles to the side of the bed where a small, upholstered stool gave him sufficient height to allow him to burrow under the covers. Just as he put his foot on the stool he heard his mother's voice murmur something. He smiled. She was awake, then. He climbed onto the stool and reached for the edge of the heavy woollen cover. But there was another voice. A deep voice. It sounded as if it had laughter in it. And something else. The covers moved, humping themselves up into odd shapes. Lex slid off the stool and made silently for the door.

Lex knew about Eumeus' girls and how they sometimes had men in their beds at night, to keep them company. He knew he wasn't allowed in the other house in the evenings when the men were there although he often went next door at other times so that the girls could spoil him. He quite liked being spoiled by Eumeus' girls. But his mother was different. She used to have Fen in her bed sometimes, it's true, and Fen didn't like him spoiling his sleep so Lex knew to go away on the days when he was there.

But then Fen had died. Quin told him he had been stabbed in the back down on the quay, a coward's death, so his friends said, who knew about it before he did. Roza cried. Fen had been her father, after all, and Lex had kindly dried her tears a few times until he got tired of doing it. Lex reached the door and had his hand on the latch when there was another movement in the bed.

'Lex?' It was his mother's voice.

He turned around. His mother was sitting up, her face flushed with sleep, her hair tangled. She was holding the covers up high to cover her body but Lex could see her smooth shoulders and knew she was naked. Next to her was a big man with thick black hair on head and chest and blue seaman's eyes. Lex could see where the sun had burnt him on his neck and arms.

'Lex, come here.' His mother spoke again.

Lex approached the bed. The stool was on the man's side so he went around to where his mother was. She reached down to lift him up, revealing the curve of her breast.

'Come on, jump in, quick! Your feet are freezing!'

Lex felt himself lifted through the air and was aware suddenly of his own small manhood on display for the big man to see. Then he was on his mother's lap with the covers over him and his cold feet tucked into her delicious warm flesh.

'So, here he is.' His mother was talking to the man, now. 'What do you think?'

The man put his hard hand on Lex's chin and turned his face around. Lex met stare for stare while his thoughts ran about inside his head like frightened mice. Suddenly the man grinned.

'He's my son. I can see that.'

Lex's mother bent her head forward, enveloping Lex in her tangled hair. 'Do you know who this is, Lex?' she whispered in his ear. 'This is your father.'

Three days later Lex and Xander walked together down the track to the harbour. The old widow who lived next door and enjoyed the small imp's daily excursions across her garden, gazed out at the pair and crossed her fingers for luck. It was a fine, fresh day which could have been spring if it were not for the patches of frost still lingering in the shadows of walls and buildings. With the great harbour laid out in front of him like a wonderful living fresco, Xander listened while Lex explained to him about the girls and how Eumeus was teaching him to count and Quin's sword that wasn't even sharp and how he wasn't allowed in the kitchen , not ever, because of the cook, but the girls always had food anyway, sweet things that made him feel sick and spoiled his dinner. And then questions, one tumbling over the other, so that Xander hardly had a chance to answer any of them.

Xander thought, he's bright but he needs schooling. All those damned women and some old slave teaching him his numbers. When I was his age I was helping my father. A real help, too, not just a nuisance tolerated. He looked down at the small child skipping along next to him and thought about Lily opening to him like a flower in the big warm bed. And he'd only stopped on Thera for a dry bed and a bite to eat.

The sleek black vessel was riding high on the water, its sail furled and the oars shipped along each side. Xander put one foot on the gang plank and turned to Lex. He was not sure how to say farewell to a small son of three day's acquaintance. He put his hand firmly on the boy's shoulder and looked down. Into a face that was ablaze with excitement.

'Can I come on board?'

Xander shook his head. 'Not this time,' and denied himself the chance to discover that Lex was not so useless after all. He strode up the short plank and was gone.

Lex waited on the dock until the ship left, nosing out into the middle of the harbour and then gathering speed as it approached the open water. He watched it go until it was lost in the sea dazzle on the far side of the caldera.

'That was my father,' he said to nobody in particular. 'He's coming back!'

10

Xander stood on the steering deck, his feet balanced against the movement of the boat, his eyes on the silk pennant at the top of the mast. He was waiting for the moment when it would reveal the direction of the wind outside the shelter of the caldera. He listened to the beat of the hide-covered drum and watched the regular dip and lift of the oars on either side of the ship. Both pride and expediency required a swift, neat transition from oar to sail. Anybody watching needed to know that the vessel was too fast to be worth chasing.

The ship rolled suddenly as it reached the long blue swell of the open sea. Xander shouted orders that were ignored by a crew that knew its business as well as he did. The sail rattled up the mast and snapped once in the brisk breeze before being brought under control. The ship skipped into speed as the oars came inboard. The men on the rowing benches relaxed, rubbed sore spots on their hands and grinned at each other.

None of them was a slave. Most were running from trouble, often not of their own making, and the rowing benches offered them a strange kind of haven. It was the times they lived in, thought Xander, that brought decent men to the rowing benches and girls like Lily, who should have been at home milking the goats, to sit on Thera and collect the liberated wealth of ruined kingdoms as it floated past her door.

And who would have thought that a man like him and a girl like her …? But, then, who was he now? Just another piece of flotsam loose in the world, serving men who, in the days of his childhood, would have counted themselves lucky to have been admitted into the presence of his father's clerks.

Xander was born in the city of Carchemish which lay at the cross roads between the middle sea and the rich delta lands to the south. The city had become rich many generations ago when the trade had been flint and obsidian from the northern mountains and, later, copper and iron ore to feed the growing needs of greedy kings. Xander had often wondered which came first, the desire for war or the ability to fight it. Certainly, with metal had come riches: stone towns grown from reed villages, wide valleys tamed by the plough, rivers busy with trading vessels. And, with riches, came the desire for more and an eye cast across the valley to a neighbour's town and the fat trading vessels tied up under his walls.

But that was not the whole story, as Xander knew quite well. There had been enough, and more, for the people of the fertile valleys to the south of Carchemish and those who lived around the middle sea. Enough, even, for the new people who moved along the river routes from the east or over the northern hills, people who settled down to learn new trades - metal work and stone masonry to serve the needs of the growing cities - or joined the armies that battered against each other in the summer months while the grain ripened in the fields and sons grew in their mothers' wombs.

But the trickle had turned into a flood and the new people were no longer content to settle among the old. Now they wanted land of their own. Now they wanted to live according to their own gods, their own ways. Now they wanted to be the kings, the nobles, the warriors. Dress their wives in gold, own their own slaves, harvest their own crops. And the only way to have these things was to take them from somebody else.

Xander's family could trace its ancestry to the Great King Shuppiluliumesh who had lived more than a thousand years ago. They were part of the Great Family, kin of the king, and Carchemish was their city, grown from their effort and protected by their strength. For a stranger approaching its walls, the city appeared a grim, formidable place with its massive stone walls and great arched gateways. But, for Xander, it was simply his home. He lived in the citadel palace which dominated the city and from which his father trained his armies, dispensed justice and levied taxes, sending always a certain proportion to Hattusas, the city of the Great King, who had been their overlord time out of mind.

In his early childhood Xander had the freedom of the women's quarters and played in the pretty courtyards and contrived wildernesses where water flowed and deer and duck gave him targets for his small bow. If he caught one, the women would praise him and have the creature cooked so he could kill it again with his dinner knife.

Later, when he was older, he joined the other boys in the training yards. Although he was destined to follow his father into one of the prestigious chariot squadrons, first he had to learn to be an infantryman, fighting on foot with the short, curved sword. Xander's father said it was important for him to know what foot soldiers were capable of doing before leading them into battle. He said there was only so much a soldier would do willingly for his leader and, after that, resentment grew and soldiers would run away from a fight.

Then, because he was his father's son and heir to his position in the Great Family, Xander had to spend time in the justice chamber listening to interminable arguments about a boundary stone missing or moved, or a beast strayed or stolen which his father appeared to treat as seriously as the first smudge of smoke on the horizon on an early summer evening which heralded the beginning of the fighting season.

Thus was his life until he turned thirteen. That summer when his father rode out to war he did not return. The smoke came close enough to catch in the nostrils of the citizens of Carchemish and the refugees struggling into town told tales of crops burnt and whole villages put to the sword. And by whom? A shrug of the shoulders. These people were lucky to escape with their lives and hadn't waited around long enough to catch sight of those that threatened them.

Within two weeks the enemy was close enough for their watch fires to be visible from the command posts on Carchemish's battlements. Xander spent his days there with boys from other noble families, angry and frustrated that war had come while they were still too young to fight. And afraid. Because the army was gone, swallowed up by the great force which was creeping closer like a black blight in the crop fields, and who was going to protect them now?

'These walls will never fall,' said the sergeant, smacking his palm against the great carved lintel of the gateway.

They were standing on the sentry walk above the gate looking down on the traffic far below them. All one way, it was, as it had been for weeks past; farmers and people from outlying towns with their possessions bundled into carts or on the backs of donkeys seeking sanctuary in the great city.

Xander had no doubts about the strength of Carchemish's walls but he knew about sieges, too. They could go on for years. The enemy, fat with plunder, camped in your cornfields. The people reduced to rat-infested grain and tainted water until the dead outnumbered the living. It's what could happen to them. Carchemish was on the easternmost boundary of the kingdom and who could tell whether the Great King knew of their plight or would come to their rescue, even if he did? All kingdoms were under pressure, even Babylon, even Egypt which had been old when Xander's ancestor Shuppiluliumesh carved out his own empire more than a thousand years ago.

Two days later Xander's mother took poison. Dressed in her finest clothes, she lay on her bed, her skin as pale as milk, her lifeless eyes staring towards the window from which the blink of sunlight on the enemy's weapons was clearly visible. That night Xander left the city by a small gate behind the barracks. In the darkness, he could smell the stench of the drain that carried water down to the river. The river itself was low after the summer drought and Xander had to wade through stinking mud to reach the water. The current, flowing south, would take him away from the city. His destination was the teeming cities that lay on the coast of the middle sea where he planned to sell his skill with a sword to whoever was prepared to give him gold.

But it was not that easy. Xander had some idea that he would find a market place with a man in it - or men - who would be like the sergeant-at-arms at home. He imagined himself walking up to them, talking to them, selecting which one he would serve. When he finally came down from the dry summer hills surrounding the long coastal strip and made his way along crowded, dusty roads into the city of Tyre he found himself in a noisy, stinking crush of humanity all bent upon business of their own. His first instinct was to find the sea, glimpsed for the first time early that morning as he began his slow descent from the hills.

When he'd thought about it at all, Xander had always imagined the sea would be just a bigger version of the river at home. Many times he had sat by his father's chair when he received visitors and heard stories of the mighty river. How it rose up following the spring melt and had to be contained in long earth dykes. How the water was drawn off through a system of channels to serve the fields on either side. How it flowed through the middle of Babylon bringing trade and wealth to the very doorstep of the city. Even at Carchemish, close to its source, the river was wide enough for traffic: trading vessels and ferries and small sailing ships. It was the river that brought the trade north from Babylon and Susa to connect with the east-west route along the foot of the northern hills, and south along the coast to the cities of the middle sea.

Standing at the top of the last pass before the hills descended to the coastal plain and squinting through the heat dazzle rising from the bare rocks, Xander wondered first what had happened to the horizon. It took him some time to realise that what he was looking at was the sea. Far from having banks on either side, its only boundary appeared to be the thin smudge of coastline lying at his feet. It took him three days to climb down to the coast and the sea was hidden for most of that time. When he entered the city his only wish was to see it again and, this time, close to.

It was the smell that reached him first, a beguiling salty freshness that came to him on the breeze, banishing the more distasteful human smells that surrounded him. When he reached the harbour the breeze was cold, licking the hair from his sweaty forehead, and the smell included rope and timber and fish. The sea was a deep blue, heaving with its own rhythm and tossing up white bouquets of foam that were caught by the wind.

Dropping his bundle to his feet, Xander stood and stared. He ignored yells as cargo was heaved ashore by sweaty slaves, was shoved out of the way by swaggering yellow-haired men with gold ornaments swinging in their ears, listened to snatches of conversation in unfamiliar languages, and changed his mind instantly about what he wanted to do. To be out there on the sea with the breeze blowing on his face. To swagger in foreign ports. He wondered how to go about getting holes in his ears.

But it was not long before Xander discovered that choice is a privilege given only to those who are sure of their next meal. Although he had received his share of beatings from his father and his father's men and had even had his ears boxed by his mother's slaves, he had never known anything in his life but kindness and a certain respect due to him because of who he was.

Now he was nobody.

The first night he had his bundle stolen. It contained a pair of sandals, a clean tunic, a small dagger with a jewelled hilt and a narrow gold ring which he had slipped from his mother's finger on that last morning before his escape from Carchemish. It was the ring he cried for most when he discovered his loss. Then he thought of the dagger and realised that he could have lost his life as easily as he had lost his possessions. He cursed himself for his stupidity. That day he realised he would have to fight for survival among a horde of urchins who had grown up on the streets and for whom stealing was a way of life. Here, his precious skills counted for nothing.

On the third day, now very hungry, he found himself outside a temple. By then he'd had his fill of beatings by market stall holders and the other boys who took from him anything he managed to steal for himself. He couldn't speak any of the languages used on the streets and he was too different, even filthy dirty as he now was, for them to accept him into one of the loose mobs that flocked around the market place and the harbour front.

Xander had heard that the gods offered protection to those who sought it and he wondered why the street urchins did not take for themselves what the temple had to offer instead of fending for themselves in the teeming streets. He discovered the answer as soon as he walked up the three shallow steps and into the courtyard that lay in front of the sacred place. This was a place where people came to die.

The courtyard was surrounded by red timber pillars and each pillar supported its own bundle of human rags. Some had lost limbs. Some were blind. Some diseased. The sound of his firm footsteps on the beaten earth of the courtyard caused the unseeing ones to cry out. He found himself a place close to the heavy wooden doors of the temple and withstood the impotent rage of his fellow beggars who wanted him to sit in a less conspicuous place.

At sunset two young girls in plain white robes came from the temple with a basket of bread. They made a slow circuit of the courtyard deftly avoiding the filthy claws of the beggars who had roused themselves from their torpor at their appearance. They ignored Xander until he raised his hand in a gesture of supplication when he received a knob of stale bread from a small, white hand.

He realised that the price of his meal was his abject submission to the authority of the temple's god. Still, he was allowed to eat it in peace and to sleep in peace, disturbed only by the snuffling and moans of the old men.

In the morning he stayed where he was, having nowhere else to go. He found himself unable to think any further than the certainty of a piece of bread at sunset. Except to mourn his inevitable death and the end of his family's one thousand year old lineage.

11

During the day the temple forecourt was busy with worshippers and with groups of men who used it as a meeting place and somewhere to transact business. Xander was half asleep in the heat when he became aware of someone standing in front of him. He squinted up into the bright light and saw a young girl. She had dark eyes and a cloud of black hair, burnished by the sunlight. For a moment he thought it was the spirit of his mother, come to call him home to Carchemish. But then he realised that she was speaking to him in an unknown language. Her voice was firm and determined. Xander had no idea what she was saying. Then she reached down her hand and, when he made no move to take it, spoke again impatiently. He came to his feet and found himself suddenly dizzy. The girl, who was about fifteen, was no taller than he was but she took his arm and held him upright until he was able to stand by himself.

When she was sure he could walk she led the way through a maze of narrow streets, turning her head every now and again to make sure he was following her. A tall white-washed wall ended in a wooden gate with a brass handle. The girl opened the gate and Xander found himself in a kitchen yard. Fat chickens pecked the ground under a line of washing. Lines of vegetables grew under the dappled shade of fruit trees. Cooking smells emerged from a dark doorway on the other side of the yard.

The girl turned around, grabbed Xander's hand and pulled him into a small, hot kitchen. She sat him down at the big wooden table, filled a bowl with stew from a pot hanging over the fire, added a thick slice of bread, then stood with her hands on her hips and watched him while he ate.

By the time Xander had been fed and washed, had fallen asleep and woken up again, it was full dark and the lamps were lit. The girl was standing in front of him, carrying a small oil lamp. Once more she beckoned him to follow her. For a moment he hesitated. It had occurred to him during the course of the afternoon that perhaps she had chosen him to be some sort of ... sacrifice. The word stuck in his throat but there was no denying he had been found on the steps of a temple and the rescuing of stray boys was obviously not a common occurrence in this city. But the place where she had brought him seemed like a family home and, now, the narrow corridor, lit by the girl's wavering lamp, gave way to a large, square salon full of furniture and trinkets.

It took a moment for Xander to locate the man who was standing with his back to the room, staring out of the open window to where the full moon was laying a shimmering golden track across the dark water of the harbour. It was a sight of such unexpected beauty that Xander had to swallow hard to keep the tears in check.

The girl spoke. The man turned. He was tall, plump, dark-skinned with a curly black beard. His head was covered by a pure white cloth, twisted into intricate folds. Around his neck he wore several heavy gold chains. The smell of perfumed oil reached Xander from across the room. For a moment neither of them moved. The girl walked into the space between them and spoke to the man, indicating Xander who stood resolutely just inside the door. The man took a step forward and held out his hands in a gesture of welcome. He spoke a question. It was obvious what he meant.

Xander lifted his head. 'I am Siskandarabba, son of Labbusilis of the Great Family of Shuppiluliumash. Governor of Carchemish,' he added unnecessarily, for he had seen the other man's reaction. Standing bare foot on another man's soft rug, he felt a quick flare of pride.

The man's name was Cyrus and he was a timber merchant. The girl was his daughter, Shyrah. Xander never knew why Cyrus offered him a job on one of his ships. A boy from the inland city of Carchemish who had seen the sea only a few days previously was hardly a wise choice to put in command of a sea-going vessel. Except that Shyrah had taken a fancy to the stray dog she had rescued from the temple. And Shyrah could make her father do anything she wanted.

Xander spent the next two weeks in Cyrus' house being fattened up by Shyrah, then he was handed over to the captain of one of Cyrus' trading vessels and let loose on the middle sea to learn his sea craft. Five years later, when he was grown into a man, Cyrus gave him command of his own ship.

Balancing his feet on the deck as the small ship began punching its way through the dark blue swell of the open water, Xander remembered his first voyage as master. It was a long journey, slipping along the low stony coastline south of Tyre, to Gaza and thence to the ancient kingdom of Egypt. Xander had hated Egypt on sight. It was a country of contrasts: the huge stone edifices with their feet in stinking river mud, high ritual and ancient ceremony juxtaposed with the toil of peasants grubbing a living out of sticky, inundated fields, and the teeming cities where the merchants lived in ghettoes far away from their dark, supercilious hosts.

Xander was amazed to discover that the Egyptian people knew nothing of metal work, had created their huge monuments by rubbing stone on stone, had achieved so much wealth and power without the aid of bronze, or iron. It took him a long time to get used to the stench of the river, the meals of dried fish and tiny birds, the clouds of biting insects that tortured visitor and native alike. It took him longer to learn to put up with his treatment at the hands of the local merchants with whom he had to negotiate on Cyrus' behalf. There was something obnoxious about them that made Xander's skin crawl: an attitude of superiority over the native Egyptians and an elevation of greed and licentiousness to the status where the satisfaction of the most vile desires was something about which a man would boast among his peers.

But Xander proved his worth as Cyrus' agent and his journeys to Egypt were frequent. He was always glad to get back to the open sea after such a visit, and the black gale which had driven him into Thera had been exactly what he'd needed to blow away the foul humour he'd carried with him from the sodden delta. And there he had found Lily, the girl he had never quite forgotten. And a son - he counted in his head - seven years old and just about to begin the growing that would make him a man. He thought of Lily, sitting alone in that big, white house while her ex-slave and her daft brother collected gold hand over fist. And I've done it again, he thought. Loved her and left her. But I'm going back. This time, nothing's going to keep me away.

Three days later, with the winter sun rolling itself into a ball to set in red splendour in the sea behind him, Xander rounded the small island that guarded the harbour at Tyre and saw the sunset light flaring from the gold and emerald pillars of Heracles' temple that crowned the citadel behind the town. At his order, Cyrus' red and green pennant fluttered up to the top of the mast. The rowers grinned at each other, spat on their palms and prepared to give their usual display of skill and precision as the small vessel entered calmer water.

It was good to be home, Xander thought, as he passed through the heavy wooden gates into the lower town and threaded his way along the narrow streets of the city towards Cyrus' house where he knew Shyrah would have a hot meal waiting for him.

After he had eaten he made his way to the big, crowded salon at the front of the house where Cyrus waited for his report. It was not good news and he wondered how he was going to explain to his patron why the timber stacked on the wharves was not worth the cost of shipping it to a buyer, if indeed a buyer could be found. At the moment it seemed that nobody around the middle sea was buying anything, not even the Egyptians.

The years had not dealt kindly with Cyrus. He had grown heavy, his face puffy, his feet swollen and painful. He ran his business from a chair by the window with his feet cushioned on a footstool and a glass of goat's milk at his side. That he had a krater of wine hidden under his chair was something his daughter knew very well but at least the subterfuge kept his consumption down to something approaching what the doctor allowed.

Tonight the shutters were closed and the heavy curtains drawn. The room was stuffy, smelling of sickness. Xander crossed the room, dodging the small carved tables, the fretted screens, the silk upholstered chairs and took Cyrus' hand in his own.

'I was expecting you three days ago.' Cyrus' voice was querulous.

'The gale drove me onto Thera.'

'Damage?'

Xander shook his head. The damage was all internal, he thought, remembering Lily's red-gold hair spread on the pillow. He pulled up a stool made from a camel's saddle, hooked the krater of wine out from under the old man's chair and made his report.

Spring arrived slowly. For Xander, kicking his heels around Cyrus' house, it was a time of intense frustration. There were no new voyages. Cyrus said he was consolidating, another word for going broke. He sent Xander on a tour of wharves and warehouses to make an inventory of what was in stock. Evenings Xander spent in the salon watching Cyrus make marks on soft clay tablets and smooth them out again. When Shyrah came in to give her father his sleeping draft she would stay and talk. She had no time for the proprieties which stated that she should not be alone with a man. She was, after all, almost thirty and had known Xander since he was a boy. Besides, her father was there as a chaperone in body if not in mind.

On the first warm evening of spring, Shyrah leaned across her father's chair and pushed open the shutters to let in the soft air. Xander rose abruptly from his seat and joined her at the window.

'I can smell smoke.'

Together they looked down at the harbour. On the island fire bloomed in the darkness. In its light Xander could see ships drifting like ghosts towards the harbour mouth.

'Raiders!' His hand went down to his waist, seeking a weapon.

Cyrus reached up and put his hand on Xander's arm. 'There are always raiders this time of the year.'

'And we ignore them?'

'We'll blockade the harbour. Look, you can see them now.'

From the dark wharf, boats were setting out across the water.

'What good will that do?'

'They won't risk a fight. There are never more than half a dozen of them.'

As he spoke, more dark shadows appeared from behind the island.

'There are more than half a dozen this night.'

Shyrah stared up into Xander's face. 'What does it mean?'

'Trouble.'

From below in the darkness a bull's horn blared, answered by another close by.

Xander turned from the window. 'I must go. They're calling out the militia. Take care of your father, Shyrah.'

High up in the citadel someone had lit the beacon and its flare sent Xander's shadow scurrying in front of him as he joined the throng making its way down to the harbour. Xander saw some of his own men. 'To me! To me!' and then they were all together, grinning and rubbing their eyes. Xander heard the kiss of metal as swords were loosened in their scabbards.

He didn't like the way his belly felt, he never did. It would be better once the fighting started.

Out in the harbour the fleet had formed itself into a solid, black wall. The sound of singing floated to them across the water. The fire on the island had subsided to a fitful red glow. The smell of smoke drifted in the warm air. By morning the militia was stood down and Xander trudged back up the hill. The raiders had made no attempt to attack. It seemed Cyrus was right.

Shyrah was waiting for him outside the salon door. She was wearing a clean white gown, her hair neatly dressed. Under her eyes purple bruises stained her pale skin. Xander unbuckled his sword belt and let it fall to the ground.

'What's wrong, Shyrah? Couldn't you sleep?'

'It's Father. I'm worried about him.'

Cyrus lay in the middle of his big carved bed, his breathing quick and shallow. He opened his eyes and stared up at Xander.

'What's the news?'

'We're safe enough, it seems.'

'Good. Now go and get yourself something to eat. And make Shyrah lie down. She's scrawny enough as she is without staying up all night. It's no wonder nobody wants to marry her.'

The raiders didn't go away. The fleet remained strung out across the harbour mouth but the enemy made no attempt to engage it. Sailors coming off duty reported that more boats had come to swell the enemy's numbers and that some of the boats were carrying women and children. Over the next few days the newcomers settled themselves down on the small, wooded island just off shore. Soon the sound of chopping wood and the smell of cooking fires became part of life for the citizens of Tyre.

It was the smell of cooking that finally brought home to the people of Tyre the trouble they were in. The blockade, far from keeping the raiders out, now served to keep their own ships in. Beyond the harbour mouth, enemy craft cruised in numbers too great to risk a fight. What was left of a caravan, sent south by land, reported the country overrun with sea wolves: villages burnt, crops destroyed, roads subject to sudden ambush. When supplies began to run short, the governor sent troops to collect what food remained in the city. It was taken to the citadel and strict rationing was imposed on the city. It was not starvation by any means but the restricted diet did little for Shyrah's looks, at least in her father's eyes.

Cyrus had not risen from his bed since the morning the raiders arrived. At his insistence his bed was moved into the salon, near the window, so that he could look out over the harbour to the island where the sea wolves were making themselves at home.

'What's their game?' he asked Xander late one night.

'A base?'

The old man shook his head. 'They want more than that.'

'What then?'

Cyrus gestured feebly. 'What we have. A harbour. A town. Wealth. Why would they settle for less?'

Xander strode to the window and stared out. 'But why here? Why now?'

'Because they are strong. And we are weak. *Stupid!*'

'Stupid?' Xander turned around.

'We've been talking about fortifications for years. Arguing about it. How long have the wolves been in the middle sea? Ten years? Twenty years?'

'A generation.'

'And what have we got to protect ourselves? A few ships. A wooden barricade. Don't get me wrong, Xander. It's a good barricade, a *fine* barricade.' There was suddenly a hint of the old charm in his voice. 'It made me my fortune, that wall. But it won't keep the sea wolves out.'

Xander thought about the stone walls at Carchemish but said nothing.

'So, what's keeping them?'

'They'll come when they're ready. Xander ...'

Xander moved quickly towards the bed. 'What is it?'

'Look after Shyrah for me, won't you? She'll be all alone when I go.'

Xander opened his mouth to protest but Cyrus grabbed his hand.

'No, listen, Xander. I'm not going to be a burden when things get bad. You understand me? The trouble is there's not much money. You know how things have gone the last few years.'

Xander nodded. He stared down at the man on the bed. The old trader had been like his father for more years than he could remember. He liked him, respected him. Loved him, even.

Cyrus was speaking again. 'I always thought the two of you might make a go of it. She's difficult, I know that. But her heart's in the right place. And she's not too old to breed.'

Xander covered the old man's hand with his own. 'I'll take care of her. Never fear.'

He thought of Lily but pushed the memory aside. There was nothing he could do about it now.

12

The raiders made their attack on a fine May evening with a full moon drifting between patches of cloud. Xander was on duty on the shore opposite the island, the place considered to be the most vulnerable to attack. A narrow strait, no more than a spear's throw in width, separated the island from the mainland. It was shallow enough to walk across at low tide, except for a deep gully in the middle where the water flowed swiftly. In the almost two months since the raiders had taken over the island they had made no attempt to cross the channel but still the militia maintained its vigil.

Even though spring was well advanced, the nights were chilly. Men soon tired of staring into the darkness across the strait and turned to the small driftwood fires strung out along the beach. Late into the night with many men dozing, Xander felt a sudden prickle on the back of his neck. It was no more than a feeling, an instinct, but it made him get up from the sand and walk the several paces to the water's edge. It was very quiet, the only noises the lapping of the water and the call of a night bird somewhere in the distance.

But there was something. Over on the island. It was the sound of movement, subdued and stealthy. Something was moving over there and it was bigger than a man. Xander could hear it more clearly now. A dragging sound as if something heavy was being pushed through the undergrowth. The moon came out from behind a cloud and he could see shadows moving between the trees. Men. The sound of whispered orders, a sudden splurge of voices quickly smothered.

Xander ran quickly to the harbour end of the beach and stood where he could see the edge of the island curving away into the darkness. The boats of the blockade rode at anchor at the harbour mouth, casting black shadows into the moon-stained water. Then he saw the first enemy ship emerge from the trees. It lay stranded on the soft sand until men ran forward with logs and rolled it into the water with a quiet splash.

Xander ran back along the beach. His yells woke the sleeping men. There was a confusion of voices as men staggered to their feet.

'What's going on?'

'Quick, sound the alarm. They're in the harbour.' Xander pointed frantically. 'They're carrying their boats across the island.'

'What about the blockade?'

Xander's gaze swept the circle of bemused faces. 'Aren't you listening? They're *behind* the blockade. They'll be ashore before dawn.'

With the bull horn blaring, the men ran towards the town. Roused by the alarm, faint pricks of yellow light showed on the ships of the blockade. But it was too late. Out on the harbour Xander counted six enemy vessels floating high on the dark water. He knew the sea wolves rowed their own boats and were not afraid to die. He could hear them yelling now as their war boats picked up speed and bore down on the unprepared blockade.

There was a sudden flurry of movement out at the harbour mouth as the ships of the blockade attempted to turn around to face the challenge. Several ships became tangled in each others' oars. One drifted away, caught in the outgoing tide. At the height of the confusion the enemy ships hit with the deadly speed of well-aimed arrows. The noise of battle carried across the harbour. Suddenly the beacon flared from the citadel, staining the water with red fire.

Xander turned to the men surrounding him. A bigger crowd, now, than the one that had maintained the watch on the beach. He recognised some of his own men, edging closer.

'There's nothing we can do for them now. We should look to ourselves.'

'What will we do?'

'The citadel. It's our only hope.'

'But the walls ...'

Suddenly there was a burst of yellow flame out at the harbour mouth. It rose quickly into the air, a column of fire that was reflected in the dark water where the living and the dead jostled for space.

'I've heard seasoned cedar burns wonderfully well,' said Xander grimly. 'It'll keep them out long enough to get the women and children up the hill. Now, come on!'

With a backward glance at the doomed fleet, Xander ran through the gateway. The men streamed through after him. He heard the creak of timber as the heavy gates were heaved shut behind them. He felt a sudden panic flaring in his chest, an almost overpowering desire to fight his way outside and run. But there was Shyrah. Her life for his was a obligation he'd accepted many years ago when she rescued him from the temple. And now he must keep his side of the bargain.

The entrance to Cyrus' house was jammed with furniture. Shyrah stood waiting for him, her eyes like black pits.

'My father's dead.'

Xander pushed his way inside. Thank the gods, he thought, the old man has kept his promise. Now it's up to me. He put his arms awkwardly across Shyrah's shoulders.

'It's for the best, you know that, don't you?'

A small nod. 'I've laid him out.'

'Good girl. What's all this stuff?'

'We've got to go up to the citadel. Haven't you heard?'

'Yes, I know. But, Shyrah, you can't take all this!'

He saw a look that was almost panic cross her face. He held out his hand.

'Take me to see your father, Shyrah. I need to say farewell.'

It was something normal, or at least more normal than the nightmare that was in front of them. Without a word, Shyrah turned and led the way into the salon. Dressed in his finest linen robe, Cyrus lay on the bed, his hands across his chest, his hair and beard combed neatly. The skin of his face was like yellow parchment. It was strange, Xander thought, how you can look at the body of a man and wonder where the essence was. He had known Cyrus for fifteen years and now he was gone. Even the room, cluttered with his things, seemed cold and dead.

'When did he die?'

'Just after midnight.'

Xander crossed to the window. The sky was washed with the pale grey light of early morning. Out on the harbour what was left of the blockade smouldered, surrounded by smoking wreckage. Below, the enemy ships lay strung out along the wharves while the sea-wolves, light glinting from spears and helmets, quested through the shops and taverns. He wondered what Cyrus had seen from this window in the depths of the night that had persuaded him his time had arrived.

'What's happening?'

'They're getting drunk. It gives us some breathing space.' He moved swiftly across the room and stood on the opposite side of the bed. 'Now, tell me, what have you packed? Clothes? Cooking gear? Bedding?'

Shyrah nodded.

'That's what we take. Nothing else.'

'Nothing?'

'Shyrah, we can't carry it! We'll be lucky to escape with our lives.' He moved around the bed and stood by her side. 'Our *lives*, Shyrah. That's the only thing that matters now.'

'What about him?' She nodded towards the bed. 'We need food and wine. Gold, to pay the priests. His own things, to take with him to the afterlife. It has to be done properly, Xander.'

Xander gripped Shyrah's shoulders and thrust his face into hers. 'You don't understand, do you? He stays behind. There's nothing we can do for him now.'

He almost told her then that Cyrus' death had been no accident but he stopped himself before the words were out of his mouth. Xander knew it was not something of which the gods approved, this taking of one's own life. It took away their power over human lives which was what made them gods after all. Cyrus would have known it, too. But his love for his child had been stronger than his fear of what might await to him in the afterlife. Cyrus had died for Shyrah and now it was up to Xander to make sure his sacrifice was not in vain.

'We can't just leave him.' Shyrah was close to tears.

'He'll have his funeral pyre soon enough. You can light it yourself, if it'll make you feel any better. But *quickly*!'

Shyrah shook her head. The tears were spilling now. 'I can't ...' A small, helpless gesture. 'It's my home, Xander. How can I set it on fire?'

'Then kiss him good bye and let's go.'

Xander's voice was harsh. He watched Shyrah lean over her father's body. Then he half-pushed, half-carried her out of the room and slammed the door behind him.

It was full daylight by the time Xander and Shyrah emerged from the house and joined the flood of people trudging up the hill towards the citadel. A flock of doves swirled around the rooftops, their white feathers shot through with gold from the sun. Higher up, an eagle and his mate soared in the clear blue sky. Behind him, Xander could hear a captive rooster crowing his displeasure. He wondered how it had managed to stay alive.

The citadel of Tyre covered an acre of rocky ground surrounded by a high stone wall. On one side was an almost sheer drop down to the bare stony country of the hinterland. On the other, an arched gateway led to a wide area of grass and trees where, in peaceful times, people gathered for a breath of fresh air away from the stink of the city. It was here too that they brought goats and chickens for sacrifice to the god, Heracles, whose temple crowned the summit of the hill. Heracles had been Xander's totem god since the beginning of his seafaring days. He had often been up here after successful voyages, or before risky ones, to ask the god's favour. But he never expected to see the temple as it was that day.

The whole area was teeming with people. Family groups crowded into what little shade there was, or erected awnings from blankets and floor coverings. Dogs growled and snapped, establishing territory. Babies cried. The smell of wood smoke and cooking added a strange, commonplace quality to what was a scene from a nightmare.

Grabbing Shyrah's wrist, Xander pushed his way through the throng until he arrived at the foot of the temple stairs. It was cooler here, under the great roof, and less crowded because most people were reluctant to invade the god's space. He dumped his bundle of bed rolls and cooking pots and pushed Shyrah down until she was sitting on the ground, her face white with exhaustion and grief.

Xander had some notion that he should go down to the walls and fight but the city fathers had other ideas. It may have been expediency, it may have been cowardice, it may have been the knowledge of the gold hidden in the temple's treasury, enough to rebuild the city ten times over. Whatever it was, there was a sudden shouted order, the horns blew, those still on the outside hurried up the hill, chivvied by men with spears, and the great gates swung shut. The citadel was secure. And we are trapped, thought Xander.

13

The town burned for three days, creating a thick shroud of choking smoke which hung around the hilltop where the townsfolk huddled in their makeshift shelters. On the fourth afternoon a violent thunder storm cleared the air. The torrential downpour left the people miserably wet but gave them an abundance of fresh water collected in dishes and cooking pots. The following morning the people crowded the walls of the citadel. The ruined town seemed deserted. The sea wolves' boats were anchored in the harbour. On the island they could see wooden dwellings with thatched roofs, goats and sheep cropping the thick grass, plots cleared for crops.

Tyre's governor, Charilaus, a stout, dark-skinned man in his forties, called together the city's leaders which did not include Xander. He sat on the temple steps and listened to their discussion. It seemed they were planning a surprise attack on the raiders. Xander wondered how much of a surprise an attack could be when it originated from the highest point of the city, in plain view of anybody who cared to look. Charilaus put the planning of the attack in the hands of his son, Cimon. Cimon was a tall, supercilious young man who had never got his hands dirty in his life. Later, Xander and his own men stood at the back of the crowd which Cimon addressed from the temple steps.

'It's an exercise in population control,' Xander muttered to the man standing by his side. Moeris was the only decent thing ever to come out of Egypt and had served with Xander for more than ten years.

The tall, good-looking man raised one eye-brow. 'Population control?'

'I know it's not your speciality,' said Xander on a spurt of laughter. 'But how many of this lot do you think will be alive after this little exercise?'

Moeris shrugged. 'I will. How about you?'

'You can count on it. Dying for Cimon is not something I intend to do.'

First find your enemy, thought Xander, as one hundred men from grey-beard to beardless slipped out of the gate in the late afternoon of the following day. They were armed with swords and spears and a miscellany of gardening implements. Many were merchants, or merchants' sons, with no experience of battle. Most of Tyre's fighting men had been on the ships of the blockade.

Xander and Moeris with the rest of Xander's men - about a dozen in all - slipped away from the main group and made their way towards the harbour through the twisting back streets and laneways which Moeris seemed to know like the back of his hand. There was plenty of cover. In many places walls were still standing, in others piles of blackened rubble provided shelter. Everywhere there was evidence of plunder. A carved chest with its lid hacked in. A handcart laden with furniture abandoned in the middle of the street. In a doorway they found a young woman, heavily pregnant, a halo of flies around her head, her dead eyes wide with horror. Between her legs, blood spilled into the gutter.

'Bastards,' muttered Moeris.

He snatched a silken shawl fluttering from a broken wall and covered her face. There was a sudden splurge of shouting away to their right and the clash of weapons.

'Come on!' Moeris ducked down an alleyway.

They found the enemy in what had once been a pretty little square. On three sides the pastel-washed walls of houses belied their ruined interiors. Windows stared like empty eyes. An old olive tree in one corner cast dappled shade onto the tiled pavement. The fourth side of the square was blocked by a rough-built barricade of burnt timber and building stones. In front of the barricade a group of sea wolves stood in a circle, concentrating on something that was happening on the ground. Two of them were crouched down and appeared to be playing a game of bones with gold pieces. The rest were shouting bets and encouragement.

Xander glanced to one side and met the gleaming eyes of

Moeris. Xander knew quite well that fighting was Moeris' passion, second only to pleasing the ladies. He had seen him in action often enough to value him above all others as a shield companion. He watched him now as he shook off the casual, friendly, charming persona which was his everyday guise and became the consummate fighting man: muscles taut, eyes keen, concentration complete.

Silently they closed up and Xander felt Moeris' shoulder touch his and heard the kiss of shield on shield as the wall formed with practiced ease. The enemy had seen them now and were on their feet yelling, the gold pieces scattered on the ground. They met in the middle of the square, the sea-wolves' ill-disciplined rabble against the steady shield-wall of seasoned warriors.

Standing in the middle of his men, Xander felt the shock of contact as the wolves' leader leapt forward. He was a yellow-bearded giant, his long hair hanging in greasy spirals beneath a dented, second-hand helmet. His breath was sour with wine which slowed his reactions so he didn't see Xander's spear thrust before the sharpened tip entered his throat. Xander yelled victory and shoved the man away. He could feel the battle madness like a hot flame thrusting through his body, burning away the fear and frustration.

It was sword to sword now, the spears gone in the first rush of battle. The ground was slippery with blood, the setting sun a sheet of golden light blinding friend and foe alike. Xander killed twice more and sang his victory song, his voice hoarse in his throat. Then he felt Moeris' shoulder slip away and reached out a frantic hand to grab him before he fell. Xander's men had fallen back across the square and stood now in the darkened entrance of a small alleyway. The sea wolves - those that were still standing - were in the middle of the square, heads lowered like bulls in a slaughter house. Death had come swiftly and unpleasantly to their companions and suddenly they had lost their stomachs for the fight.

Of the one hundred men who had set out against the sea wolves only a handful returned. Xander had lost two of his men, plus Moeris who had taken a stab wound in the thigh. It was not a wound that would kill a man normally but hunger and disease were haunting the citadel and within a few days Moeris' wound became infected. It took him three weeks to die.

When he was conscious, he cursed Xander in five different languages for not leaving him to die like a warrior at the hands of the wolves. Towards the end he lifted himself up on one elbow and prayed loudly to his gods in far away Egypt so they would know where to find him. He slept one last night, so peacefully that Shyrah thought the crisis had passed, and in the morning he was dead.

Xander had no idea what Moeris needed to help him on his voyage to the after life but he paid one of the over-worked priests to mumble some words over him before taking his body to the steep cliff at the back of the citadel and throwing it over. He was not the first to make that journey, nor would he be the last, thought Xander grimly, staring around at the emaciated figures wailing their separate sorrow against the stained wall. A hatred for Cimon, the self-styled war leader of Tyre, simmered in his chest.

'He hates you, too,' said Shyrah one night as they lay side by side, seeking sleep, 'because of who you are.'

Xander rolled over and stared at her in the darkness. 'He thinks nothing of who I am.'

'Xander, you can trace your family one thousand years to a great king. He can only get as far as his grandfather, herding sheep in the hills. Of course he hates you.' She paused. 'He asked me to marry him once.'

'Cimon did? Why didn't you take him?'

A shimmer of laughter. 'Apart from the obvious?' Shyrah sat up and rested her chin on her up-drawn knees. 'I only ever gave my heart once and that was to a scruffy urchin I found in a temple forecourt. Did you never guess?' She smiled down at Xander. 'After that I was content to stay with my father so I could welcome you home from your journey and see you off on the next. Do you realise this is the longest time we've ever spent together?'

Xander heaved himself up on one elbow. 'But why didn't you say something? Your father would have welcomed it. He told me so himself.'

Shyrah shook her head. 'It wouldn't have worked. There's something wild about you, Xander. It's what makes you a good sailor, a good fighter. You need a girl with the wildness in her, too, not a sensible little mouse like me.'

Xander thought of Lily's long, brown legs descending from the pomegranate tree in her aunt's garden. He couldn't imagine Shyrah sliding from a tree, not shamelessly as Lily had done with twigs caught in her luscious red hair.

'You're a strange girl, Shyrah. Do you want to get married?'

Shyrah put her head on one side, considering the question.

'We're going to die on this hill, aren't we, Xander?'

'More than likely.'

'So I can be your wife and ... and love you for the time we have left. You'll never have to stay with me when you'd rather go. And I'll never have to see the disappointment in your eyes.'

'It doesn't have to be like that.'

'You're saying we could live? That someone will come and rescue us?'

'Shyrah, remember when we lit the beacon the day the raiders got into the harbour? There was an answering fire that night. I saw it.'

'But nobody came.'

'No, nobody came.'

'So what was it?'

Xander shrugged. 'Someone as desperate for help as we were. Another town burning. Who knows? It's not worth bothering about now.'

'Then what do you mean?'

'I mean that I will marry you and be your husband for ever and ever. Death is not the end, Shyrah.' He leaned forward and kissed her gently on the lips. 'I'll see the priest tomorrow.'

That night he dreamed he was a boy in Carchemish. He was bare foot in the dew-wet grass of the little paradise next to the palace, hunting deer with his bow and arrow. He was in his father's chariot, peering over the edge, as he let his troops out for mock skirmishes in the marshes. He was up in the gateway guard room talking to the soldiers. In the morning he and Shyrah walked between the pillars of the temple to receive the blessing of the god.

It was an extraordinary day, the kind of day that remained in Xander's memory, clear and bright, for the rest of his life. News of the wedding spread quickly. Within minutes small groups of women had gathered. Children were caught and cleaned and had combs dragged through their dirty hair. Best clothes were retrieved from bundles. Food appeared. A jar of precious honey to spread on thin barley cakes. Beautiful old wine the colour of sunshine poured from straw-wrapped kraters. A scrawny goat was slaughtered and the meat distributed to be seethed with dried beans into a thick stew. It put the little community one week closer to starvation but nobody seemed to care.

The young girls seized Shyrah and took her away, giggling, to be rubbed with perfumed oil and dressed in borrowed finery. Older women joined in, nodding their approval and offering advice that brought a blush to Shyrah's face. Leaning against the shining emerald pillar of the temple with a beaker of wine in his hand Xander saw his bride's thin face glowing with joy. Later, after the feast, they sat side by side and watched the dancing and singing. Above them in the night sky the moon was full and yellow. Xander thought about being at sea on such a night with the moonlight like a golden pathway on the water and wondered whether the soul had any choice about where it went.

Their marriage bed was a pile of dirty blankets which someone had placed on the tiled floor of the temple courtyard. More blankets and curtains had been draped between the pillars to give them some privacy. Shyrah lay on the blankets like a sacrifice, staring up at her new husband with frightened eyes. She was very tired, worn to exhaustion by the excitement of the day. For a moment Xander wondered if he should just leave her alone and let her sleep. It was not as if he had to get children on her. There was too little future in either of their lives for that to be a necessity, or even an option. But then he remembered what she'd said the day before. About being a little mouse. Remembered, too, that she had loved him, in her own way, for half his life. He owed her love and kindness for the rest of her days. Nothing less. And the marriage bed. That, too, he must give her. He just wondered how he was going to manage it without hurting her too much.

When she was naked, Xander could see the effect of four months' starvation on Shyrah's body. Her breasts were little more than loose skin on her chest, her hip bones sharp points, her belly a pitiful hollow. She watched him as he gazed down on her.

'I'm sorry ...'

'Don't apologise, Shyrah. We're none of us any better.'

He lay down beside her and pulled a blanket over them both. Next to him he could feel her shivering. He pulled her gently into his arms. Her flesh was smooth, warmed by his hands. He could smell the perfumed oil that had been rubbed on her body. He felt his manhood rise reluctantly. He, too, was suffering the effects of the weeks of starvation and he had drunk too much of the beautiful, pale wine. For the first time in his life he doubted his ability to perform an act that had always been as natural as breathing. But this is not like other times, he thought. Tonight I have to rouse a frightened, half-starved virgin and convince her that making love to her is my pleasure and my delight and not just some awful chore I have to perform before I can go to sleep.

He thought suddenly of Lily the last time he saw her. Lily in the big, warm bed with the gale throwing itself against the window shutters and the yellow lamp flame fluttering in the drafts. Lily with her firm, smooth limbs and the look of welcome in her dark, languid eyes. His hand strayed and he felt Shyrah's body stiffen with fright. He moved closer and kissed her gently, his tongue exploring the soft cavern of her mouth. She made a noise of muffled surprise but didn't stop him. After a while he felt her hand come around the back of his head and, when he moved his hand again, the lock on her thighs was undone and he could make his way inside.

It was not perfect. It was not even particularly good. But it was done. In the end it had been quick which was perhaps as well because he hurt her. She had bitten her lip and tried to hide it but he could see it in her eyes. But there was a pride there, too, and a joy: something that Xander saw duplicated in the days that followed.

For Shyrah they were days of perfect happiness. That the well was almost dry and what was left of the grain was full of rat droppings were facts of life that couldn't be denied. That her own life was close to its end she could see in her emaciated frame and feel in the increasing weakness of her body. But it was a price she was prepared to pay to have Xander for her own.

Xander watched her as she joined the other married women waiting with their jars for their meagre rations of green water to be drawn from the well, or sitting in the shade picking the rat dirt out of handfuls of grain. There was a gaiety about her, a kind of jaunty confidence that sat strangely with her appearance. He watched her eyes swivelling around the camp, searching for him where he sat with the other men, or took his turn patrolling the walls.

At night, too, as she grew in knowledge and assurance, she surprised him more than once with the pleasure she gave him. All girls are wanton at heart, he thought to himself, but he had never expected it of this one. It was love that did it; a pure, steadfast, unselfish love such as he had never received from anyone in his life before. It made his marriage, which he had entered out of no more than a sense of duty, and this girl, who had existed for years on the fringe of his life, into something so precious that for ever afterwards he remembered those last terrible days in the citadel of Tyre with astonished delight. And gratitude to a girl who'd thought she wasn't good enough for him.

14

Xander woke from a doze to the persistent ache of his joints and the glare of the afternoon sun. Through half closed eyes he watched with astonishment and a slow-growing apprehension as Cimon walked through the camp from the temple steps to the citadel's gate. He had on his father's robes and a tall hat that should have added a certain majesty to its wearer but only managed to make him look ridiculous. He was followed by a retinue of what was left of the best men of Tyre, the beardless sons of the city's leaders all of whom had found their way to the cliff of the dead behind the temple. Xander grinned as one of them tripped over the long sword worn at his side. Next to him Shyrah stirred.

'What's going on?' She struggled to sit up.

Xander nodded in the direction of the little procession. 'Giving themselves up to the enemy. A few less useless mouths to feed.'

'*Really?*'

He grinned down at her. 'I doubt it. Let's watch and see.'

It took six of them to pull the gate open. When there was sufficient room to allow it a man walked in. To Xander he looked like the yellow-haired giant that had found death on the tip of his spear all those months ago and he made the sign against evil, glancing swiftly at Shyrah to see if she'd noticed. But two other men shouldered their way into the citadel behind him and he realised that they were all alike: huge, pale-haired men with dancing jewellery in their ears and battered swords stuck in their belts. Xander watched as Cimon bowed low then escorted the enemy to the temple steps. He watched as one of the giant warriors put out a hand to touch the golden pillar like a father caressing the face of his child.

'It's treachery,' he said to Shyrah. 'You'll see.'

But it appeared it was a miracle instead. Cimon called a meeting that evening and told the assembled townsfolk he had negotiated a safe passage out of Tyre for them all.

'The sea-wolves' leader has given me his word,' he announced. 'We leave tomorrow.'

'The sea-wolves' word is not worth *that*,' muttered Xander, snapping his finger and thumb. 'They're going to kill us for sure.'

'It'll be a death,' said Shyrah, peering up at his face. 'What's the difference? And we'll be together.'

'Not a nice death, sweetheart. Not from them.' He saw the fear in her eyes and drew her close. 'I won't let it happen to you.'

'How will you stop them?'

'I'll kill you myself. And me, after.'

But Xander felt the words in his throat and knew he was lying. Kill Shyrah, yes, he would do that to keep the wolves from their sport. But he felt the desire to live strong inside him and knew he would not lie down take his fate.

Xander approached Cimon after the meeting. 'It won't be an easy death, the one you're bringing us. Not for the women and children.'

Cimon raised one eye-brow. 'I've had their word nobody will be harmed.'

Xander turned and spat in the dirt. 'The word of the sea-wolves? It's worth nothing, Cimon, *nothing*. I've killed enough of them to know that.'

The other eye-brow joined its brother. 'I think I should *know* ... as Chief Archon of the city of Tyre, I think I have the skill to *determine* ... when a fellow leader and I negotiate a deal ... in good *faith*, let me tell you, in good faith ...'

'Fellow leader, pah!' Xander interrupted. 'Is the king of the rats less of a rat because he is a king?'

For a moment they stared at each other in silence. Then Cimon spoke again, 'What would you know? You're no more than a common sailor.' He turned on his heel and walked away, leaving Xander with the dubious pleasure of having turned the ears of the Chief Archon of Tyre bright red.

Until late the camp hummed with activity. Belongings were

packed into bundles. The shanty buildings that had been their homes for almost four months were dismantled, dragged to the middle of the citadel and set ablaze. Foul smoke rose in a thick column into air that was chilled by the first touch of autumn. Children danced, like ragged ghosts. Towards morning Xander woke to a scraping sound. He lifted himself up onto one elbow and saw Cimon and his followers dragging a carved wooden chest out of the temple.

'What is it?' Shyrah woke beside him,.

'It's the temple treasury. Heracles' gold. May the god forgive them.'

'Why are they bringing it out?'

'They think they're going to take it with them, poor fools. All they're doing is making it easier for the wolves to steal.' He bent forward and kissed Shyrah's cold lips. 'Are you ready, sweetheart?'

She nodded. 'It's going to a lovely day, Xander. Look!'

The sun was just up, gilding the pale, clear sky. The air was cool, smelling of the sea. Overhead a pair of pelicans flew in lazy circles, their feathers rose-pink in the morning light.

An hour later the gate opened and the wolves pushed their way into the citadel, headed by their yellow-haired leader. A ragged cheer arose from the townspeople, standing in groups by their bundles. Cimon appeared on the temple steps, dressed in his archon's hat. An arrow flew the length of the citadel and struck him in the chest. For an instant nobody moved. Cimon's hand plucked feebly at the feathered end of the missile, then he tumbled forward down the three shallow steps onto the dusty ground. The yellow-haired leader took two steps forwards, grabbed the nearest child and slit his throat with a single stroke.

Xander turned and took Shyrah in his arms. She closed her eyes and turned her face up to his. He kissed her, felt for where her heart beat like a tiny bird and pushed in his knife with all his strength. He disentangled himself from her clutching fingers and laid her on the ground. Then, with the sound of death close at his heels, he ran past Cimon's body and up the temple steps. The treasure chest stood open. Xander reached forward and grabbed a handful of gold. Then he stumbled around the back of the temple and climbed over the wall.

For a long moment Xander hung by his hands while his feet

scrabbled desperately for a hold among the broken rocks at the base of the wall. Below him was a sheer drop down to where the dry plain shimmering in the morning heat. On the cliff face rocky outcrops and stunted trees held the desiccated remains of the fortunate dead who would not know the terror of the massacre taking place on the other side of the wall. Finally Xander let go and he felt a stomach-churning fear as his body slid out of control down the boulder-strewn cliff. Heracles' gold tumbled from his grasp, rolling and skipping down the slope like gleaming stones. Finally his body slammed into a tree already bearing a macabre harvest of bones and dried skin. A skull toppled from its resting place and bounced away down the slope. Xander reached out his hand and grabbed at a branch. He could feel the crunch of bones beneath him.

'Oh, Lord Heracles, forgive me,' he whispered, 'my god forgive me.'

Above his head came the first wisps of smoke as the wolves fired the temple.

All afternoon Xander lay in a half-sleep while the sun drove the tree's shadow in a circle around his body. In the evening he forced himself to move. Dew was beginning to fall. A cool breath of air blew from the deep shadows at the base of the cliff. He felt the breeze pass through his body as if he had already ceased to exist, as if his life had ended here on the mountain and his soul had joined all the other souls whose voices he could hear chattering softly around him. His hand closed over something cold and smooth. It was a piece of Heracles' gold. For a moment he was tempted to hurl it from him, this useless thing for which men fought and died. Then he put it into his mouth. It lay on his tongue, cold and faintly wet from the dew. At least he had his fare into the other world, he thought, should he have need of it. He began to climb down the slope.

Later a full moon came up. It shone with a steady golden light, like a great immortal eye staring in horror at the crazy yellow flames dancing on top of the citadel. Xander was half-way down the cliff, clinging like a black insect. He thought he was back in Carchemish, climbing down the fortress walls to go fishing with his friends from town. From long practice his fingers and toes sought the cracks and niches in the huge stones. He could hear the sleepy call of marsh birds from the reeds by the river, smell the black scent of water. From above his head came the stamp of the guards' feet and the murmur of voices. He was wearing a fine linen tunic, smelling of the herbs his mother's slave put into the chest where his clothes were kept. He must be careful not to tear it. The last time it had earned him a beating.

A gasp. A slip. Rocks falling. Hands scrabbling to find a hold. Xander found himself hanging over a drop. Below him dark bushes crouched in the moonlight. The fall was too far but he had no choice. The bushes saved him, but only just. Thorns dug into his flesh. His bones felt as if they had been torn apart. The taste of blood in his mouth reminded him that he was still alive.

Another period of nightmare then he found himself face down in a small pool surrounded by the shattered fragments of the moon's reflection. The water was warm and dirty, tasting of goats. Later the goatherd found him and dragged him quickly into a rough shelter in the shadow of the black cliff.

'There are lions around. They've got used to a feed.' The boy nodded in the direction of the cliff. He was sitting in the firelight with his knees drawn up under his chin. 'You're the only one I've ever found alive. What's going on up there?'

Xander shook his head. 'It's finished.'

A tear ran down the cracked skin of his face, stinging where the blood was, and he did nothing to stop it. He accepted warm milk with herbs in it and slept until the sun was high.

It took Xander two weeks of rough travel to find a town where the wolves hadn't been. Heracles' gold bought him a berth in the first ship he could find going to Thera. He couldn't think of anything else to do.

15

Lex was running down the hill, his breath catching painfully in his throat. Rain had fallen earlier in the evening and it was slippery underfoot. Once or twice he fell on the sharp pebbles and felt the sting of blood on his knees and hands. In front of him the vast invisible sea wallowed in the darkness. In his head he could hear his mother's screams, smell the blood. Quickly! Quickly! At the bottom of the slope he plunged into the maze of alleyways that led down to the harbour. The smells were stronger here: fish and rope and somebody's dinner. It was going to be a cold night. Already the frost gleamed on walls and window ledges. His breath steamed in front of his face. He didn't see the man looming out of the dark. The man had his head down, his hands buried in the folds of a shabby cloak.

'Sorry.' Lex moved out of the way.

'Hang on a minute.' A bony hand shot out and gripped Lex's arm.

He struggled to free himself. 'Let *go*!'

'No, wait.' The man blocked Lex's path, staring down into his face. 'You're Lex, aren't you? Lily's boy. You've grown.'

Lex stared back. Saw thick, black hair, streaked with grey. A gaunt face. He didn't know who it was. Looked again. Dark eyes. He recognised the eyes. Remembered them laughing down at him on the walk down to the harbour in the sunshine. His father.

'I've grown all right. It's been almost a year since you went away. Where have you been?'

'Never mind that now. What are you doing out here in the dark? It's well past midnight.'

'I'm looking for a woman to take to my mother.' Lex jerked his head in the direction of the hill. 'She's in labour and it's not going well.'

'In *labour*?'

'Since this morning.' Lex pushed past his father. 'There's a woman along here who knows what to do. If I can get her to come with me.'

Xander stumbled after his son as he turned down a narrow laneway.

'I've got gold ...'

Lex turned his head. 'I've got *gold*. It's not that.'

'What is it then?'

'They don't like us.'

Lex stopped and hammered with his fist on a wooden door. After a long while the door opened a crack, letting out warm, stale air and the gleam of lamplight.

'What is it?'

'Please, I need the midwife. My mother ...'

The door opened further. A woman peered out. She was fat, grey-haired and not very clean. Several of her teeth were missing.

'Your mother, you say?' She held up a smoking oil lamp, creating leaping shadows. 'Hold on. You're that boy from up the hill.' Her hand gripped the door. 'Get off home to the scum you live with. I'm a respectable woman.'

'What's going on?'

A man shouldered his way into the doorway. A massively obese man with greasy grey hair and less teeth than his wife.

'It's the lad from up the hill. Says his mother needs me.'

'Be off with you! Go on, git!' The man flapped a red hand in Lex's face. His other hand wrenched at the door.

'Wait!' Xander shoved forward. He reached out his hand and grasped the woman by her forearm, his fingers digging deep into her soft flesh. 'Why won't you help us? She could die up there.'

The woman's face closed like a trap. She shook her arm trying to dislodge his grip. 'That's her business.'

'Not just hers. Mine, too.' Xander renewed his grasp on the woman's arm and shook her with what remained of his strength. 'Do you know where I have been, you miserable old hag? All these months while my lady has been carrying my child?' Another vicious shake. 'In Tyre, that's where. And I didn't escape the sea wolves' massacre to come back here ...' Shake. '... and have her die because you won't help her.'

A shudder passed through Xander's body. He dropped the woman's arm and bent over, coughing sharply.

'Tyre?' The man's meaty hand reached out and gripped Xander's shoulder. 'They said nobody got out alive. Come in, man, out of the cold.'

Lex and Xander found themselves in a small, hot room. The remains of a meal lay on a greasy table. Chairs huddled round a smoky fire. The man grabbed a clay drinking cup from the table, filled it with wine from a krater on the floor and slopped in some water. He took a metal poker from the fire and plunged it into the liquid. There was a hiss. Steam rose.

'Here, drink this.' He thrust the cup at Xander, then turned to his wife. 'Come on, woman, what are you waiting for? Get your things. There's work for you tonight.'

He reached out a dirty hand and grabbed Xander's arm, propelling him further into the room. His eyes gleamed. Like everyone who lived around the harbour he had heard about the siege of Tyre. And here was somebody who'd been there, perhaps the only survivor, standing in his house. It was the most exciting thing that had ever happened to him. His tongue dug at another loose tooth.

'Sit down and I'll get you something to eat. You look like you could do with it.'

Xander gulped the wine and put the cup on the table.

'No, I've got to go.'

'What's the hurry? It's women's work, man. No place for the likes of us.'

Xander shook his head impatiently. 'I've got to go and see her. She doesn't know I'm here.'

The man looked from Xander to Lex. 'Doesn't know you're here? Didn't you come down with the lad here?'

Xander shook his head. 'I've just got off a ship. I met the boy by chance. Just as well ...'

Xander and Lex followed the hurrying back of the midwife up the steep track. The air was clean and cold, smelling of frost and sulphur. After a while Xander put his hand on Lex's shoulder.

'Slow down!'

'What's wrong?' Lex stood by his side.

'Starvation, son. Pray it never happens to you.'

Lex saw the lines etched in his father's face. He touched his arm gently.

'We'll look after you.'

'Aye, well, there's your mother to see to first.'

They began walking again, more slowly now.

'Why did your mother send for the midwife? You must have women enough at home that could help her.'

'Some are sick. A stomach thing. My mother's had it, too. It's what brought the baby on. The rest are working.'

'*Working*? And that's more important?'

Lex turned his face towards his father. 'Eumeus sent Afrikka.'

'Afrikka?'

'She's Eumeus' favourite. He's daft about that girl.'

'Wasn't she ... working?'

Lex shook his head. 'Afrikka never works. Eumeus won't let her. He sent her to help my mother. But she won't do anything. She'll just try to run away. That's all she ever wants to do.'

'And there's nobody else?'

'There's my sister, Roza. But she's only four. I could have helped. But my mother sent me away.'

Xander dropped his hand onto his son's shoulder.

'You did the best you could. Everything will be all right now.'

Quin was in his usual place in front of the big, studded door with the flames from the brazier rippling red on his gilded breastplate. He was standing to attention, his fists clenched at his sides. His body was swaying backwards and forwards. He was gabbling wildly to himself, sometimes letting out a high-pitched giggle. His eyes were tight shut.

The midwife came to a halt just inside the gate and stared around the courtyard with ill-disguised curiosity. From inside the house the sound of screaming was very faint, overlaid with the pretty tinkle of some musical instrument. Xander started shivering again. He hunched over the brazier. The smell of damp wool singeing rose with the smoke into the cold, dry air.

Lex ran over to Quin. 'It's all right. I've brought someone to help. Let us in!'

Quin opened his eyes. He saw Xander standing by the fire.

106

He mumbled something to himself and stumbled across the space that separated them.

It was part of that strange wisdom of his, thought Lex as he watched Quin fold Xander clumsily in his arms, that allowed him to find someone he loved in the ghost he had become.

Xander, crushed against the cold metal of Quin's armour, felt an unexpected surge of feeling. A sense of homecoming. Tears rose into his throat and he swallowed hard, laughing and choking as the big man thumped him kindly on the back.

The bedroom was hot, lit by the yellow flame of oil lamps that jumped in the sudden draft from the door. Lily lay flat on the bed, her huge belly straining against the thin sheet that covered her. Her damp hair was tangled on the pillow. Her mouth was open for another scream to join the ones that had turned the warm air into jangling chaos. At the bottom of the bed stood Roza, a tiny figure in a white nightshirt, her feet bare on the tiled floor. Her eyes were shut, her bunched hands pushed tight against her ears.

By the window a dark girl of astonishing beauty was hunched over Lily's carved wooden chest, her hands scrabbling in an ivory jewellery box. Light gleamed on gold and precious stones. The girl turned her head. Her red lips parted in a snarl, showing white teeth. Her hand reached out and pushed open the window. The wind leapt into the room, carrying with it the sting of frost.

She had one knee on the sill, her hands dripping with precious things, when Lex's knife struck her. It bit deep into her back and red blood flowered on the pale silk of her gown. The gold slid from her hand like a precious waterfall. Lex burst into tears.

The midwife put her bag on the floor and shoved everyone out of the room. Behind the door Lily's screams rose and rose.

Lex and Xander went to the kitchen. Nobody was there. They sat side by side on a wooden bench by the hearth. The rising wind moaned against the shutters. After a while Xander put his arm awkwardly across his son's shoulders.

'You don't have to cry. You did the right thing.'

Lex turned his tear-ravaged face up to his father. 'You don't understand. It was my first kill. And it was a *woman*.'

'It doesn't matter. She was only a slave. Your next kill will be the one that counts. After that, you forget them.'

Xander thought suddenly of his own first kill. A border skirmish with his father. A scrawny dark-faced man in a dirty sheepskin. He remembered the look of surprise on the man's face when the spear struck his chest. The man had been armed with a wooden rake.

'How many men have you killed?'

Xander shook his head. Other memories crowded his head. The yellow-haired giant in Tyre with the dancing jewellery in his ears. His shield companion Moeris gone to join the souls on the cliff face behind the citadel. And Shyrah. His wife. The way his knife slid between her ribs. Tears choked the back of his throat.

And then the thin wail of a new born child.

Part Three

Babylon

16

'You've seen her, haven't you?'

The old man reached out a thin, sun-freckled hand. His eyes gleamed with ill-disguised lust.

'Yes, lord.'

Shutruk shrugged himself away from the fretted window and crossed the room to hand his master the fine glass goblet from the carved table next to the old man's chair. He was young, lithe, dark-haired, naked except for a linen loincloth that disguised his eunuch status but allowed him to show off a fine, muscular chest. His hair was long, greased and worn in ringlets.

He stood quietly while his master drained the goblet, refilled it from a pitcher resting in a bowl of half-melted ice, then prowled back to his position by the window. He had no interest in his master's cravings except when they created trouble for him. And this one would be trouble. He knew it already.

The girl in question was fifteen or thereabouts and already showing the promise of a voluptuous beauty. If you liked that sort of thing, though Shutruk, who found women's flesh repulsive. But it was not the flesh that interested his master - there was plenty of that in the women's rooms downstairs - but her strange pale skin and blue eyes. A collector's item, that's what she was. Pale skin and blue eyes were not common in Babylon, even these days, thought Shutruk, staring down into the street where a multi-hued throng surged under the hot sun.

'It won't be easy, lord. She's no slave. And her father has some influence.'

The old man, Mutakkil-Nusku, replaced the empty goblet on the small carved table next to his chair. 'That black-haired sailor? He's not her father. And her mother's a whore. Or was.'

'She kept a house, I know that much. It's where she got her gold.'

'Yes, but the sailor, Shutruk. You shouldn't have any problems with him.'

'Blackmail, you mean?'

'I don't think he'd respond to blackmail. I'll put a bit of work his way. He'll be honoured to do business with Mutakkil-Nusku, you'll see. And, if he's not her father, so much the better. Why should he care what happens to her?'

'He aims for a good marriage, lord'

'He won't get one. Not with her background.'

'Maybe you should try for her yourself, lord.'

'Marry her? Are you mad? It's possession I want, not ownership.' The old man, Mutakkil-Nusku lifted his thin, bloodless lip over blunt yellow teeth. 'Arrange it for me, Shutruk. You know what I like.'

'No, I won't! You can't make me!'

Angry footsteps on the tiles. Shyron waited for the slamming of a door. It came. He carried on eating. Roza's storms were a daily affair.

'What was all that about?' he asked, when his half-sister entered the room.

'Why should I marry some disgusting goat that's old enough to be my father?' Roza scraped a chair across the tiles and sat down at the table.

'Who's making you?'

'They are! They will! As if I don't matter.'

'You want to get married, don't you?'

'I don't want to do anything. Why don't they just leave me alone?'

'Want some?' Shyron pushed the plate of food towards her.

A small knife with a carved ivory handle appeared in the girl's hand and flashed down, spearing a lump of meat. Shyron didn't flinch, although he knew well enough what his sister was capable of. There was more than one slave in the household who bore the marks of her displeasure. No wonder his father was trying to marry her off, he thought. Let her be somebody else's problem!

'So who are they making you marry this time?'

Roza chewed the meat. 'Nobody yet. Your father's been invited to the palace of Mutakkil-Nusku and my mother's excited because she thinks he'll find me a rich husband.'

Shyron raised one eye-brow. 'Mutakkil-Nusku? I wonder why.'

'I've told you why. To find me a husband.'

'No, I mean I wonder why my father's been asked. I'm surprised Mutakkil-Nusku even knows we exist.'

'Why wouldn't he? We've got plenty of money.'

Shyron shook his head. 'Not that kind of money, Roza.'

Roza leaned forward and speared another piece of meat.

'What do you know about him, Shyron?'

'Not much. Wealthy, obviously. Comes from an established family. As established as anyone can be in this city.'

'Not that. Old? Young?'

Shyron pulled a face. 'Old. Don't worry, Roza. He's got a hundred wives already. And he must be past it, by now.'

Roza got to her feet and prowled to the window.

'I don't know what we're doing here, cooped up in this stinking city.'

'You'll feel better when the cold weather comes.'

'No, I won't. I'll still hate it. It's all right for you. You can go out and sail boats on that sewer they call a river while I have to stay in the house and weave things. What sort of a life is that?'

'You'd have to weave things wherever you were. It's what girls do.'

Roza turned around in a swirl of coloured silks. 'It's not what I'm going to do.'

Shyron returned to his plate of food. He wondered, not for the first time, when Roza was going to get used to the life she had. Girls stayed indoors, that's the way it was. Whereas he had the freedom to go out into the market place where spices and singing birds and straw-wrapped ice combined in a jumble of sounds and smells with sizzling food and animal dung and the raw smell of sweat from the crowded alleyways. Or down to his father's warehouse crammed up against the great outer wall of the city where the swallows nested high up amongst the roof beams and Eumeus sat in his small office clicking his beads. Or outside the city to the wharf where he could stand on the worn timber and watch the ships slipping downriver like ghosts in the early morning mist.

Roza was right about one thing. The river was a sewer, especially now after a long, dry summer when the water levels were low. And, like Roza, Shyron often wondered what his family was doing in Babylon. His father had told him his own story about being raised in the great inland city of Carchemish and how he'd made the long journey to the sea. Well, Shyron had been born in a house with a view of sparking water from every window and here he was in Babylon which was so far inland the peasants mistook rowing oars for winnowing fans.

When Shyron was two the family had left Thera and moved east. Xander had heard that the sea wolves had been cleared out of Tyre, or had left of their own accord, wolves not being the sort to settle anywhere for long, and he'd gone back to try his hand at the timber trade. They'd stayed for five years in a small, harbour-side villa while Xander made a fortune supplying timber not only for the new Tyre rising on the island that had been the wolves' lair but for all the other coastal cities which were also busy rebuilding bigger and better than ever.

Xander had a fleet of squat sailing ships and his own wharf where Uncle Quin supervised the loading and unloading of the precious fragrant cargo. Shyron spent his early childhood playing in the timber sheds. He learned to recognise the smell and feel of cedar and pine and the rarer mahogany and oak, as pale and blond as the sailors who brought it and who came to the house afterwards to drink beer and tell stories about Ocean that lay beyond the middle sea. They claimed that Ocean's water moved in and out twice a day, like a giant breathing, leaving the boats to lie stranded on stinking mud, but Shyron was never sure he believed them.

Then the family had packed up and moved again. Inland, this time. Further and further until there was not the slightest hint of salt in the dry, hot air. Only grass and goat's droppings and camel-dung fires and a vast canopy of glittering stars. Finally, when Shyron believed there was never going to be any other sort of life except riding and stopping and riding again, he saw water gleaming on the horizon and thought they'd reached the sea. But it didn't smell right. Not the salty, fishy, sea-weedy sort of smell he'd known all his life but something more like mud and weeds and damp, rotten vegetables and, when the morning haze had cleared away, there was another bank, crowded with villages and small, square fields. A great river, surely. But only a river after all.

Babylon itself was huge and noisy, blasting Shyron's senses after so long on the road. The great river Euphrates ran through the middle of the city and along each bank ran a high stone wall. Small bronze gates were set into the wall at intervals so the citizens could reach the water. Babylon was, in fact, two cities in one, each half dominated by a huge fortress. On one side of the river stood the royal palace, on the other a great temple with eight towers one on top of the other, the topmost being the dwelling place of Bel, the city's patron god.

Now Shyron shoved the last mouthful of food into his mouth and pushed the plate away. He looked up at his sister. Her temper had blown over, as it always did, and she was sitting peacefully at the table watching her brother finish his meal.

'What if you meet someone young and handsome?' he said. 'You might want to get married then.'

'No, I won't. Not even if he was the best looking boy in the whole of Babylon.'

At that moment, the best looking boy in Babylon, by his own reckoning if nobody else's, was in another part of the city preparing to do his master's bidding.

In the misty early morning Xander stood on the dock. In his nostrils was the familiar vegetable smell of the river which swirled silently below his feet. At his shoulder was Quin who never missed an opportunity to leave the city and who was, Xander knew, grinning with delight at the treat.

Quin nudged Xander. 'Coming now.'

Xander lifted his head. The faint creak of a rope, the ghost of white against the darkness of the river. Lex was as good as his father at arriving silently when he wanted to. Xander turned round and grinned at the big man.

The small boat nudged into the dock. A rope uncurled out of the darkness. Lex stepped onto the timbers of the dock. Father and son embraced, each happy to feel the solid, living warmth of the other. It was never a certainty that each would find the other alive after one of Lex's journeys.

Lex turned and wrapped his arms around Quin, slapping his hand against the big man's back. Through the thick cloak and the solid bulk of his flesh, Lex could feel Quin's bones and thought suddenly, he's getting old. Next to Eumeus and his mother, Quin was the one enduring thing in Lex's life and, he realised now, the most beloved.

Lex remembered sunny days on the hill behind the farm when he and the goats trooped after Quin's broad back from tree-shade to tree-shade until the evening when, itchy with sun burn and grass seeds, he'd climbed on Quin's shoulders to be carried home for supper. He remember leaning against Quin's knee in the red firelight sharing a bowl of bean broth spoon for spoon. Remembered Quin in his fancy armour standing by the door of the big white house on Thera. He had seemed so big then. So powerful. And then Lex's father had come into his life and Quin had never seemed so important again. From then on, only Xander mattered.

Now Lex turned from Quin towards his father. 'The river's low. What's the news from the north?'

'Drought. Here, too. It's been a bad harvest.'

The three men began walking towards one of the small bronze gates that led from the river bank into the city. Dawn had arrived pink and gold in a pale clear sky. Already women with water jars and baskets of washing were passing through the gate on their way to the river.

In the narrow street Xander turned to his son. 'So what's the news from the south?'

'Grain's fetching a good price in Lagash. They'll take as much as we can send.'

Xander shook his head. 'There isn't much to spare. We're going to need most of the harvest ourselves this year to see us through the winter. Anything else?'

'I got some of that scarlet silk Roza wanted, though why she insists on dressing like a whore I'll never know. Mother should talk to her.'

Xander raised one eye brow. 'Have you tried talking to Roza?'

Lex grinned at his father. 'Not me. I keep out of her way.'

Xander reached out and gripped Lex's upper arm and drew him close. 'Is there any other news?'

Lex turned his head. 'What kind of news?'

'About Lord Alkmon. There's a story flying around the market place that he's been stirring up trouble.'

Lex shrugged off his father's hand. 'Why ask me? It sounds as if the rumour mongers have the story already.'

'Have you seen him?'

Lex shook his head. 'He isn't in Lagash any more, Father. Didn't you know? He's back in Babylon.'

Xander raised one eye brow. 'Is he indeed? That's news to me.'

'I don't think it's public knowledge just yet.' Lex glanced sideways at his father. 'So, tell me, what have you heard?'

'They say he's planning an attack on the city.'

Lex flicked his father a dark glance. 'Babylon is due for a new master, wouldn't you say? How long since the last time? Twenty, twenty five years?'

'Twenty five,' said Xander, remembering the glint of sun on weapons seen from his mother's bedroom window the day he escaped from Carchemish. 'And you think he'll succeed?'

'There's no reason why he shouldn't. There are people enough in this city who value their treasure and don't care who rules them.'

'Traitors they might be called in other places.'

'Traitors maybe, but safe in their beds. Why should they care who's in the royal palace?'

Xander pushed open the narrow door that led through an archway into the central courtyard of their small riverside palace.

'I can't say I'm surprised. Alkmon's turned his cloak so many times I wonder he knows which side is the lining.'

'Maybe he has good reason this time. Babylon has been no friend to Alkmon these last ten years.'

Xander frowned. 'I hope you're not involved with Lord Alkmon, Lex. His affairs are not for the likes of us.'

Lex reached down and scooped up a handful of water from the raised pool in the middle of the courtyard. 'The people who rule Babylon control Carchemish, do they not?'

Xander shook his head. 'That's not my fight, Lex. Not any more. And it's not yours, either.' He reached forward and gripped Lex's shoulder. 'You may have the blood of the Great King Shuppiluliumesh running in your veins but that's no reason to risk spilling it in one of Alkmon's mad games.' He dropped his hand. 'Now go and greet your mother. She's waiting for you.'

Later in the bath house, with the slaves gone, Lex and Xander returned to the topic of Alkmon. They were sprawled comfortably on the cool stone floor with their backs to the massage benches, a jar of wine between them.

'Why exactly did the city banish Alkmon, Father? What did he do? You hear so many tales.'

'It was impiety. There was a group of them. Drunk, of course. They performed mock rites.'

'Not so shocking, surely, in a place like Babylon?'

Lex followed his father in the worship of the hero-god Heracles and had no time for Bel, the ancient god of Babylon who inhabited the high tower on the other side of the river.

Xander swallowed a mouthful of wine. 'It's true that Babylon is a city of a thousand gods. Foreigners may worship as they choose. But Bel is the guardian spirit of the city. To make a mockery of the rites due to him is no small matter, especially when your family holds high priestly office.'

'As Alkmon's family does. Yes, I can understand that. But everyone knows they're corrupt. They control the black economy. *We* pay them, for safe passage on the river. And I've seen what happens to those who don't.'

Xander pulled himself to his feet and reached for the silk robe lying on the bench. 'All the more reason for them to put on a good front.'

'The penalty for impiety is death, is it not?'

Xander nodded. 'All the others received the death penalty. A public stoning. They didn't have the benefit of Alkmon's ... connections. *He* was given ten years exile. A light sentence, given the circumstances. And now he's plotting Babylon's downfall.'

'They confiscated his property, too, didn't they?' Lex stood up and faced his father. 'You can't blame him for wanting to get it back.'

'They took *some* of his property, Lex. There's plenty more

hidden away.' Xander pushed his arms into the sleeves of his robe. 'They say Alkmon suffers from terminal boredom. Wine, women and song are meat and drink for him but what he craves most is danger. And he doesn't care how many men he drags after him when he's got some scheme afoot.' Xander draped his arm across his son's shoulder. 'I've been invited to the palace of Mutakkil-Nusku tonight. Do you want to come along? There'll be some pretty girls on display.'

'Boys, too, I should imagine. I know a little of Mutakkil-Nusku.' Lex raised an eye-brow. 'High company you're keeping these days, Father.'

Xander rolled his eyes. 'Your mother's looking for a husband for Roza. Come with me, Lex. There will be some important people there. And maybe we'll get to see the famous Alkmon. But first we'd better go and eat our dinner. It's your first night home so it's bound to be something special.'

17

Eumeus bent down and scratched the round head of Tashi the warehouse cat who had woken from her slumber next to the stove ready for a night's hunting among the grain sacks. Then he pulled his cloak off the peg by the office door, walked through the dim, dusty void of the warehouse and stepped out into the courtyard.

High above his head a haloed moon swam in the black sky. The stench of the river hung in the cold air. As he moved towards the dark square of the gate on the far side of the cobbled yard, Eumeus thought of the inventory he had just completed which had kept him late at the warehouse this cold night. Babylon will be hard pressed to feed itself this coming winter, he thought, if all the warehouses in the city are as under stocked as Xander's. He shivered and pulled his cloak over his ears.

Eumeus stepped out into street and turned around to lock the heavy wooden gate. From the corner of his eye he caught the flicker of movement as a dark shadow detached itself from the high stone wall that surrounded the warehouse. He felt someone grab his arms and twist them painfully behind his back. The key dropped from his fingers and he heard a sharp chime as it landed on the pavement at his feet. A voice, silken smooth, lisped into his ear.

'I'd advise against struggling, my friend. There's a knife at your ribs.'

Through the wool of his cloak, Eumeus felt the dig of something sharp in the small of his back. Then the man swung him around and pushed him against the rough stone of the wall. A spill of yellow lamplight from a high window in the opposite wall allowed Eumeus his first glimpse of his assailant. He was young, dark-haired, smooth-shaven. A dinner wreath of faded flowers circled his brow. His smile was lazy and charming.

'*Well*, now!'

The man leaned forward and grabbed Eumeus by the hair. He twisted his head around, revealing the old slave mark behind his ear. Eumeus felt his heart thump once, and then a strange calm.

'I'm a free man, Lord Alkmon.' Eumeus stared into the man's pale eyes.

'With a mark like that behind your ear? I think not, my friend. You belong to me.'

'It's not like that.'

'So. What is it like?'

'I was sold out of your house when I was a boy. Freed by my mistress fifteen years ago.'

'And the slave mark? There's no sign of cancellation.'

Into Eumeus' head came the memory of the night of his freedom. Muddy gold tipped over the pig pen wall. Lily, hair wild, thin clothes clinging to milk-swollen breasts. *I free you, Eumeus.* But he had never been free. His love for Lily had held him in thrall. Even when the family came to Babylon.

'No. It was never cancelled.'

The man put his hands flat on the wall either side of Eumeus' head. 'You're in a bit of bother, then, aren't you? You know the penalty for running away, I take it?'

'My mistress can vouch for me.'

'The red-headed whore who kept a house on Thera? I know about her. A fine advocate she'd make in a court of law.' Lord Alkmon thrust his face forward. 'I don't think it needs to go that far. It just so happens you can do something for me. Along the lines of your old trade. An hour's work. Maybe two. What do you say?'

Eumeus inclined his head with something approaching his normal calm dignity.

'As you wish, Lord Alkmon.'

The man pushed himself off the wall. 'Good. Then you'd better come with me.'

Alkmon flung one arm across Eumeus' shoulder, and they made their way like two drunken friends up the steep streets of the city until they came to the wide paved plazas where Babylon's notables had their palaces. Pushing Eumeus in front of him, Alkmon descended steep, narrow steps that ran down beside the front entrance of one of the palaces and led to a paved yard, slippery with damp, and a wooden door. Alkmon pushed the door open. A sweet smile, like a host to a cherished guest.

'After you.'

Reluctantly Eumeus stepped through the door. He felt the past wrap itself around him like a ghostly garment. He put his hand up and felt the raised scar of the slave mark behind his ear. Remembered the pain and the stink of burning flesh. His hatred for the man behind him rose into his throat like bile. Behind him he heard Alkmon drag the heavy door shut.

'Come on. There's work to be done.'

Eumeus followed Alkmon's hurrying back as he threaded his way through the labyrinth of narrow corridors that lay beneath the palace. Finally they emerged in a square hall with a tiled floor. Steep stairs led upwards. Alkmon turned his head.

'Up, now. I hope you're fit.'

There were plenty of times on that long upward climb when Eumeus was forced to stop and catch his breath. Each time Alkmon stopped, too, and leaned against the wall of the stairwell watching Eumeus with lazy amusement. Finally, they reached the top and Alkmon pushed open the door, revealing a room Eumeus thought he'd never see again.

It was a big square low-ceilinged room with windows on every side capturing the twinkling lights of the city far below, and the dull gleam of the river. Much of the floor was taken up with the wooden chart table, littered with maps and scrolls. Above his head Eumeus noticed the ceiling was shut but he knew that it was set on rollers and could be opened wide to reveal the stars.

The room was dim, the only light coming from a small lamp set on a table against the far wall. As Eumeus turned his head, taking in the familiar scene, a man rose from an upholstered seat by the table and moved unhurriedly around the chart table towards the door. He was of middle-years, short and bald but with an air of authority that came from accustomed wealth and power. Eumeus knew the type only too well.

'Greetings, Alkmon. You found him, then?'

'Greetings to you, my friend,' said Lord Alkmon with his slight lisp. 'May I introduce Eumeus, freedman of the house of Siskandarabba?'

In the darkness of the doorway, Eumeus snatched a breath.

122

These days Siskandarabba was nothing but a name, replaced years ago by that of Xander: sailor, merchant, father of Lily's sons. It was a powerful name, nevertheless. The kind of name people could use for their own purposes. Eumeus shivered. We should never have come here, he thought.

The other man waved his hand impatiently. 'He's an astronomer?'

'Taught in this very house, Verran.'

Verran crooked his finger at Eumeus. A moment's hesitation then Eumeus stepped forward into the room. Verran examined him closely. Grabbed his hands and inspected the palms. Eumeus' hands were soft enough now but years of hard work had left their mark.

Verran quirked an eye brow in Alkmon's direction. 'It must have been some time ago.'

'He was sold off. How long ago?'

Eumeus turned his head. 'I was thirteen,' he said. 'Lord,' he added, as an afterthought. He didn't need the prickling of the skin between his shoulder blades to remind him of the danger he was in. And not just him. He spoke directly to the man in front of him. 'But you don't forget.'

A smile lifted the corner of Verran's mouth. 'Just as well. Let me tell you what I want you to do.'

Dawn was washing the sky with grey when Eumeus lifted his head.

'I've found it, Lord.'

The night had passed slowly. While Eumeus worked, Alkmon and Verran had sat in the darkness on the far side of the room passing a jar of wine between them. An hour or so ago a slave had entered the room with fresh bread and fruit. The smell of the bread had twisted Eumeus' stomach but he had not looked up from his work. For him, it was a kind of defiance to work swiftly and efficiently in the face of these powerful men. Besides, he was enjoying himself.

The star charts had greeted him like old friends and he had found himself remembering his days as a galley slave when they dropped anchor in the shelter of some headland and he had slept with nothing but the starry sky for a blanket. Remembering the shed on Lily's farm where he had punched a hole in the stinking thatch and defied his fellow slaves to close it over. And now here he was again in the lofty tower where he had learned his trade, feeling again the sweet power of the stars beneath his fingers. And his own power over his captors. He had found the answer they wanted an hour into his search but it was his satisfaction to deny these men their sleep. And make them wait.

Alkmon stood up quickly and prowled over to the table. Verran was slower to his feet, making a show of swallowing the dregs of his wine.

'Well?'

Eumeus looked up into Verran's face. 'There'll be an eclipse of the moon seventeen nights from tonight.'

'What time?'

'Between midnight and three hours into the new day.'

Verran looked a question at Alkmon. 'Seventeen days?'

Alkmon nodded. 'It'll serve.'

He draped one long arm across Eumeus' shoulder and smiled sweetly, breathing stale wine into his face. 'And now for the other part of your ... obligation, my friend. What we want you to do is take this knowledge and give it to Siskandarabba's son. Lex. Is that his name?'

Lex? Danger yawned like a pit at Eumeus' feet.

Verran thrust his head forward. 'You know, I suppose, the greatness of the house you serve? That black-haired sailor would have been Governor of Carchemish, if the masters of Babylon had not taken the city from his father.'

Eumeus shook his head. 'It's history. Lord Siskandarabba has no interest in Carchemish.'

'But what of his son? Denied his inheritance.'

'He was conceived under a pomegranate tree in the garden of an Achaean whorehouse. What kind of inheritance is that?'

Fear had made Eumeus bold. Fatigue denied him the forewarning of Verran's hand which left a red mark throbbing on his cheek.

'You forget yourself, slave! Go back to your clacking beads and leave your betters to decide how best to order the world.'

Alkmon leaned forward, placing his hands flat on the table among the charts, and stared up into Eumeus' eyes. 'Listen, my friend. This ... thing ... that's going to happen will be all over

124

while men are in their beds fucking their slaves. Do as you're told and no harm will come to you, or the family you serve.' Alkmon smiled into Eumeus' face. 'They say your mistress is a beautiful woman. I enjoy the company of beautiful women. Don't I, Verran?' Alkmon turned his head towards the other man. His pale, lazy gaze was replaced with a look of greedy excitement. Menace chilled the room as the sun came over the horizon, bathing the city in golden light. 'Now you can go. You know the way out, I take it?'

The slave, Shutruk, dressed as a respectable merchant, loitered in the courtyard of Xander's palace. He had been to see Xander about a valuable grain franchise which would not normally come within the grasp of a small trader. Now he lingered, hoping for a glimpse of Roza or, better still, to allow the girl a chance to see him. He knew how he looked, even in the plain linen shift of his borrowed trade. In fact, the simplicity of his dress served only to accentuate his dark good looks and the charms of his fine physique.

His large, almond shaped eyes scanned the fretted screens that disguised the first floor windows of the family's living quarters. There was somebody there, he was sure of it. With a careful grace, he leaned down to the small raised pool in the middle of the courtyard. A flower floated there, its rich pink petals heavy with water. With one eye on the window, he scooped it up and tucked it down the front of his tunic.

The flower, dried, pressed, and drenched with perfume was delivered to Roza the following day. She knew exactly where it had come from. The previous evening she had questioned her stepfather closely about his young visitor and knew as much as Xander could tell her. He was young, respectable, wealthy. Xander had met him at the palace of Mutakkil-Nusku whence he had gone with Lex several nights ago. At the time Roza had been more interested in hearing about Lord Alkmon who had entered the party an hour after everyone else dragging a crimson cloak behind him and left before dawn with a giggling slave-girl in tow.

He was famous for his red cloak, was Alkmon, and for the soft lisp of his voice and his easy charm. That he had just returned from ten years exile for a crime vile enough for his accomplices to have been put to death by public stoning was forgotten within a moment of his arrival. He had toured the room, greeted everyone by name and asked after their families as if he'd been away a week instead of a decade. By the time he left he was everyone's best friend and had invitations enough to keep him amused for the decade to come.

But now, with the flower lying on the table in front of her and the memory of Shutruk's dark eyes staring up at the window, Roza forgot about Alkmon and turned her mind to thoughts of the young man without his shift. Naked on a bed.

At fifteen, Roza knew well enough what went on between a man and a woman, having learned the art of pleasure from a certain eunuch slave of Xander's who was employed, after the tradition in the city, to attend the women's quarters. That he took his duties beyond flower arranging and the provision of sweetmeats was his revenge for what had been done to him. He had been a warrior before his capture and it had been his misfortune to have the kind of looks valued by Babylonian matrons and worth preserving by the cut of a knife. He had found in Roza a willing pupil for the things he had to teach.

The following day brought an invitation for Shutruk to call on Roza's mother. The salon overlooking the courtyard was hot and stuffy. Sweetmeats were served by a pretty boy with a look in his eyes that Shutruk did not quite like. Faint tattoos chased themselves up the boy's well-muscled arms. Not slave-bred, then, thought Shutruk. A dangerous breed, captive boys. It was something he'd learnt to his cost.

Roza sat by her mother, plainly dressed, hair neat, eyes downcast like every other well-bred maiden in the city. But Shutruk caught a glance from her startlingly blue eyes and knew that she would swallow the hook when it was dangled. As her stepfather had swallowed his. Grain franchise indeed! What fools these people are, he thought. He glanced again at the boy slave. Perhaps ...

Two days later Lex returned south carrying with him a piece of information to be delivered to certain people in the city of Lagash. From the chart room at the top of his palace, Alkmon watched the boat move downstream until it rounded a bend in the river and was lost to sight.

18

Roza disappeared three days before the eclipse of the moon. Eumeus came back from the warehouse to find the house in uproar, Lily in floods of tears and the eunuch slave standing next to her chair with a bowl of rose-water in his hands and a knowing look in his dark eyes. Eumeus found him in the slave quarters later and questioned him closely.

'It's my belief she's gone off with Shutruk, Lord.' Eumeus was one of the few men the eunuch respected. And, in answer to Eumeus' puzzled look, 'He's been to the house a few times. To see Roza.'

'And what manner of man is this Shutruk?'

"A merchant. Or so he says.'

'And Roza liked him?'

'Yes, Lord Eumeus. They seemed well pleased with each other.'

'But?'

'My lord?

'Come on, Zaagor! There's more to this than you're telling.' Eumeus walked to the table, poured wine into two beakers, splashed in water and handed a beaker to the young slave. 'Tell me what's been going on.'

Zaagor took a gulp of his wine. 'Shutruk is one of the old ones, the ancient people who lived in Babylon before the invasions.'

'So?' Above his wine beaker Eumeus quirked an eye brow at the young slave.

'So, my lord, the old ones are not traders. Not in this city. Some are servants of Bel ...' With a nod of his head Zaagor indicated the great temple on the other side of the river. 'Most are slaves.'

Suddenly Eumeus remembered seeing a dark-skinned young man in a white linen shift leaving the women's quarters.

Remembered thinking that the plain garment sat ill on such a man and that, despite his impeccable bow and polite greeting, there was something not quite right about the look he received from the young man's almond-shaped eyes.

'So this man has been courting Roza?'

'That's what it looked like. My lady had high hopes he'd make her an offer.'

Eumeus took a deep draught of his wine. 'And you think she's gone off with him? Why would she do a thing like that?'

Zaagor shook his head. 'Why Roza's gone off with him isn't important, Lord Eumeus. It's why he's taken her.'

'They've run away together. That's obvious.'

'No, Lord. That man ... I believe he is as I am.'

There was silence for a long moment.

'A eunuch?' Eumeus started at the young man in front of him. It was a subject that was never mentioned, never discussed, even among the slaves themselves. Eumeus wondered at the effort it had cost Zaagor to speak to him of such a thing. 'How can you tell?'

Zaagor drained his wine. Crossed to the table to pour more. 'They do it to preserve our looks.' The slave indicated his own unlined face. 'I am as I appear. Eighteen, as near as I can make out. That man is nearer thirty. You can see it in his eyes.'

'But why ... why would a man like that take Roza?'

But Eumeus didn't need Zaagor's reply. The answer dropped complete into his head.

'To please his master,' said Zaagor.

Xander searched the city. He visited his fellow traders, the brokers, the dealers and middle men who had been his friends and neighbours since his arrival in Babylon. They all shook their heads and Xander watched their eyes slide away from his face. With Eumeus, he went to the office where he had gone to stitch up the lucrative grain deal that Shutruk had brought his way. The secret deal, he remembered now, that Shutruk had told him not to mention for fear of arousing envy. But this time he could get no further than the door. He cursed himself for a fool. Returned home to Lily's tear-streaked face and tried to imagine what she was feeling.

Two days went by. Lex was due back from his trip south.

128

And in just over twenty-four hours the moon would go into eclipse.

It was cold. Freezing. Lying on the straw mattress on the stone floor, Roza curled herself into a tight ball. She clamped one hand over her face to block the stench from the bucket in the corner which was full to overflowing. She knew it was evening. She'd learned to tell the difference between daylight and lamplight as it lay in a narrow strip at the bottom of the door. Three days it had been. Three days since Shutruk lured her away with promise in his dark, almond-shaped eyes. A secret meeting, he'd said, to talk and kiss and touch hands. Then he'd talk to her stepfather, nothing surer. And she'd fallen for it like some silly maiden.

The first night Shutruk had appeared in her cell dressed in his loincloth with oil on his smooth chest and greased ringlets in his hair. He had put her into a white dress, placed a circlet of fresh flowers in her hair and taken her to his master. It was the original old goat, Mutakkil-Nusku, and she'd laughed to think how he had fooled her stepfather with his favour and his grain. But the old man was not fooled by her.

The old man had an appetite for young maidens and he liked them to be afraid and to shrink from his touch. It added to his excitement. Allowed him to do what was impossible with the compliant, experienced women he kept in the palace harem. But Roza was not afraid and she did not shrink. She allowed him to lie on her body, grunting like a rooting pig. She stared up at him with a steady blue gaze and, in the end, he decided she was not what he wanted. Not what he wanted at all.

The next night the white dress was replaced with a short tunic and a pair of baggy pants gathered at the waist and ankles, both in a sheer silk fabric that hid little of her naked body. This time Shutruk took her to a room hung with red drapes and lit with perfumed lamps. A large table in the middle of the room was set for a dinner party. Bronze tripods stood at each corner of the table holding kraters of wine cooled with crushed ice. Shutruk told Roza to sit at the end of a padded bench and to please the man who sat there.

The man was young and dark. He came into the room with feast flowers in his hair, trailing a long red cloak behind him.

He smiled at her and touched her breasts. He tipped wine into her mouth and down the front of her tunic. He didn't ask who she was – he probably didn't care – but Roza could see a look of desire in the back of his eyes that she returned ardently. To go with this man. That was her aim. She'd be his slave. She didn't care. Anything would be better than the stone cell and the cool, careless hands of Shutruk, her gaoler.

The wine made her dizzy. She was not used to drinking it neat. But the men were worse. By dinner's end she was on the man's knee with her arms around his neck. She was well aware of his interest, which accorded well with her plans. But all of a sudden the situation went from quite promising to very bad indeed.

The man pushed Roza off his lap. 'Over there.' Roza heard a curious lisp in his voice she hadn't noticed before. She stood against the wall where the man had indicated while the table was cleared by soft-footed slaves. When they'd finished, Roza noticed with a sudden chill that she was the only girl left in the room. The other dancing girls – the real ones – had gone out with the food and the slaves. With rowdy good cheer the dinner guests pushed the empty table against the wall. Wilting dinner garlands were discarded. Wine beakers drained. All the lamps were pinched out except for two burning each side of the table. There was a moment's silence. And the mood in the room changed.

The men were nervous now, their drunkenness replaced by a sort of manic excitement. One by one they left the room and returned dressed in rough linen gowns. One man's face was covered by a gold disc upon which was etched a four-point star. One had a horned cap on his head. Several were carrying weapons: a gilded axe, a bow, a short bronze sword. Then the man, her man, the one whose dinner she'd shared, came towards her. His eyes were glittering with excitement.

He held out his hand. 'Come.'

Roza shrank back against the wall. 'No! I can't do this.'

The man reached down and grabbed Roza's hand. 'You will do it.'

He pulled her away from the wall and dragged her into an adjacent room. He dropped his loose dinner robe to the floor, revealing a taut, muscular body. A puckered purple scar seamed his torso, marring his beauty. He pulled one of the rough gowns over his head and reached for the mask lying on the bed. It was a gilded disc painted as a dreadful head. Four piercing eyes dominated the centre. Four ears decorated the edge. The mouth roared flame, red and black and gold. He turned to Roza and smiled his lazy, charming smile.

'So, what is it to be? I can kill you or wed you. Wed first, perhaps. You will not be opposed to that, I'm sure. I saw it in your eyes at dinner.'

Suddenly Roza recalled a conversation she'd heard between Lex and Shyron in the salon at home. It was about the Lord Alkmon and why he had been banished from the city for ten years. He had taken part in false rites, an abhorrence to the people of Babylon and usually punishable by death. And she knew who this man was smiling down at her with menace lurking in the back of his eyes. She knew what lay in store for her in the darkened salon next door. She knew, too, that Alkmon would kill her for sure, either now or later, and it would make no difference to him. Terror suffused her body like a black wash.

Lord Alkmon picked up a shimmering white gown from the bed.

'Come along, my dear, don't be shy. This is your wedding night, remember? You are Tiamut, goddess of love and fertility, and I am ...'

'No! Don't say it.'

'... and I am Marduk, king of heaven, that these people call Bel. That is my shrine on the hill across the river. We will go there together, you and I.' He reached forward and touched her hair gently. 'You are very beautiful, you know that, don't you? And soon you will be the queen of heaven.'

In a daze of terror, Roza allowed Alkmon to dress her in the white gown and put a gold circlet on her head. Then he picked up a gold goblet from a small round table by the bed and forced a bitter liquid between her chattering teeth. Within moments the world seemed warm and distant, and her feet were very far away as she took Alkmon's proffered arm and returned to the other room.

And now, dazed and bruised, Roza was lying on the filthy

straw mattress of her cell to which Shutruk had returned her some time in the early hours of the morning. Soon he would be back to prepare her for the evening's entertainment. She knew what it would be this time. Through the drug-filled haze, Roza remembered Alkmon's words: *We will go there together, you and I.*

Roza had lived in Babylon long enough to know the stories of the city's gods. From the scared girls who did her hair she'd heard of the sky god Marduk's battle with Tiamut, which ended with the goddess' death. It was rumoured that the battle was re-enacted every year in Marduk's temple on the other side of the river but whether it was by priests, or others, nobody seemed to know. Those who lived in the merchants' quarter, few of whom thought of themselves as native Babylonians however long their families had lived in the city, believed they were too civilized to condone human sacrifice, but they didn't mind the thought of others doing it.

Roza reached under the mattress and touched her knife. They had brought her food that first night while she was waiting for the old man and she had hidden the knife in the folds of her maiden's costume. It was only a blunt dinner knife but Roza had sharpened it on the stone walls of her prison until it was a thin stiletto. She was not going to die for the amusement of her captors, especially Lord Alkmon with his lisp and his lazy smile who called himself Marduk, the king of heaven. She would die here in her cell, by her own hands if need be. And Shutruk would die with her. Of that she was very sure.

But nobody came. The long day dragged towards night. Cold seeped in from the stone walls. Feelings of hate, anger, fear and revenge were replaced by a nagging hunger and, finally, sleep.

Eumeus left the warehouse early in the afternoon. It was the eve of the eclipse. The sun was the colour of copper, stained by the dust blown from fields that were bone dry. It had not rained for weeks. The river was lower than he'd ever seen it. Even where it flowed between the twin walls of the city it was no more than a sullen stream between banks of shining mud. On the paved footpath along the river bank where on a normal day women gossiped and washed clothes, and young boys came to swim and play, knots of anxious people were watching the water level dropping rapidly to reveal the skeletons of old boats lying on the stinking mud. Pushing his way through the crowds, Eumeus entered the city by one of the bronze gates and began walking up the steep street that led to the merchants' quarter.

Inside the city there was a different anxiety. Dressed in ceremonial costume, groups of men were heading towards the market square. Some wore the winged bull head dress of Nannar, the moon god. Some had dyed their long, curled beards blue to represent lapis lazuli, sacred to the god. All carried musical instruments: drums, cymbals and long trumpets. Later that night they would help the priests rescue Nannar from the grasp of his enemy, the sun god En-kidu.

In the market place, stall holders were preparing for the night's trade. At one stall spicy kebabs were cooking over a charcoal brazier. At another a sweating man tossed flat bread from one hand to another to cool it then wrapped it swiftly around a mixture of burghul and vegetables. On a bloody block a squawking chicken was beheaded with a blow from an axe. The middle of the square had been left clear for the dancing and, across that empty space, Eumeus saw someone he knew. He felt his heart turn painfully in his chest and was annoyed with himself. Would there ever be a time when the sight of the Lord Alkmon did not have that effect on him? Perhaps after tonight he would be free of the man at last.

But there was something familiar about the man walking at Alkmon's side. Dodging a peddler with a basket piled with sweet oranges, Eumeus moved swiftly to the edge of the square. And it was Lex. There was no doubt about it. But surely Lex was not back yet? Could not get back with the river as low as it was. It was the one thing Eumeus had counted on. That Lex would not be in Babylon on the night of the eclipse.

But there he was, sauntering through the market place with the Lord Alkmon's arm draped across his shoulder. And, even if Alkmon looked as if he had nothing whatever to occupy him except a stroll with a friend looking for something to buy, Eumeus knew this night's work had Alkmon's name written all over it. Eumeus watched until, trailing his long, scarlet cloak, Alkmon steered Lex through an archway and they disappeared from view. Then he turned and hurried home.

He heard the commotion before he was through the door. He ran up the stairs and into the main salon. Zaagor, the eunuch slave, stood in the middle of the room. He was holding another man by one arm twisted behind his back. The man had dark skin and long hair. He was dressed in a short embroidered kilt. His chest was smooth and well muscled. He was struggling violently and screaming obscenities in a high, shrill voice. A small carved table fell over with a loud clatter and rolled across the floor. At that moment Xander ran into the room, followed closely by Quin, his mouth agape with excitement. For a moment nobody spoke.

Then Eumeus took a step forward. 'What's going on?'

Zaagor's eyes swivelled round to Eumeus. 'It's him, my lord. This *thing* is the one who took Roza.'

Eumeus ignored Zaagor's familiar use of Roza's name. 'How did you find him?'

'This piece of slime fancies me, Lord Eumeus. He came up to me in the market today. Offered me sweetmeats and gold pieces for an afternoon of pleasure. I may be a slave and a eunuch but I am no *whore*.' Zaagor twisted Shutruk's arm violently, making him squeal with pain.

Xander took a step forward. He grabbed a handful of greasy hair and pulled Shutruk's face close to his own. 'Your master is Mutakkil-Nusku?'

A whimper.

Xander pushed Shutruk away. 'I might have known'

With a roar Quin launched himself across the room. His huge hands closed around Shutruk's throat. Held as he was in Zaagor's grasp, there was little Shutruk could do to save himself. Neither Xander nor Eumeus were inclined to stop the big man, except that Shutruk was their best chance of finding Roza and he was therefore more use to them alive than dead. From behind, Xander wrapped his arms around Quin's body.

'Come on Quin, stop it now.' Xander spoke in the voice he used to Quin alone. 'You can have him, I promise you. But first we have to find Roza.'

It took a while for Xander's words to penetrate. Then Quin let go of Shutruk's neck and stood panting, with his hands by his sides. Zaagor dropped Shutruk's arm and he fell to the floor, gasping and choking.

Xander gripped Zaagor's shoulder. 'Well done, lad.' He didn't know the slave's name. 'Now let's go and find Roza.' He turned to Eumeus. 'Are you coming?'

Eumeus did not move. 'My lord, there's something else.'

Xander turned. 'Something more important than this?'

'I saw Lex just now in the market place. He was with Lord Alkmon.'

'Lex? I didn't know he was back.'

Eumeus took a step forward. 'Xander, there are things you don't know. Things I haven't told you.'

Xander looked at Eumeus. Looked down at Shutruk gasping and retching on the floor.

'Take him away and do something with him,' he said to Zaagor. Then, to Eumeus, 'Now, my friend, tell me what's going on.'

'There's going to be an attack on the city tonight during the moon ceremony. Alkmon is behind it. And Lex is involved.'

'How do you know?'

'Because I told Alkmon when the eclipse would be. And I told Lex. I don't know what Lex's involvement is in all this ...'

'I can guess. He wants Carchemish. And Alkmon's promised it to him. *Stupid* boy!'

'I'm sorry, Xander. There wasn't anything I could do. Alkmon made threats against the family.'

'And now he's got Lex sucked into his madness.' Xander reached down instinctively to where his sword should be. Suddenly he was sick to the stomach of Babylon and everything in it. 'Eumeus, can you get Lily and Shyron down to the warehouse? No fuss, just quietly. Wait for me there. Quin, you and ...' He turned back to Eumeus. 'What's his name? The slave?'

'Zaagor.'

'You and Zaagor take that piece of filth and find Roza. Bring her down to the warehouse. Quick as you can.'

"What are you going to do?'

'I'm going to find my son.'

Roza woke. A strip of yellow light had appeared under the door. She slipped her hand under the straw mattress for her knife. Her heart banged in her throat. A movement, rehearsed so many times in her head, took her to the wall next to the door. She could feel the rough stone through the flimsy fabric of her gown. A long way away, beyond the stillness of the stone cellar, she could hear cymbals and drums. A festival. Bel was coming down from his temple to claim his bride. Fear and hate swirled in her mind, a heady mixture. The door opened. More light now, making her blink. Her name was spoken. 'Roza?' It was Quin's voice but her mind rejected it. Shutruk was very near. She could smell the oil he put in his hair. She pounced.

Her knife met the barrier of smooth flesh and pushed through. She ripped it out and struck again. A high-pitched screaming echoed in the stone hollow of the cell. Hands on her throat forced her head back. She stumbled. Fell back on the mattress with Shutruk's body on top of her. Her knife hand rose and fell. She could smell his blood, taste it at the back of her throat, feel it hot and sticky between their bodies. Joy rose in her body, fierce and wonderful. Then Shutruk was gone, lifted from her and tossed aside. Someone else stood above her, his body silhouetted against the lamp light.

'Come on, Roza love. I'm taking you home ...'

'No!'

A fierce shriek. Roza's knife, slippery with blood, lashed out towards the sound of the voice. A cry, a scream of pain and bewilderment. Quin staggered back, his hand clamped over his eye, fresh blood spurting between his fingers. Zaagor stepped forward and gripped Roza's wrist. There was a brief struggle. The knife dropped to the floor. Another swift movement and a heavy cloak was wrapped around her flailing arms. She was pulled upright onto legs that refused to take her weight.

'Quin, can you walk? Come on, man, we haven't got much time.'

Zaagor turned and saw the big man stagger to his feet, his hand still gripping his bloody eye. He kicked the lantern towards the blood-drenched mattress. Watched the eager flames lick at the filthy straw. There was a quick sizzle as Shutruk's heavily oiled hair caught alight.

'A funeral pyre,' Zaagor grunted. 'It's more than he deserves.'

He dragged Roza from the blazing cell, glanced over one shoulder to make sure Quin was following, then made for the stairs.

Outside the air was cold and crisp. The moon was in the sun's grip, casting a bronze glow over the city. The streets were full of shifting crowds. Avoiding the central plaza where the wailing of the priests rose above the crash of cymbals and drums, Zaagor carried the half-senseless girl through narrow alleys towards the river with Quin staggering behind him, moaning with pain.

19

Inside the warehouse Lily paces to and fro, her shadow leaping against the walls. She is wrapped in an old cloak which covers the thin dinner gown she was wearing when Eumeus hustled her from the house. Eumeus is crouched on a grain sack, his hand gentling the ears of Tashi the warehouse cat whose tail is twitching with frustration at the interruption to her night's hunting. Shyron is making himself useful by the door, knife in hand, wondering what would happen if he found himself having to use it. Lily halts in front of the old slave, her shadow falling behind her on the dusty floor.

'Tell me again, Eumeus. What are we doing here?'

'There's going to be an attack on the city. Xander thought we would be safer here. In case we have to leave in a hurry.'

'And Quin?'

'Gone to fetch Roza.'

'And Xander's gone to find Lex. Yes, I know. You've told me already. But, Eumeus, what's going on? I don't understand.'

'Someone's coming.' Shyron fingered his knife nervously.

Eumeus twitched a corner of his cloak over the lantern. The warehouse was plunged into darkness. Brown moonlight seeped through a high window.

Shyron put his eye to a crack in the door. 'It's all right. It's Quin and the slave. They've got Roza with them.'

He unlatched the big door and pulled it open. Zaagor slipped inside dragging Roza behind him. Quin stumbled through the gap after them and collapsed on the floor.

'Get that door shut.'

Eumeus picked up the lantern and hurried forward. In the feeble yellow light Quin's face was black with congealed blood, his hand clamped firmly over his eye. Zaagor lowered Roza to the floor and bent over, his breath coming from him in gasps.

'Got her … my lord.'

'And Shutruk?'

'Dead.'

Lying on the floor, Roza began screaming, her body flailing from side to side. The heavy cloak fell from her, revealing a flimsy white gown stiff with blood. Her hands tore at her hair as her screams rose higher.

'Roza!' Lily stared down at her daughter. She turned to Zaagor. 'Is she hurt?'

'It's not her blood, my lady. It belongs to the slave, Shutruk.. She killed him. And did that … to Quin.'

'Grab her, someone,' said Eumeus. 'Shyron, you.'

Shyron approached his sister. He picked up one edge of the cloak and wrapped it firmly around Roza's body. A shriek of fury. Roza bared her teeth.

'Get her away from the door.' Eumeus reached down and grabbed Quin's arm. 'You, too, old mate. Come on.'

They huddled in the corner of the warehouse, the lamp making a pool of light at their feet. Roza, held tight in her brother's grip, had shuddered herself into an uneasy sleep. Eumeus had fetched a jar of wine from the locked store at the back of the warehouse and they passed it around between them. It was the finest Sumerian vintage, worth a fortune, and its fragrance uncurled its tendrils into throats that were dry with the reek of blood and smoke and dust.

Zaagor took his turn with the rest and felt the wine's fumes rise into his head. He had the girl's knife tucked in his belt and freedom was but a step away through the warehouse door. But he made no move. Somehow he felt he owed Eumeus something because the old slave had trusted him to rescue Roza. Besides, just then he preferred the outside of the city to the inside, and life to a death that could come to him easily enough on Babylon's streets that night. He took another long pull from the wine jar and wiped his mouth with the back of his hand. He leaned forward to pass the jar back to Eumeus.

'You know they're armed?'

'Who?' Eumeus' voice was urgent.

'The men at the festival. I saw them on the way here. It's not usual … is it? … for men to go armed to a religious festival?'

'No, it's not usual.' There was silence for a long moment. Then Eumeus spoke again. 'Now I understand. That's why Alkmon planned the attack for the night of the eclipse. It's what he was counting on. That men would leave their weapons at home. Easy enough to take a city against unarmed men.'

'But they didn't.'

'No, they didn't. And that means only one thing. Alkmon's been betrayed.'

Eumeus gripped the mouth of the wine jar between his teeth and tipped the wine into his mouth. It tasted of hot sunshine and reminded him suddenly of the old farmhouse in Achaea and the ruined palace against the sky. His mind returned to the dusty warehouse, the eerie copper moonlight and the quiet moans of pain from Quin who lay at his feet like a felled ox.

'Alkmon said it would happen while men were in bed fucking their slaves,' he said. 'Wake up to a new master. Like a dozen times before.'

'But not this time.'

'No, my friend. Not this time.' Eumeus glanced across the circle to where Lily sat half asleep, cradling the head of her daughter in her lap. 'Babylon's not so easily taken, if it puts up a fight. And you know what that means, don't you? It's what cities like Babylon are made for. Repulse the enemy, lock them out, wait for them to go away.'

'A siege.'

A weary nod. 'All well and good when the storehouses are full of grain. But after the harvest we've had this year ... I'm telling you, Zaagor, Babylon won't last a month. What we're sitting on is all that stands between this city and starvation.'

'So, we leave.'

'We're dead if we don't.' A sudden splurge of shouting from the street brought Eumeus to his feet. 'Whichever way it goes.'

Shyron sat next to his mother on the dusty floor of the warehouse and watched the quiet bustle of the slaves. From the moment Eumeus had hurried into the living quarters and told them they had to leave, he had been waiting his chance to take command. Obeying Eumeus was not so bad. It was a habit he was used to. Besides, he knew the old slave spoke with his father's voice when he told him to look after his mother. It's what he had done. Got her down to the warehouse. Soothed and persuaded her. Kept her calm as they passed through the madness of the streets. He hadn't noticed that the revellers were armed. Only that they were drunk and inclined to be belligerent.

But then their eunuch slave had arrived with Roza and Quin. Shyron was shocked by the sight of his sister, her eyes staring wildly as if they saw some hidden horror. And Quin, his great hand clamped to his face, keening his pain in a high-pitched moan. That was when Shyron should have taken charge. Started telling people what to do. He was, after all, the master's son and, therefore, the head of the household in the absence of his father and older brother. But Eumeus had spoken to the eunuch – whose name was Zaagor, apparently – and shared wine with him. And now it seemed the two of them were hatching some sort of plot to leave the city.

'Eumeus?'

The two slaves, old and young, were crouched over Quin's prostrate body. They had torn strips of linen from a bale of cloth stacked in one corner of the warehouse and were working on the dried blood that had stuck Quin's hand to his face.

'Easy now, old friend. Easy.' Eumeus rinsed the bloody cloth in a bowl of wine and applied it again. He turned his head. 'What is it, Shyron?'

'That's my father's wine.' It wasn't what he'd meant to say.

'It's going to spoil anyway, now it's been opened. And it's cleaner than water. Move out of the way, there's a good lad. You're in my light.'

Shyron clenched his fists but moved as he was bid.

Eumeus returned to his task. 'That's it,' he murmured to Zaagor who was dipping strips of linen into the wine jar and giving them to Quin to suck. 'Inside and out, that's the best way. Makes the job easier for everyone. But not too much inside. He'll have to walk later.'

With Quin's hand free at last, Eumeus began to work on the swollen, pulpy mess that Roza's knife had made of his eye while Zaagor, gentle as a mother, cleaned the dried blood from between the big man's fingers.

Finally with his wound clean and bound up tightly, Quin lumbered to his feet. The wound was no longer bleeding but oozing a pale serum and the pain seemed to have receded because the big man took two paces across the dusty floor, grabbed the wine jar and gulped down the rest of the wine. Then he straightened up, swaying slightly on feet planted some distance apart, and grinned down at his family squatting on the floor.

'Strong as an ox, that one,' said Eumeus fondly.

'So what now?' asked Zaagor.

'Now we get out.'

'But how?'

Eumeus nodded towards Shyron. 'Ask him. He knows.'

And Shyron grinned, realising suddenly what they were going to do.

'The water stairs!'

Like many of the traders in Babylon, Xander's warehouse had a set of stairs built into the thickness of the wall which led down to his wharf outside the city. This staircase not only made communication between the two areas of Xander's business more efficient, it also provided a means of bringing certain goods into Babylon without going through the city's custom sheds. Xander's main business was in grain, linen, wine – bulk cargo upon which he paid import duty to the city. But there were other things: luxury items such as perfume and fine silks, as well as special orders for Xander's wealthy clients, which came up the water stairs no questions asked. Shyron had known about the water stairs for as long as he could remember. It was a quick way down to the river when he wanted to go swimming with the other boys on hot afternoons.

Shyron moved swiftly into the small office at the back of the warehouse. He pushed aside a desk holding a pile of scrolls and began pulling on a metal ring in the wooden floor. Behind him the scrolls dropped one by one onto the floor and unrolled themselves with a whisper of sound. The trap door was heavy but eventually it yawned open to reveal stone stairs leading down into blackness, and the smell of water. He stood aside as the others came crowding into the small room.

'Watch it, the steps are slippery.'

Quin first, lumbering down into the darkness with the ease born of long experience. Then Roza and Zaagor, and Lily and Eumeus. Finally, Shyron stepped down into the stair space and pulled the trap door shut behind him. In the sudden darkness he could hear the quiet drip of water, feel the soft wet slime on the stone wall as he used his hand to guide his descent, smell mud and vegetation which was the familiar stench of the river. There was something missing. But he didn't know what it was. Not yet.

The stairs ended at a wooden door inside the small watchman's hut which stood at the back of the wharf. Xander's dock lay on the outside perimeter of the city walls with its feet in the wide moat that surrounded it, and a view across the fields to the east where the thin line of the Zagros mountains joined earth to sky. Tonight a band of dense clouds hung over the mountains and obliterated the horizon.

By the time Shyron reached the bottom of the stairs, the others had crowded out of the hut onto the smooth timber of the dock. The eclipse was at its height. The moon was a bronze disc riding in a sky like brown velvet. From the city a crescendo of sound from flute and cymbals and drums, then silence. For a long moment the moon hung in the sky, shedding its weird brown luminescence. Then appeared a spark, a sliver of pure silver light, growing rapidly. A roar of voices from the city streets. The air became cold as the strengthening moon brought down a frost that laid seeds of white on the boards at the edge of the dock. Shyron could see the cloud of his breath in front of his face. The clash of cymbals began again. And suddenly Shyron realised what was missing. It was the rush of the river, the background to his life in Babylon.

He walked to the edge of the dock. Peering down, he could see the slick shine of mud. A boat was hanging on the end of its rope, hull deep in the thick slime. Across the river a rock wall dripped with dark weed. Beyond the wall the fields began, a neat patchwork seamed with irrigation channels.

Shyron turned his head. 'Come and look. The river's dry. There's no water in it.'

A movement behind him and Zaagor stood at Shyron's shoulder. He pointed beyond the dry river. 'The fields. Can you see something moving?'

Under the clear silver light of the returning moon Shyron could see a dark flood moving towards the river. 'Eumeus. Come here. What is it?'

As Eumeus approached the two boys standing at edge of the dock, the dark flood reached the river bank and revealed itself. It was men. An army of men. One by one they slipped down the wall into the river bed, replacing the lost water with a flood of warriors.

'What's going on?' Shyron's voice was a whisper.

'They're attacking the city. The bronze doors will be no defence against such an army. Look at them! Still they come.'

'They think the city is given over to revelry,' said Zaagor quietly. 'But the men in the streets are armed. There will be more of a fight than these soldiers are expecting. And men fight hard to save their own.'

Shyron turned his head. 'So what do we do?' From long habit, his question was directed towards Eumeus.

'We leave. Before the fighting starts. The mud looks thick but we can cross. The moat is paved with stones. We'll get dirty, but no more.' He pointed. 'There's a ladder over there that leads down from the dock. It's rough but it'll do. Think you can manage it?'

Eumeus didn't wait for the nods. He strode back to where the others were huddled just inside the doorway of the hut. 'Come on. We're leaving.'

'But what about Xander. And Lex?' Lily looked pale with shock and exhaustion.

'They can look after themselves. With a bit of luck it'll be over by morning and we can come back.'

Eumeus crossed his fingers behind his back, a defence against the necessary lie. It was Lily's safely he cared about, and Lily in hysterics would not help his cause. He had enough to think about with Roza. And Quin. He had no idea how long the big man would remain on his feet. But not long. Nobody could, with a wound like that.

Once across the moat they found themselves in a fallow field, the soil hardened into ridges by the frost. Eumeus found a path along the top of an earth embankment that ran between the fields. Here the irrigation channels were as dry as the moat. Stranded fish flip-flopped in the mud. Ducks sat in silent rows along the edge of the embankment with their heads tucked under their wings. Ahead, a willow tree arched naked branches across the ditch. Under the tree a deeper shadow. A hut with woven wicker walls and a straw roof, abandoned and dilapidated, the frost lying white and pristine on rotten thatch. Shivering with cold and with stinking mud to their knees, they crawled through the doorway into a dark, animal-smelling space. The smell of straw and dung reminded Lily of the old farmhouse in Achaea and offered her a strange sort of comfort as she fell into an uneasy sleep.

20

Dawn. The city lies silent under oppressive, snow-laden clouds. A bitter wind swirls through the broken bronze gate at the end of the street, stirring dead leaves. Xander pulls his cloak around him and moves cautiously along the wall of his warehouse. At the corner of the street he steps around a tangle of bodies. Raiders in bronze helmets carrying round bull-hide shields. Citizens with leather jerkins hidden beneath their ceremonial dress, swords grasped in their hands. There is the sharp smell of blood in the air.

An old crone is huddled over a body prising a gold tooth from its mouth with a blunt knife. She looks up as Xander passes. 'I'm not doing no harm, master,' she whines then, seeing Xander has no intention of harming her, she parts her bloodless lips in a smile and opens her hand to reveal her booty: tiny nuggets of white and gold smeared with blood and slime.

The gate is unlocked but the yard is deserted. The warehouse greets Xander like an old friend. Scents of grain and oil and spices. Grey light from a high window lancing the dust-laden air. In one corner Tashi is crouched on a pile of grain sacks, tail twitching.

Xander's eyes scan the empty warehouse. 'Lily? Lily? Eumeus, are you here?' The sound of his voice fades into the stillness.

Hearing a familiar voice, the cat condescends to come down from her perch on the grain sacks. She winds herself around Xander's legs, demanding food. Xander bends down and scratches her head.

'Where are they, Tashi, eh?'

There is a lamp on the floor at Xander's feet, the flame a tiny bead of yellow light in the gloom. Scuffle marks in the dust. Blood. Xander bends down and touches the brown stain. He lifts his fingers to his nose and sniffs. Fresh. His head whips round, scanning the empty space. He crouches on his haunches. Torn cloth, blood stained. Not dead, then. Whoever it was that had bled on the floor last night. And someone was there to tend the wound. He reaches out for the stained rags and knocks over a wine jar which rolls elliptically across the floor, spilling meagre drops onto the scuffled dust.

Xander picks up the jar. Eumeus, then. He smiles. Eumeus is fond of wine, good wine especially, and would have lost no time justifying to himself the opening of this jar of finest Sumerian vintage which, in better times, would have graced the dining salon of some wealthy lord. Xander grabs a handful of the bloody clouts and sniffs the vinegar odour of stale wine. 'Inside and out, that's the way.' He can hear the sound of Eumeus' voice inside his head.

The scuff marks on the dusty floor lead Xander to Eumeus' office in the far corner of the warehouse. Inside, the clerk's desk is pushed aside, its load of scrolls lying where they have fallen on the floor. Some have unrolled themselves, revealing columns of neat script. Xander bends to pick one up, then drops it back on the floor. Worry about it later. The trap door is closed but the cracks are clear of dust, a sure sign it has been opened recently.

On the dock the freezing wind whips Xander's face. Thick grey clouds are massed on the horizon. Beneath his feet a flood of brown water plucks at the wooden pylons holding up the dock. He can feel the vibration under his feet. The boat that brought Lex to Babylon has been torn from its mooring. Thick hemp rope dangles into the rolling water. Xander scans downstream and finds the boat caught in a tangle of willow trees, its mast lurching as the flood works to dislodge it. Xander wraps his arms across his chest against the bitter wind and retreats to the small hut at the back of the dock.

They have escaped then, he thinks. Across the moat when the water was low. Lily, Shyron and Eumeus. Those three at least. Beyond the grimy shutters covering the small window Xander sees a single flake of snow spiral slowly from the grey sky. It lays itself gently on the worn timber dock, a tiny speck of white, and is gone. Xander's thoughts begin to move quickly. Lily, Shyron and Eumeus. Maybe Quin and that slave – Zaagor – with Roza, if they managed to find her in time. Someone injured, don't know who, or how badly. A storm coming. They will have no shelter. Nothing warm to wear. An image opens in his mind. Lily in a thin silken gown, a cloak thrown hastily across her shoulders, her eyes wide with fear. I must find them and bring them back into the city.

But there is another image, this one told with Eumeus' voice: Lex in the market place with Alkmon's arm draped across his shoulders just hours before the raid. Alkmon the traitor, his insurrection crushed, his fellow conspirators rounded up, his life forfeit to anyone who finds him alive. And Xander knows with a certainty that clutches his heart that Babylon is no place for any of them any more. Himself included.

Back on the street, cloak muffling his face, Xander hurries uphill towards the main road that bisects the city and leads to the big bronze gates where the toll booths are, and the customs sheds. A motley tide of humanity fills the street, moving slowly towards the gates. Poor citizens with bundles on their backs and small children hand fast at their sides. Ox-drawn wagons laden with household goods with matrons and daughters riding atop, faces covered with silk wraps. Over the heads of the crowd, Xander sees soldiers moving among those waiting patiently at the gates. Wagons are unpacked, bundles examined, faces exposed. Occasionally someone is pulled roughly from the crowd and forced through the doorway of the customs shed where two of the palace guard, gigantic men with ebony skin, stand bare-chested in the bitter wind. He'd have to find another way. No good standing in line to be picked off when he reaches the bronze gates. But home first. Something to eat and pack some clothes. Then think what to do.

Xander walks swiftly through the familiar lanes and alleyways towards the merchant quarter. The snow is thicker now, whirling from the heavy clouds and laying a freezing mantle on the roofs and spires of the upper town. There are few people around, a combination of snow and soldiery keeping prudent folk indoors. Xander's breath steams in front of his face. I'll go back to the warehouse, he decides. At least I can get outside the city. Hide out on the dock until things calm down. Maybe float out on the flood, like I did from Carchemish all those years ago. They'll take my property, I know that. It doesn't matter. We can start again somewhere else. Xander's hand reaches down to where his sword should be. I just have to find Lily. That's all that matters now.

The palace is deserted. From the shelter of the gateway, Xander watches the snow drifting silently across the tiles of the courtyard. Water lilies lie clamped in ice in the little raised pool where a duck stands on pink webbed feet, feathers fluffed against the cold. Xander raises his eyes to the fretted windows surrounding the courtyard. No movement. Again his hand clutches his thigh, seeking the familiar reassurance of his sword. He grits his teeth and steps forward out of the darkness. He feels the sudden prickle of the skin on the back of his neck. It is all the warning he has. The heavy blow fells him breathless onto the cold tiles. Another blow and he is plunged into oblivion.

With grey dawn came the sound of water. Leaving the hut to relieve herself, Lily saw that the irrigation channel was filling up. A group of white storks, feasting noisily on dead fish, flew up when they saw her. She shielded her eyes against the morning glare and watched the heavy birds winging away towards the hills. In front of her the great stone city of Babylon lay quiet behind its walls. A twist of grey smoke rose into the pale sky. Nothing moved.

But there was something moving on the dirt road coming from the city. Dust to start with, like a summer whirlwind. In the middle of the swirling dust Lily could see a man on horseback leading a heavy wagon pulled by two slow oxen. Another horse trailed behind the wagon. Lily hitched up her muddy skirts and scrambled across the channel, now half full with swirling brown water. She stood by the side of the road and waited for the man to draw near. Living so long in the city, a sheltered, pampered life, she had forgotten to fear a man on horseback and wanted only to ask for news from the city. She reached up her hand and picked dry straw from her hair.

The man was dressed in leggings, fur boots and a thick tunic. A wolf skin cloak was fastened around his neck with a plain metal fibula. He looked like one of the northern tribesman that Lily sometimes saw in the market place with their animal skins and their smoked fish and, sometimes, lumps of raw amber that reminded her of her own piece of amber hidden near the pigsty back home on the farm. She remembered when Xander gave her the amber. How he'd said it was the colour of her hair. But not any more. Now there were grey threads among the russet curls. Lily shivered and pulled her cloak tighter around her.

But this man was no tribesman. He had a long, pale face. Hooded eyes. A thin, mobile mouth. His fine black horse was dancing under him, unused to the slow pace of the oxen. The wooden wheels of the wagon ground to a halt. The dust drifted in the air, settling on the frost bitten grass on either side of the road. The man dismounted and bowed to Lily, a curiously courteous gesture in the circumstances. He spoke with a lisp so Lily knew who he was before he said his name.

'I am the Lord Alkmon. At your service, my lady.'

Lily watched his eyes appraise her and felt a frisson of excitement because he found her attractive. Neither of them noticed Eumeus leave the hut and step across the channel until he appeared at Lily's side. Alkmon recognised the small, quiet man and knew instantly who the woman was with the tumble of red-blond hair and the manner of a queen, even though the hem of her gown was mired with mud.

'My lord Alkmon.' Eumeus bowed his head, then moved closer to Lily. 'We seek news of my lady's husband. Have you come from the city? Is it yet safe to return?'

Alkmon indicated the wagon behind him. 'As you can see, I am leaving the city. There are better places to be than Babylon just now.'

'So, what's the news?'

'This is your slave, madam?' Alkmon did not like the insolence in the old man's eyes, nor his familiarity towards Lily. He wanted to see him brought down to size.

Lily tipped up her chin. 'He is my freedman, Lord Alkmon.'

Alkmon raised one eyebrow. 'He was my slave once.'

'He is nobody's slave now.' There was a challenge in her dark eyes.

Alkmon bowed his head. He was beginning to enjoy himself. A beautiful woman in trouble. On the wrong side of the city walls. Husband within. Never mind the slave. There were plenty of ways of getting rid of one old man. And he must die anyway because of what he knew. Especially now that things had gone so horribly wrong.

'My lord, can you tell us what's going on in the city.' Lily's voice roused Alkmon from his thoughts.

'Madam, Babylon is sealed up as tight as a drum. Nobody is getting in or out.'

It was a blatant falsehood, but Alkmon had no trouble with that if it got him what he wanted.

'So what happened? Last night?'

'There was an attempt to liberate the city. It failed.' For a brief moment Alkmon wondered if it had been Eumeus who had betrayed his plans. 'Now there is an army camped on its doorstep.'

'A siege?'

Alkmon shrugged. 'Call it that, if you wish. Though Babylon can live on its fat for as long as it chooses. As it has done many times before.' He stepped forward and cupped Lily's chin in a gentle hand. 'So don't be concerned for your husband, my lady. He'll be snug at home like all the other good citizens. It's you we need to think about out here without shelter. There's bad weather coming.'

Lily turned her eyes towards the eastern horizon. Half the sky was covered with thick grey clouds. There was a brooding stillness in the air. Lily noticed suddenly that the temperature had lifted.

'Snow,' she said.

'Not just snow. That's a big storm. And it'll be here before nightfall.'

Lily turned to Eumeus. 'What are we going to do?'

Alkmon bowed his head. 'I can offer you shelter, my lady.'

'Lily, no!' Eumeus put his hand on Lily's arm.

'But, Eumeus, what else can we do? We have to think of Quin. And Roza.'

'There are more of you?' Alkmon's expression was almost comical.

Lily stared up at Alkmon. 'My brother is injured. My daughter is ...' Lily couldn't say what was wrong with Roza.

Alkmon thought swiftly. A man and a child. A nuisance, sure. But it gave him a chance to show Lily his generosity.

He nodded. 'Fetch them. Old man, you.'

Eumeus crossed the channel, now churning with a brown flood, and ducked into the hut. He emerged several moments later with Roza, wrapped tightly in a blood-stained cloak and held by a lithe, dark-skinned youth. Behind her came a giant of a man with one eye bandaged with fine linen, followed by a half-grown boy with frightened eyes.

It was all Alkmon's worst nightmares rolled into one. With Lily's husband in Babylon he could risk befriending her – and befriending her was something he wanted to do very much. But now here by some ghastly mischance was the very girl who'd taken part in the mock rites at that fool Nuttuk's house not two nights ago. The girl he'd drugged and forced to play the part of Tiamut to his Marduk. She was still dressed in the costume he'd made her wear. A costume that was stained brown with dried blood. He didn't like to think whose blood it was. A second glance revealed her wavering, unfocussed eyes. Maybe not such a danger after all.

He examined the two boys. The younger one seemed harmless enough. Lily's son at a guess. City bred. No good for anything except flicking the beads of an abacus. But the other one ... The dark skin on his arms was tattooed with intricate swirls. He was not yet fully grown. But he was strong. Under the tattoos the muscles in his arms moved like silk. There was no doubt he would know how to handle himself. And he had a knife in his hand.

Alkmon was outnumbered. His instinct was to attack the greatest threat.

'Hey, hill man,' he called to Zaagor in the Scythian language, for the young man's tattoos identified him as a member of that tribe. 'Let's see if you can ride.'

Zaagor grinned. He dropped Roza's arm and stepped forward. But the sound of Alkmon's voice made the girl scream and roll her eyes. She fell to the ground, clawing at her face.

'Roza!' Lily bent over her. But Roza lashed out at her mother with bloody hands. Lily stepped back, a hand print livid on her cheek.

Zaagor lifted Roza to her feet, speaking quickly to her in an undertone. He wrapped her cloak around her body and held her tight until she stopped screaming and thrashing, and stood quiet. Then, 'Shyron, you take her.'

Relieved of his burden, the young slave vaulted athletically onto the back of Alkmon's black stallion. The horse tossed his head but made no objection to its new rider. Zaagor gripped the horse's body between his knees, grasped the leather reins, and kicked the horse's flank lightly with his bare foot. The horse took off at a gallop along the hard dirt road. Just as Alkmon was beginning to wonder if the young Scythian tribesman had run off with his best stallion – and Scythians were well known for their horse thievery, as he belatedly remembered – Zaagor wheeled the horse around in a flurry of dust and galloped back to the odd collection of people waiting by the side of the road. He brought the beast to a trampling halt, jumped from its back while it was yet stamping and pawing the ground and handed the reins back to Alkmon.

'Nice. Very nice. My lord,' he added very much as an afterthought. Zaagor knew a great deal about Alkmon and was not disposed to offer him any sign of respect.

But Alkmon ignored the slave's insolence, or didn't hear it. He lifted his head and stared at the eastern sky from whence the clouds were approaching rapidly. A freezing damp wind was blowing steadily, bringing with it the smell of snow. He turned back to the little group and pretended to think, though his plan had been forming in his mind ever since he first saw the knife in Zaagor's hand. Finally he turned to Lily.

'Lady, the storm approaches rapidly. It is my wish to have you and the young lady in shelter before nightfall. Will you allow me to offer you and ...?'

'... my daughter, Roza.'

Alkmon bowed his head. '... you and Roza the hospitality of my keep? Your slave can act as your escort and care for your daughter. He seems to be able to handle her.'

Zaagor was once again holding Roza, her terrified whimpers muffled by his chest.

Then Alkmon turned to Shyron. 'You, sir, I put in charge of my wagon and the injured man. It will take you two, maybe three days. Take the road north past the marsh. My keep is in the hills beyond, near a lake.'

Eumeus he ignored. In his mind the old slave was already dead.

Shyron nodded eagerly. 'Yes, lord.'

So easily did Alkmon gained Shyron's devotion. Shyron was completely unaware that his life or death was a matter of supreme indifference to Alkmon, with his inclination rather towards the latter. All that mattered was that Alkmon had given him his first command.

'And take care. There are things in that wagon I'd rather not lose.'

'Yes, Lord Alkmon.'

Alkmon nodded his head, then mounted his horse. He reached down for Lily and settled her in front of him. He turned to see that Zaagor had Roza on the second horse, the chestnut which had been tethered to the back of the ox wagon. He dug his heels into his horse's flank and sped off up the road.

Thus did Alkmon divide his foes and capture Lily. With the freezing fitful wind at his back and the hard road under his horse's hoofs, he offered a prayer of thanks to Adad, the god of storms, who had come to his aid at a time of great need.

21

The wild storm was howling at their heels as Alkmon and Zaagor rode their exhausted horses under the rough stone arch of the keep into a paved yard with a thatched stable and a stinking midden, barely visible in the dwindling light. Rough steps led up to the keep's living area, a circular room with animal pelts spread-eagled against the stone wall, damp rushes on the floor and a cold, ash-strewn hearth. At the narrow windows wooden shutters rattled in the rising wind.

Alkmon carried the almost senseless Lily to a wooden settle by the fire. He pushed aside stained silk cushions to lay her down, then covered her with the wolf skin cloak which had warmed them both on the journey north. Zaagor followed with Roza in his arms. There was no other furniture in the room except for a table pushed against a far wall so Zaagor laid his burden on the stained rushes then followed Alkmon from the room. A blazing fire and a stew of dried beans and salt meat, washed down with an evil wine diluted with snow melt, was the best the uninhabited keep had to offer. But it was enough to bring sleep as the blizzard took possession of the night.

Zaagor's resolve to hunt the following morning was defeated by the weather. A late dawn revealed whirling snowflakes and drifts against the keep's wall that were already the height of a man. An exploration of the kitchen area downstairs revealed a jar of wine, nearly full, a sack of the vile beans and an ancient unidentified carcass from which last night's meat had been stripped. However, one of the stables held a number of scrawny chickens and a goat that stared at Zaagor with mournful eyes.

When Zaagor returned with the chickens hanging from one hand, he saw that Alkmon had made an effort to make the living space more habitable. Embroidered hangings had joined the pelts on the wall, sacks of straw created make-shift beds and a wood pile by the hearth promised warmth, at least for the front of those that gathered around it, their backs being at the mercy of the freezing air that filled the rest of the chamber.

It was not pleasant but they survived. For three days Alkmon and Zaagor laboured to keep the fire burning and bring in enough snow to keep them supplied with water, mainly to dilute the filthy wine that got progressively worse the further down the jar they went. The horses were brought into a space under the keep and kept alive with straw pulled from the stable's thatched roof. Just melting enough water for the horses was work enough for both men. Any thoughts Alkmon had of seducing Lily were lost in the struggle to stay alive. On the fourth day the wind died down. Snow flakes fell softly from thick grey clouds. The temperature rose slightly then plummeted as the short day gave way to night. At midnight, stars showed like stab wounds in a pitch black sky.

The first flaw in Alkmon's plan was that Zaagor refused to steal a horse and make his escape. The morning following the storm he went out early, returning with a deer, its hide flecked with white marks. The second day it was two fat ptarmigan in their white winter plumage. On the third day, with the snow melting rapidly into brown slush, Alkmon's servants drifted in, a motley collection of old women and wizened men carrying a miscellany of ancient weapons. For Alkmon, the sacks of grain, goats' cheese and rough barley beer they brought with them were more than welcome. Less welcome were the long-winded conversations they had with Zaagor discovering family connections that went back for several generations and established him as the acknowledged kin of every one of them. By nightfall they were all comfortably drunk before a roaring fire in the downstairs kitchen and Alkmon, finding himself outnumbered yet again, chose to leave well alone. But the young slave was beginning to be a problem.

The next morning Zaagor took one of the horses and rode south. He returned as the fading sun was splashing yellow light across the pale, cold sky. With him were the ox cart and the rest of Lily's family: Shyron leading the oxen, Quin walking strongly, his eye still swathed in its filthy bandage, Eumeus sitting on the tail gate of the wagon, his face grey with exhaustion.

Though much enhanced by the lavish contents of Alkmon's wagon and the sacrifice of the melancholy goat, dinner that night was not a happy affair. Upon Eumeus' entry into the keep's living area, Roza had rushed towards him and, for the first time since her arrival, spoken aloud to beseech the old slave to take her home. When Eumeus said he could not, Roza had retreated to the wall furthest from the fire where she squatted down, wrapped her arms around her knees and rocked back and forth, moaning piteously.

So much did this behaviour enrage Alkmon, even though he was the cause of it, that he ordered his servants to prepare a room for her on the floor above to which she was removed as soon as the old starlings' nests had been poked out of the chimney and the fire lit. Her moans then became howls which accompanied every mouthful eaten by Alkmon, Lily, Quin and Shyron sitting before silver plate and fine wine in the malodorous room below.

Quin, too, was unhappy. He was unused to fine dining and was distressed to be served goats meat because it reminded him of his beloved animals left behind in Achaea. Tears flowed unheeded down his cheeks while he ate, wetting the new bandage which Eumeus had applied to his ruined eye. Alkmon gritted his teeth and wished them all a thousand cubits away. His patience was at an end and not even Lily's charms could restore his good humour. Surrounded by so many members of her household her virtue seemed unassailable.

Eumeus and Zaagor ate their meal downstairs in the kitchen where Eumeus decided they better belonged. Besides, nothing would induce the old man to share a meal with Lord Alkmon. Zaagor served dinner upstairs then gleefully reported the gloom with which it was being consumed to Eumeus who sat by the roaring kitchen fire with his feet up and a beaker of Alkmon's finest vintage in his hand. His self-imposed ban on enjoying Alkmon's hospitality did not extend to his wine of which Eumeus was only too happy to deprive him.

It was late when Eumeus went upstairs to make sure Lily had all she needed, an unconscious habit that had started in the house on Thera. The snow was falling again, softly this time, cocooning the tower in stillness. Quin and Shyron were asleep on the straw mattresses, wrapped in their cloaks. The fire was a dull red glow. Lily sat on the floor in front of the hearth with a blanket around her shoulders.

'Everything all right, mistress?'

Lily looked up, smiled and hugged her knees like a girl.

'How about you, old friend?'

'A good meal and a beaker of Lord Alkmon's Sumerian vintage will restore any man.'

'It's good to have you here, Eumeus. The snow was so heavy I wondered if you'd make it.'

'It wasn't so bad down by the river. And the wind kept the road clear enough for the oxen.' Eumeus sat on the settle and leaned forward, his hands between his knees. 'You know, Lily, I think I've solved the problem of the disappearing river.'

'But the drought …'

'Not just the drought. The water dropped too quickly.'

'So what was it?' Lily turned her face towards the old man.

'There's a big marsh north of the city. You might know of it?'

Lily nodded. 'It's where the men went hunting for duck.'

'Well, someone has been digging there. A vast number of men, by the look of it. They dug a channel and diverted the river into the marsh.'

'But the water was back the next morning.'

'Yes, it was coming back. Once the marsh was flooded, the water started to return to its normal course. Except now it's frozen solid. The whole marsh is one great sheet of ice.' Eumeus glanced down at Lily. 'It is to be hoped there is enough water in the river to serve the people in Babylon.'

'What do you think is happening in Babylon, Eumeus?'

'I don't know, Lily. There are as many factions in Babylon as there are snow flakes falling from the sky. There'll be new alliances by now.'

'Yes, but what about Xander. And Lex?'

'I don't know,' Eumeus said again. He reached out and took Lily's hand. 'There's no good fretting over something we can't fix. We're here now and we're safe. And here we'll stay until the weather clears.'

While the weather alternated between snow fall and freezing, life in the tower settled into some sort of routine. Roza remained in her room, whether by choice or compulsion

Lily didn't enquire, and was tended by Quin who carried food up and soil down with the same tender intensity he would have shown towards a sick kid back in his goat herding days. His wound healed to a mess of puckered purple scars in the socket where his eye had once been. That Roza had caused such disfigurement he seemed to have either forgotten, or didn't care. That he was living in a snow bound stone tower instead of a palace in Babylon excited no interest. He stumbled up and down the freezing stone stairway between the kitchen and Roza's upstairs chamber, grinned stupidly when he encountered Alkmon, whom he somewhat feared, and was otherwise as he had always been.

Eumeus took charge of what he thought of as Lily's household. With his own brand of quiet authority he had Alkmon's rough servants take away the soiled rushes from the living area floor and lay fine patterned rugs in their place. The table was scoured clean, then rubbed with oil. A search of store rooms and outhouses unearthed lamps, chairs and tables, all filthy, which were scrubbed and sent upstairs to create a suitable living space for Eumeus' beloved mistress. The whole process drove Alkmon quietly mad but there were too many secrets behind the old slave's dark, unblinking gaze for him to risk a confrontation. So Alkmon took himself and those of his possessions that were left to him upstairs to a chamber at the top of the keep where much of the floor space was taken up with a vast bed piled with furs and windows on four sides allowed him to observe any movement in the surrounding countryside.

Zaagor continued to hunt when the weather allowed, riding out on the chestnut mare that he had taken for his own and returning with deer, or birds, or a brace of hares and, one time, a huge grey fish with sharp teeth that he said the goddess of the nearby lake had given him as a gift. Sometimes he stayed out overnight, always returning in the late afternoon of the following day. One afternoon, he came back accompanied by a band of young men from his own tribe who rode bareback on short-legged, curly-coated ponies. They crowded into the kitchen and had a noisy party that lasted into the early hours of the morning. When they rode off the following morning, they left one of the ponies behind and from then on Shyron rode out with Zaagor, returning to the keep high-coloured and exhilarated as the pale winter sun dipped behind the hills.

In his thirteenth year, Shyron was already taller than Alkmon and had the promise of strength in his broad shoulders. Born in a brothel and raised in a merchant's house in Tyre and Babylon, he knew more than any young man should about warehouses and women's business. For him, the high plains beyond Alkmon's keep were a place of delight and freedom such as he had never known before. Scythians are great archers and Zaagor taught Shyron the bow craft he himself had learned as a toddler, and shook his head in wonder at the clumsiness of the city boy. He taught him, too, his tribe's customs relating to the kill, and what was owing friend to friend and between kin. Through Zaagor's eyes Shyron began to see Babylon as a vast stinking heap of vice and corruption, and he was ashamed.

Alkmon stood in his tower room watching the two boys gallop away across the bare uplands and thought about Lily. She was alone now, isolated in the pretty room her freedman had created for her, in need of conversation and eager for company. And Alkmon was the best company any woman could wish for, when he was in the mood. Now was the time to make his move.

With the sun conducting its daily love affair with the western hills, darkness came early to Lily's window. She was standing there this evening gazing east towards Babylon as the room behind her sank into gloom. When someone entered the room carrying a lamp she turned, expecting it to be Eumeus. But it was Alkmon. She felt her stomach twist painfully the way it always did when she saw this man. Despite being confined together in the restricted space of the stone tower, Lily had seen little of her host. He respected her right to the women's room Eumeus had created, allowed the old slave to take care of her daily needs and imposed his company on her only at the evening meal because it was fitting that they should eat together, separate from the servants.

Since their arrival at the keep, Alkmon had been wearing tribal costume, for warmth, and every evening she had watched him come into her living space dragging his great wolf skin cloak behind him, bringing with him the smell of frost and horses.

He would toss his cloak onto the wooden settle by the fire and sprawl on top of it with the kind of sinewy grace that reminded Lily of a cat. He had the wildness, too, that even a pampered Babylonian house cat possessed somewhere inside its sleek fur coat, the wildness that would make it stretch out its claws in its make-believe sleep, ready to swipe the nose of a passing dog.

But Alkmon kept his wildness well hidden beneath the smooth, city-mannered demeanour he displayed in all his dealings with her. Lily had seen Alkmon from her window as he galloped his black stallion across the wind-swept plain, heard him in the stable yard making ribald jokes with his men in their own rough tongue, watched him stride into her room with snow flakes clinging to his hair, then down would come the sheen of politeness and the wildness would disappear beneath his pussy-cat exterior. It was driving her mad. With desire. Yes, it was desire. She acknowledged that. Acknowledged, too, the pleasure she'd taken from the look he gave her when they first met on the road outside Babylon, the look that told her he found her attractive. And, no, she didn't want to sleep with him. Not really. She was loyal to Xander and that would be betrayal.

She thought about the years they'd lived together in Babylon. A comfortable existence. Xander's familiar body a little soft, now from easy living. Making love on warm nights under the ceiling painted with stars, with the noise of the city coming through the fretwork window. And her mind, as often as not, on something else. The number of guests at her next dinner party. Some embroidery thread she needed from the market. Now here she was in this bleak stone tower with her husband and son lost in a besieged city and all her mind could do was ponder the lean, lithe body of the Lord Alkmon, who was her captor or her protector, she wasn't quite sure which, and long for his touch.

Alkmon put the lamp on the table and came over to the window.

'Come and sit by the fire, lady. I'm going to close the shutters.'

Lily did as she was bid and watched him close and bar the wooden shutters over the window, shutting out the fading light. The wind began whistling through the gaps in the ill-fitting boards creating a feeling of warmth and sanctuary in the lamp-lit room. Alkmon bent down and threw a log onto the fire, then draped himself gracefully on the uncomfortable wooden settle. After a while Eumeus came in to set the table for dinner. He glanced across the room at the two by the fire but said nothing. Lily sensed his hostility but thought nothing of it. Eumeus made no secret of his hatred of all Babylonians. She thought it had something to do with the slave mark behind his ear.

Lily and Alkmon sat opposite each other at the table. The wind at the window had been replaced by the hush of snow. The fire flared ruddy in the hearth. Alkmon poured wine the colour of pale sunshine and raised his fine silver goblet. His dark eyes caressed her face.

'To you, my lady. Health and happiness always.'

Halfway through the meal Alkmon started talking about Tyre. Giddy with warmth and wine – she seemed to have drunk more usual – Lily found herself telling him what she knew about the siege, a subject she normally shunned because it caused Xander pain. It didn't occur to her to wonder how Alkmon had acquired his knowledge about an event that, so far as she knew, lived in one mind only. She reached into the bodice of her gown and showed Alkmon the gold disc hanging on a chain between her breasts.

'Xander is a follower of the hero-god Heracles,' she explained. 'This is a piece of the gold his god gave him when he escaped from Tyre. It allowed him to pay for his passage across the sea to my house on Thera. He arrived the night Shyron was born.'

Lily remembered that freezing night so long ago. Xander bursting into her bedroom like a black ghost as his child tore her body apart trying to be born. The blast of cold air from the window as the dark slave Afrikka made her escape, her hands dripping with jewels. Lex's knife between her shoulder blades and the bloom of blood on her silk gown, like a great, red flower.

Alkmon leaned forward and refilled Lily's cup. 'It was generous of you to let him name your son after his wife. Didn't you mind?'

His wife?

Lily didn't speak but Alkmon read the look in her eyes and allowed himself a smirk of triumph. He thought about the slave girl he'd bought in Lagash, a pretty little thing halfway to going mad from the treatment she'd received from the sea-wolves who'd taken her from the citadel at Tyre with the rest of the women, once the men were dead.

The slave's time with Alkmon had not been long; she'd died playing one of Alkmon's after-supper games, as so many of them seemed to do, but not before she'd told him everything she knew about the siege, including Xander's marriage to Cyrus' daughter, Shyrah, and the rumour of his connection with Carchemish.

Alkmon had used the information the slave girl gave him to persuade Lex to act as his messenger when he was making his plans for the invasion of Babylon, and now he was using it again. It's not often you get such value from cheap slave trash bought off the docks, he thought. He buried his pleasure in his wine cup and quirked one eyebrow at Lily over the rim.

'Did he never tell you about her? Xander's wife was the daughter of the timber merchant who employed him as ship's master before the siege. How do you think he gained that timber concession when Tyre was being rebuilt? It was his business, Lily. He inherited it. From his father in law.'

'But nobody owned anything in Tyre after the siege. Xander told me so himself. Not even the land. The city was rebuilt in a different place.'

'On the island, yes, I know. But there was more to the business than just the land. There were the cedar forests up north at Ugarit. Transport. Warehousing. It all belonged to someone.' Alkmon was improvising, guided by the look in Lily's eyes. 'Xander took what was his. His by right. And it was accepted by others that he had the right. Why was that, do you suppose? And him no more than a common sailor. That's all he was to *them*, for all his noble connections.'

'And her name? Xander's wife. What was her name?'

'Shyrah. Her name was Shyrah.'

Lily felt a pain in her heart like the twisting of a knife. She thought about the months after Shyron's birth. There had been something about Xander, a barrier of grief and pain that she had been unable to cross. And ever afterwards in all their years together there had been a part of him that had remained remote and unreachable. Now she knew why.

In the depths of the winter night with the snow turned to sleet that hissed on the dying coals of the fire, Lily woke up under the heavy wolf skin that covered Alkmon's bed. She lay on her back aware of his long, lean body touching hers and remembered the feel of his warm hands on her skin. At first, it had been a rough, urgent coupling, a tangle of frozen limbs as need called to need in the icy bed. Then, as the hastily rekindled fire warmed the air in the room and a semi-sated desire made their bodies damp with heat, they had lain naked in the golden lamplight, drinking wine from a single cup and exploring all that had been hidden in the weeks since their first meeting. She had arched her body to take him deep inside her and voiced her mounting pleasure into the howl of the wind, then raked her nails down the smooth skin of Alkmon's back as his voice mingled with hers. Now she turned her body into the curve of her lover's back. She touched the long scar that seamed his ribs, then slid her hand down his belly, to see if he was awake. And he was.

When Eumeus entered Lily's living room the following morning and found she was not there, he didn't need the single silver goblet upturned on the hearth to tell him where she was. He'd seen it coming. His beloved Lily was the mistress of that monster, the architect of the invasion which had separated Lily from Xander and brought her here to this desolate place.

Eumeus knew what everyone else in Babylon knew about Alkmon: that he had been exiled for ten years for taking part in false rites, that he had a reputation for using pretty slave girls at a rate that was beyond what was acceptable even in that most corrupt of cities and that his name had been linked with a group of noblemen who enjoyed bizarre and illegal pastimes, though nobody could describe exactly what they did. A group that included Mutakkil-Nusku, the man in whose palace Roza had been found. And that he would turn traitor for a price, or for revenge, or for amusement, for all of which he had an insatiable appetite.

That Alkmon had been intending to seduce Lily had been obvious right from the start. Eumeus had watched him isolate her from her family. From Shyron. From Quin. Even from himself. But Eumeus believed Lily was safe from Alkmon's wiles. She was, after all, devoted to Xander. What had Alkmon done to change her mind? Eumeus laid down the bundle of logs in his arms. Then he kicked the silver goblet with all his strength and watched it skitter across the stone floor. Damn him, *damn* him.

22

A month later Alkmon found Lily near the little stream that ran through a sloping meadow close to the walls of the keep. The stream was frozen now in the depths of the winter and Lily was on her knees digging in the snow with her bare hands.

'What are you doing out here? Come inside before you freeze.'

Lily turned her face up to his, her eyes welling with tears.

'My daughter Roza is with child. I need the herbs that will bring a termination.'

'With child? How do you know?'

Lily dropped her gaze. 'The usual way, my lord.'

'And who ... who is the father?'

'She says it is the lord of heaven.'

It was only when Lily's monthly courses began for the second time since her arrival in the tower that she thought to enquire about her daughter. Quin could make nothing of her questions, and Eumeus responded with an embarrassed shrug, so Lily had gone to see Roza for herself. What she found was a credit to Quin's care. Roza's room was cold, sparsely furnished but clean, as was the girl herself. She lay in a narrow bed with her face turned towards the wall. She didn't seem deranged as she had on the journey north when her hair was wild and her face torn with her own nails. More than anything else, to Lily's eyes, she appeared frail and infinitely sad. She turned her head and stared up at her mother with blank, hard eyes as if she was lying in wait for something to happen, something that nobody was going to like.

Lily crossed the room to Roza's bed and looked down at her daughter. For a moment she was reluctant to speak. Then, 'Roza ... I've come to ask you ... Do you think you might be pregnant?'

Roza nodded her head, her eyes not moving from her mother's face.

Lily sat down heavily on the bed. 'Who is the father?' she asked gently. 'Do you know?'

'It is the lord of heaven.'

'The lord of heaven?' Lily could do no more than repeat her daughter's words.

'First he loved me. Then he was going to kill me. But Quin came and rescued me. And the boy slave, I forget his name. I hurt Quin. I didn't mean to do it.' Tears welled in Roza's eyes. 'But I killed Shutruk, Mama. I had a knife and I killed him.'

'Shutruk?'

'He was the slave who made me dance for the gods.'

Lily remembered Roza on their last night in Babylon. Remembered her white gown drenched in blood. She shuddered at what her daughter had been forced to do.

'Do you want to keep the baby?'

Roza struggled to sit up. 'Help me get rid of it, Mama. Help me!'

And so Lily had gone out to the stream to gather the herbs she needed to kill her daughter's child. But she saw nothing familiar. So far from home she was unable to find what she needed even for so simple a task. Alkmon reached down his hand and pulled her to her feet. He held her in his arms.

'Don't worry. I'll get one of the women to deal with it. Come on, Lily. Come back inside.'

And Lily allowed him to lead her back into the tower.

A few days later Lily entered the bedroom she shared with Alkmon. He was sprawled on a chair in front of the fire, staring at the flames. Lily sank to the floor at his feet. She laid her arms on his knees and stared up into his face.

'Thank you, my lord.'

Alkmon lifted one eye brow. 'Thanks? For what, my lady?'

On her way upstairs Lily had called in to see her daughter. The room was vastly changed. Fur rugs covered the cold stone floor. Vivid embroidered tapestries hung on the walls. The wooden shutters had been repaired to keep out the wind. In a chair by the bed sat one of the kitchen women spinning lumpy yarn from a bundle of fleece. From the door Lily had been aware of the sour smell of her unwashed body.

'For taking care of my daughter.'

Alkmon lifted his lip in a smile. 'But I am only doing what I should have done before. A young girl in my care. Your daughter.' He reached down and cupped Lily's breasts in his hands. 'However, if you wish to display your gratitude, I would have no objection to that.'

A month later it was obvious that Roza was still with child. On so frail a frame the small mound of her belly was painfully obvious. Lily found her daughter's servant, whose name was Djana, in the kitchen preparing Roza's evening meal. There was a language barrier between them but Lily was given to understand that Roza's pregnancy had been too far advanced for the treatment to have any effect. Lily was not convinced. She reckoned Roza's pregnancy from the time of her kidnapping in Babylon barely three months ago. Procuring so early abortion was within the knowledge of any women who was familiar with herb craft, even a barbarian like Djana. So why had it failed? But Djana had nothing further to say and stumped off with the tray of food.

There is a fine line between protection and captivity, and Lily wondered which was Djana's role when she followed the kitchen woman upstairs into Roza's room. As always, Roza lay in bed perfectly still. But now her eyes were like those of a dumb beast that sees the sacrificial axe ready to fall. She stared at her mother with a look of such pleading that Lily forced Djana to leave the room, then closed the door behind her. She moved swiftly to the bed and took hold of her daughter's hands.

'You don't have to keep it, you know, Roza. The child was forced on you. And there is no father to claim it.'

Roza's eyes were unreadable. 'The father is here, Mama. He comes to see me in the night. He wants me to bear this child so he can have it for his own.'

Lily tightened her grip on Roza's hands. 'No, Roza, no. You're wrong. There is nobody here for you to fear.'

But Roza refused to be consoled. She turned her face to the wall and wept.

168

Much later that night Eumeus sat in front of the embers of the kitchen fire, twisting a cup of wine in his fingers. There were two pieces of information inside his head that were begging to be joined together, despite his reluctance to connect them. The first was a conversation he'd just had with Lily. It was the only time he'd commented on her liaison with the Lord Alkmon. He'd pleaded with her to take care, to avoid creating a child that would have to be explained to Xander when they met again, as they surely would, once the winter was over.

And Lily had said, 'There doesn't seem to be much possibility of that, Eumeus. The lord Alkmon has never fathered a child. He told me so himself. Isn't that sad? It's no wonder he is so kind to my children.'

Secondly, there was this strange business of Roza's pregnancy. Eumeus had been born and raised in Babylon and knew all the city's gods. The lord of heaven, or Bel, or Marduk, was a fearsome creature with four eyes and four ears set in a fiery visage. Strange, then, that Eumeus had found a golden mask with those exact features wrapped in a piece of cloth in Alkmon's ox wagon when he'd been rummaging for food during that terrible journey through the blizzard. Eumeus remembered Roza's screams when she heard Alkmon's voice that first morning outside Babylon, and her insistence to her mother that the lord of heaven was visiting her in her room.

So was Alkmon the father of Roza's child? It would explain why Alkmon was so careful of Roza's health, Eumeus thought. And why he had entrusted her care to one of his own people who made it difficult for Lily to spend time alone with her daughter. Either that, or Eumeus was allowing his dislike of the man to overcome his reason. Eumeus took a deep draught of his wine. Either way, Lily must never know.

It became Lily's habit to sit in her daughter's room during the short winter days. Ignoring the stolid presence of Djana in the corner of the room, Lily retold the ancient stories from Achaea that she hadn't thought about for years and sang the songs Roza had liked when she was a little girl. After a while she persuaded Roza to leave the bed and sit by the window in the thin winter sunlight. It seemed to Lily that they had gone back to the days on Thera when they used to sit together in that high, white room with the blue water sparkling beyond the windows. It surprised Lily how much Roza remembered of those days when she had been such a little child. She asked about the man who had been her father and Lily dredged up from her memory images of Fen who now seemed no more than a boy. Roza had the look of her father, she saw now, that pale northern colouring that had made her seem so exotic in Babylon. And so the weeks of Roza's pregnancy passed while, outside the window, winter softened slowly into spring.

In Roza's sixth month Lily began to be concerned about her daughter's health. Roza's pregnancy had shown very early and it had seemed for a while that she was carrying twins. She had grown greedy and lethargic, complained of heart burn and swollen feet and Lily could do nothing for her. Lily thought of her well-stocked medicine chest at home in Babylon and could have wept with frustration. Her knowledge of herb craft did not extend to this northern plateau and, besides, everything was still buried beneath a thick blanket of snow. But now, six months into her pregnancy, Roza's whole body was bloated, her face white and puffy, her legs and feet so full of fluid that Lily's finger pressed into the flesh left a dent that was slow to disappear. Lily went to the kitchen to find Djana. By now they could converse in a strange mixture of words taught to them by necessity.

'I need someone to look at Roza, Djana. Do you know if there is a midwife hereabouts?'

It was a vain hope. But Djana turned from her slow stirring and stared pityingly at Lily.

'My mother. In the settlement yonder. I'll send someone to fetch her.'

In the afternoon of the short winter day Djana's mother arrived riding a stocky hill pony. She thawed herself out in front of the kitchen fire, ate a bowl of rich venison stew, then heaved herself to her feet and waddled upstairs. Lying on the bed, Roza submitted to having her huge belly exposed to the old woman's exploring hands. No words were spoken. When she'd finished, the midwife pulled Roza's gown down and her blanket up, nodded at Lily waiting by the window and left the room. In the corridor she leaned her back against the rough stone wall.

'Is it her first?'

Lily nodded.

'She's young.'

Lily nodded again. Knowing what was coming.

The old woman rubbed a grubby hand over her face. 'She's holding a lot fluid. And the head's too big.'

'What can you do?'

The woman shook her head. 'There's nothing to be done except get rid of it. It won't live anyway. And if you wait until term she won't be able to deliver it and she'll die too.'

'Can you do it?'

Another shake of the head. 'I've got nothing with me.'

'Will you show me?'

Gaze met gaze.

'We'd better hurry. It'll be dark soon.'

Wrapped against the cold the two women slipped out of the keep and went down to the stream. The snow lay on the meadow knee deep, the top freezing into a hard crust. The last of the daylight revealed a thread of dark water under the trees. The old woman found a stick and dug holes in the snow along the bank of the stream. She collected brown roots and white sappy stems just beginning to push themselves out of the hard ground. She showed each one to Lily and explained its use, then stowed it away beneath her cloak. Under a blanket of brilliant stars they returned to the keep. In the kitchen the midwife wrapped the herbs in a piece of cloth and gave them to Lily.

'Now remember. Soak them tonight. Tomorrow you must boil them in fresh water for an hour. Strain the liquid. Give her just a sip to begin with until the pains start. And don't worry. She's a strong girl.' She leaned forward and brushed Lily's cheek with her dry, cold lips. 'Now I must be off. There's another in the village will be wanting me by now.'

Lily woke in the depths of the night when Alkmon left their bed. She lay awake for a while thinking about what she had to do the next day. She was glad Roza was to be rid of a burden that seemed to trouble her so profoundly. Yet the induced labour would not be easy. And, even now, it might be too late.

She woke again towards morning to a steady drip, drip

outside the window. The air in the room was damp, releasing all the odours of a long winter spent indoors. Alkmon's side of the bed was cold now but Lily heard a drift of cheerful voices from the stable yard and assumed he was going hunting. Grey dawn was filling the high chamber but Lily turned on her side and pulled the wolf skin over her shoulders.

She came fully awake some time later to a strip of warm sunshine lying across the bed and the sound of Eumeus' voice outside the door. Lily dragged the wolf skin around her and padded across the cold floor.

'What is it?'

Eumeus pushed the door open and came into the room. A glance showed him the tumbled bed, the cold ashes in the hearth, the windows covered by heavy wooden shutters. Lily stood bare-foot on the stone floor, her eyes heavy with sleep, her hair tangled on her shoulders. It took all his strength not to turn on his heels and walk away. But old habits are not so easily shed.

'They've gone.'

She nodded. 'Hunting. I heard them earlier.'

Eumeus shook his head. 'They're not hunting, Lily. They've gone. Cleared out.' There was a look of triumph, of gloating, not quite hidden at the back of the old slave's eyes.

With the wolf skin dragging behind her on the rough stone floor, Lily made a tour of the keep, seeing for herself the things Eumeus already knew. The walls of her living room were stripped of hangings, there were no cushions on the bench by the fire. The silvers dishes and plates and goblets were gone. There was a fire burning downstairs in the kitchen but no pots to boil up the scraping of mouldy grain which was all that remained in the store. Lily sank down onto the ash strewn hearth and held her hands out to the sullen flames. The heavy wolf skin almost upset the bowl of herbs she had left by the fire the night before. With a painful thump of her heart she remembered Roza.

She turned her eyes up to Eumeus. 'I need to boil them up. What can I use?'

"Lily, there are more important things ...'

'No! No, Eumeus there are not. I must abort Roza's child today. I don't want to lose her, too.'

Her eyes, full of anguish, beseeched him. Eumeus felt a rush of pity wash away the jealous rage that had lodged in his throat ever since he saw his beloved mistress warm from the bed of that ... that ... But Eumeus had no words for Alkmon's treachery.

Eumeus knew now why Alkmon had left. It was because of Roza's child. The promise of that child had kept him in the stone tower all winter, amusing himself with Lily's body while he waited for his child to be born from the body of her daughter. Now he had discovered there would be no child. And he had gone. Lily was right. Removing that monster's spawn from Roza's womb was the most important thing to do right now.

There was a silver bowl under Eumeus' bed. It had a raised pattern around the rim which seemed to be of people chasing each other. Eumeus' somewhat feeble eyes were unable to work out exactly what they were doing. He thought it was probably pornographic. Eumeus had lifted this fine silver vessel from the ox wagon during the confusion of their arrival at the keep and it had been his pleasure to use it as a piss pot all winter. Now he brought it out and set it on the fire to boil the herbs for Roza's abortion. He watched as the hot flames blackened and distorted the soft metal of the bowl, watched the tiny rubies that had made up the eyes of the romping figures drop one by one into the flames. Watched carefully as the mixture seethed into a brown stinking liquid. Then he drew the bowl from the fire and went upstairs with Quin to fetch Roza down to the kitchen.

She lay as she had lain all winter flat on her back in bed with her face turned to the wall. It was almost as if she had laid herself out, thought Eumeus, a corpse that was not yet dead. He and Quin raised her vast bloated body and set her small white feet onto the stone floor. Roza said nothing. Her eyes were distant, staring at some inner horror. They half carried, half dragged her across the room towards the door. But she would not go through. A throaty growl of fear rose and rose to a high-pitched shriek of terror that made Quin's damaged eye weep tears of pity. Eumeus stopped and took her in his arms. He felt the hard lump of the child inside her swollen belly. Felt it move sluggishly. Roza struggled to be free of his embrace but he held on tightly

'It's all right, Roza. It's all right. He's gone. Nothing to fear, now. Come on, child. Downstairs where it's warm.'

His voice was warm and soothing. He felt Roza relax in his grip. Saw her eyes focus and stare into his own.

'Gone?' Her voice was a whisper.

Eumeus nodded. 'And now we'll be rid of the child and all will be well.'

'When?'

'Now. Today. Come on. Your mother's waiting.'

A look of understanding, of trust, of love passed between the old man and the girl.

And then, 'I'm ready.'

It was afternoon before Roza's labour was established. Lily had begun by dosing her daughter sparingly, unaware of the strength of the potion she had prepared. Eumeus stoked up the fire, then made a thin porridge in what was left of his silver bowl. Towards evening Shyron and Zaagor came home with a day-old fawn dropped by its mother on the half melted snow. They set to work to skin it, then put the tender meat to seethe in the old leather pot they used when they camped out on the steppes. In the flickering light of the fire Zaagor began working on the soft, dappled pelt.

'It's for the child,' he said, looking up as Eumeus bent to throw more wood on the fire. 'This is what our women use for their new babies.'

Eumeus shook his head. 'It won't live.'

'You'll need something to wrap it nevertheless.'

It was a long night. A frost came down after sunset and gripped the thawing land in its iron fist. The young men took themselves off to the stables to sleep with the horses, leaving Lily, Eumeus and Quin to tend Roza as pain took control of her body. Towards dawn there was the soft hush of rain. The smell of water and damp grass crept into the dark foetid room. An oil lamp flickered and smoked. With her hand clamped on her daughter's belly, Lily felt Roza stiffen to take the next wave of pain. On each side of the bed the two old men held on tight to hands that were convulsed with agony.

Lily looked up. 'I think it's going to be all right.'

She went to the window and pushed open one of the heavy

shutters. A breeze rushed into the room stirring the damp wisps of hair on Roza's forehead. Roza turned her head towards the window. A pale blue sky. Small white clouds tinged with the pink of sunrise. She struggled to sit up. Pushed fiercely at the hands that tried to force her back.

'Mama, tell them to let me go.'

Lily nodded to the two men.

Free of the men's hands, Roza sat up and swung her legs over the side of the rough bed. Another pain gripped her and she paused until it passed. Then she was up and moving towards the kitchen door. The door led to a yard surrounded by a high stone wall. An arched gateway framed an image of a steep, brown meadow crowned by a rocky tor. Close by, the stream chuckled at its freedom from the ice.

Roza crossed the yard to the gate then, gripping her belly, she stumbled down the shallow steps that led to a narrow path beaten into the frost-brown grass of the meadow. Another pain. She paused again. Lifted her head exultantly as rain dashed briefly across her face. At the end of the meadow the land tilted upwards, studded with rocks. The path ended and the cold grass stung her feet. Slender birch trees grew in the shallow ground, their bark ruddy with new growth.

Roza climbed further until she reached the base of the rocky plateau, then she collapsed to the ground in the shelter of the naked swaying branches of the trees. She was pushing now, forced by the pain. She felt the child shift within her and widened her legs. Another pain and she grunted with effort. The child slithered onto the cold grass.

For a moment Roza lay still. The child moved feebly between her legs, the thick grey umbilical cord still pulsating. She saw blood smeared limbs, red balls and a tiny pink penis, a huge grotesque head. The child had no face, no features. Just a red mucus-filled hole that gaped for air. Another effort and the placenta slipped from Roza's body. She turned over and pushed herself upright. Reached down and grabbed the slippery child from the ground. Her sharp teeth severed the cord. The placenta fell, a bloody mass onto the stained grass.

There was a gurgling sigh from the tiny, hideous body and then silence. With the dead child gripped in her hands, Roza scrambled onto the high rocky platform. Stood with her legs apart for balance against the cold wind. With both hands she held the child above her head.

'Here he is, my lord of heaven. Take him! Take him!'

The child hung in her hands, its great deformed head lolling. And an eagle came out of the sky.

The bird filled Roza's vision. Fierce yellow eyes. A cruel curved beak. Talons reaching out. Standing on tip toe, she held up the child. Her laughter was a thin thread of sound in the warm air. The bird's claws gripped the child's body, lifting it from her grasp. Roza felt the rush of its wings and ducked her head instinctively as the bird bore her child aloft.

Part Four

The High Plains

23

When Roza left the tower Lily hung back, awed by her daughter's need and her strength. She watched her move through the open meadow and climb the rocky hill beyond. Saw her collapse onto the ground under the trees. At that point anxiety got the better of her and, with Eumeus and Quin trailing behind, she hurried across the kitchen yard and out of the gate into the meadow. As she toiled along the path through the frost-dried grass, the rocky plateau was hidden from her sight. It was not until she began the climb up the hill that she saw Roza standing at the highest point with something in her outstretched hands. Lily saw the great bird of prey coming out of the sun dazzle and opened her mouth to cry out some sort of warning. But Roza stretched out her arms to offer her burden to the bird.

When Lily reached her, Roza was still standing on the rock but she was shivering violently. She turned as Lily took her in her arms and buried her face in her mother's shoulder. The tears came then, great heaving sobs that shook her body. After a while she lifted her wrecked face.

'It had no face, Mama. Now I know why he wore a mask.'

'Who, child?'

'Its father. Now I know why he wore a mask.'

Then the sobs began again.

High in the blue sky the eagle spiralled upwards, the child's body held in its claws. Its wild scream was answered from below by a piercing whistle. For a long moment the eagle hung in the air. The whistle came again. Then, as if making up its mind, the eagle let go of its burden, bent its wings close to its body and shot swiftly towards the ground. Over the top of her daughter's head Lily traced the child's descent. The body fell with agonising slowness, twisting in the air currents. Finally it dropped out of sight in a thicket of grey-leaved bushes that clung to the side of the hill. Lily blinked the sun from her eyes and sought the eagle's flight.

Beyond the rocky tor where Lily stood, the grasslands of the high plain stretched towards the horizon, patterned with a patchwork of melting snow. A knot of horsemen was crossing the plain at high speed. Like a flung spear the eagle was heading for the man at the head of the group. Lily watched as the man reined his horse to a trampling halt and leapt from its back. With the other horsemen in disarray around him, he stood erect, holding out one arm that seemed to be clad with thick leather. The eagle put up its tail, let down its great feathered feet and landed on the man's arm as gently as a snow flake on a window sill. The bird folded its huge wings and bent its head to receive the man's caress. With one hand stroking the eagle's head, the man stared around until finally he spotted the two women standing on the rocky hill. Holding his arm aloft, he sprang onto his horse's back and headed at a gallop towards the hill with his men streaming behind. As he came closer he cried out in a language that stirred in the back of Lily's memory.

'Are you all right? What has happened?'

Roza wrenched herself from her mother arms and took off down the hill towards the horsemen, scrambling and slipping on the uneven surface. She called out in the same language. And Lily remembered what it was. It was half a lifetime since she had last heard it spoken by the man who had captured her, along with her farm, in the dark days of conquest after her father and brothers left to defend Achaea against the invaders. Roza had been a small child, barely two, when that man had died with a dagger in his back in the alleyways of Thera's harbour town. Fen, Roza's father, never loved, long forgotten.

But he had given his language to his child and now that unwanted gift could be the saving of them all. Because at that moment with the short spring day dipping towards evening and thick grey clouds a familiar menace above the northern hills, and no food or drink in Alkmon's abandoned keep, they were in dire need of succour from whatever source. By now Eumeus and Quin had caught up with Lily. Together the three of them began the long scramble down the hill. There was bright blood on the rocks where Roza had passed. Another thing to worry about.

By the time they caught up with Roza she was on her knees in front of the leader. He was a short man, bandy legged, barrel chested, his rusty beard clipped neatly, his hair tied back in a leather thong. His eyes were blue, reflecting Roza's own, and they were staring intently at the girl in front of him. A young girl, beautiful perhaps when she was clean. Her hair was tangled. Her face pale like death. Her gown, white once, was drenched with blood. Between her legs more blood dripped, scarlet on the snow. She was gabbling in a high keening murmur something that sounded as if it had been learned by heart. But her accent was so strange and unfamiliar it was a while before he understood what she was saying. It was a genealogy. Her folk. From the beginning.

The eagle on his arm rose up and opened his wings, excited by the smell of blood. An impatient gesture and one of the men came forward and took the bird. The girl was coming to the interesting part. Her father and her father's father. His own kin. They had left the high plains a generation ago, seeking their fortune in the west where, it was said, there was land for the taking and no-one to protect it. And now here she was returned to her ancestral homeland. Though how she got here... and why she was in such a condition ... there were many questions to ask. He raised his eyes to Lily and the two old men. How many more were there who would demand hearth rights? At the end of a harsh winter there was little enough food as it was. But the girl was not finished.

'Lastly there is my son gotten on me by the sky god, Marduk, and born this day ...'

The man stepped forward. 'A child? Where is he?'

Roza lifted her eyes to his. 'He has gone to his father.'

In the blue depths of the girl's eyes the horseman looked for signs of madness. But there was none to be seen. He remembered the eagle soaring upwards in the air with something gripped in his claws. The bird had been trained to take meat only at his master's command. Perhaps he had been obeying a higher master – a god. And it was not surprising that the sky god would call upon an eagle, lord of the air, to do his bidding. It pleased the horseman to think that Marduk, the most powerful of all the gods, had chosen his kin for a mate. He would ask his minstrel to make a song about it. Something like that could do nothing but good to his reputation amongst the neighbouring tribes. But in the mean time ...

He bent down and raised the girl from the ground. Beckoned the others forward. A woman with tousled red-gold hair which she was attempting to bundle into some sort of order behind her head. Two old men. The first was tall and strong, despite his age. Huge hands. One naked eye socket seamed with purple scars. The other was ... small, dark, proud. A man not to trust, at least not straight away. Supporting the girl with one strong arm, the horseman turned to the woman now standing before him.

'Madam, I am Allyn, leader of one hundred spears, and I claim you as kin to my family. It is many years since Fen, your husband and my kinsman, left these plains to seek his fortune in the south. It seems that he met with success.' A small bow. 'A beautiful wife. And a daughter who has received the favour of a god. You bring honour to us all. Is your husband with you?

A shake of the head. 'He's dead.' The language sounded rough and unfamiliar in her mouth.

'And your companions?'

'My brother, Quin. And my ... uncle. His name is Eumeus.'

Not true, thought Allyn. Not with that look in his eyes. Maybe he's a eunuch. That would explain the expression of doting adoration. A slave anyway. Allyn had spotted the Babylonian slave mark behind Eumeus' ear. He prided himself on having eyes as sharp as those of his hunting bird.

Now he bowed again. 'You have much to tell us. But, come, we must seek shelter. Night approaches and your daughter needs care.'

Allyn's camp lay to the north of the tower. Hunched in the sea of brown grass, the leather tents looked like boulders marooned on the windswept plain. As they came closer Lily could see lines of horses tethered for the night. Goats were penned in a thorn bush stockade. Lamp light and fire light shone through the low doorways of the tents. A flurry of sleet at their backs hurried the horses towards home.

Ducking his head, Allyn carried the half-unconscious Roza into the largest of the leather tents, beckoning Lily to follow.

Inside, the tent was lined with richly embroidered hangings, the floor piled with rugs. Lamps were lit. Cooking smells from the large pots huddled over the central hearth reminded Lily that she had not eaten that day. A group of women and girls sitting by the hearth raised their eyes as the newcomers entered the tent but said nothing.

At a word from Allyn they came forward, took Roza to lie on a soft bed piled with furs, motioned Lily to sit by the fire and dished out steaming bowls of the delicious food. Outside, the wind rose, throwing spitting handfuls of sleet through the open smoke hole in the roof of the tent. From her place by the fire Lily watched the women tending her daughter. She felt that she should be doing something to help but the delectable warmth of the food had saturated her senses. All she wanted to do was sleep.

Several days later the camp was packing up ready for the next stage of the journey to the tribe's summer camp by a vast lake further west. Lily spent the day helping Allyn's women pack up his tent and load it onto the mules and camels. In the early afternoon a drumming of hooves made Lily raise her head. She recognised the two horses – the chestnut mare and the stocky hill pony – and the boys riding them. Each horse was laden with what Lily recognised as the gear the boys took on hunting trips when they planned to be away for several days. The boys slowed their horses to a walk as they began threading their way through the dismantled camp. Lily dropped what she was carrying and stood waiting for them.

Lily had seen little of her son during the winter just past and it seemed to her now that in the few months since leaving Babylon he had grown from a child to a man. His skin was weathered from a winter spent outdoors, his hair grown long and tied back tribal fashion with a leather thong. He will be a big man when he's finished growing, thought Lily, as he came towards her. Big, like his uncle Quin.

'Greetings to you both,' she said when the horses reached them and the boys swung down to the ground.

'Greetings, Mama. We heard you were here.' Shyron leaned down and brushed a kiss onto his mother's cheek. 'How's Roza?'

The question was asked reluctantly. Lily sensed Shyron was embarrassed by what had happened to his sister.

"She's fine. Recovering.'

'We brought her this.' Zaagor held out the soft fawn skin he had been working on the night of Roza's labour. 'I know she has no need of it, now her child has gone to his father. But maybe for next time.'

News travels, thought Lily. She wondered what they'd heard. Already the story had grown far beyond the truth. She reached out her hand.

'It's a beautiful gift. Thank you, Zaagor.'

For an instant Lily wondered what would happen if she claimed the young man as her slave. Wondered if he remembered that she was still his mistress. It seemed ridiculous, looking at him now, to imagine him in the ladies' quarters of a Babylonian palace handing out sweetmeats.

'There's something else.' Shyron turned to the pony that was nuzzling his neck and pulled something off its back. It was Alkmon's wolf skin cloak. Lily shook her head. But Shyron reached out and put it into her arms.

'Go on, Mama. Take it. It's yours.'

She felt the familiar rough texture of the fur under her hand. Suddenly she wanted to cry for all the things she'd lost. And what she was about to lose. Her son. Her baby. She wondered when she'd see him again. Or if she ever would.

'So you're off, then?'

Shyron looked uncomfortable. 'We're going to visit Zaagor's kin in the east. I just wanted to make sure you were all right. What's happening here?'

'The tribe's leaving for summer camp. I'm going with them.'

'But why? I thought you'd want to go home.'

Lily reached up and pushed a strand of hair off her forehead. 'Look, Shyron. These are Roza's people. They've accepted us as kin. And she's … getting better. I'm not taking her back to Babylon. Not after what happened. And there's your uncle Quin.' Lily swept one arm towards the goat pen. Quin was there surrounded by animals and children as he had been ever since their first day with the tribe. 'Look at him, Shyron. He's happy. He's doing what he's good at.'

'But what about my father?'

Let him go back to his wife, she thought bitterly, even though she knew Shyrah had been dead these many years. She stared up at her son with his hated name. Perhaps it is as well he is going, she thought, before I learn to hate him too. Perhaps with him gone I can begin to forget.

'I'm not going back to Babylon, Shyron', she said in a voice that Shyron knew allowed no argument. 'Any more than you are. Now, good bye, I've got work to do.'

'Good bye, Mama.' Shyron turned away, eager to be gone.

As he turned to follow him, Zaagor bowed his head to Lily.

'I wish you happiness, lady.'

Beneath his calm demeanour, Zaagor's heart was soaring with joy. He had taken a risk coming to the camp knowing Lily could claim him as her slave. He knew, too, the risk was unnecessary, that he could ride away and Lily could do nothing to stop him. But his honour had demanded he take his freedom from her hands.

Lily bowed her head, then looked up into his eager, joyful eyes.

'Thank you for your good wishes, Zaagor. But I think my days of happiness have gone forever.' And then, 'Take care of my son.'

But the last words were spoken only in her mind. She stood and watched as the two young men galloped away into the distance.

24

Another spring day. From the open field outside the walls of Chalcedon, Xander looked down to the blue water of the Hellespont. A ship under sail was tacking briskly towards the narrow straits that lay just beyond the headland. On the far shore the mountains of Thrace came down to the water's edge, green upon green, topped by snowy peaks, stark against the clear sky. Many days had passed since Xander first smelled salt on the wind and knew he was close to the sea. It was a knowledge that had sustained him during the final days of the long march across the high plains of Anatolia and now the sight of that ship beating against a freshening breeze filled Xander's heart with something akin to joy – a rare emotion indeed in the days since his capture in Babylon.

The hasty rattle of a chain and Xander felt a sharp elbow in his ribs. He dropped his eyes quickly to the ground. With an imperceptible movement of his head he acknowledged his thanks to the man next to him. One of the things Xander had learned swiftly after he joined the slave caravan in Babylon was that a raised head attracted the sting of the lash. Another was the ephemeral but intense loyalty of slave to slave. He had been shackled night and day to this man, Borg, for two turns of the moon in the sky and had forged a relationship of mutual trust with the big, pale-haired man. It was the only way for either of them to sleep at night and conserve what energy they had for the hardships each day brought.

'It smells good, even if I can't look at it,' he murmured.

Borg quirked the corner of his mouth. 'Mebbe you'll get yourself a spot on the rowing benches. They say drowning's a fine way to go.'

An answering grin. 'At least it's quick. Better than being worked to death in the silver mines.'

'That's where we're headed, I reckon.'

'We'll find out soon enough.'

The two men were standing on a low wooden platform. Their leg shackles, and those of their fellow slaves, were fastened to rings set in a long beam that ran along the front of the platform. Their hands were chained loosely in front of them, so the buyers could see what they were bidding for. For the same purpose, they were dressed in no more than loin cloths, their chests bare to the cool breeze blowing from the hills on the far side of the strait.

Borg shook his head. 'Nah, they'll be a while yet. May as well enjoy the sun on your head. It might be in short supply where we're going.'

The slave market was part of a spring festival that had brought the citizens of Chalcedon out of the gates and on to the big open field. Booths were set up selling food and pretty trinkets. A group of young girls with flowers in their hair danced slowly in a circle. A gang of small boys ran after an inflated pig's stomach, yelling with excitement. Some of the bigger boys sauntered along the line of slaves amusing themselves by darting forward and rattling the slaves' leg irons. Xander and Borg took no notice. It was nothing new for them. Even the smell of roasting meat and fresh bread did not entice their appetite, dulled by a constant diet of thin barley broth. While he stood at the edge of the field, half-asleep in the noon day heat, Xander's mind wandered back to the time of his incarceration in the dungeons deep beneath the palace of the governor of Babylon.

Xander had spent all winter in a cell where foul water ran down the walls freezing and thawing as night followed day. Every now and then he was taken out and tortured in all kinds of cunning and painful ways in an attempt to extract from him information he did not possess. At least the torture chamber was dry and relatively warm, a chance for him to thaw out a little before he was tossed back onto the stinking slime of his cell floor.

Xander gained from the persistent questioning of his torturers the certain knowledge that none of his family had been captured in the days following the raid. Safe, then. Or dead, which was much the same thing. By the end of his ordeal, Xander knew that death was a safe haven compared with the dank, subterranean dungeon and the close attention of the governor's black guard. It was something he had wished for often enough himself.

He was still not sure why they had let him go instead of leaving him to rot where he lay. Maybe his tormentors had grown tired of trying to extract information about something so trivial as a failed uprising and had decided to exchange their prisoners' bruised and battered bodies for the meagre pickings of the slaver's purse. Or maybe they needed space for the victims of some new intrigue. Babylon was full of them and the dungeons saw a regular traffic of poor souls caught up in some lord's game.

There was snow on the ground the day Xander was released but signs of spring were all around from the pale blue arch of the sky to a tiny plant putting out tender leaves in the shadow of a grimy wall. After spending so long underground the light of the spring morning roared into Xander's eyes and made him blink. Half-blinded, he was led to where a blacksmith was working his forge and heavy iron shackles were hammered onto his wrists and ankles. Thus burdened and with tears of pain in his eyes, Xander stumbled through the bronze gates and out of Babylon for ever.

There was no time for Xander to become accustomed to his shackles, which rubbed him raw over the first few days, because the slave master was in a hurry to get to the markets in the north where the overseers from the Thracian silver mines would be seeking fresh slaves to work the narrow seams underground. The silver mines had a voracious appetite for strong men and it was well known that few came out alive. Thus Xander had little time to appreciate the irony of marching in a slave caravan across the ancestral lands of his own one-thousand-year-old dynasty. He did, however see the signs of a civilisation fallen on hard times. Empty cities infested with bandits. Shanty towns of tents and hovels, teeming with traders and thieves. And everywhere the lines of abject slaves.

It was on this long march across Anatolia that Xander's pride in his name flickered and died. Never again would he be able to stand, as he had stood in Cyrus' crowded salon all those years ago, and declare, 'I am Siskandarabba, son of Labbusilis of the Great Empire of Shuppiluliumash,' and wake respect in another man's eyes.

Roused by his friend's sharp elbow Xander returned to the reality of the slave market.

'Look at this fine fellow,' whispered Borg. 'How would you fancy working for him?'

Xander leaned forward and glanced in the direction of Borg's nod. A man was strolling along the slave lines. A tall, lean man in tribal dress with long hair falling across his forehead and a rough woollen cloak trailing behind him in the dust. It was a man that Xander had seen only once before but he recognised him instantly. No other man walked with that particular indolent grace. Or smiled with such easy charm at the slave master who trotted eagerly at his side. Instinctively Xander jerked his head back. He stood perfectly still and stared unseeing at the wooden boards between his feet while his heart thumped frantically in his chest.

'You know him?' asked Borg with surprise.

'Aye, I know him right enough. Just pray to the gods he doesn't recognise me.'

But Alkmon had seen him. He took his time but eventually he arrived at the place where Xander stood in the line of slaves.

'Well, well.' Alkmon turned to the slave master. 'You didn't tell me you carried such superior stock. Let me introduce you to Lord Siskandarabba of Carchemish. Last seen keeping fine company in the salon of my good friend, Mutakkil-Nusku in Babylon. Very fine company indeed. Namely, my own. Though I have not seen you since then, have I, my lord?'

Silence.

'*Have I?*' Alkmon's voice was insistent and Xander could see the short metal-tipped goad flicking in the slave master's hand.

'No, my lord Alkmon. Not since the day of the invasion.'

Xander was aware of the quickening interest of Borg at his side.

'Ah, yes, the invasion. It's interesting, is it not, the opportunities that present themselves on such occasions? In my case, it was the opportunity to spend time with a beautiful woman.' Alkmon's voice was silken. 'A beautiful red-haired woman. A woman you lost and I ... I found.'

Alkmon's words fell into Xander's ears like drops of searing oil. The sounds and smells and sights of the market place retreated, leaving in their place a profound, heat-soaked silence in which he faced his enemy and waited for the torment to begin.

'It never ceases to amaze me how a respectable city matron turns into a whore the minute you get her into your bed.' It was as if Alkmon was settling down to gossip with a friend. But Xander could hear the malice beneath Alkmon's smooth, conversational tone. 'But you'd know all about that, wouldn't you, my lord? Because she wasn't always a fine lady, your Lily, was she?'

'She is no whore.'

Anger diffused Xander's face. He ignored - or didn't feel - Borg's warning jab in his side.

'So what was she doing in that nice white house on Thera? She was a whore and you were her pimp. That's the story I heard. Isn't that where you got your wealth?'

'She is no whore!'

A violent movement snapped tight the shackles on Xander's wrists. Alkmon took a step backwards. The slave master, agog at the tale, was too late with the goad and earned himself a flash of venom from Alkmon's pale blue eyes before he returned to his prey.

'She behaved like a whore in my bed.' A slow smile. 'Did she never arch her back and scream her ecstasy for you, my lord? Did she never rake her nails down your back? I'll show you the scars, if you like.'

Xander clenched his fists. 'Where is she?'

Alkmon quirked an eye brow. 'You think she'll want you back after she's been with me?'

'Where is she?' Xander repeated while despair gripped his heart.

'You'll not find her in this world, my friend. Not any more.' Alkmon was turning away. 'I was finished with her, you see, and I am a tidy man.' He beckoned the slave master. 'Is Jeoge here yet?'

'The mine master? Yes, my lord.'

'Give him my compliments and tell him this man ...' Alkmon flicked a slender finger towards Xander. '... comes with my special recommendation.' He turned his head and favoured Xander with a cool stare from his pale, hooded eyes. 'Don't die too quickly, Lord Siskandarabba. I want you to have plenty of time to think about your beautiful lady and all the things we did together. Let your imagination roam as far as you like. Because we did it all. Believe me. We did it all.'

When Alkmon had strolled away with his cloak dragging in the dirt, Borg turned towards his friend, eager with his questions. But Xander's cheeks were wet with tears and Borg left him to his grief.

25

'We're nearly there.'

Lily turned and smiled at her daughter. In front of them the waters of the vast inland sea sparkled under a pale spring sky. Despite being on horseback since before dawn, the excitement of arriving at the summer camp made up for the discomfort of the long day's ride. Lily knew they would do no more than erect the small travelling tents when they arrived before settling down to a night of singing and celebration. She had been with the tribe for two years, and this was her third camp, so she knew what to expect.

All around her Lily felt the pace of the long dawdling caravan pick up as the excitement spread. A group of young men passed by at a gallop. Lily watched as each one turned to steal a glimpse of Roza. It was not surprising. With her flawless honey coloured skin, thick pale hair and wide-set blue eyes, Roza was the acknowledged beauty of the tribe and this, together with her position in the tribe leader's tent and her well-known connection with the sky god Marduk, made her the object of desire for every young man in the tribe.

It had taken a long time for Roza to recover from her ordeal. Her young body had healed quickly but it was her emotional state that had caused Lily the most concern. Eumeus counselled Lily to be patient. Roza had gone through a terrible ordeal and it was not to be expected that she would return to normal straight away.

During their first months with the tribe, Lily watched her daughter closely. Roza was willing enough to join the other young women in their daily activities, even to the extent of learning their songs and dances, but she continued quiet and inward looking. While the other women in the tribe congratulated Lily on her modest, hard working, obedient daughter Lily was waiting for the first flash of rage that would herald the return of the daughter she knew. It was a strange thing to wish for: Roza's spit-cat, fiery temper that used to set the whole house ablaze. But as month succeeded month and the tribe moved on its slow routine from summer camp to winter quarters, Lily gave up waiting.

Lily glanced across at Roza now. The girl had ignored the young men, as she always did. She seemed completely unaware of her power over them, or chose to disregard it. And, although her refusal to acknowledge all the hot male glances that came her way was to be commended, her complete indifference to the serious and acceptable suitors that Allyn paraded in front of her at every summer camp was beginning to be a problem.

Perhaps she will see things differently after I am married, thought Lily. At the end of last summer camp Lily had accepted the proposal of Allyn's brother. Vyk. By then the heat of Alkmon's love making had died in her loins and the pain of Xander's betrayal had faded to a dull ache, and Lily could think calmly about the advantages of such a match. She was aware of her position as a female without status in Allyn's tent and had found herself, on more than one occasion, on the receiving end of the ill-temper of his latest wife, a girl young enough to be Lily's daughter.

Vyk was known as a fine horseman and a brave warrior but he was kind to his women, in fact a soft touch according to his chief wife, Retta. Lily saw Vyk as a stiff old man, past his prime, under whom she could to lie and think about the morning's yoghurt or the next line in the pattern she was weaving on the loom. It was all she wanted. The wedding would take place at mid-summer, time enough for Lily to enjoy the beauty of spring in the high plains, something which she had anticipated all the long, hard winter.

Mid morning and Eumeus was sitting with his back to the warm trunk of an alder tree frilled with pale green leaves. The sun was warm, the grass soft and starred with flowers. Birds flitted above his head, busy with insects and nest building. In front of the old man the water of a narrow stream flowed smooth and dark, full of snow melt. At one end of the small glade the stream gurgled between moss covered rocks before widening into a shallow pool fringed with sedge and hawthorn. Eumeus could hear the voices of children calling excitedly from the narrow gravel beach that edged the pool.

Since Lily's decision to accept Allyn's hospitality, Eumeus had found it difficult to find himself a place in the tribe. His experiences as astronomer, galley slave, brothel keeper and warehouse tally man were of no value in a tribe of nomadic horsemen. He had never been comfortable on a horse and the yearly round of migrations when he had to choose between days on horseback or riding in the wagons with the old and weak was a particular torture to him. Nor could he assume his best-loved role as manager of Lily's household, something he had been able to do even in Alkmon's tower.

In the tribes only close relatives were allowed inside a man's tent. Wives, daughters, slaves and unmarried kinswomen, such as Lily herself, attended to the household chores and prepared meals for their lord and his sons and brothers, should they choose to eat with the family. Other men were excluded. Thus, Eumeus had been forced to find himself a bed in one of the communal bachelor tents that were set up near the horse lines, taking what comfort he could from the cheerful and familiar companionship of Lily's brother Quin. But now, listening to the excited cries of the children from the downstream pool, Eumeus allowed a smile to creep over his face. He was tired of living like a poor relation on the fringes of Allyn's tribe. This summer he was going to make a place for himself. And it was gold that was going to do it for him.

All the creeks around Allyn's summer camp bore gold and this one seemed to yield more than the rest. The children down on the beach were busy picking through the gravel for flecks of the precious metal. Soon they would grow tired and the more serious fossickers would move in. But it was a slow, tedious business and often there was little to show for the aching back and cold feet brought back to camp at the end of a hard day's work. Beside, all the gold in the stream belonged to Allyn who was the lord and protector of the tribe and to whom all things flowed.

It had taken Eumeus a while to understand why men were willing to hand over to the chief the results of their own hard labour until he realised the reward was Allyn's favour and the gifts that he gave to those who had his approval. It was just like trade, Eumeus thought – you gave and you got back – except that everyone pretended the transaction had more to do with loyalty and mutual esteem. Well, he could play that game. But first he had to think of a way to extract the gold without getting his feet wet.

There were two things Eumeus had learned about these gold-bearing streams. First, he knew the gold was not a component of the gravel that formed the chilly little beach where the children yelled. Otherwise the gravel would have been picked clean by now, instead of which there was always gold to be found, especially in the early spring after the stream had been in flood. So that meant the gold was carried by the water and was dropped when the current slowed, as it did in the little pool below his vantage point. The question that had been teasing his mind all winter was how to collect the gold before it fell into the gravel. But now, with the sun as high in the sky as it was going to go on this early spring day and his stomach growling with hunger, Eumeus climbed stiffly to his feet and made his way back to camp.

Eumeus sat down near the communal fire and a slave girl handed him a bowl of the goats' meat stew which, along with unleavened bread and fermented mares' milk, was the staple fare of the bachelors' camp. While he chewed the tough gristle, he watched a group of women making cheese. Two of them held a piece of clean linen across the top of a large leather basin. Two others hefted a jar full of milk which had been sitting by the fire. Eumeus watched them tip the jar and empty its contents onto the stretched cloth. He saw the thin whey trickle through the linen into the basin below. He saw the curds caught by the cloth settling in thick creamy clots. The girls gathered up the edges of the cloth around the soft cheese and squeezed out the rest of the liquid.

It was a process Eumeus had seen many times before. Lily and her mother had made goats' milk cheese on the farm in Achaea. It had been made by the kitchen slaves when they were living in Tyre and, sometimes, in Babylon although it was the habit of householders in that extravagant city to buy their cheese ready made in the market. Wiping a piece of bread around the inside of his bowl, Eumeus got to his feet and went in search of Quin.

Quin was with the goats. Surrounded by a gaggle of little children he was feeding a new kid with a handful of soft fleece dipped into a bowl of milk. The little creature was sucking furiously while its small feathery tail wagged itself into a blur. Seeing Eumeus, Quin handed the fleece to the nearest child and lumbered to his feet. He dropped his arm heavily across Eumeus' shoulder and they walked a little way from the pen.

Eumeus said, 'Quin, I need a goat skin.'

'I don't have one. You'll have to ask the tanner.'

'No, Quin. If I wanted a nice tanned goat skin I wouldn't be asking you, would I? What I want is a bit of old skin. I don't care what it looks like. I just need it without the creature inside it.' Eumeus ignored the look of pain that crossed the other man's face. 'Just some old beast that wandered off and died. That nobody will miss. Do you think you can help me?'

'One that nobody wants, you say?' Quin's face was creased with thought. Then he grinned. 'There's that old billy that isn't up to the job any more. He's going into the pot if he doesn't watch out.'

Eumeus winced. 'Let's save him from the pot, eh, Quin? I've got a better use for him.'

Two days later Quin approached Eumeus at the cooking fire and with a series of theatrical nods and winks let him know that his mission was accomplished. Eumeus followed Quin to a thicket of scrubby trees behind the goat pen where a freshly skinned hide patterned in dirty black and white hung from a branch, surrounded by a buzzing horde of flies.

'Poor old fellow wandered off and died,' grinned Quin.

'Who skinned it?'

'I did.'

'Does anyone else know?'

A shake of the head.

'Good. Come on, then.'

Eumeus was hoping he wouldn't have to touch the stinking hide. But Quin reached up, unhooked the bloody skin from the branch and flung it over his shoulder. Then he followed Eumeus out of the trees.

It took the rest of the short spring afternoon for Eumeus and Quin to suspend the goat skin in the stream at its narrowest point just above the little pool. In the end they were both soaked through and icy cold, but content: Eumeus because he had high hopes for what the morning would bring, Quin because he'd had a good time. He still had no idea what his old friend was up to.

Eumeus knew his plan had failed long before he reached the place where he'd left the goat skin the night before. What was left of it was strewn in tatters along the shore of the little pool, obstructing the fossickers in their search. Gloomily he crouched down on the dry pebbles at the edge of the gravel beach. At his side Quin crouched down too, and waited for what would happen next.

Finally Eumeus swore. 'Damn!'

He had suddenly remembered the goat skin that Shyron and Zaagor had used to seethe the deer meat the day Roza was struggling in labour. Granted it was tanned leather and seasoned with the fat of a thousand meals but Eumeus realised now that a goat skin was never going to let the water through the way that piece of linen had let through the whey when the slave girls were making cheese. And anything suspended in the part of a stream where the water flowed swiftly would be torn away by the force of the current. Obviously.

'Damn,' he said again. He turned to Quin. 'What I'm trying to do is catch the gold before it lands on the gravel. It's carried by the water, you see, and I thought I could trap it in the goat skin.'

'Like a fish net?'

One of the chief pleasures of summer camp was the sturgeon in the lake, especially the females with their rich, red roe.

'Yes, something like that.'

Quin shook his head. 'A fish net would be no good. The holes are too big.'

He sunk his head between his hands and stared at the pool. The fossickers had gathered up most of the bits of skin now and piled them in a stinking heap on the grass beyond the shore line. There was a long silence.

Then, 'Why do you want to stop the gold from landing on the gravel?'

'Because it's hard to pick it out.'

'Then why don't you put the goat skin on top of the gravel?'

Eumeus turned and stared at Quin. 'Laid out flat, you mean?'

Quin nodded. 'Then the gold would land on the skin instead of on the gravel.'

A slow smile spread across Eumeus' face. He reached out his hands and put them either side of the big man's face.

'Don't ever let anyone tell you you're daft.'

Quin grinned. 'It's a good idea, then?'

'Yes, it's a good idea. It's the best idea I've ever heard.'

'We haven't got a goat skin any more.'

Eumeus stood up. 'I'll use my cloak.'

'You'll freeze.'

'It doesn't matter. Come on, we'll try further upstream.'

Together the two men walked alongside the stream until they came to another place where the narrow torrent widened into a pool. This pool was deep and boggy, reflecting the blue of the sky. Kneeling down, Eumeus reached into the water and brought up a handful of stinking mud.

'Look.'

He stirred the mud with one finger and they both saw the gleam of gold.

'Perfect.'

They laid Eumeus' cloak on the bottom of the pool and anchored it with rocks so it wouldn't float away. Then they returned to camp.

Over the next few days a number of goats wandered off never to be seen again. A wolf was heard howling near the camp and several young men went off to catch it. However, they could find no trace of it, not surprising because the noise they'd heard had been made by a certain one-eyed goatherd with a talent for mimicry.

The moon had gone a full cycle in the sky when Eumeus approached the fire outside Allyn's tent where the chieftain sat with his warrior companions. He waited until Allyn noticed him, then walked around the fire until he stood in front of the leader. He took a small, though satisfyingly heavy leather pouch from under his tunic and laid it on Allyn's outstretched palm. Allyn felt the weight of the pouch, nodded his approval, then stowed it under his cloak. Not a word was spoken but two days later Eumeus became the owner of a pretty white mare and a young lad to care for her. Not something he would have chosen for himself but at least he knew the system worked, even for a low status Babylonian ex-slave who'd never killed a man in his life and rode like a bag of chaff.

Eumeus and Quin moved to their belongings to a camp close to the muddy pool. They let it be known that they had been commanded by the sky god Marduk to build him a temple in the little grove near the pool. As proof, Eumeus pointed to a bright planet hanging like a yellow lamp in the eastern sky. He had been tracking its trajectory for some time, thinking it might be handy in his dealings with these superstitious people. Not that he needed the star to convince them the sky god had spoken to him. Everyone knew that Eumeus' family had a special kinship with Marduk through the beautiful Roza who had been the sky god's paramour and had borne his child.

From then on Eumeus and Quin were left to their gold gathering in peace. Often they would find small offerings by the hawthorn tree which formed the entrance to their camp: a young kid fresh from its mother, a chicken trussed for the pot, a bunch of flowers with a twist of dried grass to hold them together.

By late spring when the hawthorn was full of creamy scented blossom, there was a place for Eumeus at Allyn's fire and a turn at the strong mare's milk brew as it circulated the group. For some reason that he'd never been able to explain, Eumeus had a strong head for liquor and his ability to drink tougher men senseless did nothing but good for his position in the tribe. The men even gave him a nickname: *Sæf Hans* which meant soft hands – an insult turned into a mark of respect, typical of the tribes.

By midsummer, Eumeus had been invited to stand up as Lily's sponsor at her wedding, even though his status as her uncle was no more believed now than it had been on the day Allyn found them outside Alkmon's abandoned keep. But, as Eumeus was beginning to appreciate, a rich man high in the chief's favour could be anything he wanted to be.

26

On midsummer day Eumeus stood next to the woman he adored and prepared to give her to another man. The irony was not lost on him, yet he wished to be in no other place. It was the closest he'd been to Lily since their arrival in the tribe. And he hoped to be able to get nearer to her, now he was a great man and accepted as Lily's kin. He understood without the need for explanation that Lily's decision to marry Vyk was no more than a strategic choice, just as his was to collect wealth for the tribe. Women had only their bodies for barter and Lily had done well with hers, though the gleam in Vyk's eye when Eumeus, as Lily's sponsor, handed over the wolf skin which was all she had for a dowry made him wonder which was more precious in the tribesman's eyes.

The wedding was a grand occasion, involving as it did the houses of both the chief and his brother, and funded lavishly with Eumeus' gold. For a week before the big day families from the other tribes camped around the lake rode into Allyn's camp, setting up their household tents in the area set aside for them on one side of the vast open space where the feasting and dancing would take place.

While the older men went hunting in the forests surrounding the lake, the young warriors kept themselves amused with horse races and games of polo using a goat's head for a ball. Matrons took the opportunity to parade their unmarried daughters under the critical gaze of the mothers of sons. Sweetmeats were sampled, weaving examined and temperaments tested before the young men returned from their day's sport and the girls were whisked away into their own tents.

The day itself dawned fresh and clear. Dressed in fine linen with a garland of summer flowers on her hair Lily felt a surge of excitement. It was, after all, the first time she'd been a bride.

Standing just inside Allyn's tent with Eumeus by her side, she had a sudden sense of what a wedding meant: that she was valued enough for all this to happen because of her.

'Are you ready?'

Lily turned and looked into the eyes of her faithful friend. She nodded and laid her hand on his arm.

In the middle of the meeting ground stood an arch made of willow wands and woven with fresh flowers. Under the flowery arch Vyk waited, a tall grizzled warrior looking ill at ease in so unfamiliar a setting. Next to the arch was a small bright fire where the tribe's shaman, a stooped ancient with filthy hair, was muttering spells over a handful of bones tossed onto the ground. For a long slow moment the old man studied the bones, then he let out a high cry of triumph and capered around the fire, throwing aromatic herbs into the flames which gave off a heady fragrance into the warm morning air. With visible relief, Vyk squared his shoulders and awaited his bride.

Apart from the annual migrations to and from summer camp when it couldn't be helped, a wedding was the only time when men and women mingled freely. Seated in the place of honour next to her new husband, Lily watched as a group of young women performed a graceful dance in the middle of the square. Roza was among them and Lily was aware of the young men's eyes following every movement made by the beautiful girl.

'We'll have to find her a husband,' said Vyk, following Lily's gaze and Lily nodded. It was a relief to have someone else to worry about Roza. She had done enough of it to last a lifetime.

After the dancing came the feast. Great pits had been dug in the earth and filled with meat and fish to roast on the hot coals. Fresh greens and root vegetables, still young and tender so early in the season, had been steamed in leaf-lined baskets. At the bridal table Lily and Vyk were presented with a great golden jar full to the brim with rich crimson caviar. Lily tasted it cautiously but was enchanted with its rich salty taste.

She turned and smiled at Vyk. 'It's good.'

Vyk tipped back his head and roared with laughter. 'Good, she says! I can see I've got an expensive wife on my hands.'

When the sun had gathered itself into a red ball and rolled behind the purple hills, and the sparks from the fires rose like spits of flame into the velvet sky, the women from Vyk's tent took Lily away from the feasting. They removed her wedding finery and bathed her body in warm water scented with rose petals. They led her to Vyk's bed upon which lay the wolf skin – strange to see it on her bridegroom's bed when it had been a witness to all the wanton excess of her time as Alkmon's mistress – blew out the lamps and left her lying warm in the firelight to await the best her new husband had to offer. Thus it was that Lily did not know until the following morning that Roza had gone missing.

In the gloom of the small tent Roza lay still, listening to the unfamiliar sounds of the night. Around her she could hear the soft breathing of the others girls. Outside, the horses shifted quietly in the picket lines. A dog whimpered, dreaming of the chase. Just above her head light filtered through the thin hide of the tent wall as the short midsummer night lost its grip on the sky. She hadn't slept. Over and over in her head she replayed the events of the previous day.

Firstly, her mother and that old man standing under the ridiculous flowery arch as Lily bartered her body for property and status. She'd watched Lily and her new husband share a spoon that dipped in and out of some red gloop in a golden bowl. Then the dance out in the middle of the square, round and round in their white dresses, followed by the stares of the young men. Roza knew people were talking openly about who she would wed, now her mother had married into the ruling family of the tribe. She'd overheard Vyk's son, Pell – a bandy, splay-toothed lad with pocked skin – boasting that he could have Roza any time he liked, now his father had married her mother.

Before the women of Vyk's household came to take Lily away and prepare her for the sacrifice, Roza slipped away from the fire. She followed the cool whisper of the stream until she left behind the roar of voices and the stench of bodies. Above her head stars dripped from the luminous midnight sky. She heard the quiet plop! of a fish. She leaned her arm along the low branch of a willow tree and stared down at the black water. Her heart ached with misery.

The girl came along the edge of the stream walking softly on bare feet. She was wearing a short leather tunic. Her long dark hair was fastened behind her head with a leather thong. Her bow was across her shoulders and a brace of duck hung from her belt. She saw the gleam of Roza's white dress under the shadow of the willow tree and stopped a heart beat away from the beautiful girl. Gaze locked with gaze.

The girl spoke. 'Excuse me.' Her voice was low and husky. She turned to leave.

'Don't go.' Roza reached out her hand and laid it on the other girl's arm. She felt the warm skin under her fingers.

'Are you waiting for someone?' asked the girl quietly.

'Yes,' replied Roza simply. 'I think it is you.'

Without another word the girl took her hand and led her upstream to where a small brown mare was waiting patiently, huffing at the thin grass. She helped Roza onto the horse's back then sprang up behind her. Behind them the fires burned upwards towards the midsummer sky.

'She's not the first to go off with the Amazons,' said Retta, Allyn's chief wife. Her voice was sympathetic but it was clear she was enjoying Lily's discomfort. 'They were hanging around the camp last night. They come in when we have a gathering looking for young men to lie with.'

'The Amazons?'

'That's what we call them. It's not what they call themselves.'

'And isn't anyone going to rescue her?'

A shrug. 'They go because they want to.'

'Your daughter suffered at the hands of a man,' said Retta. The women drew closer together. 'A god, they say.'

'They all think they're gods.' A splurge of laughter.

'So let her run with the Amazons for the summer.' Retta's big dry hand came down and grasped Lily's knee through the thin linen of her skirt. 'It won't do her any harm. She'll be back before the autumn journey, you'll see.'

'And when she comes back?'

'Don't worry, she'll still get a man. It won't make any difference to them where she's been. They're all mad for her.'

In the autumn Roza and the sisters moved from the lake to their winter quarters. Roza rode her own pony now and carried a bow across her back although it would be some time before she could use it with the skill of the other girls. Over the summer Roza had lost the slight heaviness left behind by her pregnancy and her body was lean and fit with exercise. Her skin was tanned by the sun, her long thick hair curling wildly around her face. She had allowed her friend Dyann to cut it short while she lay blissfully with her head in Dyann's lap staring up into the depths of the summer sky as the pale curls fell onto the grass like shaves of wood.

The sisters' home for the winter was a squat stone dwelling tucked under an outcrop of rocks that sheltered it from the east wind. A paved yard enclosed by a high wall sheltered turf-roofed stables and a barn full of freshly cut hay. An underground larder held a stock of root vegetables. Salt meat and fish hung from the ceiling in the snug kitchen. Here lived the girls who had received the goddess' blessing the previous year and whose babies were too young to take to summer camp. Apart from the babies, there were three small children in the winter house, including an enchanting curly haired boy about three years old.

'What will happen to him,' Lily asked Dyann after dinner the first night when the children had been put to bed and the sisters were gathered around the fire.

'He'll go back to his family and learn to be a man. That's one thing we can't teach him.'

'And they'll take him?'

'Of course they will,' said Mahra, the mother of the group. She was old and heavy, twisted with bone pain so she spent most of her time in a chair by the fire. 'There is no animosity between the tribes and the sisters. We take nothing from them except their young men's seed. And there's plenty of that to spare.'

The girls laughed. Many of them lay with the young men of the tribes during summer camp: some because they wanted to receive the goddess' blessing, others because it gave them pleasure.

Mahra noticed the closed look on Roza's face. 'Have you never received pleasure from a man, my dear?'

Roza shook her head. Then she remembered Zaagor who had taught her much. 'There was a eunuch once. In Babylon.'

'A eunuch?'

The girls gathered closer.

'What was it like?'

'It's said they can go all night.'

'And that nice, soft skin. Like sleeping with a girl.'

'Only one big difference!'

Roza smiled and shrugged. 'It was a long time ago.'

She found herself embarrassed by such lewd talk among a group of girls.

Later when she and Dyann were laying their blankets side by side on the straw pallets Roza said, 'What happened to Mahra?' She touched her own breast. Even under the thick woollen shawl Mahra wore around her shoulders it was obvious that Mahra had lost her left breast.

'You noticed, did you?' Dyann took Roza's hand and they sat down together on the bed. 'In the old days many of the sisterhood had one breast removed. It was said the nipple became caught in the bow string when the arrow was loosed. That was the reason they gave for doing it. But really it was a symbol that a girl had committed her life to the sisterhood. She could never go back to the tribes once she had taken that step. And she knew that no man would look at her.'

'And now?'

Dyann laughed and put her arm around Roza's shoulders. 'Mahra says we are all growing soft. But, really, why go through such a thing? There are other ways of showing your commitment.'

As the days shortened the household settled down to its winter routine. To begin with the girls went out every day to the meadow by the stream to practiced archery and take part in running races and their own brand of bare-handed combat. Roza discovered the pleasure of pushing her body to the limit and gloried in her young strength.

As the weather closed in, the straw targets were set up into the paved yard that could be kept swept of snow. The girls moved indoors into the living area where the fire burning in the central hearth created light and warmth. They brought out their weapons and repaired the damage caused by the summer's hunting. They fashioned new arrows from bundles of thin straight sticks they had collected from the hedgerows.

They trimmed wild birds' feathers –each girl had her own favourite –to fletch the arrows.

In the corner of the living room stood a loom. Next to it was a basket of yarn spun from all the bits of animal hair the girls had collected from thorn bushes and hedgerows, as well as the thick wool from their own small herd of goats. The colour of the yarn varied from white to black with every shade of brown in between but what astonished Roza was the uneven quality of the yarn itself which went from fine to thick to fine again. If she'd produced such work as a five year old her mother would have made her do it again. And what was on the loom was no better. The girls took turns at weaving whenever they had a spare moment and, as Roza knew quite well, each girl had a different technique, a different tension so the piece of cloth looked like some old floor rag before it had even been taken from the loom.

When Roza grew tired of trying to bind flint arrow heads onto little bits of stick, she would get up from the fire and seat herself on the stool in front of the loom. She sorted out the yarn into dark and light and smoothed out the lumps and bumps as best she could between finger and thumb. She unpicked the worst of the work and began again. Almost without thinking her fingers began to create the intricate Achaean meander pattern taught to her by her mother in that high white room on Thera. She had been happy then, the only time in her life when she had been truly happy, and the familiar pattern brought with it memories of the sparkling blue sea, the scream of the gulls and the bowls of ice shavings sweetened with syrup that she'd eaten with a small silver spoon.

One evening when she was at work Mahra got up from her chair by the fire, lumbered painfully across the room and sat down heavily on a stool next to Roza. She put out one finger and traced the half-finished pattern.

'Ah, yes, I see how it goes. It's clever.

Roza was pleased. 'My mother taught me how to do it.'

'Where's she from? Your mother?'

'From Achaea. A long way to the west.'

'But you are kin to Allyn's tribe?'

Roza nodded. 'My father came from here.'

'And what do you call this pattern?'

'It's called a meander pattern. Because it's all one line. Or, at least, that's how it will look when it's finished.'

Mahra leaned forward. 'Did you wonder why the work you found on the loom was so very rough? Compared to yours?'

'I just thought the sisters hadn't been taught to do it properly.'

'And what would you say if I told you they produce that kind of work because they see no value in doing it ... properly, as you call it?' Marah pointed to the rough work at the bottom of the loom. 'This cloth will keep the sisters just as warm on the hunt as any of the fancy work your mother taught you how to do. And every cloak that comes off that loom has the sisterhood woven in it because they all have a hand in making it. To us, the cloaks we make represent something very precious. I don't know if you understand what I'm trying to say?'

Roza shook her head.

'You see, Roza, this work you're so proud of is just a trick that men play to keep their women in the tents. The women believe they are busy and their work is valued. They don't realise they are being excluded from the important work of the tribe – hunting, trading, making decisions. The things men do.'

'But it's the mothers who teach their daughters. Not the men.'

Mahra nodded slowly. 'Because the mothers want their daughters to marry. In the tribes that's all there is for a girl to do. And they know what men want in a wife. Someone meek and obedient. And this ... this weaving you're doing is the perfect occupation for a meek obedient wife. Look at the way you're sitting now. You try doing this work and see what's going on in the rest of the room. Never mind in the world around you. It's designed to keep your focus narrow, Roza, can't you see that?'

Roza was silent. She was finding it difficult to accept this kindly old woman's dismissal of the way of life which was accepted as natural and normal by every women she'd ever known, while the other girls sat peacefully by the fire carrying on with their work as if they'd heard it all a hundred times before. Yet when Roza looked back over her life she realised that she had rebelled against the stifling confinement of a woman's lot without understanding why she did so.

Roza stood up and helped Mahra to her feet. Together they went back to the fire and Roza picked up her abandoned arrow. In the silence that followed, Mahra's words spiralled in her mind. Finally she said, '... but women have children to raise. Isn't that why they are taught these skills and expected to stay at home?'

Mahra smiled gently. 'We raise children, too.'

Roza stared across the big central fire to where the sisters' children slept snuggled in their warm fur blankets. The little boy, Eryk, was flat on his back with his arms spread out, his hair damp on his forehead.

'Yes, but it's different here. You have a choice.'

A sigh as if Mahra had reached the finish line after a long race.

'Yes, we have a choice.'

27

'Me and my big mouth. One of these days I'm gonna learn to keep it shut.' Pell, son of Vyk, stared morosely at the small yellow puddle soaking rapidly into the dirty snow at the back of his father's tent. Above his head a skein of geese was etched against the sunrise sky. The signs of spring were all around him but he was not happy.

It was not as if he had been promised the girl, more that he thought he could have her, if he liked, once his father married her mother. But then he had to blab it out to the other young men on the very day of the wedding. Roza was supposed to move into his father's tent that very night and Pell's plan to get to know her better could have begun. The thought of getting to know Roza had been a like a warm patch in his mind ever since she arrived in the tribe.

And what had the bitch done? Run off with the Amazons. That very night. Well, girls did that every now and again, everybody knew that. And it did no harm to their prospects in the tribe. The boys fell over themselves to marry them when they returned. There was something exciting about a girl who'd been with another girl.

Pell asked his father if he could have her when she got back and Vyk said, 'Have her, if you think you can manage her. But I always thought you'd make a match with that young lass Sahr, Roget's daughter. She's fond of you, and there's nothing wrong with her apart from that limp.'

It was true Pell liked Sahr. He liked the way she gazed at him with her soft, brown eyes and how she ducked her head shyly every time they met. And he knew her father would give her a good dowry so they could set up their own tent straight away. But how could he marry Sahr when he'd told everyone he was going to have Roza, the most beautiful girl in the tribe?

Then autumn came and Roza did not come back. Pell rode out to the Amazons' camp and saw her wearing a short leather tunic with her cropped hair gleaming like a golden cap. Saw her laughing with a brown haired girl as they rolled up their bedding and loaded it onto a sturdy pony, ready for the trek to their winter quarters. She had a bow across her back and a flint knife stuck in the belt circling her slender waist. And now here was spring again and Pell had to ride to summer camp and face the taunts of the other boys who found it amusing that Roza had ridden off with the Amazons, rather than marry him.

The arrival of the wild geese on the lake was a sign for the sisters to begin preparations for the new season. There was still snow on the ground but the horses were turned out into the meadow to enjoy the new grass while the stables were swept clean. In the house the doors and window shutters were flung open. Children and chickens were shooed outside into the brief spring sunshine while each room was cleaned and fresh straw sweetened with herbs was laid on the floor. Bedding and clothing were flung outside and laid out to air on walls and hedges. Even old Mahra consented to leave her chair by the fire and sit in the sun-drenched courtyard watching the children while the girls worked.

When the house was clean, the girls who were going to spend the summer out on the plains began packing their camping gear. With a full turn of the moon before the tribes arrived at summer camp, the girls took advantage of the warmer weather by wearing nothing but short leather kilts, leaving their breasts bare in the spring sunshine. Even Mahra unwound herself from her heavy layers to reveal the ancient scars of her mastectomy seaming the left side of her chest.

However delightful it would be to dress that way on hot days, it was not something the sisters chose to do at the height of the summer. They considered it prudent to dress more modestly when they shared the plains with men. Despite the good relations that existed between the tribes and the sisterhood, there were always young men who considered the Amazons easy pickings and the sisters did what was necessary to discourage their advances. They could defend themselves well enough if they had to but blood spilled on either side was something to be avoided. So it was only in these early days of spring that the sisters dressed as they pleased and enjoyed the warm sun on their bodies as they worked.

With the first showing of the new moon that would be full when the sisters left for their summer camp, Saera went into labour. She was one of the girls who had sought the favour of the goddess last midsummer on the day Roza left the tribes to live with the sisters. Saera spent the first part of her labour walking outside in the sunshine with one or two of the other girls walking with her. As dusk fell the girls went inside. Supper was eaten and cleared away. The children were put to bed. Then Saera was drawn close to the fire where a bed of fragrant straw covered with fine deer skins had been prepared for her. She was stripped naked and fragrant oil was rubbed on her distended belly. Her hair was combed and twisted in a leather thong. Eager hands rubbed her back and smoothed cool water on her face. As Saera's labour progressed Mahra began singing a low rhythmic chant. Eyes shut, the old woman's body swayed to the pulse of the song. Others joined in until the room seemed to be full of a soothing, steady beat like the sound of a single heart shared by many. Outside in the darkness the wind had arisen and rain was rattling the wooden shutters that covered the windows.

For Roza, it was a reminder of her own labour three – no, four – years ago. She remembered the pain as her mother's poison gripped her body. Remembered the two old men, Eumeus and Quin, hanging on to her hands. Remembered Shyron and Zaagor crouched over the tiny body of the fawn they had taken from its mother a few hours before. The stone tower had been cold and empty, a place of fear and madness. It was no wonder she had escaped outside when the time came for her to expel that hated burden from her body. She shuddered and felt Dyann's warm arm come around her shoulders. Dyann knew from the silvery lines on Roza's belly that she had borne a child but she had never questioned her about it. Somehow she understood that Roza's present happiness depended on her past remaining unspoken between them.

Dyann had heard the story about the eagle and Roza's supposed relationship with the god of heaven. She didn't believe a word of it. The sisters worshipped mother earth from whom all good things come. They believed the sky god had no connection with earthly creatures but concerned himself solely with his endless pursuit of the moon goddess who shared his celestial kingdom but never submitted to his love. Dyann believed whatever happened to Roza had nothing to do with a god but with a man. Dyann had been born into the sisterhood and had no experience of men and no desire to gain any. However, she knew well enough that some men forced themselves onto women for no other reason than their own pleasure. It was a thought that appalled her.

Midnight had come and gone and dawn was approaching when Saera's baby was born, a tiny girl. The sisters lifted her onto her mother's bare stomach while they waited for the placenta to come. The thick grey cord that connected mother and child continued to throb. Saera's hand caressed the baby's small round head and she cried with joy that she had a daughter who would never have to leave her. Finally the cord was cut and the child was wrapped in a soft kidskin and taken to Mahra for her blessing. Then the sisters went to bed hand in hand and arm in arm, leaving Saera drowsing by the fire.

Under the warm furs of the bed she shared with Dyann, Roza was shivering. At first she thought she was cold but, even after Dyann had enclosed her body in her arms and rubbed warmth into the thin bones of her back, still she shivered. Finally she thrust her face into the soft hollow of Dyann's neck and abandoned herself to tears. Dyann said nothing. She continued to hold Roza as close and as tight as she could, willing the warmth in her own smooth limbs to enter the body of her lover until she was shivering too. Finally she extricated her hands from the covers and placed them either side of Roza's tear-swollen face.

'Come on, let's get up. I'll make us a warm drink. Saera would probably like one, too.'

Saera was asleep with the tiny child clasped in her arms. Dyann bent down and covered them closely. She stirred the fire and added wood, watching the yellow flames waken into light and warmth. The room was cold and quiet. Still Dyann said nothing as she seethed milk over the new fire and added chamomile and honey. She took a beaker to the old mother who slept propped up because her lungs were bad and who was never fully asleep. Then she and Roza took their drinks to the other side of the fire where they would not disturb Saera with their talking. But for a long while they sat in silence.

Finally Dyann spoke. 'You lost a child. This I know. Is that why you are so upset? You can have another baby, you know that, don't you? At midsummer ...'

'No!' Roza turned her face towards Dyann. 'No. And it wasn't a child. It was a monster. We destroyed it, my mother and I.'

'A man misused you. Didn't he?'

Roza nodded. 'It was in Babylon. I can't believe, now, the things he did to me. The things he made me do.' A sob, quickly suppressed. 'I was mad for a while. Coming here saved me. You saved me.'

'Oh, my dear.' Dyann turned and took Roza in her arms. 'I'm glad I am of the sisterhood,' she said fiercely, her voice muffled in Roza's hair, 'if that is what it is like in the world of men.'

There was silence for a while then Roza said, 'I ... I don't have to leave, do I?'

'Leave? What gave you that idea?'

'In the tribe they said girls went with the Amazons for a season, then came back to find a husband. I ... I thought ... I just thought maybe I'd have to go back. At midsummer ...'

Dyann pulled away and stared into the other girl's eyes. 'You don't have to go back, Roza. If you want to stay here, then stay. You are one of us now.'

Roza shook her head. 'Not quite one of you. I wasn't born into your tribe. And I feel ... tainted ... by the man who used me. I can't forget what he did. It doesn't matter how hard I try. Dyann ...'

'Yes, my love?'

'You know how Mahra is? You are not like that, I know. You and the other girls. And you've told me why. How you can be a sister in your heart and not need to lose a breast to know who you truly are. But I can't do that. I've tried and tried. Always I feel that man's hands crawling on my skin. I can't be free of him. I think ... if I lost a breast ...'

'But, Roza, you can't lose a breast just so men won't be attracted to you.

Roza shook her head. 'I don't care what men think. I want to do it for my own sake.'

Dyann kissed Roza softly. 'You have made your arrows. Killed your deer. You don't have to do this.'

'Yes, I do. I need to. I need to carry my loyalty to the sisterhood on my body for everyone to see. So everyone will know what I have chosen to be.'

'But Roza, it's a sacred ceremony. It's not something to be undertaken lightly.'

'That's the whole point, don't you see? If ... if I take part in the most sacred ceremony of the sisterhood. And I share it with everyone. It's a way to become truly a sister. I think it's the only way for me.'

'My poor darling.' Dyann drew Roza into her arms and laid her cool face against her lover's flushed cheek. Their tears mingled for the sorrow of Roza's past.

The ceremony took place two nights later. The old woman, once persuaded, decided to conduct the ceremony with a minimum of delay to allow Roza's body time to heal before she left for the summer camp. She did not want Roza too sick to travel so that Dyann was tempted to stay behind. She needed Dyann to lead the summering girls, now she was too old and ill to travel herself. But the decision did not sit well with her. The sacred words were known to no one but the wielder of the knife and she upon whom the knife was wielded, and should take longer than a day to learn. But Dyann would be the mother after Mahra and she must have her way in this matter of her lover's choice. Though Mahra might wish that the next leader of the sisterhood had chosen someone less troublesome than Roza to be her partner in life. But Roza learned swiftly and well, absorbing the words eagerly and repeating them back to the old women with no hesitation. Perhaps it would be all right, after all.

From sunrise to sunset Roza was secluded from the other girls, eating nothing and drinking only water scented with herbs. She knew enough of herb craft to know she was being sedated but she let the slow drug take her body while she chanted over and over the sacred words Mahra had taught her. Finally darkness fell and Roza was drawn forth eagerly into the warm, lamp lit room. She was stripped of her clothes and the girls drew their hands over her breasts and down her body to the hollow of her belly where the silver lines served as a reminder of the child she had borne.

She was laid high on a bed where the old mother could reach her without bending painfully. Mahra was stripped to the waist, her grey hair plaited into snakes and sacred symbols painted on her chest with ash from the fire. Surrounding them - the sacred, silent heart - the girls crowded eagerly, holding up torches.

The chant was different from the one used for Saera's labour. The sound went from mouth to mouth around the circle of watchful faces, weaving a pattern in Roza's brain that brought a heavy peace. With her eyes closed and her hand held firmly by Dyann, Roza felt the tug of the knife against her skin, the whisper of Mahra's touch on her breast, and then a long slow darkness where only the sound of her breathing reminded her that she was still alive. When she came round, she was lying under a mound of furs with the bright fire flickering against her eyelids and Dyann's arm under her shoulders, lifting her up.

'Drink this.'

It was warm milk mixed with poppy and it made her sleep. She woke at the breaking of a new dawn. Her hand explored the tight binding around her chest and her heart sang with joy because now she was one of the sisterhood truly and for ever.

A week later the sisters set out for the summer pasture with Roza in their midst. Her wound had healed cleanly and the intense pain that had swamped her after the drug wore off was now a dull throb that grew towards nightfall when she was tired. The sisters believed pain was essential in the healing process but Roza did not have the ability to block its intensity with the power of her mind, as the other girls did. Still the pain was welcome to her, reminding her of her choice and her sacrifice. As she rode out from the winter quarters, she carried the livid scars with pride, only regretting Mahra's insistence that she cover her wound with a linen shirt to protect it from the dust of the journey. What she longed to do was to wear the new leather vest presented to her by the old mother at the dawn of their leaving which would reveal her status as a member of the sisterhood to all who saw her.

Pell saw her.

For several days he had been watching out for the sisters'
arrival and now, alerted by the dust raised by their horses'
hooves, he was skulking in a grove of hawthorn at the edge of
their summer camp hoping to catch a glimpse of his quarry. She
seemed much the same. Paler, perhaps. But still as beautiful as
ever. He watched her dismount from her horse and put her arm
around the waist of the dark haired girl who had been riding at
her side. He watched her turn her head and smile at something
that was said. Toss back a remark that made them all laugh. He
felt a stirring in his loins at the thought of what he was going
to do to her. Because he would have her. One way or another.
This summer Roza would be his.

28

'Take her.' Bran turned his head and squinted at his cousin. 'She's yours, isn't she?'

Pell was silent. He stared down at the lush, shaded meadow where the Amazons had made their camp. The thump of arrows on straw targets and the sound of laughter floated up to where he and Bran were crouched under a tangle of thorn bushes.

Bran spoke again, 'Your father said you could have her, didn't he? She'd have your child in her belly by now if she hadn't run off with the Amazons.' His small eyes gleamed from their pouches in his pale, freckled face. 'You're not afraid, are you?'

'No, I'm not afraid. Why should I be? They're girls, aren't they?'

'They're warriors. You wait until you see them fight.' Bran, whose chief pleasure was violence in any form, felt his loins tighten with anticipation.

Pell turned his head. 'We're not supposed to fight them. They're our neighbours. You heard what Allyn said.'

'So it's fine for them to come and take us when they want the blessing of the goddess but we're not supposed to take them? That's not very neighbourly, is it?'

Again Pell said nothing. He knew there was a flaw in Bran's argument somewhere but he couldn't figure out what it was. Not without an effort. And it wasn't an effort he was keen to make.

'Come on, Pell.' Bran's voice broke through Pell's thoughts. 'Nobody's going to blame you for rescuing your own woman from the Amazons.'

'I don't think she's being held captive.'

Pell stared morosely at the scene below him. Roza and the brown haired girl were standing at the edge of the archery range with their arms around each other's waist. Pell saw Roza turn her head and laugh at something the other girl said. She had not taken part in the archery practice and was still wearing her linen shirt to protect her wound. But Pell knew nothing of that. He just felt the familiar pull of desire for the beautiful young girl.

'That should be you.' Bran was reading his thoughts. 'Look, Pell, think of it as your duty. If you don't want to do it for yourself, do it for the tribe.'

Pell dragged his gaze from the scene below. 'How do you mean?'

'A girl like that. She should be in some man's tent. Under his body on winter nights. Not running wild with the Amazons.' He grinned. 'Anyway, you'd be doing her a favour. Once she's felt a man's rod between her thighs, do you think she'll want to go back to pussy?'

'You think so?'

Pell's rod, untried except by his own hand, strained against his leather trousers.

Bran grinned again, triumphant.

'I know so.'

They were seven. Pell, Bran and a handful of other boys who'd come along to share the spoils, in the unlikely event there were any, or to watch Pell make a fool of himself, something that would give them equal satisfaction. It was the night of the new moon. Dark. Warm. Silent. They assembled by the thorn trees at the edge of the meadow. They had no plan. Boys are different from men because they focus their attention on the outcome of their actions without bothering their heads about how to achieve it. Those who survive boyhood learn that lesson when they hunt with men. There was one boy in Pell's gang who was destined never to learn.

Bran had a skin of the potent goat's milk liquor, flavoured with last year's berries to hide the bitter taste. He passed it around. All drank and wiped their mouths with the back of their hands, grinning with bravado. Some drank more than others and it impaired their judgement and their aim when Pell gave the order to attack and they stumbled down the hill towards the sisters' camp.

When Roza came awake, shaking the remnants of a dream from her head, Dyann was already up, strapping on her quiver of arrows.

'What is it?'

'A gang of boys. The heat's got into their loins.' Dyann turned swiftly and kissed Roza. 'You stay here. That's an order.'

Dyann's words were echoed by the dull thud of pain from Roza's chest which reminded her every day that she was far from healed.

Roza watched from the tent flap as Dyann ran swiftly towards the ragged shadows that were heading for the tents. There were other girls there now, their bows at the ready.

'Don't shoot! Let them attack first.' Dyann pitched her voice high over the boys' yells.

The moon was a thin sliver in the sky but the summer night was not dark. As Roza watched, the running shadows detached themselves from the ground and became solid bodies. Bodies running in the open with the luminous sky behind them. Bodies in leather vests and bare feet.

The line between life and death was invisible to the boys running headlong down the slope. But the sisters had paced it out when they made their camp and they knew the moment it was breached.

Dyann took a step forward. She raised her hand. 'Stop now. One step further and we shoot.'

The sister stood in a line, bows raised, bodies sideways to show the least target. At Dyann's words their hands reached backwards and each one notched an arrow into her bow.

The attack wavered. Then a high-pitched cry, 'There she is. There's the bitch who took our woman. Get her!'

A flint-tipped spear came out of the darkness and thumped into the ground at Dyann's feet. The sisters drew their bows.

'Yes,' said Dyann wearily. 'Just one.'

The thrum of a bow string. An arrow loosened. A boy lay screaming on the dark grass as his life blood pumped out of the wound in his chest. The others turned and fled.

In the clear early-morning light the sisters bathed the boy's body. Anointed it with oil. Wrapped it in clean linen. Laid it on a wooden sled. They ate bread and honey and drank watered wine. Poured the goddess' share onto the thirsty ground. Then Dyann dressed herself in her finest red-dyed leather tunic while the sisters harnessed the sled behind her white mare.

'I'm coming, too.' Roza stood by the horse's head.

'No ...'

'Dyann, it was me they were after.' Roza had recognised Pell's blundering, awkward silhouette as he fled from the camp. 'And I need to let them see me. Know whose side I am on. Now and for ever.'

A silence. Then Dyann nodded. 'Come, then. As mother of the summer camp, I command it.' She turned and laid her arms on Roza's shoulders. Stared into her eyes. 'As Roza's lover I wish it could be any other way.'

Roza shook her head. 'You can't protect me for ever, Dyann. I know what I must do.'

It was a slow journey. The sled dragged over the rough stony ground and the mare tired quickly. She rolled her eyes in her head and listened reluctantly to Dyann's voice coaxing her to keep going. The body's white shroud became covered with dust, the fresh-picked flowers laid by the sisters drooped their heads and faded under the hot sun. In the late afternoon they reached a low ridge of land and saw the tribe's camp below them next to the dull sheen of the vast lake. Two sisters who were acting as outriders to the cortege reversed their spears as a sign of peace and rode down into the camp to prepare the tribe for the return of their dead son.

It was a dangerous moment. Blood demanded blood, as Dyann knew well enough. But she trusted in the ancient alliance between the sisterhood and the tribe, and the old friendship that existed between Mahra and Allyn, to hold revenge in check. Halted on the rocky ridge, Dyann watched as the sisters rode unmolested into the meeting ground at the centre of the great camp. Saw Allyn and the tribe's elders emerge from the chief's tent and greet them. Saw the tiny black figures of the tribespeople emerge from their tents and surround the space where the sisters stood with Allyn and the old men. She turned to Roza across the horse's drooping head.

'Are you ready? It's time to go.'

For Roza it was the hardest journey of her life. To leave the safety of the ridge and walk down among the tents of the tribe. To smell the goat smell, the dog smell, the man smell of the great camp. To see the eyes of the women following her from the tent doorways as she walked with Dyann at the horse's head with their long, black shadows laid out behind them. There was silence. An intense, oppressive silence. Not a dog barked. Not a child wailed. Within her bruised and aching chest, Roza's heart cried bitterly for what she had suffered and what might yet be to come. But she raised her chin and looked straight ahead. Ignored the whispering that surrounded the pool of silence in which they walked and which filled her ears with a sibilant roar.

Roza and Dyann led the white mare into the circle of watching faces. The sled's runners bruised the summer grass, raising the fragrance of wild herbs. The two sisters already there moved either side of them as they came to a halt in front of Allyn's tent. The mare turned her head this way and that to touch the soft noses of her stable mates.

Dyann's words dropped into the silence. 'I have brought you the body of your fallen warrior, as is the custom between your tribe and mine. His death is a sorrow to myself and to my sisters.'

Allyn raised his own voice so all would hear. 'He died attacking your camp. For that I offer my apologies. And I thank you for his safe return.'

A murmuring sigh swept the circle. All was well. The body had been returned. The traditional words spoken and accepted. Honour had been satisfied. There would be no war with the Amazons. There was movement in the crowd as people began to turn away. The boy's mother could have his body back to mourn over while his father decided how many beasts to kill for the funeral feast. Pell would be punished, but lightly because of who his father was. His real punishment would be to see the young girls sniggering behind their hands as he walked through the camp. It would make a good story for the winter fires.

Out of the crowd flew a flint-tipped spear thrown strong and true with the setting sun behind it. Roza cried out and moved her body to shield her lover. The spear thumped into her chest. She staggered back under the force of the blow, her eyes wide with astonishment. Red blood fell like rain onto the dusty grass. For a heartbeat Roza stayed on her feet, her hands clawing uselessly at the wooden shaft of the spear. Then she fell backwards into Dyann's arms. A howl like a wounded animal rose from Dyann's mouth as she laid Roza on the ground. A scream echoed from the tent of Allyn's brother and Lily came running across the narrow circle of beaten grass to kneel at her daughter's side.

Lily stared down at Roza's chest where the spear had split her linen shirt. Saw the livid scars and thought they were part of what the spear had done. Then realised they were old scars, half-healed, and knew the truth. Above them Allyn loomed. He leaned down and snapped off the spear close to Roza's chest. A gush of blood like a well of black water. He straightened up and held the spear shaft aloft.

'A life for a life. It is done. Now let our guests depart in peace. Tomorrow we will build the funeral pyres for the bodies of these our children.'

Lily stared across her daughter's body into the tear-filled eyes of Dyann. Slowly she raised herself to her feet. She faced Allyn as she had faced him once before. Spear-straight she stood with her gown stained with her daughter's blood, as it had been that last time out on the snowy plains after the doomed child was born. But now she stood in the meeting place where women did not stand. Stood shameless before the silent circle of men. She was breaking tribal law. Then she broke it again.

'Hear me, oh men of Allyn's tribe.' Her voice was high and clear in the evening air. 'I give the body of this my daughter to be buried by her own tribe. If Roza found happiness with the sisterhood I am glad of it. She found none in the world of men.' There was a break in her voice. Then she continued, 'I demand you give my daughter's body the same dignity the sisters bestowed on that young man ...' She gestured towards the wrapped body still lying on the sled. '... and you offer them guest rights tonight and a safe departure in the morning to take the body of their sister back to their own hunting grounds.'

The tears were flowing freely now and Lily could speak no more. She sensed someone behind her, standing at her back against the vast disapproving silence of the tribe. It was Eumeus. He stood with Lily in the circle of watching faces and sealed his own fate along with hers. One sign from Allyn and they would die where they stood. Dyann, still kneeling by Roza's stiffening corpse. Lily, who had broken tribal law by speaking out in a public place. And Eumeus, who had supported her. The dying sun lit the scene blood red. But the sign did not come.

'It shall be done,' Allyn said curtly.

A nod of his head brought men to take the body of the young man from the sled and carry it to his family tent where the women were already beginning the mourning chant that would continue all night. Roza's body was lifted from the bloody ground and taken to Vyk's tent for his women to tend.

Then, 'Show them to the guest tent,' Allyn said gruffly to Lily, avoiding her eyes. 'And you ... you go with them.'

Thus did Lily receive her punishment from the tribe's leader. There would be no return to her husband's tent, not even to attend the laying-out of her own daughter. From this night forward, she was banished from the tribe. And good riddance, thought Allyn, as he turned on his heel and retreated to his own tent.

But it was not over yet.

29

Towards midnight Allyn came stooping into the guest tent where the women sat sleepless before the dying fire. He waited until he was invited to sit, then turned to Dyann.

'My apologies for the intrusion at this time of sorrow,' he said with a dip of his head. 'But we must talk together now. The situation is a dangerous one. I have been with my men all night. They feel ... unhappy that Roza's body will be given to the sisters in the morning. They think she belongs to the tribe and should receive her funeral rites here in the camp.' A pause. Allyn sighed deeply. 'And there are hotheads among us who seek revenge.'

Dyann lifted her head. 'Revenge? For what?'

'They think there have been two deaths on our side. None on yours.'

'Our arrow, your spear,' said Dyann carefully. 'That's clear enough, surely?'

Another sigh. 'That spear was meant for you, Mother.' He gave the young girl the title of respect. 'Because you took away our jewel. That's how the men feel.'

'Roza came to us of her own accord.'

'Yes, I know she did.' He stared across the fire at Dyann. 'But perhaps it was not wise to take her in. Roza was a high-status female here in the camp.'

'Love is not always wise.'

'True, but sometimes we are not at liberty to love as we choose. We who inhabit high places in our tribes.'

It was a mild rebuke but Dyann heard the flint behind Allyn's words. It hit her like a thunderbolt. It seemed there were things to learn about men that Mahra had not taught her. And perhaps the sisters' position on the high plains was not as secure as she had always believed. Men were strong, and women must submit. It was a hard lesson.

Allyn pressed home his point. 'And now this woman ...' He averted his eyes from Lily sitting silently at the edge of the group. '... this woman has spoken out where she had no right to speak. The men are saying women have usurped their power in the world. They say women should be made to learn their place.' He lifted his head and stared at the girl across the fire. 'It will be war if we don't stop it now. The men are thirsty for blood.'

Dyann made a swift gesture with her hand. 'Blood they have. It nourishes the grass in your meeting ground. Roza's blood. Yours and ours.'

'Yours and ours. Yes. You are right.' Allyn leaned forward. 'This is what I propose. We will escort Roza's body with full honour to your burial ground. We will participate in her funeral ceremony. She will leave this world as a woman of both tribes. Yours and ours. In return you will welcome us into your territory. Provide us with a feast fit for such an occasion. What do you say?'

Dyann opened her eyes wide. 'The whole tribe?'

'As many as wish to attend.'

'We cannot afford to feed so many. It will take all our reserves. We will starve come winter.'

A dismissive gesture. 'Food there will be. You hunt. We hunt. Then we share. Are you agreed?'

Dyann nodded. 'I agree.'

Allyn stood up. Straddled his legs. Stared down at the women by the fire. He wanted to ring their necks. Every one of them. Longed for the feel of those brittle bones crushed between his hands. Dyann's dog lifted up his head and growled a warning.

Dyann laid her hand on the dog's head. Looked up at the man. 'Tomorrow, then.'

Allyn nodded. 'Tomorrow send your outriders to your camp. Tell them to make all preparations. The funeral will be in three days.'

'That's midsummer.'

'Aye, midsummer. What better day to bury this girl and put to rest the animosity between your tribe and mine? I, Allyn, have spoken.'

With his fists clenched by his sides the man ducked his head and left the tent.

Another midsummer night. Another fire reaching to the velvet sky. But no singing. No celebrations. Not this time. It was the night of Roza's burial. The men were restless, aware they were in women's territory. Missing the reassuring kiss of a sword against their thighs. The women huddled together, watching the sisters walking freely among their men.

They had set out at first light, a long caravan of horses and wagons. Goats for sacrifice and feasting. Grain and fish. Fermented goats' milk sweetened with honey. But not too much. Allyn was being careful. Leading them was the funeral procession. Roza's body lying in state on a wagon decked with flowers and drawn by two white horses, their harnesses hung with gold accoutrements. Girls and boys walking alongside, equal numbers from each tribe, garlanded with white flowers to denote Roza's virgin state.

It was something to which Dyann had objected when she heard of Allyn's decision: one of many short, sharp battles she fought with the wily old leader in the days leading up to the funeral. This one she conceded because she knew that public acknowledgment of her place in Roza's life would cause offence to the people of the tribe. Dyann was learning to think with her head rather than her heart. Besides there was some comfort in it, too. If her own status as Roza's lover was to be unrecognised then so, too, was the man who had abused her body and driven her mad. At last Roza was free of him.

Once he had got what he wanted from Dyann, Allyn tried hard to make things easy for the sisterhood. He sent young men to help dig the grave. It had to be especially large because he intended to sacrifice two horses, in the way of the tribe. Usually the horses were burned on the pyre along with all the belongings of the deceased. This time they would have to be buried. He had taken Dyann aside and explained to her that it was the custom in the tribe for them to appear to sacrifice the young horses drawing the funeral cart but in fact to slaughter two old nags with ground-down teeth whose working days were over. For once Dyann was in agreement. It made perfect sense not to waste valuable horses on ceremony.

Mahra, the old mother, greeted Allyn at the entrance to the grove where Roza was to be buried. She was standing up, her massive bulk supported by two girls either side. Over her head arched a rowan tree in full green leaf. A shady track led uphill to where a mess of dirt and timber revealed the site of Roza's grave.

The wagon came to a halt and the young boys and girls lifted Roza's body and carried it to the grave. The white horses were led away, to be exchanged for the old nags that would die that day. The tribe unpacked the wagons, pitched their travelling tents, dug trenches to hold their pit ovens and settled down to wait in the hot sun, the men's eyes firmly on the wagon that held the goats' milk liquor.

With the linen wrappings removed, Roza lay on a carved wooden bier, a concession to the funeral customs of the tribe. She was wearing a fine leather tunic, dyed red and richly decorated with shells and quills. Her bow and quiver lay at her side. The skin on her arms and face was patterned with the sisters' ceremonial marks painted on with wood dye. Her hair had been braided with beads and over her brow was a thin coronet hastily created by the tribe's master smith from some of Allyn's abundant stock of gold.

The horses were led forward and slain by the tribe's shaman with an ancient stone axe. Laying them in the grave proved to be more difficult and less dignified than Allyn had anticipated. He cursed the sisters' funeral customs as he watched the young men heaving the heavy bodies over the edge of the pit. The young girls came forward with the things Roza would need for her journey to the next life: plates and goblets, jars of grain and oil, a deer, freshly killed, and a pair of fat ptarmigan in their brown summer plumage.

Then Roza was laid in the grave while Mahra spoke the sisters' timeless words of farewell. The body was covered with fresh grasses and flowers, picked at first light. Asking nobody's permission, Dyann stepped forward and threw the first handful of dirt into her lover's grave. Then she turned and bowed her head to Mahra, and received a reassuring smile from the old women. At Allyn she did not look. Now it was Mahra's turn to play power games with the old man and she could be left to mourn in peace.

As the sun dipped towards the western horizon the cooking pits were opened and the food distributed. The children from both tribes stopped their games and sat quietly to receive their share of the meat and bread. Allyn and Mahra sat together and dipped handfuls of bread into the pot of caviar that stood on the table between them. For both it seemed that a good thing had happened that day. The uneasy peace that had existed between the sisters and the tribe had become something more. They watched as boys and girls slipped away from the feast to seek the goddess' favour on the warm grass beyond the light from the fires.

'Perhaps it is better this way,' said Allyn to the old woman. 'To let your girls seek the goddess' favour openly instead of stealing into camp when their need is on them. It is a way to share her abundance more freely between us.'

'And it is good to see the children play together,' answered Mahra. 'Especially our boys who will return to the tribe when they leave their mothers' care.'

'Dyann is a good girl,' said Allyn. 'She has behaved well though burdened with her own grief. She will make a wise leader when you are laid to your rest, oh Mother.'

Mahra chuckled. 'Wise under your tuition, my friend. She has much to learn. And now you must deal wisely with Roza's mother. It was she who brought to pass this new understanding between us, even though she broke your laws to do it.'

A flicker of rage, quickly suppressed. Sometimes the old woman went too far. Allyn inclined his head politely. 'The lady Lily is not of our tribe, Mother. She received our hospitality while she chose to stay. If she decides to leave she will do so with the honour her status deserves.'

'That husband of hers won't have her back, eh?' Mahra's finger scooped the rich red caviar into her grinning mouth.

Allyn's eyes hardened with anger. 'My brother, has been shamed by his wife's behaviour. It is his right and duty to cast her from his tent.'

'Yes, yes. So she's leaving. Who is going with her?'

'An escort to our boundary. Then it will be up to her. There's her brother, the goat-herd. And that ex-slave of hers. She will not leave alone.'

'Ah, yes, I've heard about him. A sharp fellow, so I'm told.'

'Sharp enough. But he leaves with his mistress. Tomorrow.'

Mahra leaned her head towards Allyn. Her eyes gleamed with malicious sympathy.

'Perhaps it is as well she is leaving, my friend. Sometimes it is not wise to welcome strangers into our midst.'

30

Lily stared in amazement. 'Where did it all come from?'

After the funeral procession had left that morning, she had walked the short distance between the visitors' tent and Eumeus' camp. Now she had been cast from the tribe there was no shame in entering a bachelor's tent. Besides, she had nowhere else to go.

'I knew you had moved to a tent of your own,' she continued. 'But I had no idea it was anything like this.'

'I am high in Allyn's favour,' smiled Eumeus, trying to hide his delight at Lily's nearness. 'Or was. Therefore he gave me things. Not always things I wanted.' He put his hand under Lily's elbow and guided her to a leather stool under the shade of a thorn tree. 'Sit here. It's out of the way of the packing.'

Lily sat down. 'I heard you took gold from the rivers and gave it to him. Why didn't you just keep it for yourself?'

'It doesn't work that way here. In the tribes your status grows according to the gifts you give to the leader. Then the leader gives to you according to your status. Yes, yes, I know it's crazy. But that's where all this stuff came from.' He grinned. 'But he didn't get it all. Remember how we robbed the palace graves to get the gold for our journey from Achaea? This time we've robbed Allyn. How does that please you, my lady?'

A commotion by the horse lines made Lily look up. A small girl with black hair was waving her arms and yelling at a slave boy who was loading cookware and bedding onto the back of one of a number of camels standing in a patient line. The girl finished her argument then came stumping towards the shade where Lily sat with Eumeus.

'Who's she?' asked Lily.

Eumeus pulled a face. 'That's Suza. One of Allyn's gifts that I didn't want. She's my slave.'

230

The girl arrived in front of Eumeus, nodded at Lily, then attacked her master with rapid words. 'Those lazy scoundrels don't know what they're doing. I'd hit them with a stick, so I would, if my master let me. Shall I get them to start pulling down the tent? It's empty now.'

'Don't hit them with a stick, Suza,' said Eumeus when the girl paused for breath. 'You wouldn't like it if I did it to you. And leave the tent. We need somewhere to sleep tonight.'

'You and me?' The girl's face brightened

'No, not you and me. The lady Lily will be sleeping in the tent. Now I'm off to help Quin with the goats before it gets dark. You make sure Lily has all she needs. She is our guest and must be treated with respect. And we'll need something to eat when I get back.'

As soon as Eumeus was gone, Suza sat herself neatly at Lily's feet and stared up at her with dark eyes that gleamed with curiosity.

'My sorrow at your loss, mistress,' she said formally. Then,' My master says he has known you a long time. He is your lover perhaps?'

Lily opened her eyes wide with amazement. 'No, he is not my lover.'

'He is a man that loves men, I think.'

'No, I don't think he is.'

'But he must be. I have been with him while the moon travels thrice through the sky and he has never touched me. What's wrong with him?'

Lily leaned forward. 'How old are you, Suza?'

Suza spread out her fingers and counted carefully. 'Eleven. Twelve at the next snow fall.'

'That's too young to be given to a man.'

'At home I would be.'

'You are not slave born, then?'

'No.' The word was spat out of her. 'Why does he not touch me, mistress?'

'He was a slave himself once.'

'Whose slave was he?'

'He was my slave. I freed him long ago. When my daughter was a baby ...'

'The one they are burying today? Aieeee! They say she rode with the sisters. Better than being the slave of an old man.'

'You don't have to come with us. Not if you don't want to.'

'Pah! That's what he said. I was a gift from Allyn himself. Do you know what they would do to me if he left me behind?'

'I can imagine.' Lily had learned a great deal about the tribe since she had left her husband's tent. She placed her hand carefully on the girl's thick, black hair. 'Suza, will you look after me? I think I will need someone in the days to come.'

Suza turned her head swiftly. 'Thou art sad, mistress,' she said in the dialect of her tribe. 'Suza will take care of you. Anything you want, Suza will get.' And she laid her small head on Lily's lap.

When Eumeus returned, the camp site was in chill shadow. Lily was still sitting on the stool under the thorn tree with the dark-haired child asleep at her feet. She looked up and met her old friend's gaze. 'It seems she is my slave, too.' And smiled.

Four days later, in the late afternoon, Lily, Eumeus, Quin and Suza were camped on the outskirts of a vast tent city on the western side of a low range of hills that marked the edge of Allyn's territory. As promised, Allyn had provided the travellers with armed men to escort them from his hunting runs, probably more for his own benefit than theirs. Despite the satisfactory outcome of Roza's funeral, he was glad to see the back of his brother's troublesome wife. And he wanted to make sure Eumeus did not help himself to any of the gold that rightfully belonged to the tribe. When they reached the tribe's boundary marker – the blackened stump of an ancient tree daubed with red symbols - Eumeus had no trouble persuading several of these young warriors to stay with them for a few days until they could pick up a caravan travelling west.

Now the young men had gone off into the market to spend the gold he gave them, leaving the camel boys to put up the tent under Suza's merciless supervision. They came back cheerful and boisterous having been cheated outrageously by the stall holders selling the pretty trinkets they wanted to take back to mothers, wives and girlfriends. They brought with them fresh bread and soft cheese, vine-leaf parcels of fragrant rice, figs and pink-fleshed pomegranates, and jars of pale wine carrying in its taste the warm sunshine of the south. It was a feast they gladly shared, laying it all out on their cloaks because the dishes were packed away.

Lily watched as Eumeus picked at the food Suza had heaped in front of him, a grimace of pain creasing his face. Afterwards when the young people were singing round the fire she went into the tent where he was lying on a heap of cushions with one arm across his eyes. An oil lamp lit by the vigilant Suza and placed by his side was casting leaping shadows on the tent walls.

Lily sat down by the bed. 'What's wrong, old friend? You were not hungry tonight.'

Eumeus moved his arm and squinted up at Lily. 'All the liquor I had to drink at Allyn's fire has taken the lining off my stomach. That and the rancid goats' meat which is all I've had to eat the last three years. Think yourself lucky, my fine lady, you were in Vyk's tent and had better food.' He winced and gripped his stomach. 'Give me a diet of bread and milk for a few days and I'll be fine.'

But Lily was not sure. Eumeus was losing weight, shrinking before her eyes into the old man of Suza's imagination. Eumeus had never seemed old to Lily, although he had been a grown man when she was a little child.

'So what do we do tomorrow?'

'Tomorrow we send those lads home before they start getting themselves into trouble. Then we sell everything except what we need for the journey.' And then, in answer to Lily's look of surprise. 'I brought everything Allyn gave me because I didn't want to cause offence. He's a powerful men and we'd have no defence against him should he decide to seek vengeance for some imagined slight. Believe me, Lily, we're lucky to get out alive after what happened.'

'So why not keep it? Won't we need it when we come to settle down? Wherever that happens to be.'

Eumeus shook his head. 'We don't need all this stuff. Tents and carpets and cushions and fancy dishes for our food. Camels and mules to carry them. Boys to look after the camels and mules. It's rough country ahead and we must travel light. Besides, if we look too rich we will be robbed. There's nothing surer in this part of the world.' He smiled up at Lily. 'And don't worry about what's going to happen at the end of our journey. Do you really think your old friend would leave Allyn's camp empty-handed? Now go and see if you can find me some warm milk, will you please, my dear? I think it might help me sleep.'

After Lily had taken Eumeus his milk in a ridiculously ornate silver goblet that Suza insisted she use, and had blown out the lamp, she sat alone outside the tent listening to the noise of the camp. The murmur of voices and the splurge of laugher. A swift fight swiftly ended. The dust shimmered golden in the last of the evening light, its sharp odour mingling with the more earthly smells of wood smoke and camel dung, spilt wine and dirty bodies. Despite Roza's death and Eumeus' illness, Lily felt a sudden surge of joy fill her chest. She was free. And it was good.

The following morning Eumeus dismissed Allyn's men with elaborate words of thanks to be conveyed to the camp. Then he and Quin took themselves off into the market place. There was a little colour in Eumeus' cheeks and he walked erect, as he had always done, but there was no disguising how thin he was under his plain linen gown. They were back after a couple of hours and spent the afternoon overseeing the removal, bit by bit, of Eumeus' vast array of possessions. Camels and boys. Donkeys laden with household goods. The tent in which they had slept the night before with all its rich carpets and bed ware.

Finally they were left with what Eumeus deemed necessary for their trip: a small travelling tent, a box of household gear, warm cloaks for the mountains. He'd kept the pretty white mare which had been Allyn's first gift, a pair of mules and a sturdy wagon. Once he and Lily were alone, he showed her the gold and they hid it in jars and wheel hubs, rolled it up inside their blankets and sewed it into the hems of their clothes, just as they had done all those years before.

When all had been achieved and the sun was setting ablaze the dust of the market place, Eumeus sat down on a three-legged stool next to the fire that burned in the middle of the trampled space that had been their camp site. He accepted a bowl of seethed kids' meat from Suza and held it in his hands.

'It seems the roads are safe, or safer than I thought they'd be. I've paid for a place in a caravan that leaves in the morning, heading west. It will take us through the mountains to the next market. At a place called Carchemish ...' He turned to meet Lily's surprise. 'Yes, my lady, Carchemish lies three days journey to the west.'

'Can we go there?'

'Not to the fortress, no. My information is that it's infested with thieves. But Carchemish is a meeting place of two roads. One goes west towards your old home in Achaea. The other south towards Tyre.'

'Tyre?' Lily spat out the word. 'Why would we want to go there?'

'Not there necessarily,' said Eumeus quietly. 'But it is a rich coastline. We could have a good life.' He grimaced and clutched his stomach. 'Buy a farm. That would please Quin, wouldn't it, old lad?'

Quin lifted his face from his bowl of food. 'Settle down. Breed goats. Maybe get a wife. I've never had a wife.' A smile creased his scarred face. He scooped another spoon of goat's meat into his mouth. 'No more travelling. That would be good, eh?'

'I think it would be good for all of us.' Eumeus lifted a spoonful of thin broth to his mouth and sipped carefully. 'In the meantime we have to make our plans for the journey.' He put the bowl of food on the ground. 'We will travel as a family. It is the only way to avoid suspicion. Husband, wife, brother ... and child.'

Suza lifted her head, her eyes alight with excitement. 'I am to be your child, master? Aiee! Thou art kindness itself. Where is the dress that I must wear? The shoes?'

Eumeus smiled. 'No dress, Suza. No shoes. We are a poor family looking for a new place to settle. That's the story we're going to tell. When we get to Carchemish we need to have it straight. That gives us three days to learn to behave like a family.' He turned to Lily. 'I'm sorry, my lady, but there is no other choice.'

Lily leaned forward and laid her hand on Eumeus knee. 'I think I can learn to behave like your wife, old friend. The question is, can you learn to act like my lord?'

'I also can learn.' Suza jumped to her feet. 'Watch me.' She stamped her foot. '*No*, I will not. *No*, I don't want to.' She grinned widely. 'How will that do, oh master?'

'I was thinking more of a dutiful daughter, my dear,' said

Eumeus. He was finding it hard to keep a straight face. 'And you'll have to stop calling me master. I am your papa now.'

Suza clapped her hand over her mouth and dissolved into helpless giggles.

The market at Carchemish was a huge, dirty, semi-permanent camp of tents and stone huts. Dusty roads led from the outskirts of horse-lines, wine shops and whore-houses, past dirt-coloured hovels crouched in chicken-scratched yards, to the banks of a wide river where commerce took a more recognisable form: laden barges with coloured sails, warehouses with dusty interiors glimpsed through open doors, inns with whitewashed walls from which drifted the tantalising smell of fresh bread and roasting meat. To the north the vast deserted city of Carchemish – Xander's birthplace and the inheritance of Lily's sons – showed as a gap-toothed silhouette against the evening sky. Lily felt sudden tears sting her eyes. Not immune, then. Xander still had the power to hurt her. Or maybe she wept for her sons.

Suza noticed. 'Aiee! My mistress … Mama … weeps.' The girl was walking at the head of the white mare, now dun-coloured from the dust of the road.

Lily shook her head. 'It's nothing Suza. Just some grit in my eye. Let's hope there's some clean water in this place so we can wash ourselves.'

But the sight of the ancient city had put thoughts of Xander into her mind and they could not be dislodged. Xander in her aunt's garden laughing up at her in the pomegranate tree. Xander in her lamp-lit salon on Thera, twirling her around with delight while the gale raged outside the shutters. Xander who'd named his son Shyron after the woman to whom he'd been married in Tyre. But she didn't want to think about that. Even after so long, the knowledge of Xander's betrayal remained as a dull ache in her mind.

31

Early next morning Lily and Suza were sitting at the open window of their bedroom enjoying the cool, clean air before the heat of the day drew up the smells of dung and dirt from the dusty ground. Eumeus was below in the stable yard arguing with a man with a black moustache and a crooked red turban. The sun flashed on the various gold rings the man was wearing on his fat fingers as he gesticulated wildly. His voice floated up to where Lily sat.

'No, no, my lord. First you have to pay me for your passage. A place in my caravan to the next trading stop. Then there is the cost of your protection while we are in Lord Alkmon's territory. Alkmon keeps the roads safe but he charges a high price.'

'Alkmon? I know that name.'

The man turned his head and spat in the dirt. 'A thief from Babylon, that's what he is. But at least he keeps the roads open and we can do a little business.'

Lily turned to Suza, her eyes blazing with excitement. 'It's Alkmon! At Carchemish.'

Suza shook her head. ''T'isn't a name I know, my lady.'

'He saved our lives after Babylon was attacked. Kept us safe through the winter. I wouldn't be here, if it wasn't for him.'

'That man calls him a thief.' Suza gestured towards the window.

'He's a thief himself. Men like that always are.' She leaned forward and took Suza's hand. 'Everyone said bad things about Alkmon. But I don't think he was as bad as they made out. He treated me well. Me and my family. That's all that counts.'

When Eumeus returned to the room, Lily turned to him. 'Eumeus, that man said Alkmon's in Carchemish. Is it true?'

A weary glance. 'Yes, it's true. I've just paid him a fortune to let us use the roads.'

'But, Eumeus, we have to let him know we're here. He'll help us, I know he will.'

A brief shake of the head. 'We don't need his help.'

Eumeus sat down on a wooden chair by the window. Suza moved swiftly to his side. 'Do you need anything, Papa?'

'A beaker of milk.'

Eumeus clutched his stomach in what was now a familiar gesture. Lily turned from the window and stared down at the old man.

'We could send him a message at least.'

'No, Lily. There will be no contact. Not with that man. Let's just leave in the morning and forget about him.' Eumeus reached out his hand and took the milk from Suza. 'Thank you, child.'

Lily lifted her chin. 'Three days masquerading as my husband and you have forgotten who you are.'

A careful sip of the milk. 'I am your loyal friend, my lady. As I have always been. And I still say no.'

'No to my wishes? That's not loyalty. That's disobedience.'

Lily turned her back and walked to the table where their breakfast lay untouched. There was a dish of purple grapes, the first she'd seen since she left Babylon.

From behind her came Eumeus' quiet voice, 'You can call it what you like, my lady. On this matter I will not be overruled.'

Lily turned to face him. 'You never did like him, did you, Eumeus?'

'No, I never did. And for good reason.'

'You were jealous of him.'

Eumeus lifted his hand and touched the slave mark on the side of his neck. 'It's not a word I'd use to describe my feelings for the lord Alkmon.'

'What then?' Lily moved back to the window, a silhouette against the glare of the sun. 'Eumeus, what's this all about?'

Eumeus turned his head to where Suza sat on the stool by his chair, her eyes alight with curiosity. 'Leave us, please, child. Your mistress and I have things we need to say to each other.'

But Suza didn't move. 'She is my mama. She needs me. I will stay.' She turned her head. 'You will let me stay, won't you, Mama?'

Lily ignored her. She leaned forward and took Eumeus' cold hands in hers. 'Tell me, old friend. I see anger and hatred in your eyes. I want to know what the Lord Alkmon did to put those feelings in your heart.'

Eumeus sighed. 'What if I told you Alkmon was the mastermind behind the conspiracy to overthrow Babylon's rulers?'

'But that's old history, Eumeus. Why drag it up now?'

'Because Alkmon involved your son Lex in that plot, Lily. He was using him to carry messages between Babylon and his allies in Lagash.' Eumeus pinched finger and thumb either side of his eyes. 'You remember the night of the eclipse? I saw Alkmon and Lex together in the market place that afternoon. That's why Xander went into the city to find him. He knew Lex's life would be in danger, if the plot failed. And not just his life either. All our lives.'

Lily narrowed her eyes. 'How do you know all this, Eumeus?'

'I know because I was involved in the plot myself, my lady. At my lord Alkmon's insistence.'

'*You* were? How?'

'He … persuaded me to locate the moon's eclipse on the star charts in his astronomy room. One of the messages Lex carried south was the date of the attack. Which I gave him.'

'But *why*, Eumeus? Why did you do such a thing?'

'Because Alkmon said he would harm you, if I did not.'

Lily's eyes flashed fire. 'I don't believe you. Why would Alkmon want to harm me? He was so kind to us that winter in the tower. Especially poor Roza.'

'Ah yes, Roza.' Eumeus reached for the beaker of milk. A deep breath. 'Lily, do you remember how Roza used to cry out that the god of heaven was in the tower? We thought she was mad and maybe she was. But she was right about that. It was Alkmon who assaulted her in Babylon, disguised as Marduk, the god of heaven. I found his golden mask in the wagon when Quin, Shyron and I were left to fend for ourselves after Alkmon took you and Roza to his keep. He expected us to die on that journey. It would have been more convenient for him, if we had.' Eumeus leaned forward. 'Alkmon hid his face while he raped your daughter, Lily. But he couldn't disguise his voice. Remember that lisp? She knew who he was all right.'

'It can't be true,' Lily cried, her eyes wide with horror. Knowing suddenly and completely that it was. She sat down abruptly and put her face in her hands. 'I thought he ... loved me, Eumeus.'

'No, it was never love. He fancied you, that's all. You could see it in his eyes.' Eumeus lay back in his chair, his face white with exhaustion. 'And that's the thing I could never understand. I knew he'd fooled you into lying with him. I just never knew how.'

Lily rubbed her hands over her face, scrubbing away the tears. 'He told me Xander was married to a girl in Tyre. A girl called Shyrah. That he named our son after his wife. Is that true?'

'Yes, it's true.' Eumeus' voice was weary. 'But it wasn't what you think. What Alkmon let you think.'

'What was it then?' Lily felt Suza creep closer and lay her head in her lap.

'Xander's marriage was a gift ... a kindness ... a reward, if you like. Shyrah was the daughter of Xander's patron in Tyre. She rescued him from a temple forecourt after he escaped from Carchemish. He would have died but for her. They loved each other as brother and sister for many years. But Shyrah felt more than that. Xander never returned her love. Not in that way.' Eumeus lifted his dark eyes to Lily's face. 'He married her when Tyre was besieged by the sea wolves. They were close to death by starvation. There was no hope for any of them. He married her and made her happy for a week, maybe two. When the wolves broke in he killed her himself to save her from what they would do to her. Then he made his escape and came back to Thera. To you.'

There was a long silence. Lily was aware of a hot gust of air from the window, the silky feel of Suza's hair under her hand, the painful rasp of Eumeus' breath. The tears were gathering in her throat but she pushed them down.

Eumeus leaned forward. 'It's a different story from the one Alkmon told you, yes?'

Lily shook her head. 'He didn't tell me anything about the siege. He just let me ... assume Xander had been married to this girl in Tyre the whole time he and I had known each other. That I was just ...'

'His whore? You were never that.'

'Alkmon said Xander inherited the timber yard from his wife's family. He said that was why Xander went back to Tyre after the siege. But that doesn't make any sense. If what you say is true.'

Eumeus shook his head. 'Nobody owned anything after the siege, Lily. How could they? There wasn't anybody left alive who'd lived in the city before the sea wolves came. Xander saw his opportunity, that's all. He knew the timber business. And he had his patron's good name to trade on. Nobody knew about him and Shyrah. Except Alkmon. I wonder how he found out?'

'He said a slave ...'

'Ah, yes, that makes sense. The sea wolves would have taken the women, what was left of them, after they'd killed the men. That's what would have happened to Shyrah, if Xander hadn't saved her.'

But Lily wasn't listening. With her head bowed she ran her fingers through and through Suza's hair. Then, 'So Alkmon tricked me. Tricked me into lying with him that whole winter. To amuse him while he waited ...' She lifted her tear-swollen face. 'Eumeus, why didn't you tell me?'

'Mistress, I couldn't tell you. You were amusing him, that's true enough. But you were keeping us alive, don't you see? All that winter we had food and shelter because of you. How much harder would it have been for you to keep on doing what you were doing, if you'd known the truth?'

'I would have killed him.'

Eumeus shook his head. 'We would have died, Lily. Not him.'

A long silence. Then Lily leaned forward and kissed Suza's tangled curls.

'Eumeus, which way are we going in the morning when we leave this place?'

A tentative smile. 'Whichever way you want. There are caravans leaving every day.'

Lily returned the smile. 'So we could go west? To Achaea?'

'You want to go home? Back to the farm?'

Lily nodded. 'Yes, I want to go home. If Xander ... if he's alive and he's looking for me, that's where he'll go. That's where the amber is ...' Lily lifted Suza's head from her lap and gripped her shoulders. 'There's a piece of amber, Suza. Xander gave it to me the first time ... I was in a pomegranate tree, you see. I wasn't much older than you.'

'Where is it, mistress? This ... amber?'

'I buried it by the pig pen wall. The night I gave Eumeus his freedom.'

Suza giggled. 'By the pig pen wall, my lady?'

'I haven't always been a fine lady, Suza. I was a farm girl once. And I worked in a harbour whorehouse.'

'You owned one, too,' said Eumeus. 'Don't forget that.'

'Ah, yes, we owned a whorehouse once, didn't we, old friend? That beautiful white house on Thera.'

Suza's wide gaze went from one face to the other. 'So how did you end up ... here?'

A quick glance between the two.

'That's a long story. But we'll have many a night to tell it on the journey ahead. We're going home, Suza. *Home.*'

32

The smell of raw wine was the first thing to greet the travellers as they came over the hill and looked down on the village. As they approached, they became aware of the sound of singing and the shouts of children. For Lily it seemed like a scene set in crystal from the years of her childhood. It was the day of the wine crushing.

The great wooden vats were set up in the middle of the market place and sweaty young men were trampling the grapes to the rhythm of pipes and whistles, and the beating of a drum. Young girls, squealing with excitement, tossed in basket loads of the fresh purple fruit, as the thin red juice trickled out into the waiting barrels. Long tables laden with bread and cheese, and jars of wine and barley water were set up under the trees. Old women sat nodding in the shade, or gossiped while their spindles twirled ceaselessly in their fingers, spinning wool into yarn.

Suddenly a shout. A pointing finger. The music faltered and died. The young men stood in the vats, their legs stained with purple mash. Children stopped their play and ran forward, only to hesitate and stand with their fingers in their mouths. Finally a group of men who had been quietly finishing off last year's vintage climbed unsteadily to their feet to see what the children were staring at.

Lily was riding the white mare with Suza walking at the horse's head. Both were swathed in silken mantles which covered their heads and their mouths to keep out the dust. Behind them came the wagon in which Eumeus lay in a nest of pillows and rolled-up blankets to cushion him from the jolting of the road. Behind the wagon was Quin leading the camels they had bought to carry their belongings, once the wagon was given over to Eumeus. Lily had lived in the east long enough to be accustomed to camels and she had forgotten her astonishment the first time she'd seen one. And these were a pair of two-humped, rough-haired Bactrian camels Eumeus had picked up from a merchant in Tarsus who'd won them in a bet and wanted to offload them before he moved on.

As the men approached, the big bull, who was docile enough under Quin's care, sensed an opportunity to show off. He curled back his mobile top lip to reveal long yellow teeth. He tossed his head, making the ornaments on his harness jingle, although the attempt to loose himself from Quin's grasp was a half-hearted one. From long experience, the camel knew his limitations.

However, the camel's show of strength had the desired effect. The village men stopped in mid-stride just behind the line of children and dropped their jaws in amazement. The stand-off could have gone on for ever had not one of the old crones recognised Quin. She dropped her spindle in the dust and came forward, a smile of delight creasing her ancient face. She grabbed one of his huge hands in her two wrinkled claws.

'It's Quin, isn't it? I haven't seen you for many a long year. Been in the wars, have you, my lad?'

At that the whole village surged forward, each eager to claim friendship or kinship with the travellers. Lily and Suza were taken indoors to wash their faces and braid their hair. They were given fresh linen to replace their travel-stained silk, which was fingered and admired by all the women in the village. Eumeus was helped from the wagon by the men, thumped heartily on the back and offered wine before he was rescued by a toothless crone who, seeing his emaciated frame and grey skin, took him home and tucked him into a bed which, though none too clean, at least did not sway and jolt as the wagon had done day after day on the long journey from Carchemish. Quin was surrounded by the children, eager to get close to the strange beasts and the giant man with an empty eye socket who seemed to be someone the old people knew. The young men and women got on with the grape pressing, because it had to be done, though it was less fun now with the attention of the village diverted to the newcomers.

The travellers spent two days enjoying the hospitality of the villagers, paid for with oft-repeated stories of their journeys.

On the third day Lily and Quin walked up to the old farm, leaving Suza to tend Eumeus who was growing stronger under the influence of rest and good food. It seemed, too, that the old man drew comfort from the knowledge he'd brought Lily and Quin home, and pleasure from the company of his little dark-haired slave who was now a daughter to him in everything except fact.

Nobody had lived at the farm in all the years since Lily had been away. The fields were overgrown, the house was hidden under a tangle of thorn trees, the pig sty, where lay Lily's precious amber, was lost to weeds and bracken.

'What are we going to do?' Lily asked her brother in despair.

'Ask Eumeus,' said Quin. 'He'll know.

And Eumeus did.

They took lodgings in the village while Eumeus put his long-held plan into action. He was now strong enough to spend some part of every day sitting in the weak autumn sunshine and, watched by a circle of curious village children, he set up his abacus and got down to work. Eumeus knew the villagers placed no value in gold so he bought goods in the harbour town – grain and oil and cooking pots, wine and cloth and pretty trinkets – and offered them to his neighbours in exchange for their labour. The exchange worked well. Before winter set in, the fields had been cleared, the well cleaned out and a snug house built from limestone blocks dug from the quarry on the far side of the hill. One time Eumeus brought home some bales of silk and almost caused a riot as the women in the village rushed to the kitchen door hoping for work in the new house. But Lily had no need of their help. Before they moved from the village she had taken on a young widow, a comely dark-haired woman with a little boy just old enough to help Quin with his goats, as Lex had done all those years before.

In the beginning the poor woman had to bear the brunt of Suza's jealousy until the young girl realised the newcomer had no intention of usurping her place in the family. The woman, whose name was Ella, was a simple soul who wanted nothing more than a kitchen and a cleaning rag to make her happy. The fact that she had accepted without question Suza's status as a daughter of the household – a situation which the rest of the villagers took with a healthy dose of scepticism – brought Suza's grudging acceptance. That, and her skill as a cook.

Eumeus said Ella had the hands of a goddess when it came to baking bread and pastries, and the sweet little biscuits he especially liked. To say nothing of her chicken broth made with herbs and wine and olive oil which was often the only thing Eumeus could keep down when the griping pain was at its worst. Suza was prepared to accept anyone who could ease the suffering of her beloved papa. After a while Ella turned her beautiful dark eyes in Quin's direction and courted him with honey cakes and sweetmeats. Eumeus smiled when he heard what was going on and ordered his workers to add another room to the house, even though Quin insisted they would be quite happy sharing the new shed with his goats.

In spring Lily gave Quin and Ella a wedding feast which was attended by the whole village who were eager to see for themselves the family's fine new house. To Lily, it was no more than a simple farmhouse built to an eastern pattern with the women's quarters, Eumeus' office and bedroom, a large living salon, and the kitchen quarters on three sides of a paved courtyard where Lily planted flowering trees and pretty gardens, a new idea to the villagers who'd never thought of growing anything except things they could eat. On the fourth side was a low wall and an arched gateway – a break from eastern style but Eumeus said it was a pity to waste the view over the valley and the warmth of the afternoon sun. An ancient olive tree guarded the gateway and it was here Eumeus sat on his good days, his sharp eyes missing nothing of what went on in the village below.

Quin and Ella's first son was born the following autumn. Quin brought him into the salon and laid him gently on Eumeus' bed which was close to the central fireplace, the only place he could keep warm as the first gale of winter rattled the window shutters. The child lay in the crook of Eumeus' arm and stared solemnly at the old man from dark, fathomless eyes. It was a moment of supreme joy for Eumeus. He smiled up at Quin.

'What are you going to call him?'

'I want to call him Lexy. Like our Lex that was lost in Babylon. Rot that place!' Quin spoke with sudden and unexpected venom. 'We're better off here, so we are, thanks to you.' He reached down and picked up his child with his big work-hardened hands. 'Lexy boy,' he crooned. 'How are you, my little Lexy boy?'

Eumeus smiled and turned away to hide his tears. It's a good thing Ella's the one making milk to feed the little mite, he thought. Otherwise she'll never get near him. And he treasured up the look on Quin's face for the dark times ahead where he knew the pain was waiting.

Eumeus died the following spring. The winter of his decline had been a time of peculiar pleasure for him. When the pain became unbearable Lily prepared the poppy draft but he would not always take it because it made him sleepy and unaware of the life around him. From his bed by the fire he watched Lily and Suza, the pale head and the dark, working on their looms by the window as Lily taught the young girl the secret of the Achaean meander pattern. Laughter and conversation came from their corner of the room with every now and again a swift glance in his direction to make sure he was included in the joke. The new baby lay in his basket next to Eumeus' couch, cooing and kicking his sturdy legs. At night when the pain kept Eumeus from sleep he watched Ella sitting in the firelight as she fed her baby and crooned to him, and listened to the child's contented suckling.

On fine days he saw Quin, followed by Ella's son, Jonni, followed by a new puppy, still wobbly on his feet, cross and recross the open doorway as they went about their outside chores. Or the door would fly open, bringing in the swoop of the wind and mud on Jonni's feet as he brought in the things he had found to share with the old man. A skeleton of a leaf, delicate and perfect. A brown egg, warm from the nest. A newborn kid, protesting for its mother, and Ella bustling from the kitchen to shoo it outside and complain about the dirt on her floors. It was a good time. In some ways, the best time. Because he was truly a part of Lily's family. Because he loved them and knew himself loved in return. Because he had brought the family safely home, and they were happy. That, perhaps, most of all.

On a morning in early summer, six-year-old Lexy sat in the old olive tree by the gate. His bare, scratched legs hung either side of his favourite branch from which he could survey the whole of the valley below the farm while keeping an eye on the courtyard behind him for his mother's approach. He knew she would give him a sharp slap if she found him because he hadn't finished his chores, but this morning it was worth the risk. Because there was a man on horseback coming up the track towards the farm – a stranger. If Lexy was the first one to carry the news into the house he'd probably get away without the slap. Strangers were a rare event in the valley and even rarer up here where no road passed the farm gate.

As the man came closer Lexy could see he had pale reddish hair and a curly beard cut square in the eastern style. Lexy had seen beards like that worn by the slave masters who came through the valley from time to time with their strings of slaves to sell in the market place. Lexy was never allowed into the village when the slave sales were on, even though they were exciting events with wine stalls and sweetmeats for sale, and music and dancing. But Lexy knew his father and Aunt Lily had an unusual abhorrence for a situation that everyone else accepted without question and that they ran their farm with free labour. Secretly Lexy thought a slave or two around the place would make life a lot easier for him, and save the back of his skinny legs from his mother's stinging slaps when he didn't do his work.

Now the man was almost under the archway. Lexy could see the gleam of gold around his neck and the rich lustre of his crimson cloak. He had a dagger with an enamelled hilt in his belt and heavy rings on his fingers. A rich man, then. Lexy had just made up his mind to climb down the tree and run to the house with his news when he saw his mother come out of the kitchen door and advance purposefully towards the tree.

'Lex? Lex, where are you?'

Lexy withdrew his legs into the shelter of the leaves. His mother was using his formal name, so he knew he was in trouble. But Ella had spotted the stranger now and she halted five paces away from the gate and bowed her head respectfully.

'Welcome, lord.'

The man didn't return the greeting. He leaned forward on his horse's neck.

'You said my name just then. I am Lex, son of Xander. Does that mean my family is here?'

There was a long silence. Then Ella screeched loudly, gathered up her skirts and scuttled towards the house.

The man looked up through the leaves and grinned at Lexy. 'You can come down now.'

Lexy climbed off his branch and slid down fearlessly onto the horse's neck. He turned his head and stared up at the red-bearded man.

'I know who you are.' Lexy had heard all the old stories. 'You're my cousin Lex. But I've never met you before.'

Another silence. This time while Lex absorbed what the urchin had said, dismissed it as unlikely, then realised there was no alternative.

'You're Uncle Quin's son?'

'Aye, we all are.'

A smile quirked the corner of Lex's mouth. 'How many of you are there?'

'There's me and Little Quin and Max. But Max is only a baby. Oh, and Jonni. Ma had him before she met my dad.'

'So who else is here? Apart from you and Little Quin and Max and Jonni, and your ma and pa? Is your aunt here? My mother?'

'Aye, she's here.'

'What about Eumeus?'

A shake of the head. 'No, he's dead. He died when I was a baby.' The boy indicated a carved wooden stele daubed with ochre and decorated with a wreath of withered flowers. 'That's his grave down there.'

'Well, then.' Lex dug his heel into the horse's side. 'Let's go and meet everybody, shall we?'

It was a long time later before Lex could speak with his mother alone. His arrival put the farmhouse into an uproar. Quin was sent to kill a kid, something he was always reluctant to do even on an occasion like this, which was why Ella sent Jonni along with him to make sure the job was done. Summoned by one of the farmhands, Suza arrived from the village with her handsome young husband at her shoulder and Mina, their dark-haired minx of a daughter in her arms, wriggling to be put down. Set on her feet, she ran to curtsey to Lily, as she had been taught, then made straight for the tangle of little boys puppy-fighting by the fire place. Later, flushed with excitement and the heat from the oven, Ella presided over the long table set outside in the courtyard lit by lanterns hung in the trees and a full moon that rose from behind the hill and filled the sky with golden light. Then, with the visitors gone, the children finally packed off to bed and Quin and Ella clattering dishes in the kitchen, Lex and Lily sat together by the fire in the salon, newly lit against the chill of the evening.

'It's wonderful to find you so well settled, Mother,' said Lex, holding out his silver cup for a refill of Lily's excellent wine. 'I've been up this way a few times over the years but there's never been anyone here.'

He sipped his wine. He was feeling a little drunk and very tired but he knew there was talking to be done before he could go to bed.

Lily smiled. 'I knew if I came home someone would find me. I thought maybe your father ...'

'You've never heard from him?'

Lily leaned forward. 'Lex, I haven't seen your father since the night we left Babylon. You were in the city that night. What happened?'

Lex shook his head. 'I don't know what happened, Mother. I got out as soon as I could. I knew I was in danger of arrest because of my connection with the rebels ...'

"... with Alkmon, you mean.'

'Yes, with Alkmon. I'd been seen with him in the days leading up to the attack. Fool that I was ...' Lex sunk his face into his hand. '... to believe all that nonsense he fed me about Carchemish. I should have known better.'

'You're not the first person to be taken in by that man,' said Lily acidly.

Lex looked up, surprised, but Lily hid her face in her beaker and refused to meet his eyes. Her relationship with Alkmon was not something she wanted to reveal to her son.

'Go on,' she said finally. 'What did you do after you got out of Babylon?'

'I found a boat going south to Lagash, then I made my way back to Tyre. I've been in trade there ever since, working the overland routes north and south. I've always kept my ears open for news of my father. But I've never heard a single word.'

'And I came back to the farm thinking he'd turn up here.'

'I'm glad you did.' Lex reached out and grasped his mother's thin, dry hand. 'It's good to know you're safe and you've got Quin to look after you.'

'He's all the family I've got now, Lex. With Roza dead and Shyron somewhere a year's journey to the east, I'd be very lonely without Quin and his little boys.'

'Is Carchemish really a year's journey from here? I suppose it would be, travelling by land.'

'*Carchemish?*'

'Yes. That's where Shyron is. Didn't you know?'

Lily put her wine beaker very carefully on the tiled floor next to her chair.

'The last I heard Alkmon was in Carchemish. Eumeus had to pay him a fortune to let us pass.'

'Alkmon isn't in Carchemish, Mother. Unless you count what's left of his body hanging on a spike over the gateway. And I doubt there's much of that any more.'

'Alkmon's dead?' Lily leaned forward and fastened her gaze on her son's face. 'Tell me how it happened.'

Part Five

Carchemish

33

Shyron and Zaagor returned to Allyn's camp in the autumn of the year that Roza was killed. It took several evenings around several fires for the two young men to hear all the different versions of what had happened to Shyron's sister, and a frank conversation with Allyn alone to sort out the facts from the various fictions and exaggerations that had been presented to them as truth. Shyron's first reaction was anger that Allyn had forced his mother onto the road with no other protection than her old slave and the half-blind Quin. He and Zaagor decided to follow their trail as far west as they could go before the winter rains closed the roads. In the Carchemish markets they found a number of people who told them their quarry had set off west in a caravan several days after leaving Allyn's territory. They had been conspicuous enough by all accounts: the beautiful red-headed woman, the sick old man, the young girl masquerading as their daughter and the giant with the ruined face.

'They had gold, too,' said one trader. 'They tried to hide it, but the old man had plenty to pay the caravan master. For their passage and to pay Alkmon his ransom ...'

'Alkmon? Did you say Alkmon?'

The trader spat eloquently into the dust. 'Aye, that's right. He's holed up in the citadel with his gang of thugs. Nothing goes in or out of Carchemish unless he gets his cut.'

'How long has he been there?'

'Three years, or thereabouts.'

Shyron turned to Zaagor. 'So that's where he was going when he left the tower.'

Zaagor shook his head. 'That's where he was going when he left Babylon. The tower was just a distraction.'

Shyron said nothing, knowing full well what the distraction had been.

The two thanked the trader with a gift of gold they could scarcely afford, then took themselves off to where their small camp was being guarded by a gap-toothed urchin. They kicked the fire into life and set a pot of beans and salt meat on the flames. The meal was eaten in silence.

Then, 'So now what? Are we going to follow them any further?' Zaagor was busy picking shreds of meat from between his teeth.

'Not much point. They're off home, by the sound of it.'

'So what do you want to do?'

Shyron was silent for a long time, staring into the fire. Then he looked up at his friend.

'I want to get that man out of Carchemish.'

'You want to do *what?*'

'You heard.'

'But why?'

'Because it's mine, that's why. Carchemish belongs to my family and I want it back.'

Zaagor lifted an eye brow. 'You make it sound like a squabble over a cooking pot. Look, friend, we can't take Carchemish. Nobody can.'

'He did.' Shyron stared over Zaagor's head at the dark mass on the horizon.

'There wasn't anyone for him to take it from, except ravens and foxes. The place had been deserted for years. Now he's locked himself up in there, how do you propose to get him out? The place is impregnable.'

'My father used to climb the walls when he was a boy.'

'And what good will that do? A couple of lads like us.' Zaagor leaned forward. 'Look, Shyron, Alkmon was inventing dirty tricks when we were puking in our mothers' arms. The only way to defeat someone like that is to play him at his own game.'

Shyron grinned. 'Now you're talking.'

'You're serious, aren't you?'

'Of course I'm serious. I owe him vengeance, Zaagor, for what he did to my family. He wanted them dead. Why else did he burn down that stinking keep?'

'They weren't in the keep when the fire started.'

'Burned to death in the keep or dead by starvation outside it.

Do you think Alkmon cared how they died? It was only luck that Allyn found them when he did.'

Zaagor rolled himself in his cloak and lay down, pillowing his head with his arm. 'In that case, I think we'd better pay a visit to the sisters.'

'D'you fancy one of their arrows through your eye? It would spoil your looks considerably.'

'No, no, Shyron. You're not thinking. Your sister was initiated into the sisterhood, remember? She's buried at their winter quarters. We'll go and visit her grave. They'll let us do that, surely?'

'And ...?'

'And talk to them. The sisters are wise in the ways of men. They watch us from a distance and mock our vanity. If anyone knows a way to trick Alkmon, they will.'

They arrived at the sisters' winter quarters as the first flakes of snow drifted from a leaden sky. The door was opened by a small child with tousled hair, revealing a chink of golden lamp light and the smell of food. The child stared up at them, then turned her head.

'Two lords are here, Mother. In cloaks,' she added unnecessarily for the east wind was bitterly cold.

'Tell Mother Mahra it is Zaagor of the Scythian tribe and Shyron, son of Xander who wish to speak with her. And it's damned cold out here,' Zaagor muttered under his breath.

The door opened further. A tall girl with dark hair and fine skin still retaining its summer tan stared out at the strangers. Her gaze went from one to the other, then rested on Shyron. 'You are Roza's brother,' she said simply. She stared past them at the whirling snow. 'I am Dyann. Please, come in.'

'My sorrow for your loss, lady,' said Shyron, as soon as the door was shut behind them.

'And mine for yours,' answered Dyann. 'And your mother? Do you have news of her?'

'She's travelling west. We tracked her as far as Carchemish.'

Dyann quirked an eyebrow. 'And then you came here.'

Shyron bowed his head. 'I wish to see my sister's grave.'

The eyebrow was lifted higher. 'In a snow storm? It will still be here in spring.'

Shyron stared into Dyann's eyes. It was odd, that shiver of recognition. It was as if he'd known her all his life. 'There's something we'd like to discuss with you.'

Dyann nodded. 'You had better eat first.'

At first sight, the hall was like any other women's quarters in a prosperous household. Women and girls gathered around the central hearth. Children on the floor intent on a game. A wooden cradle. But the loom was abandoned in a dark corner of the room and the women were busy with their weapons. They lifted their heads and stared boldly at the men as they walked past.

Dyann led the two men around the fire to a table holding the remnants of a meal. She helped them to bowls of good venison stew and hunks of fresh bread. Filled their beakers with wine. She sat down and watched them while they ate. Finally Shyron wiped the last of his bread around the inside of the bowl and pushed the bowl away.

'My thanks, lady.'

'It was my pleasure.' Dyann smiled. 'It is not often I get the chance to watch young men eat.'

When Zaagor's bowl was empty too, Dyann rose to her feet. 'Come, now. I'll take you to the guest quarters.'

The room was small and square, icy cold despite a new fire burning in the hearth. Two narrow beds were made up with straw mattresses and woollen blankets. The men's saddlebags had been brought in and were propped against the wall, dripping water onto the stone floor. Dyann leaned her arm against the wall above the fire place and stared down at the yellow flames.

'So, what is it you want to talk to me about?'

Shyron and Zaagor looked around for somewhere to sit, then perched themselves awkwardly on one of the beds.

'There is a man in Carchemish. His name is Alkmon. We want your help to get him out.'

'Why do you want to get this ... Alkmon out of Carchemish?'

'Lady, I am Shyron, son of Siskandarabba of the Great Family of Shuppilumish. Carchemish belongs to my family.'

Dyann was unimpressed. 'What has that to do with me?'

Zaagor leaned forward. 'We want your advice only, lady. This Alkmon is a thief and a trickster. He gains by lies and stealth.

We wish to defeat him with a trick of our own. We thought you might be able to tell us what we should do.'

Dyann dismissed his words with a shake of the head. 'But this is men's business surely. Why come here to seek advice?'

Zaagor bowed his head. 'The sisters are wise in the ways of men.'

'Hah!' Dyann was silent. The boys waited, watching her face. Then she left the fire and moved swiftly across the room. She sat down on the other bed and stared across the narrow gap at the two young men.

'So, this Alkmon. What manner of man is he?'

Shyron spoke. 'He is a Babylonian from a noble family. He was exiled for ten years for mocking the city's gods and came back just before the uprising three years ago.' He turned to Zaagor. 'Or was it four? I've lost track'

'Four years ago,' said Zaagor who still counted the years of his freedom.

'A wealthy man, then. So how did he end up in Carchemish robbing travellers of their gold?'

'His property was forfeit when he was exiled,' said Shyron. 'And he ended up outside Babylon after the attack. My family spent the winter in his fort.'

'In Alkmon's fort?' Interest quickened in Dyann's face. 'Roza carried a child that winter did she not?'

'The child died.' Shyron was sitting with his arms across his knees, leaning forward towards the young woman opposite.

Dyann nodded. 'This I know. But you have not answered my question about Alkmon. I wanted to know what he is like, not who he is.'

'He's like this ...' Zaagor stood and swept up a blanket that was folded at the foot of the bed. He draped it around his shoulders and paraded up and down the narrow space, dragging the blanket behind him. He turned his head towards Dyann and imitated Alkmon's lisp:

'Good evening, my lords and ladies.'

He was showing off for this attractive young woman but he didn't get the reaction he expected. Dyann's face was a mask of horror.

'Is that how he speaks?'

'Yes, my lady.'

'Then he is the man who violated my Roza. A man with a golden face and a lisp in his voice. That is what she said.'

'Alkmon?' Shyron looked up at Zaagor. 'But Roza's child came from the time of her captivity. Nobody knew who the father was.'

Zaagor dropped the blanket on the floor and returned to his place on the bed.

'Do you remember, in the tower? Roza screamed every time she heard Alkmon's voice. We thought she was mad but maybe ...'

'... it was because of what he'd done to her.' Shyron's eyes were wide with shock.

'I'll tell you something else. There was a ... a dinner club that met in the palace of Mutakkil-Nusku. Alkmon was on the invitation list.'

'How do you know that?'

Zaagor bowed his head. 'Slaves know many things. It is one of their pleasures to gossip about great men.'

'But what have these dinner parties to do with Roza?'

'That's where Roza was held captive. In Mutakkil's palace.' He looked at the girl on the opposite bed. 'Mutakkil had a eunuch slave called Shutruk. It was his job to procure the girls for these ... parties. Roza killed Shutruk. The night we went to rescue her. I've never seen such blood.'

Dyann nodded gravely. 'She was a sister in her heart, even then.'

'What went on at these parties?' asked Shyron.

Zaagor turned his head. 'Any kind of abomination you can think of. Men dressed up as gods using girls for their own pleasure. Slave or free, it made no difference to them. And Mutakkil had a liking for free-born virgins.'

'Which my sister was.'

A quick look. 'Well, yes.'

Dyann's eyes were wide with dismay. 'I cannot believe men would behave in such a way.'

'They do,' said Zaagor shortly. 'In the cities they are worse. They hide behind their noble names and their palace walls and they do what they like.'

'He drove my Roza mad, you know that, don't you? This ... Alkmon.' Dyann was on her feet, prowling restlessly back and forth across the narrow chamber. She came to a halt in front of the two young men. 'If I help you get him out of Carchemish, you will have to do something for me.'

Zaagor inclined his head. 'Anything.'

'Let me have him.'

A cold shiver ran down Shyron's back. 'What do you want him for?'

Dyann's eyes were hard as flint. 'There are one or two things I'd like to discuss with the lord Alkmon. Before he dies.'

Zaagor nodded. 'We agree.' He nudged Shyron.

'Aye, we agree.'

'Good.' Dyann strode towards the door. 'You will have to stay with us for a few days while we make our plans. Please, go anywhere you choose outside and in the yard. Our hall is forbidden to you unless you are invited inside. Understand?' Dyann lifted her lip in a smile. 'If the sisters want you they will come here. There will be some who will seek the goddess's gift. It is for you to decide if you will bestow it.'

Zaagor turned his dark eyes towards Dyann. 'My lady, I do not have the gift to give. Tell them that so they do not waste their time.'

Dyann bowed her head. 'I have been told that the gift of the goddess is more than the seed that makes a child. But I will tell them, my lord, if you wish it.'

The following morning Zaagor and Shyron went hunting, hoping they could repay the sisters' hospitality with a gift of fresh meat. But they returned empty-handed with nothing to show for the day's exercise except high colour and healthy appetites. Not long after they returned to the guest quarters a small boy arrived at the door carrying carefully a jar filled with warm water.

'Mother Mahra requests your presence at dinner tonight,' he said formally while his gaze darted around the room with lively curiosity.

So Zaagor and Shyron washed, dressed in their freshest tunics, and braided each other's hair in the tribal manner. Then they walked the short distance across the yard to the sisters' hall. Frost was forming on the rough cobblestones but inside it was warm and full of the smell of food. Dyann came forward and took the two young men to where the vast bulk of Mother Mahra was crammed into a huge carved chair at the head of the table. Her swollen hands were trembling on the arms of the chair and she had difficulty raising her head which was sunk onto her chest. But her small, black eyes were full of intelligence as her gaze darted from one face to the other.

'Aye,' she said finally, nodding her great head ponderously. She turned stiffly to where Dyann stood at the side of her chair. 'It is as you say, child. The warrior brothers, Enlil and Enki, have come down from the sky seeking vengeance in the world of men.' Mahra turned back to Zaagor and Shyron. 'You are twice welcome: for yourselves and for what you bring.'

'What does she mean?' asked Zaagor as the old woman's head fell slowly forward.

'It means we will help you get what you want,' Dyann said shortly. 'Now eat.'

She led the young men to seats at the bottom of the long table, then motioned the sisters to join them.

Later, Zaagor and Shyron stood by the door of the guest house breathing gulps of the cold air. It was a moonless night and the frosty sky was ablaze with stars. Neither of them noticed the chink of yellow light as Dyann slipped from the hall. But Shyron turned his head as she approached, aware suddenly of the warm perfume of her body.

She stood between them and stared upwards. 'What are you looking for?'

'We're looking for the twins, the ones Mother Mahra was talking about,' said Shyron. 'But the stars are different here.'

'They are brighter out here on the high plains than they are in the city, so I believe.'

Shyron shook his head. 'I'm not talking about Babylon. I was raised in Tyre far to the south. My mother's old slave taught me star craft when I was a little boy.'

'What happened to him, this old slave of your mother's?'

'He's with her still. But he's no slave now. My mother freed him years ago, before I was born.'

Dyann nodded. 'I have heard of him. It is said he took gold out of Allyn's streams.'

Shyron and Zaagor grinned at each other.

'That sounds like Eumeus.'

'She is lucky to have someone like him to take care of her. But why did he stay when he was free to go?'

'For friendship,' said Shyron.

'And love.' Zaagor thrust forward his arm and showed Dyann a small white scar on the inside of his wrist. 'I, too, was slave to Shyron's family. Now we are brothers.'

Dyann's eyes opened wide. 'It is as our mother said. You are the twins. Two halves of a whole. Dark and fair. Man and eunuch. Slave and free.' She pointed into the sky. 'There are your stars. Low in the sky. Two bright stars in the east, one above the other.'

'Ah, yes, I can see them now.' Shyron gripped the back of his friend's head and directed his gaze upwards. 'See? Those two stars are their heads. Their bodies point towards the west.'

Zaagor turned to Dyann. 'Mother Mahra called us Enlil and Enki. Are they the twins in the sky?'

Dyann nodded. 'Enlil and Enki are the gods of earth and water, cattle and grain, city and farm. Equal and opposite. Rivalry and harmony. Enlil rules over the destiny of beasts and men. Enki is the guardian of water from which all things grow.'

'So what does that mean? For us?'

Dyann said, 'You are the genesis of a great dynasty. Two bodies, one man, one seed. You and your heirs will bring a time of peace and prosperity. So the legends tell.'

Shyron's gaze darted to his friend's face. 'Carchemish.'

Zaagor laughed shakily. 'We have to win the place first.'

Dyann smiled. 'Tomorrow we send out the arrows so the sons will muster to our aid.' And then, in response to the young men's puzzled looks, 'Before our sons return to the tribes of their fathers they take an oath to fight for the sisterhood if our need is great. At dawn we will sacrifice a bull calf and dip our arrows in his blood. Then runners will take the arrows to those tribes that are blessed with our sons. Thank the gods the snow has cleared away because some will have a long journey.' Dyann looked up at the clear sky. 'When the moon is full in the sky we will ride for Carchemish and meet them there. In the mean time ...' Dyann laid her hand on Shyron's arm. '... I was born into the sisterhood and never thought I would seek the goddess' favour, but I will lie with you, Shyron son of Xander.

I wish to have a child for Roza's sake: a daughter to warm my hearth or a son to go with his father where his father goes.'

Shyron stared down into the girl's dark eyes. 'Your son will be heir to Carchemish.'

34

The gaily decorated wagon swayed ponderously as it wended its way up the steep track towards the main gate of Carchemish. The driver's whip cracked over the shoulders of the oxen as they strained at the yoke. The driver was one of the sons, summoned to Carchemish by Dyann's messengers. He was not just any son but the son of Mahra, the ailing mother of the tribe and, therefore, the leader of the men who had answered the call. His name was Neym and he was a powerful man with a greying beard, hiding his bulk beneath a soiled cloak and his lordly status beneath a generous layer of grime. Inside the painted canvas awning that covered the back of the wagon rode Zaagor and six sisters.

Underneath his heavy cloak Zaagor was shivering in an embroidered vest and a short leather kilt. His body was oiled, as was his hair which had been taken out of its tribal braids and dressed in greasy ringlets. The sisters, who were huddled together for warmth, were likewise dressed in party costumes. In their case, their tanned and muscled limbs were hidden by long silken pants and sleeves sewn with sequins and small chiming bells. At home the sisters danced for their own pleasure. Now they must dance for the pleasure of men. The only consolation Dyann could offer the girls she chose was that they could kill the men afterwards. They were armed with flint skinning knives, tucked into the waistband of their trousers and warmed by their skin.

Gradually the walls of the great citadel loomed up before them, blotting out the stars. Towers built of smooth stone blocks flanked huge wooden gates, shut fast. In both directions massive walls disappeared into the darkness. In the left hand gate tower a narrow window showed the gleam of yellow lamplight. Neym swung down from the wagon. He approached a small postern door set in the gate and knocked loudly with his clenched fist. The door was opened by a dark-skinned rogue in a leather jerkin who leered past Neym to where the wagon stood with its bright silken flags fluttering in the freezing wind. Neym allow himself to be frisked for weapons, then walked back to the wagon while the guard yelled over his shoulder for help to open the gate wide enough for the wagon to pass through.

The wagon rumbled through the gate and halted on the other side. Two of the guards climbed onto its tailboard, grinning at the others left behind. As the wagon began the long pull up the cobbled road towards the citadel, the guards amused themselves by peeking through the thin curtains and whispering obscenities to the girls inside, while the girls gritted their teeth and managed with a supreme effort of will not to kill them where they sat.

As soon as the wagon had passed through the gates a man detached himself from the shadows by the wall and ran swiftly down the track towards the town, his breath steaming in the freezing air. He pushed aside a stained leather curtain covering the door to a tavern on the outskirts of town and went into the warm sour-smelling room roaring with the sound of men's voices.

He made his way to a wooden bench near the fire where two men were sitting. These were sons, as he was, but showed nothing of their heritage, being the kind of tough-looking men produced by the hard life of the open plains. They moved up reluctantly to make room for the newcomer to sit but took no further notice of him. Within a few minutes they began arguing loudly.

'You took that ewe of mine, Zahr, I know you did. You think nobody saw you but you were seen all right.'

'Who saw me?'

'My son, that's who. Plain as I'm looking at you now.'

He crashed his beaker onto the table in front of him. Wine splashed out onto the greasy board. They were beginning to draw an audience.

'Your son? Ha! That's a laugh. He's as blind as his old man, that one. Except for seeing things that aren't there.' Zahr fumbled under his shirt for an old wash-leather pouch. 'Tell you what, we'll toss for it. Let's the gods decide.' He pulled open the pouch and emptied a set of yellowing knuckle bones onto the table. 'I win and we'll call it quits. You win and you can come over and take your pick of my flock. What do you say to that?'

The other man nodded. 'Fair enough.'

With a grin, Zahr picked up the knuckle bones, shook them in his hand, then tossed them onto the table. The other man scooped up the bones and threw them down.

'Looks like I won. I'll be over tomorrow and take your best ram.'

Zahr thumped the greasy table, making the bones jump. 'Damn you, Keyn, you ill-gotten son of a raddled whore.'

'Toss again?' Keyn was unmoved by Zahr's insult. 'I'll give you the chance to win back your ram.'

Zahr was aware that they were the centre of attention in the small room. Time to increase the stakes. 'Never mind my ram. Let's make it interesting. We'll throw for a slave, how about that? I've a fancy for that pretty little wench of yours. The one with the black hair. And I've got a young lad you can have. Set him guarding your sheep and you won't lose them so easily.'

There was a murmur of laughter from the crowd of men as they shuffled closer.

The bones were tossed. Zahr lost his fictitious slave to a triumphant Keyn. He became reckless. Lost the next three throws. Stood up angrily.

'No, I'll not play you again, you scoundrel. You own half my flock. My wife's going to kill me when she finds out.'

'I'll play.'

A man stepped forward. He was dark-skinned, his grimy face crossed by a deep scar. His long black hair was bundled under a greasy leather cap. He was from the Carchemish garrison. Keyn and Zahr had tracked him from the fortress earlier that evening in a gang of some twenty men. There were two of them in the tavern. The rest had dispersed around the town. But two was all they needed.

The man pulled out a stool and sat down opposite Keyn. 'You've been lucky so far, mate. Let's see how you like playing against an expert.'

The other soldier came from the bar with two brimming

beakers. He slapped one down on the table in front of his mate then stood back, rocking a little on unsteady feet. They were playing for gold, now. To begin with Keyn continued his lucky streak, accumulating a small pile of the precious stuff. Finally the man pulled a fine enamelled brooch from his cloak and tossed it on the table.

'It's worth a bit, is that. It came from Babylon. My master gave it to me with his own hands.'

The toss was lucky for the soldier. He leaned forward and dragged his precious brooch and Keyn's stake of gold to his side of the table. Tossed again. Won again. There was a leer of triumph on his face. He picked up a piece of gold and reached behind him to hand it to his companion.

'Come on, what are you waiting for? Drinks for me and my friends.'

Keyn rested his elbows on the greasy table. 'Who is your master, then? He must be a fine man to give you something like this.' He reached out for the brooch and rubbed his thumb over its surface.

The man hoisted his eye brows in surprise. 'Where are you from that you don't know who my master is?' He jerked his thumb. 'I work for the lord Alkmon in that fortress yonder.'

'You are Lord Alkmon's man?' Keyn feigned astonishment and respect. 'I didn't realise I was gambling with so worthy an opponent.'

'Did you hear that?' The soldier turned his head to the other soldier. 'Worthy he called me. You wouldn't call us worthy if you saw us doing his lordship's bidding. Dirty work it is, most of it. And Alkmon's dirty work is dirtier than most. ' He turned back to Keyn. 'You should join us, my friend. You wouldn't be worried about losing your sheep then. He's got treasure enough for all.' Then he laughed and sunk his face into his beaker of wine.

By the time Keyn had finished losing his gold to Alkmon's soldier, the bar was empty of all but the hardened drinkers. The two soldiers staggered across the floor and thrust their way unsteadily into the freezing air. The sons followed them out into the dark street. They had matched the soldiers beaker for beaker all evening but had tipped most of the sour liquid onto the dank and stinking straw that covered the floor. Silently and efficiently they slit the throats of Alkmon's men, dragged their bodies into a narrow laneway beside the tavern and stripped them of their clothes. Keyn fished the gold pieces from the soldier's pouch and weighed them in his hand.

'A cheap night,' he grinned at Zahr.

Zahr grinned back. 'And the fun's about to begin.'

They pulled the soldiers' greasy leather tunics over their own clothes and wrapped themselves in the other men's thick woollen cloaks. Keyn fastened the enamelled brooch at his neck.

'It's nice, that. I'll give it to my wife when I get home. She was none too pleased when I took the arrow from Dyann's messenger'

'Neither was mine. But there was no way I was going to miss out on something like this. Now, come on, let's get a move on. And, remember, we're drunk.'

'Best night I've had in my life.' Keyn's teeth were white in the darkness. 'Let's get back and tell our mates all about it.'

Zahr wrapped his arm around his friend's neck and together they staggered up the long road towards Carchemish.

Alkmon stood at the high window staring out into the freezing night. Below him he could see the smoke from the market town laid flat by the cold air, and the pale gleam of the river. To the south, in the direction of Babylon, there was nothing but darkness. With an impatient gesture Alkmon closed the shutters and turned to the warm room where a cheerful blaze burned in the hearth and clean clothes were laid out on the bed, just the way he liked it. The fact that he had laid the clothes out himself because there was nobody in his service who knew how to do it properly brought another hiss of impatience. At least there was water, he thought, stripping off his leather gear and bending his face to the bowl.

Alkmon had taken the room of Xander's mother for his own. He liked being high up, for its own sake and because a man with as many enemies as he had was wise to make sure he could see who was approaching. The first time Alkmon entered the room he found the remains of the Lady of Carchemish still on the bed where they had lain since the night Xander escaped the citadel and began his journey south. They were now no more than a dried up bag of skin and bone from which all semblance of humanity had disappeared many years before. Alkmon had bundled up the lady's mortal remains with the stinking sheet upon which they lay and tossed them out of the window.

It reminds me of the chart room at the top of my palace in Babylon, he thought now as he reached for a linen cloth to dry his face. That was where Lily's old slave had plotted the moon's eclipse which had triggered the invasion. The invasion that should have given him the governorship of Babylon, if things had gone to plan.

Alkmon rubbed the cloth over his wet hair, then shook his head vigorously.

A dangerous man, that slave. I should have killed him when I had the chance. But at least he wasn't able to stop me bedding the lovely Lily, he thought, his memory lingering on that other tower room with the wolf skin on the bed and the snow against the shutters. A whole winter, the longest I've ever been with one woman in my life, all those months while I waited for her mad daughter to whelp my pup. Another disappointment.

Alkmon screwed up the wet cloth and threw it down.

Well, they're all dead now, or should be, if my people carried out my orders to burn the keep to the ground after I left. Dead and gone, the lot of them, while here I am in Carchemish. Snug enough and growing fat on the caravan trade, even if the place is somewhat lacking in style. And even in this outpost of civilisation things sometimes come my way to remind me of the old days in Babylon. Tonight it's a wagonload of dancing girls. It's a pity I lost that golden mask I used to have. I fancy myself as Marduk tonight and the prettiest of the girls can be Tiamut. Just like Roza. My best and finest Tiamut ever.

Alkmon felt his manhood rise and smiled to himself as he pulled the clean linen tunic over his head.

Time for some fun.

35

There were six men in the room, Dyann saw with dismay when the girls danced lightly in with smiles on their faces and murder in their hearts. Five of them were rough men, the captains of Alkmon's guard. The sixth was Alkmon himself dressed in clean linen and wearing a dinner wreath of ivy around his head. To her eyes, the wreath made him look absurd and effeminate in the chill, unkempt room. But Dyann knew very well how dangerous this man was.

By the time dinner was over and it was time for the dancing, Alkmon's captains were the worse for drink with glazed eyes and slurred speech. The Lord Alkmon had drunk as deeply as any of them but still his eyes were alert, glittering with ill-disguised excitement as his gaze darted from one girl to another.

Dyann's soft fingertips beat a rhythm on the stretched kidskin of a small tambour held in the crook of her arm. Bone flutes took up the beat in a wild shrill of music. The girls were naturally fit and athletic and combined acrobatics with a fierce tribal dance which left them breathless and the men lusting for more.

Lounging in his carved wooden chair Alkmon allowed a smile to play across his face. Compared with the jaded courtesans that were standard fare in all the big cities to the south, these provincial girls were hot stuff, managing to combine an exciting allure with a delicious kind of artless innocence. He liked them. Oh, yes, he liked them very much indeed. He clapped his hands and the flutes started up again, a wild, sweet sound that set his blood racing.

"Oh farewell to you Babylonian ladies,
I'm off to the west and will see you no more.
I'll bring back some gold for to buy you sweet favours,
and love you and leave you a dozen times more ..."

Keyn and Zahr's voices rose in noisy song as they approached the gates of the city. Keyn banged loudly on the postern gate with the handle of his dagger.

'Come on, you bastards, let us in.'

A creak and the small window in the door opened. 'Who is it?'

'Who do you think it is? Open the door. It's freezing out here.'

'You're late. The others have been back a long while.'

'We were on a winning streak.' Zahr jingled the gold in his pouch. 'Anyway the captain's up the hill with Lord Alkmon. Why should he care if we're back late? He's got better things to do, or so I hear.'

'Aye, you're right there. They've got dancing girls in their laps while we're standing out here in the freezing cold.'

The window shut, then the postern door creaked open. For an instant the guard stood silhouetted against the light from a smoky torch. From somewhere in the shadows a bow string was released. The arrow flew from the darkness and buried itself with a quiet thud in the guard's throat. Zahr and Keyn kicked the body to one side, then pushed the door wide open. Keyn turned and beckoned into the darkness. Out of the shadows came a rush of men, excitement replacing the bone-numbing chill in limbs stiff from the long wait. The last man through the gate was Shyron. He looked around quickly then gestured to the left.

'Up there.'

Two men ran up the twisting stone stairs to the guard room in the gate tower. They peered in and found everyone asleep with the sour stench of wine heavy in the stale air. With a look of disgust exchanged between them, the men pulled the door shut and prepared to wait it out. Two more mounted guard on the gate itself and the rest ran up through the empty echoing streets towards the citadel. At the top of the hill their way was blocked by an arched gateway set in a high stone wall. A guard, muffled in his cloak and half-asleep, fell to an arrow before he knew anyone was there.

The sons pushed open the gate and followed the wagon tracks into the wild and overgrown paradise that surrounded the citadel itself. They heard the stampede of tiny hooves and a soft thump, thump as deer and rabbits fled before them. Doves rose with a clatter of wings before settling back into the trees.

Shyron slowed to a walk and indicated with his hand for the rest to do the same. Moving stealthily now, the sons approached a low building in a clearing beyond the trees where there was a glimmer of yellow lamp light and the muffled sound of music. Another few steps and they found the wagon with the silken flags hanging from their poles and the oxen grazing patiently on the thin winter grass.

Zaagor and Neym slipped out of a painted porch. 'Everything all right?'

Shyron nodded.

'Come on, then. You're just in time.'

The girls were reaching the climax of their dance. They had practiced it for weeks while they waited to start their journey to Carchemish. A pyramid – three, two, and one – hold it for a moment, then a soft collapse that would land a girl in the lap of each man. They had hoped for fewer men, so there would be someone to help Dyann with Alkmon. Now they had to take a chance that the sons were outside and would come to their aid.

They threw away their flutes and the tiny kid-skin tambour. Three girls made a circle and held out their hands for the two who leapt laughing onto their shoulders. Then it was Dyann's turn to climb nimbly to the top of the pyramid and stand triumphant with one foot on the shoulder of each girl. She stared down into the eyes of her enemy and saw the tip of his tongue dart out and lick his top lip. In anticipation of something. Whatever it was, he wasn't going to get it.

With a shrill cry, Dyann leapt from the girls' shoulders, went into a tight somersault and landed on her feet in front of Alkmon's chair. Behind her the other men died where they sat as the girls sunk warm flint into ripe bellies. For an instant man and girl stared at each other, eye to eye. Dyann saw Alkmon's eyes flick to the scene behind her. His face changed instantly from a look of lazy anticipation, to understanding, then ...

The sons burst through the heavy curtains that covered the arches surrounding the dining room. Two grabbed Alkmon's arms, preventing any movement. Dyann took a step back into the space in the middle of the room where lost sequins winked on the bare floor boards. She stared across at Alkmon and smiled in triumph.

'Greetings, Lord Alkmon of Babylon,' she said in a clear, calm voice. 'I am Dyann, daughter of Mahra, mother of the sisters in the east. Lover of Roza, daughter of Fen of the tribe of Allyn. You remember Roza, do you not, my lord?'

Gaze met gaze. Alkmon knew his enemy. And that there would be no mercy.

On a freezing Thracian hillside in a flimsy reed-thatched hut among the rough grey slag heaps of the silver mines Xander woke suddenly from exhausted sleep. He propped himself up on one elbow and stared through the black square of the doorway at the blaze of stars in the midnight sky. He nudged his companion.

'Borg. Borg. Are you awake?'

A grunt. 'What do you want?'

'Look at the stars. There, on the horizon. It's Gemini, the twins. I've never seen them so bright.'

Borg was properly awake now. 'Enlil and Enki, we call them. The warrior twins.'

'So, what does it mean?'

Borg grinned in the dark. 'There's trouble afoot for somebody, this night. And there's Ishtar, the goddess of war. She's bright, too.'

'Show me!'

Xander felt Borg grab his hand and guide it upwards. 'See? Higher in the sky than the twins. You can see her hunting bow.'

Xander's eyes followed the dark line of his arm and found the constellation of the huntress high in the eastern sky. His mouth twisted in a smile.

'Ah, yes. I can see her now. Where I come from she is called Diana.'

'It's a powerful combination,' murmured Borg. 'Three gods walking abroad in one night. Something's going on, I'll warrant it. Something big.' He dropped Xander's hand. 'Go back to sleep, man. It'll be dawn soon enough.'

Xander lay down on the stinking straw and put his hands behind his head. Through half-closed eyes he watched the stars blaze and flare in the night sky. Just before he returned to sleep he felt his heart gripped by a feeling of intense joy.

At dawn Alkmon woke from a restless, wine-fuddled sleep to the hollow sound of arrows hitting straw targets somewhere beyond the window of his narrow cell. The grey light of morning was seeping through the shutters but it brought no warmth. Alkmon was still dressed in his linen dinner outfit and he felt the humiliation as much as the chill from the stone walls. He wondered if they would allow him to change before his execution. He gathered the thin bed cover over his shoulders and crossed to the window.

The room looked out onto an oval of rabbit-nibbled turf where, dressed in their hunting gear, the sisters were busy at practice. It was a sight that would have raised Alkmon's desire on any other morning than this. He noticed that one of the targets, bigger than the rest, stood at the end of a wide lane created by lances stuck into the ground. The lances were decorated with coloured silk flags taken from the wagon that had brought the girls to the citadel the night before and looked like something you'd see at a fair, not an execution ground. The shred of passion raised by the sight of the girls' strong, brown limbs died as Alkmon realised how he was to die.

He turned from the window, cursing himself for every kind of fool under the sun. But who could have predicted the chain of events that had brought an Amazon to his door seeking revenge for something she should have known nothing about? And how was he supposed to guard against such an eventuality when it had never crossed his mind it could occur? And now the great Alkmon had been brought down by a gang of girls. It was almost laughable. And they would laugh, curse them. The whole world would laugh when they found out. Alkmon crouched on the bed and covered his face with his hands.

36

'So they shot him?' Lily leaned forward, her gaze fixed steadily on her son's face. It was late into the night. The fire had sunk down to a red glow. Beyond the still room a cock crowed loudly.

Lex shook his head. 'They didn't just shoot him, Mother. Dyann wasn't going to let him off that lightly.'

It was Dyann's womanly desire to humiliate her enemy but her honour as a warrior allowed Alkmon to wash himself and dress in an plain tunic and a fine leather kilt as befitted a soldier about to die. He was led out to the target where the sons had formed a guard along the lane of decorated lances. Four sisters were lined up at the other end of the lane with Dyann in the middle. A young girl, hardly more than a child, stood next to Dyann. She held a quiver of arrows which had been dipped in the sacrificial blood a month before and which she had been given the honour of carrying on the long journey west to Carchemish.

There was a short silence broken only by the fluttering of the silken flags on the lances and the liquid sound of a bird singing from a tree nearby. Then Dyann spoke. Her voice was clear in the still air.

'Lord Alkmon of Babylon you stand here accused of sins against the gods who rule us and crimes against your fellow men and women. How do you answer?'

Alkmon said nothing. The remnants of the wine he had drunk the night before rose up into his throat.

'How do you answer?'

Still no reply.

Dyann turned her gaze to the girl at her side. 'Begin.'

The girl stepped forward. The small child handed her an arrow which she notched into the string of her bow.

'This is for your dishonour to the gods. How do you answer?'

Alkmon did not speak.

'How do you answer?' repeated the girl.

Still no reply.

The nearest son grabbed Alkmon's upper arm and shook him hard.

'Answer the lady.'

Alkmon raised his head and stared at the girl.

'It's none of your business what I do.'

The girl raised her bow. 'Elbow.' Her voice was a crystal of sound.

The arrow flew down the lane of lances, pierced Alkmon's elbow and pinned him to the target. Alkmon gave a whimper of pain and slumped a little where he stood. Blood flowed down his arm and dripped from his fingers.

The second girl stepped forward. The small girl gave her an arrow which she notched into her bow.

'This is for destroying families through your senseless, greedy wars. How do you answer?'

'I don't know what you're talking about.'

'There are families broken and scattered because of your part in the invasion of Babylon. How do you answer?'

'It had nothing to do with me.'

'Arm.'

The arrow pierced skin and sinew and buried its head deep in the straw target. A slick of sweat covered Alkmon's skin. He gritted his teeth and made no sound.

The third girl. 'This is for defiling the sacred gift given by the goddess to men and women. How do you answer?'

A defiant sneer. 'I've enjoyed that gift more than most, my dear. I could teach you a thing or two, if you're willing to learn.'

'Knee.'

Crack! Her arrow buried its head in Alkmon's knee cap. A shrill squeal of pain, bitten off.

The fourth girl stepped forward. 'This is for denying life to your victims, slave and free. How do you answer?'

Alkmon lifted his head. He was shivering now from pain and shock.

'Yes, yes, a few girls died. I played a bit rough now and then, I admit it. Just get on with it, will you?'

'Ankle.'

The arrow left the girl's bow and pinned Alkmon's foot to the ground. Without warning Alkmon let go of his bowels. A foul mess dripped onto the pale grass to mingle with his bright blood.

Neym, the captain of the sons, turned away his head in disgust. To kill in the heat of battle, that he understood. To kill in the heat of passion, that, too, was something he could accept. But this slow, relentless torture was beyond his comprehension. He was glad not many women chose the warrior path.

There was a long silence. Alkmon was half conscious now, slumped against the target. Only the arrows through his elbow and forearm kept him from collapsing onto the ground. Neym stepped forward and grasped Alkmon by his arm. He dragged him upright. At least the man could die on his feet instead of cowering on the ground in his own dung.

Now there was Dyann.

She stood relaxed, leaning on her bow. Only her eyes betrayed her emotion as she stared at her enemy down the avenue of lances.

'Let's talk about Roza, shall we? She was happy with me. Did you know that? I showed her what love was. What trust was. She died for me, my Roza. Did you know that? She took a spear that was meant for me. She died for love. Has anyone ever died for love of you, my lord Alkmon?'

Alkmon dragged up his head. Half blind with pain, his dark eyes stared back at his tormentor.

'No, my lady. Nobody ever has. Not friend, not lover, not child. There are no people in the world who love Alkmon. There are only enemies.' He was sobbing now, the tears flowing unheeded down his grey cheeks. 'Is that what you wanted me to say? Is it? Because I've said it. All right? I've said it. Now finish me off … please.'

Dyann reached out her hand. The youngest sister laid the last arrow on her palm. Dyann kissed the blood-soaked tip. 'This is for Roza,' she said and shot Alkmon through the heart.

Lily wrapped her arms tightly around her chest to stop the shivering. Lex went into her room and dragged the great wolf skin off her bed. He put it over her shoulders, then sat down and watched her carefully. It was full dawn. Outside the birds were shouting their greeting to the sun. Ella came out from the kitchen with a beaker of hot milk. Lex could smell honey and spices. She handed it to Lily.

'Here, drink this, my dear. You've been up all night. Bread's a-baking.'

Lily sipped her drink and gradually the shivering stopped. She handed the beaker to her son. 'You finish it.'

Now it was her turn to watch him. He was growing plump, she noticed. Underneath his fine linen tunic she could see evidence of a middle-aged paunch.

Then she said, 'But, Lex, it isn't right that Shyron is ruling Carchemish, even if he did take it from Alkmon. You are the eldest son. It should be yours by rights.'

Lex shook his head. 'I am a trader, Mother. It's what I've always been. A house in town. A farm in the hills. I have no desire to swap my life for Shyron's. And don't think for a moment that Carchemish has been restored to what it was in my grandfather's day. It's true some of the richer merchants have moved inside the walls and taken over the houses in the lower town. People are growing crops in fields that had been abandoned for twenty years. They have confidence in the peace that Shyron and Zaagor have brought.'

'So they rule together?'

'They do. People believe they are the warrior twins Enlil and Enki come down from the sky to rule men but, of course, that's not true.' Lex spoke with the disdain of a southerner for northern gods. 'But they fit well together for the job they have to do. Shyron has the blood of the ancient rulers of Carchemish. Zaagor has kinship with the local tribes.'

Lex turned round and smiled at Ella who had emerged from the kitchen with a plate of bread and cheese.

'Some of the sons decided to stay behind and serve the new masters of Carchemish. The people believe the sons took the fortress with a single arrow, which is true enough in its way, so there are few who want to challenge their authority. And everyone knows the sisters used their magic to fly over the fortress walls and capture Alkmon alive in the citadel. Plenty of people claim they saw them that night crossing the sky like a skein of geese. Everyone knows, too, how Alkmon died. His body was displayed at the gateway so all could see the sisters' revenge.'

'And Dyann? I met her once, you know. A fine young woman. She was going to be Mother when the old mother died.'

'She is Mother now.'

'Did she had children with Shyron?'

'She gave him a son - a true heir for Carchemish - and a fair-haired daughter.'

'Like Roza?'

'Like enough, so they say.'

Lex could hardly remember his sister except as someone to pity when they were children.

'They are my grandchildren,' said Lily wistfully. 'I'd love to see them. But it's too far to go for an old woman like me.'

'You don't have to go to Carchemish to see your grandchildren, Mother' said Lex with a smile. He leaned forward. 'Come back to Tyre with me. Spend the summer with my family. I want you to meet them all.'

'All?'

'I have three daughters. And a baby son still in his cradle. The youngest girl is called Lilleth. Named for the grandmother I thought she'd never see.'

Lily smiled back at her son. 'I'd like that. And now I think we'd better go to bed.'

Lex stood up and helped his mother to her feet. Leaning heavily on his arm, Lily allowed him to escort her across the tiled floor of the hall to the door of her bed room.

'I'm glad Alkmon is dead,' she said, turning to kiss her son. 'He was an evil man and he deserved his fate. And I'm glad Shyron is master of Carchemish. And that you are happy in Tyre with your family. It's more than I ever dreamed of. I just wish I knew what happened to your father, that's all.'

Lex leaned down and hugged his mother. How frail she is, he thought. Nothing but skin and bone beneath her fine clothes.

'I don't suppose we'll ever know that. Not now.'

37

On a sweet spring morning Xander sat on a hillside watching a gang of sweating slaves run a ship across the narrow isthmus between the Gulf of Corinth and the Aegean Sea. At the end of winter the silver mine had spewed him out and left him to die with the coughing sickness that had taken the life of Borg, his long time chain mate. He had watched the blacksmith cut the chain from Borg's lifeless body and wept briefly for the only friend he had in the world. Then, against the bitter urging of his mind, his body had begun to heal and he had been sold to a slave master running the dregs of humanity down into Achaea to end their lives as beasts of burden in the fields of poor farmers.

Despite the breath still entering and leaving his body, Xander felt death close to him now. He remembered the macabre slope behind Heracles' temple at Tyre where the ghosts of the fortunate dead had chattered to him all that moon-struck night. Then he had been eager for life. Now he welcomed death like a friend too slow to arrive. And he would die in Achaea, that he knew. He would die in Lily's land.

Xander stared across the wind-chopped water to the steep, bare hills and narrow, fertile valleys falling away towards the south. He thought of the piece of amber he had given Lily after they had lain together under the pomegranate tree in her aunt's garden. He knew it was buried by the pig pen wall of a little farm in the shadow of an ancient palace somewhere among those hills. Buried years before when Lily had followed Fen, her invader husband, across the sea to make a new life in the east. Buried so it would draw the two of them, Lily and Xander, safely home one day. In his mind, Xander tracked his journey since he left Babylon: north, then west and, finally, south. The amber was calling Xander to a home he had never known.

At first Lily and Suza didn't notice that Lexy has slipped away. They were standing at a market stall examining a pile of soft fleece that Lily wanted to buy so she could make a shawl for Suza's next baby. When they did notice they were not concerned. Quin and Ella had a stall of their own selling soft goats' cheese and Ella's delicious sweet pastries and Lexy had likely gone back there seeking something to fill his ever-empty belly. With Suza's daughter Mena swinging on their hands, they wandered towards a shady bench where they could sit and rest their feet. Although it was yet early spring, the day had turned warm.

Chained one behind the other, Xander and his fellow-slaves stumbled into the village, following behind the slave master on his white stallion. Xander was exhausted, his throat choked with dust from the road, but still he lifted his head and looked around. It was a pretty little place. More prosperous than the places he'd been in lately. The villagers had planted flowering shrubs in old wine barrels and the sight of their cheerful colours brought a smile to Xander's haggard face. In the open space in the middle of the village a market was in full swing.

Under the shade of the trees, tables were laden with farm produce, jars of oil and wine, bales of woven cloth, and rough-glazed pottery stamped with crude geometric patterns. A smith had set up his forge and was busy mending tools and cooking pots. A gaggle of women, their hair covered with white linen kerchiefs, was crowded around a table laden with pretty trinkets.

The slave master led the chain gang to a field at the end of the village. Xander allowed himself to be chained to a stake hammered into the hard earth. He looked neither left nor right. He had no friends in this gang, nor wanted any. Quite soon the young lads arrived in the field and began to amuse themselves by darting forward and rattling the slaves' chains, as young lads had been doing at every slave market since Xander left Babyon.

'Hi!'

Another boy entered the field. Brown skin, blue eyes, a thatch of reddish hair. Skinny legs and scabbed knees protruded from a grubby, too-small tunic. It was Lexy, drawn like the other boys to see the slaves. He ran up to the nearest boy and grabbed him by his tunic.

'You leave them alone, d'you hear?'

The other boy was bigger than him but eight year old Lexy, built like his father and fed by his mother, was tough and fearless.

'Go on, git,' he said, his face red with anger. 'My father says slaves are men like other men. He'll beat you, so he will, if he sees you behaving like that.'

The bigger boy shrugged himself away from Lexy's grasp. 'I'd like to see him try.' He raised his voice. 'Come on boys, let's go. We'll come back when the auction starts.' And the gang of lads drifted away moodily in the direction of the village.

Lexy stood in front of Xander, legs slightly apart, and looked up at him. 'They're only stupid boys. I could lick 'em all if I had to.'

He had a pomegranate in his hand and Xander watched his small white teeth stripping off the golden skin to reveal the pink, juice-filled globules inside. The smell of the fruit invaded Xander's nostrils and his mouth watered involuntarily. Lexy tore off a hunk of the fruit and handed it to Xander.

'Here, help me eat it.' The boy gestured with his head towards the market. 'I pinched it off old Aggie's stall and I'll get a beating if I get caught. I'm going to get a beating anyway for running off and coming here.'

Xander reached out and took the fruit from the boy's grubby hand. He crushed it into his mouth and felt the sweet juice on his tongue. It's a strange thing, he thought, to share a piece of fruit with such a boy with his open, honest face. He has never known anything bad in his life, living in this pretty place. He reminds me of my son Lex when I first saw him on Thera. Xander remembered walking down to the harbour on that chilly morning with his new-found son skipping beside him. His son, lost in Babylon all those years ago. He thought of Alkmon and felt his hands clench into fists.

He looked down at the boy in front of him. 'I hope he doesn't hit you too hard.'

The boy shook his head. ''tisn't my father that beats me. It's my ma. My father couldn't hurt a fly, even if he wanted to. He can't even kill a kid unless my brother goes with him.'

Xander grinned. 'I knew someone like that.'

'We'd better go and find Lexy.'

Lily stood up and turned around to pull the heavily pregnant Suza to her feet. Together they wandered through the market, beginning to pack up now as the day dipped towards afternoon, until they reach Quin and Ella's stall.

'We've lost Lexy,' said Lily. 'Has he come back here?'

A quick glance between Quin and his wife.

Ella said, 'How long since you saw him?'

'Not long. We were looking at some fleece and then we sat down for a rest.'

Another glance between the two.

'There's a slave market at the edge of the village,' said Ella. 'That's why we wanted Lexy to stay with you.'

'You think he's gone to see the slaves?'

Quin nodded. 'Surely. Isn't that what all boys want to do?'

Ella snatched up a square of linen and wiped her hands. 'I'll go and find him.'

But Quin put out his hand. He knew his wife's temper better than most and he felt for the backs of his son's skinny legs, as if they were his own.

'No, you stay here. I'll go.'

Xander sucked the last of the juice from the pomegranate skin and dropped it onto the ground

'So why will your mother beat you for visiting the slave lines? All boys like to see the slaves. Most rattle our chains, like the one you chased off. Bigger than you, he was, too.'

'My family won't have anything to do with slavery, that's why. Our farm is run with free labour.'

Xander lifted his head and stared up at the dry hills surrounding the village.

'Where is your farm?'

'Up yonder.' Lexy pointed a grubby finger.

Xander's gaze followed the boy's finger and found a low, white house surrounded by olive trees and patches of green fields. A hill rose up behind the farm, crowned by a massive ruin.

'What are the ruins on top of the hill?'

'An old king's palace, burned down when my father was a boy.'

Xander's heart wakened. 'And … and do your pig pen walls have pictures on them?'

'Aye, they do. Pictures you can feel with your fingers.' Lexy was unmoved by the man's question. He couldn't imagine a world beyond the valley and everyone in the valley knew about his pig pen walls.

'A man in a chariot?'

Lexy shrugged. 'I dunno what a chariot is. There's a horse on one of 'em. Standing up on its hind legs.'

But Xander had stopped listening. I know what this is, he thought. It's a dream. This pretty village with its flowers and its cheerful market. This beautiful mellow afternoon, the warmth of the sun, the taste of fruit lingering in my mouth. This boy, so familiar somehow, talking about his farm and the pig pen walls where, maybe, my piece of amber lies hidden. I used to have dreams like this when I was in the silver mines. The emotion so real, the colours so rich, the smells so seductive, and then I'd wake up on that harsh hillside and another day to endure.

But this dream continued.

'Lex?'

Both heads turned.

A big man, burned brown from working outdoors, one arm held slightly askew, one eye replaced by silver scars. He reached the boy and grasped him firmly at the back of his neck.

'Lexy boy? What are you doing here? Your mother's after you.'

'I've been talking to this man. We …'

Xander and Lex glanced down guiltily at the pomegranate rind scattered on the ground. But Quin took no notice. His gaze rose to Xander's face. Pity first, and then a shift somewhere in the back of the big man's remaining eye. And, once again, there was that curious gift Quin had always possessed: to recognise the ones he loved, even in the ruin of what they had become. Xander returning to Thera from the siege of Tyre, half-starved and full of grief. Xander, now, after the agony of Babylon and twelve years hard labour in the Thracean silver mines. He lumbered forward and grasped the other man's hands, oblivious to the rattle of the chains.

'Xander? Remember me? I'm Quin.'

'Quin?' Xander stared at the big man's ruined face. 'Quin, what *happened* to you?'

'What, this?' Quin touched his empty eye. 'It happened a long time ago. The day we left Babylon. *Curse* that place.'

'You're a long way from Babylon now. How did you make it all the way back here?'

'It was Eumeus that brought us home. Me and Lily. And Suza.' Quin's slow mind was reviewing that long-ago journey. 'I've got goats again now. A wife. Four sons. I never thought I'd have such things when I was living in that accursed city.'

But Xander wasn't listening.

'Lily's here? I thought she was dead.'

'She's no more dead than I am. What made you think she was?'

Xander shook his head. 'It doesn't matter. Where is she?'

'In the village.' Quin put his hand on his son's shoulders. 'Lex, go and find your aunt. Bring her here. Quick as you can.'

Within moments Lexy returned dragging Lily by the hand. Behind her came Suza with Mina riding her pregnant belly, and Ella, out of breath but agog with curiosity.

'Quin, what's going on?' Lily tried to avert her eyes from the line of slaves staked out like beasts in the dusty field. 'Why did Lex bring me here?'

'It's Xander. He's come back.'

Lily lifted her eyes to the man in front of her. He was dressed in a dirty loin cloth, his wrists tied in front of him, his ankles shackled to a stake driven into the ground. His skin was sun-dark and ingrained with dirt. His black hair was streaked with grey. There was no sign here of the man she had lost in Babylon all those years ago.

Xander, too, was nonplussed by the woman presented to him as his long-lost love. He could hardly believe this village matron with wisps of grey hair escaping from her white linen kerchief was his Lily. And these other women, who were they? The plump one with her hand on her heaving bosom appeared to be Quin's wife. But the young girl? A dark-haired wench with a child in her belly and fire in her eyes. As he watched, the girl reached out her slim hand and laid it on Lily's arm.

'Mama, what's going on? Who is this man?'

Xander stared from one to the other. So now the dream begins to unravel, he thought. Because how could this young woman be Lily's daughter? He tried to calculate how many years they had been apart.

Quin spoke. 'This is Suza, daughter of Lily and Eumeus.' Forgetting that Suza had once been Eumeus' slave in Allyn's camp.

And Suza, seeing the shock in Xander's eyes, said quickly, 'It is true I am the daughter of the lady Lily and Papa Eumeus. But not in the way you think. Aiee, it is a long story!'

'And worth the telling,' said Lily gently. 'But first we have to get you free.'

It was then that the slave master came strolling back from the market place. He had eaten a plate of roast kid and drunk a beaker of wine which – surprisingly – was as good as anything he could get back home in the east. He had already decided to move on. He knew he was unlikely to offload any of his moth-eaten crew on these people who obviously could afford better. As he approached the picket line he saw the eager group clustered around one of the slaves at the far end. So all is not lost, he said to himself. It looks like there might yet be a chance to do myself a bit of good. He addressed himself to Quin, the only man in the group.

'Three gold pieces.'

But it was Suza that replied. 'Three gold pieces? We could buy the whole lot of them for that. And that fancy horse of yours.'

'Yes, but you want this one. So it's three gold pieces, or he comes with me when I leave.'

'No.' Lily this time. 'I have something else. A piece of amber. Will you take that?'

The slave master's lips curled in a smile. Amber was rare. Rarer now the sea wolves had all but halted trade with the west.

'Bring it to me and we'll see.'

'Wait.'

Lily turned and picked up her skirt. She began running out of the field towards the track that led to the farm. Up the hill, breath short, chest heaving, dust in her throat. Through the farm gate and around to the yard where the animals were kept. The pig pen wall with its carving of a chariot, horses prancing under the moss and the grime. She knelt down and began digging frantically in the damp earth. Dirt lodged under her finger nails. Deeper and deeper. Her white kerchief fell from her head and her hair tumbled unheeded down her back.

And then her fingers felt something smooth. Her hands closed around it and she pulled it clear. Rubbed it clean on her skirt. The amber. She held it up and lit its hidden glow. Then she tucked it into the bosom of her gown and began the return journey to the village. But, when she got back, the field was empty.

'Xander!' She turned around frantically, searching for the slave caravan.

'Aunty Lily! Over here!' Lexy was beckoning from the edge of the field.

Lily followed her nephew into the village and found Xander sitting on the old wooden bench under the big shade tree in the middle of the market place. He had a chunk of bread in one hand and a beaker of wine in the other. Around him were clustered the villagers, watching every move he made.

Xander looked up and Lily saw recognition flare in his eyes. She pushed her way through the throng and sat next to him. 'Ah, you know me now!'

Xander reached out his hand and touched Lily's tumbled hair. 'How could I not, now I can see your hair?'

Lily gazed around at the villagers. 'What happened? Where did the slave master go? Is Xander free?'

'Aye, he's free all right,' said Quin, his arm across his wife's shoulders. 'And the slave master's gone. He got his three gold pieces and took himself off as quick as he could before we changed our minds.'

'But ... where did the gold come from?'

'We paid it, my lady,' said a village crone. 'Your family brought prosperity to our village. We've have a good life, thanks to the gold you and the lord Eumeus brought back from the east. We owed you a debt of gratitude and now we have paid it. We will all sleep well in our beds tonight.'

There was a grumble of assent from the assembled villagers. They all knew the story of Lily and Xander, how they had travelled east to the city of Babylon and how their son Shyron had taken the great citadel of Carchemish from the robber

Alkmon. Now they had played their own part in the tale. It was something to tell their children and their grandchildren in the years to come.

By now it was late afternoon. The sun was dipping towards the hill behind Lily's farm. Above, the first star had appeared, hanging from the tail of a new moon. Lanterns were lit, creating a golden bowl of light where young girls and boys had started dancing to the music of drums and pipes. Wine jars appeared from house doorways and there was some good-natured banter about the relative merits of each man's vintage. Housewives brought out baskets of fresh bread and platters laden with cheese and olives.

In the midst of the celebrations, Xander and Lily sat together on the old wooden bench. Lily took out the amber, warm from her body, and gave it into Xander's hand. He held it up to the flaring lamp light. 'Ah, yes, I had forgotten. It is the colour of your hair.'

'Not any more.' Lily put up her hand and touched her wild mane, aware of the grey threads running through the gold.

Xander turned his head. 'What do I care about the grey? You are still beautiful. My beautiful Lily.' He reached forward and put his work-hardened hand against her cheek. 'He told me you were dead. Alkmon ...' The name tasted foul in his mouth. '... he found me in a slave market. Years ago now, it was. He told me you were dead.'

'It's Alkmon who is dead, Xander. He was killed by our son, Shyron, and the lady Dyann, who was Roza's lover.' Lily shuddered, thinking again of the manner of Alkmon's death. 'Together they avenged all the wrong that evil man had done to our family.' She reached for his hand. 'He's dead, Xander. We can forget about him now.'

Into Lily's mind came an image of Alkmon's eyes gleaming over the rim of his wine goblet as the snow fell outside the stone keep and he dropped poison into her heart. It was an image that had haunted her over all the lost and lonely years since Eumeus brought her home to Achaea. But now, as she leaned into the familiar curve of Xander's body, she knew she could let it go finally and for ever.

She turned her head and smiled at Xander. 'Remember that day under the pomegranate tree when you first put the amber into my hand? You told me you would come back one day to claim it. And so you have, although I had no idea it would take you so long to get here.' She gave his hand a little tug. 'Come on, sweetheart, let's leave these good people to celebrate the loss of their three gold pieces. It's time we went home.'

www.ingramcontent.com/pod-product-compliance
Lightning Source LLC
Chambersburg PA
CBHW070838250626
47159CB00003B/825